A

LOST

Book two of the Legacy series

RONON dropped into the chair beside Radek, his water in his hand. "Dead world. Nobody lives there, but somebody dialed New Athos three times." He took a gulp of his water. "Where'd they come from? If nobody lives there and they dialed New Athos three times, but nowhere else, those are our guys."

"I don't see…" Woolsey began.

"They came from a hive ship," Teyla put in. "It is the logical conclusion. The ship remained in orbit around an uninhabited world while the Darts attacked New Athos. Once they had what they sought they returned through the gate and rejoined the hive ship. They did not dial anywhere else, and they are not still there."

"Three times?"

Teyla nodded. "Once to scout, once to send the message that lured us to New Athos, and once to seize… their prize." She could not quite bring herself to say, 'to seize Rodney.' That was too raw.

John sat up straight, his eyes meeting Woolsey's down the table. "If we get a jumper and go back…"

Woolsey frowned. "What will that give you?"

Radek glanced from one to the other, addressing himself to John rather than Woolsey. "The hive ship has certainly opened a hyperspace window. We did not detect them in orbit and they have had three days to go anywhere they wish. I do not think there is more information we can gain on M40-P36."

John's hands opened and closed in frustration. "We have to," he began tiredly.

"We have to find another means of intelligence," Woolsey said.

"Rodney…"

"We will find Dr. McKay," Woolsey said. "But if there's no more information to be had this way, we need to find another way."

STARGATE
ATLANTIS™

THE LOST

Book two of the Legacy series

JO GRAHAM & AMY GRISWOLD

FANDEMONIUM BOOKS

An original publication of Fandemonium Ltd, produced under license from MGM
Consumer Products.

Fandemonium Books
PO Box 795A
Surbiton
Surrey KT5 8YB
United Kingdom
Visit our website: www.stargatenovels.com

STARGATE
ATLANTIS.

METRO-GOLDWYN-MAYER Presents
STARGATE ATLANTIS.
JOE FLANIGAN   RACHEL LUTTRELL   JASON MOMOA   JEWEL STAITE
ROBERT PICARDO and DAVID HEWLETT as Dr. McKay
Executive Producers BRAD WRIGHT & ROBERT C. COOPER
Created by BRAD WRIGHT & ROBERT C. COOPER

ISBN: 978-1-905586-54-7
Printed in the United States of America

To my parents, Bill and Carolyn Griswold

Down, down, down into the darkness of the grave
Gently they go, the beautiful, the tender, the kind;
Quietly they go, the intelligent, the witty, the brave.
I know. But I do not approve. And I am not resigned.
—Edna St. Vincent Millay

CHAPTER ONE

Quicksilver

HE WOKE in darkness, in the comforting dark. His throat was raw, and when he tried to speak only a strange croak came out, like some primal bird strangely shaped and grotesque.

"Here," a voice said, and he felt the metal pipette at his lips, cool and slick. A few droplets of water slid onto his tongue, and he swallowed greedily. "Not too much at first," the voice said. "Slowly."

He had dreamed that he opened his eyes to see nothing but blackness behind them, but this time his eyes did open, and for a moment he recoiled. It was just shock — how not? The face that bent over his was concerned, eyes searching his own worriedly. And what a face. Pale gray and seamed with the dark whorls of spiral tattoos, silver hair rising from a widow's peak above slitted yellow eyes, the other stared down at him, the pipette in his hand.

"There, now," the other said. "Can you speak?"

He might. He might force something from his raw throat. It came out weak and thready. "Who are you?"

The other's eyes were compassionate. "I am your brother, Dust. You have been sick these many days, and I have worried about you."

Dust. His brother. Pictures should come with that, pictures and stories. Words. And yet where they should be was nothing.

"Would you like another sip of water?"

Dust put the pipette to his lips. A few more drops of cold water, soothing his aching mouth.

"Thank you," he whispered.

Dust shifted, and he saw the lines of arm and sleeve, black

cloth embroidered in rich purple, the shades so close that to any eyes other than their own it might have seemed black on black. "Better?"

"Yes," he said. He. A frisson of terror ran through him for all the things that ran away when he tried to think them, ran like water from a pipette. "Who am I?"

Dust's voice was patient. "You are my brother, Quicksilver. You have been very sick, and we have all been greatly concerned about you."

Quicksilver. His own name. And yet it meant nothing. "Quicksilver?"

"Quicksilver," Dust said with a smile, and he saw the picture in his mind, liquid mercury running in a thousand directions, scattering in a hundred rolling balls on the table, glittering and cool. Quicksilver, like his mind. A thousand projects, a thousand ideas, too many gleaming thoughts to pursue before they escaped.

And now he had no thoughts. He was empty. He could not summon a single idea, a single memory. Fear chorused through him. "I can't remember," he said.

"You will," Dust said soothingly. "You will. You have been very sick. I have tended you twelve days. It is not to be expected that you recover in an hour."

"Where…" There was something missing, some place. Some other thing. Some other person. Some other hands. "She…"

"She will be very glad to hear that you have awakened," Dust said quietly. "She has worried too." Dust lifted a soft cover around him, tucking him in as though he were small. "Rest, my brother. Sleep, and let yourself heal."

He knew he should protest, but the cushions beneath him were warm and the covers soft. And he was so tired. He meant to speak, but instead he slept.

The second time Quicksilver awakened he felt stronger. He

lay for a long moment, looking up at the curves of the room in the soft shiplight, rose shadows near the ceiling shading soothingly to gray. He lay in an oval nook, soft cushions beneath him to ease every part of his body. Three coverings lay about him, two to warm him against any chill, while a third was folded across his feet where even to an invalid it would be close to hand. A small table beside the bed held a deactivated light pod, and the steel pipette in its stand, the bottom chilled and sweating in the humid air. Water.

Quicksilver turned, trying to reach it. His eyes focused, and he shook.

His hand was grayish green, dark nails lacquered in midnight blue, carefully tended with no chips, as though someone had carefully groomed him while he lay ill. Such tenderness ought to please him, and yet he shook. His feeding hand extended, raw slit gaping. Where it touched the pipette the cold shocked him to the bone, ice on tender tissues biting with cold. The pipette overturned with a crash, falling to the floor.

The door irised open and Dust rushed in.

Quicksilver could do nothing but clutch his hand in horror, rocking, while some sound came out of him that might have been keening.

"It is all right, my brother," Dust said, kneeling and picking up the pipette. "It is nothing. Just some water spilled. Do not be distressed." He lifted it up and put it again on the table.

Quicksilver could not speak. He could not speak for the waves of horror flooding through him. And yet…

Dust put his hand in his, back to back, leaning close. "Quicksilver, it is nothing. Just water spilled. Be content, brother."

"Water," he whispered.

"I will get you more," Dust said. "You are clumsy from being ill. Your strength and your coordination will come in time. You will heal."

"What happened?" he asked. "I remember nothing…"

"You have been very sick," Dust said, but he thought his eyes evaded him. "In a few weeks you will be yourself again. Come. Lie down. Let me make you comfortable and bring you more water."

His legs were better to look at, loose black pants that showed nothing. His limbs were shaking as he let Dust settle him back on the cushions again, Dust's head bent and his long, fair hair falling forward. He lifted a hand to his own head. No fall of silver, no braids. "My hair…" he whispered. It was shorn close to his head.

Dust did not look up. "It will grow in time," he said.

"I don't remember," Quicksilver whispered. As Dust straightened he caught at him, hand to wrist. "Tell me the truth. What happened?"

Dust let out a long breath, but his eyes did not evade. "You were captured," he said. "You were captured by the Lanteans. We do not know what they did to you. You were found wandering disoriented on an uninhabited planet, wounded and near starvation. We think…" His voice trailed off, then began again. "We think you somehow managed to escape and dialed a random gate address. We don't know, and until your memory returns we may never know."

Quicksilver swallowed. "I don't remember anything."

"You have been very sick, but it looks as though you are mending. I am glad that it is so."

He flexed his hands on the covers, taking warmth from the smooth threads, from the slight spirals of stitching beneath his fingers. "Captured. And I escaped."

"We do not know how," Dust said. "But you did." There was a spark of amusement in his eyes. "But you are the cleverest of clevermen."

"Who am I?"

Dust plumped one of the cushions behind him for him to

lean on. "You are my brother, Quicksilver of the lineage of Cloud, ship's officer and lord among the Queen's Clevermen. The Queen herself has been to see you while you slept, and offered her own blood if it might avail you. We have all worried about you and are relieved to see you becoming yourself again."

"The Queen's Clevermen…" He ought to know what that was, but didn't.

"You are a master of sciences physical," Dust said. "You have your own laboratory, and many men follow you."

That sounded right. For a moment he could almost see a lab, streaming data on a screen.

"If you would like, I will bring you a data reader," Dust said. "Though you should rest as well."

"Thank you," Quicksilver said. A data reader. Yes. That was more right. That was more as it should be.

"Soon you will be better," Dust said, "And then perhaps you will remember what happened. Perhaps then you can tell us of Atlantis."

CHAPTER TWO
The Searchers

"OFFWORLD activation! Colonel Sheppard's IDC."

They came through the gate in good order, the ninth passage in three days, Teyla last on six, herding Radek Zelenka ahead of her. Zelenka clutched his laptop case, and Ronon, just ahead of him, looked back over his shoulder.

Above, Richard Woolsey hurried out on the walkway from his office, looking down over the railing with scarcely concealed worry. "Anything, Colonel?"

John shook his head, dropping the muzzle of his P90 down. Woolsey's face fell. "Come up and tell me, all of you."

Wearily, the team climbed the stairs, Teyla reaching up to catch Zelenka's arm when he stumbled.

"I am fine," he said quietly.

"Of course," she said. He did not look fine to her. Unshaven, his hair in need of washing, Radek looked like all of them did at this point, a bunch of scruffy renegades and madmen who had not slept in days. "But I do not think you should go out again right away."

Radek shrugged, preceding her up the stairs and around toward the conference room. "If we need to go, I will go," he said.

John had already fallen into one of the chairs, while Ronon poured himself a big glass of water from the pitcher at the back of the room. Woolsey lowered himself into his usual chair at the end of the table. Radek sat down to his left while Teyla went around the table and sat beside John.

He looked at her sideways, dark circles under his eyes like bruises. "You look like hell."

"Thank you," Teyla said politely.

"What do you have?" Woolsey asked.

John stirred, his finger tracing patterns on the surface of the table. "M40-P36 was the right planet. Rocky, cold, uninhabited. Some ruins a few miles away, but nothing around the gate worth looking at. No life signs. The gate had only been opened three times in the last six months, and all three times were to dial New Athos."

"Which means?"

Radek put his laptop on the table in front of him. "The buffer on a Stargate is roughly six months or fifty dialings. The Athosians had dialed thirty seven addresses in the last six months, which I recovered from the gate on New Athos. After talking with the Athosians, Teyla could account for twenty eight of the addresses—allies, trading partners, and us of course. Having checked out the other nine addresses, I am confident this was the gate where the Darts that abducted Rodney originated."

"Why is that?" Woolsey asked, frowning.

Ronon dropped into the chair beside Radek, his water in his hand. "Dead world. Nobody lives there, but somebody dialed New Athos three times." He took a gulp of his water. "Where'd they come from? If nobody lives there and they dialed New Athos three times, but nowhere else, those are our guys."

"I don't see…" Woolsey began.

"They came from a hive ship," Teyla put in. "It is the logical conclusion. The ship remained in orbit around an uninhabited world while the Darts attacked New Athos. Once they had what they sought they returned through the gate and rejoined the hive ship. They did not dial anywhere else, and they are not still there."

"Three times?"

Teyla nodded. "Once to scout, once to send the message that lured us to New Athos, and once to seize… their prize." She could not quite bring herself to say, 'to seize Rodney.' That was too raw.

John sat up straight, his eyes meeting Woolsey's down the table. "If we get a jumper and go back…"

Woolsey frowned. "What will that give you?"

Radek glanced from one to the other, addressing himself to John rather than Woolsey. "The hive ship has certainly opened a hyperspace window. We did not detect them in orbit and they have had three days to go anywhere they wish. I do not think there is more information we can gain on M40-P36."

John's hands opened and closed in frustration. "We have to," he began tiredly.

"We have to find another means of intelligence," Woolsey said.

"Rodney…"

"We will find Dr. McKay," Woolsey said. "But if there's no more information to be had this way, we need to find another way."

John's brows knit, graving deep ridges across his forehead. It was a wonder any of them were making sense, Teyla thought. If they were. "They were after Rodney," she said. "These were not simply Darts culling. Nor were they merely seeking a prisoner from Atlantis to interrogate. They could have picked up half a dozen Athosians, and at one point they abandoned a run on me that could have been successful." She looked around the table, as they were all staring at her. "They were after Rodney specifically, and as soon as they had him they disengaged. This is about Rodney. Which means there is a plan, a careful plan that has involved many Wraith. And where there is a plan that involves many, there is talk."

"Among Wraith," Ronon said, leaning his elbows on the table and looking at her.

"The one who dialed our gate pretending to be Athosian was not Wraith," Teyla said. "There is a Wraith Worshipper or an agent among them, someone who might speak with humans." Her eyes met John's. "We know Rodney is alive. They would not go to such trouble to capture him only to kill him."

"That's what I'm afraid of," John said grimly.

Woolsey cleared his throat. "We all know Dr. McKay could be a valuable intelligence source for the Wraith. And we all know it's a priority to find him and recover him. If there's no further information to be gained from the DHDs of various Stargates, then we need to consider other methods."

"Such as?" John asked. He looked like he wanted to go out again. John was not usually this dog-headed, but Teyla knew he had not slept in seventy-two hours. Caffeine and adrenaline were no substitute for sleep, and robbed a man of common sense.

"The Genii have the best intelligence in the Pegasus Galaxy," Woolsey said. "They may have heard something."

"We're not exactly on the best terms with the Genii," John said. "I don't think…"

"Radim has assured us of his good intentions," Woolsey interrupted. "Now is a good time for him to show us. And passing on rumors costs him nothing."

Ronon snorted. "For whatever they're worth."

Teyla took a deep breath. "There is Todd," she said.

To her surprise, John didn't dismiss it. "There is," he said.

Ronon put his hand down on the table, fingers clenched. "You're talking about trusting Todd."

"Todd's more likely to know what the Wraith are up to than the Genii are," John said.

"If he didn't do it himself," Ronon said.

"We can only hope we are so fortunate," Teyla said. "If Todd wanted to kidnap Rodney to help with some plan of his, we know Rodney is unhurt."

John glanced at her, as though that thought brightened him. "That's true. And if it's some other hive, he may be able to get us the lowdown on it."

She did not mention Queen Death. None of them did, though she was certain that the image from Manaria hung over them all.

Woolsey nodded. "Our next move is to shake the bushes, as it were. And while we do that, I want you and your team to stand down, Colonel Sheppard." John started to shake his head, but Woolsey did not wait for him to. "Your team is in no condition to go back out again, and yes, that includes you, Dr. Zelenka. If you're going to be ready when we get word, you need to stand down now."

She expected John to argue. Perhaps once he might have. Perhaps his respect for Woolsey had increased. Or perhaps he was also so tired that it seemed that the briefing room swam gently before his eyes.

"You've done your part," Woolsey said quietly. "Let me do mine. When we hear anything I'll call you."

John nodded slowly. "Ok. Ronon, Teyla, get some rest. You too, Radek. That was a good job out there."

"Thank you," Radek said. He sounded vaguely surprised.

"We're standing down," he said. "This isn't going to be over in a couple of days. Let's get some rest."

Woolsey got to his feet and went to the door. "Banks, get me a radio link and open the gate for me. I need a line out to Ladon Radim."

Ronon headed for his quarters, brushing past people without speaking. They would have questions, want to know if they'd found Rodney yet, and he was too tired for any more words. He'd end up stumbling over them the way Zelenka had stumbled on the gateroom steps, the way when he had first come to Atlantis it had been an effort to remember how to talk to anyone.

The halls were still too crowded with all new people who were still being herded through trainings and were free at weird hours rather than busy with work all day. There were too many people he didn't know, and too many people he did, scientists who didn't seem to know what to do with themselves without Rodney around. It wasn't like they didn't have work to do, but they kept gathering in little knots in the corridors and the mess hall, repeating the obvious as if that would somehow help.

He didn't want to talk. He didn't much want to sleep, but it was probably true that they should sleep while they could. Every instinct was telling him to keep moving, that doing anything would be better than doing nothing, and instead they were sitting around waiting to find out if their allies — such as they were — were going to talk to them. It rankled, and there wasn't anything to do about that either.

It would help if he could stop running over the fight on New Athos in his head, with every wrong move clear to him now. His last shot had been off, clipped the Dart's stabilizers instead of crippling its wing, and even the one that had told best hadn't brought the Dart down. Even if the Dart carrying Rodney had gotten away, if they'd had a prisoner to interrogate, they could have found out a lot that would help them now.

If they'd seen the trap sooner, they could have all taken cover, tried to take out the Darts from the shelter of the trees. If he'd seen the pattern in the dives sooner, seen that the Darts had a single target, he would have gotten Rodney to shelter, left him there and come back to fight. Or at least have stuck close, close enough to dive into the culling beam when it took Rodney.

They'd escaped a hive ship before. And, all right, neither of them could fly a Dart, but they'd have figured something out. The Wraith wouldn't have killed them right off, not if they were after information. Ronon would have gotten Rodney free, and then Rodney would have figured out a way off the hive ship, and then they wouldn't be searching empty planets and coming up with nothing.

He could still remember how much he'd wanted to kill Rodney himself if Rodney didn't shut up, that first time they'd been captured together. It wasn't like he liked being trapped in Wraith webbing so that he couldn't move, struggling for every finger's-width that he could move his hand toward his knife, for every deep breath. He didn't see how it could possibly help to give voice to every terrified thought in your head while you waited.

It had still been better than being alone. Better than waking up in a cell, or cocooned in the long rows of people who were going to be somebody's next meal, and knowing that there was no one to help you. He was trying not to think about that now, but it wasn't working very well.

If he'd stuck close, the way he would have back in the days when Rodney couldn't yet be trusted to hold his own in a fight — but John had said spread out, and there were too few of them to lay down a crossfire otherwise. And Rodney had done everything right, shot straight and true, dodged when he should have. He'd never had a chance to see the second Dart coming in.

No one had seen it in time. They should have done better. For that matter, they should have left men at the gate, or waited at the gate ready for the trap, but John had been convinced it was a trick, children playing games.

He'd heard the distress call played back, and seen Teyla's face when she heard it. It hadn't sounded like a boy playing the kind of game he ought to be beaten for. It had sounded like raw panic. A man in fear for his life, or a good actor, a good liar. An agent of the Genii, or a Wraith worshipper.

Ronon had thought it at the time, but he hadn't said it. It was New Athos, the fields heavy with grain and sleepy in the hot sun, children playing the same games they'd all watched a hundred times. They'd all wanted to believe it was a safe place, the kind of place where a strange call for help was probably just another children's game.

They'd all spent too long on Earth. He'd still run every morning, sparred with whoever was around when John and

Teyla had both been too absorbed in worrying about the future to spend much time in the gym, but it wasn't enough to keep from getting into the habits of safety. Five months idle was too long to go straight back to the field without time to retrain, to get their edge back.

That apparently wasn't how John's military did things. He wasn't going to argue, but either it was getting to them, or they'd just screwed up with no excuse. They couldn't afford any more mistakes like that. And now they didn't even have their scientist to help them figure out what to do next. If Rodney were here, he'd figure out some solution, some way to find whoever they'd lost.

He'd keep working until he found some solution, complaining the whole time, which was all that they could do now. Without the complaining part, which he still didn't think helped. They'd get information from somebody, and then they'd go get Rodney back and kill the Wraith who took him. They'd make this right.

His mind was on New Athos, not on where he was going, and he nearly ran into someone as she stepped into his path. He was ready to shoulder her aside and keep moving until he saw it was Jennifer. She didn't ask him anything, just looked up at him with eyes that made her question clear enough.

He shook his head, and then realized she might take that to mean they'd had bad news. Worse news than none. "We don't know," he said.

She nodded, her chin up. "Just let me know if you hear anything."

"Woolsey thinks he can talk to people," Ronon began, but he really didn't have the words. "We're going to find him."

"I know," Jennifer said. She nodded and walked on, back straight.

Now he didn't feel like sleeping at all, but he knew it

was time to sleep while they could. He knew the difference between a sprint and long days of running. He could see well enough that was what they were in for.

That didn't mean he had to like it.

Radek had barely set foot in the infirmary before he was brought up short by Jennifer's weary "And what happened to you? Slipped on the stairs? Frostbite?" She was cleaning up what he thought looked like the preparations for putting on a cast. He wondered who had broken what.

"Neither," he said. "I don't think it is actually cold enough for frostbite."

"You'd be surprised," Jennifer said. "You'd think no one had ever seen it snow before." It was true that the outdoor stairs and walkways were slippery that morning, and metal railings cold, but Radek had sensibly enough changed his usual shoes for the military-issue boots he rarely wore, and also put on gloves when he went outside. Apparently some had not, and were regretting it.

"I have seen my share of snow," Radek said. "I am from the mountains, you know."

She nodded absently. "I'm from Wisconsin. Where it snows. But I think everybody got used to living on a nice warm island."

"And we are all simply going to have to learn to cope with living on a colder one. The energy consumption that would be required to keep the shield up every time it is snowing…" He was getting a little tired of this explanation. Perhaps it would help if he sent a memo. "It is prohibitive."

Jennifer shook her head. "I'm not asking you to put up the shield so that it won't snow."

There was a momentary pause. "Then…"

"Why are you in here? That was actually my question."

It took a moment. There had not been much sleep for anyone

in the last few days, which might have something to do with a tendency to fall down icy stairs. "I came to see if you were all right," he said simply.

There was still hope, of course. They had lost people to the Wraith before and recovered them again after it had seemed that all hope was lost. But it did not look good, and he thought it might be the first time that it was personal for her. She and Rodney had been seeing each other for months, had been sharing living quarters since they returned to Atlantis, and now he was gone, and it might end just like that, quick and sudden like a candle being blown out.

Jennifer's expression was more awkward than anything else, as if trying to remember how one responded to such remarks. For a moment she reminded him oddly of Colonel Sheppard. "I'm good," she said. "I mean, as much as possible, considering that we're kind of in a holding pattern right now."

"We must be patient," Radek said. "But it is frustrating."

"It's probably best to just get on with everything else," Jennifer said, looking up as one of the Marines entered the infirmary with a sheepish expression and a pronounced limp. "It's not going to do any good to fall apart until, you know, we're there."

"I hope we will not be there," Radek said, but he could recognize a request to be left alone when he heard one. They were hardly close, and he was sure he was not her first choice for a sympathetic ear. It was only that he suspected she might not have one, and at a time like this, sometimes anyone would do to tell about one's troubles.

No, not only that. What he wanted to say was: *The first year, when Peter Grodin was killed, it was hard for me to take, and I said nothing about it because everyone was unhappy, what else was new? And Rodney, who had been his friend, tried awkwardly to say something comforting, although it came out more 'when you think about it, we're probably all going to die,' and I told him to please be quiet so we could get on with work. And now I am sorry I did, because Rodney is terrible at such things, but he tried instead of saying nothing, and to say nothing would have been so easy.*

Jennifer was already crossing the infirmary to greet her new patient, though, and maybe there really was nothing more to say. Radek left her to her examination and ducked out of the infirmary. He nearly ran into Major Lorne, who looked distinctly troubled. That in itself was probably not a surprise.

"Hey, doc, have you got a minute?"

"Not really, but tell me your problems," Radek said. "I will add them to the list."

"The short-range scanners keep cutting in and out," Lorne said. "And when they're in, we're getting some weird readings off them. I don't think it's really likely that we've got company here, but back on Lantea there was that business with the whales —"

"There could be whales here," Radek said. "Dangerous space whales intent on battering themselves against the city suicidally, or possibly on eating military personnel. I would not at all be surprised."

"I'm just saying it would be nice to check it out," Lorne said. "I don't really want to be on a new planet with scanners that don't work."

"I see that," Radek said. "It is possible that the weather is causing some problems. The city was surely once equipped to handle cold and snow in Antarctica, but that was literally thousands of years ago, and it may be that given Lantea's milder climate, keeping those systems working was not a priority."

"But now maybe we might want to rethink that. I've also been noticing that it's a little cold in here."

"People keep opening and closing the exterior doors," Radek said. "You see, without the shield, we have no control over exterior temperatures, and while the city's heating system is very good, we cannot heat the entire outdoors."

"My mom used to say that," Lorne said. "Maybe you could send a memo."

"Yes, that will be sure to help." Radek spread his hands in surrender to the uselessness of attempting to teach all Atlantis personnel to keep doors closed. "I will add it to the list, but at the moment we have worse problems to deal with."

"I know," Lorne said, all humor gone. "Believe me."

Teyla came into the gateroom twelve hours later, cradling a cup of coffee in her hands. Sleep and food had made her feel human again, capable of taking up the search for Rodney with competence.

Radek was there ahead of her, frowning into one of the monitors, his glasses askew. His hair was still wet, so he had not been there long. His usual travel mug of coffee was beside him.

Teyla came and stood beside him, looking over his shoulder at the screen filled with incomprehensible code. "What are you doing?"

"Locking Rodney out," he said. "Which is pretty much an impossible task."

"I don't understand."

Radek spread his hands, flexing fingers above the keyboard and reached for his coffee. "Rodney is in the hands of the Wraith. Rodney has access codes to every one of Atlantis' systems, from power to the shield to the gate codes to the requisition order forms for Earth! He has the codes for the auto-destruct system. He has the codes to drop the shield on the gate. So I am changing everything."

"Rodney would not tell..." Teyla began, and stopped. Of course he would tell. He would have to. She had touched the mind of the Wraith far too often not to understand what it was like, what a Queen's telepathy was capable of. The first time, she had folded like bent paper. When faced with a great queen, the one they had discovered aboard the lost power station beneath the sea, John had crumpled in seconds. Taken by surprise, she had crumpled as well.

But later, knowing and expecting the strength of the mind that wrestled with her own, she had won.

Coldamber, Todd had named her, the queen Teyla defeated. Coldamber, he had said, with a kind of wonder in his voice, and through the corners of his mind she had seen what he remembered, Coldamber in her beauty and pride, while Todd fell to his knees before her in homage, as helpless as John. She had seen his wonder that she, Teyla Emmagan, had defeated Coldamber.

This was the Gift, the remnant of a long-ago medical experiment when a renegade Wraith scientist had combined his own DNA with that of captive humans. Some few of them had survived. Some few of them were her ancestors. Among her foremothers stood a Wraith Queen, the mother of the scientist who had done this, and from that tainted blood sprung her Gift. She was strong enough now, strong enough with Todd's tutelage, that she thought she could face a Wraith Queen and give away nothing.

But Rodney had none of her defenses. He had none of the protection offered by her tainted blood, by the strand of Wraith DNA among her own. His mind would be open to a queen, as surely as the mind of a captive Wraith could be opened to her. She had not tried that. She hoped she would not need to, and yet she held it in reserve, a hidden dagger that no one had as yet realized she carried.

None but Todd. He had opened his mind to her willingly during her charade aboard his hiveship to teach and counsel. But he had been aware, before the end, that if he did not give she could take. It was a curious kind of power, and one that sickened her as much as it pleased her.

Radek mistook her hesitation for disapproval. "I must do it," he said. "I will let Rodney back in when we get him back, but I cannot leave the codes as they are."

"No, of course you cannot," Teyla said. "It would be much too dangerous."

Radek ran his hand through his damp hair. "As it is I make no guarantees. Rodney has backdoors for everything. I have found a few of them, but I know there are many more." He shook his head. "After the time the Replicators took over the city, Rodney swore he'd never be locked out. He would always have a way to get back in. I do not know what they are. And as many as I find, we will never be certain that we have them all." He looked at her and shrugged self-depreciatingly. "Not to mention that he is a genius. I say that without him standing here. He knows my code, knows my style. I do not think I can build something he cannot hack."

"We will get him back," Teyla said, her voice filled with a certainty she did not feel.

"If Rodney gives over to the Wraith what he knows, we cannot stand against them," Radek said.

CHAPTER THREE
Quicksilver

THE THIRD time Quicksilver woke he felt stronger. The data reader lay on the bed beside him, just as he had put it by before he slept. It had been hard to read. He'd had to make an effort, like a child who has not learned properly, and sleep had overtaken him before long. Now he felt better, as though clarity was returning.

Yet he remembered nothing of what had happened to him. A prisoner of the Lanteans, Dust had said. When he closed his eyes he could find a vague impression of towers that stretched against the sky, of a control room with windows of colored glass. Before that nothing. Why could he could not remember Dust, nor this, his home?

He was Quicksilver, one of the foremost of the Queen's Clevermen. These were his rooms aboard the shipworld Bright Venture, large and private rooms as befitted a cleverman of his stature. He had a laboratory as well and eager assistants. Trouble had come to him, but surely he had risen above much in his life. This illness and the mistreatment that had preceded it were only one more thing. In time it would all be behind him.

Quicksilver sat up slowly. Though his limbs were weak they did not tremble. His arms on the side of the bed seemed his own, though marred with the tiny pinpricks of needles. He must have been very ill indeed to have been given medicine straight into the blood, and for the pricks not to have healed almost instantaneously. But then, he had been. Dust had said so.

Carefully he got up and crossed the few steps to the press where his clothes hung. Clean clothes were worth much. Soft black pants to replace the ones he had slept in, those would do. A shirt of dark blue silk, midnight to match the lacquer on his nails, deep bands of embroidery at neck and sleeves, black on blue in an intersecting pattern that looked oddly familiar. It took a moment, but Quicksilver's mind found it. The pattern was that of a circuit board. This was his dress shirt, its embroidery proclaiming his position as a master of sciences physical. With effort, Quicksilver lifted it over his head, letting the soft folds cascade around him.

The door irised open to admit Dust, who started. "Quicksilver? You are standing!"

"I feel better," he replied. "Much better."

Dust nodded gravely. "I am glad. The master of sciences organical has been to see you, and he said that you would wake much restored. I shall be glad to tell him he was correct." Dust came beside him, looking at Quicksilver half dressed, his shirt ballooning around him. "Let me cinch that for you." A few quick ties of threads Quicksilver hadn't even seen, and the shirt fit tightly, only the sleeves billowing while the rest clung to his form.

"I wondered if I could go to my laboratory," Quicksilver said.

"The Queen has asked you to attend on her when you're fit. If you are feeling well enough to be up and about, you must see her first," Dust replied. "She has been concerned. She will not tire you," he said, seeing Quicksilver hesitate. "It is a courtesy only. You need not attend her more than a few minutes."

He could think of no reason to refuse, though the idea filled him with a sort of anxiousness. Perhaps he feared she had been displeased with his work? Or that she would blame him for his capture? It had surely been a great expense and bother.

While he considered, Dust brought his coat and set it to his shoulders, a knee length coat of black silk, not leather as a blade would wear, quilted and trimmed with embroidered facings, black on black.

"There. You are ready," Dust said. He touched Quicksilver's

hand encouragingly. "It will be short, I promise you."

They made their way through the corridors of the shipworld, cool mist blowing caressingly against their faces from the vents, doors opening before them. At the Queen's doors two blades waited, their faces stilled to perfection.

"It is Dust of the Queen's Own Clevermen to see Her Grace," he said. "With my brother Quicksilver, who has been Chief among the Queen's Own."

There was a pause, and the elder of the blades, a tall man with hair worn in long braids, stepped back. "Queen Death will see you."

A frisson ran through Quicksilver, but Dust propelled him forwards, his hand at his back comfortingly.

The lights were lower, amber instead of blue, and Quicksilver caught his breath.

"Come closer, my paladins," she said. On a throne carved of a single piece of glowing coral was a beautiful young woman. Her hair was a river of black silk down her back, bound at her brow with a fillet of silver set with fine stones. Her features were even and proud, and her skin had the glow of youth, high cheekbones arching beneath amber eyes that laughed and danced with pleasure.

When she saw him she rose with one graceful movement, her skirts sweeping around her, and came forward. "Quicksilver!" she said, and her voice was melody and delight. "I am very relieved that you are much better. When you were missing we were all terribly worried, and when you returned so injured…" She broke off, smiling at him. "My dear, we feared the worst! And now you are nearly well again."

"My Queen," Quicksilver murmured, stricken to the core. He could barely speak, and it came to him that he should bow. He bent his head.

"I commend you for your good care," she said to Dust.

"Thank you, My Queen."

"And you, Quicksilver." He raised his eyes and saw that she spoke with mock severity, as though they were very old friends indeed. "I know that you will want to exhaust yourself returning to your laboratory as soon as you may. But I do insist that you rest yourself and do not exert yourself too much. It is not necessary, as we are in no peril, and it is of great importance to me that you be restored."

"You are too gracious," Quicksilver muttered. It was an effort to speak at all, so overwhelming was her beauty and her presence. That she should speak to him thus, dulcetly, and full of appreciation for his work was...

"We were much relieved when we found you," she said. "Do you have any idea how you came to be alone on Fyvera?"

"None, My Queen," Quicksilver said truthfully. "I do not even know where Fyvera is."

She shook her head sadly. "Perhaps you will remember in time how you came to escape. I do not know. But trust that I will avenge you upon the Lanteans, that did this to you!"

"That is kind, My Queen," he said.

"Do you remember aught of your captivity, of Atlantis?"

"No," Quicksilver began, but it seemed to him that he did, a brief impression of a chamber with soaring walls, an Eye set in the middle of a floor of unbearably bright stone. And then it was gone. "Not really," he said.

Her eyes sharpened, and he knew her power as well as her grace, a fluid shift of feature beneath tranquility that reminded him of some other he knew, though her face escaped him. "Do you recall something?"

"Nothing of consequence, My Queen," Quicksilver said. "A brief impression of a room. Nothing of note."

She nodded once. "You should write down that which you remember, or tell Dust if writing tires you. Anything you can remember may be of use to us in the future, either to recover another if they are also unfortunate, or to defeat Atlantis in the end." She looked away, her gaze ranging over the blades assembled in their beauty and honor. "My far-mother tried and failed to take the City of the Lanteans, and she died when her ship crashed in the sea. But her blood is stronger for the centuries that separate us, and I am her true heir! I will not fail! We stand in the age of silver, and our best days are before us!"

Quicksilver felt rather than heard the ripple run around the room, the assent and desire that flowed to her. Who could not desire to serve such, beauty and glory and strength in one?

"I shall give you all you can hope for, My Queen," Quicksilver said, and bent his knees to her in homage.

CHAPTER FOUR
Reluctant Allies

JOHN SLID into a chair at the briefing table nursing a cup of coffee. He'd slept badly, but enough coffee would take care of that. Teyla and Ronon were already there, and Carson and Keller came in together. He wondered if they'd actually been invited to the briefing or were just hanging around to find out what the plan was. It wasn't really a situation where they needed medical advice.

Keller took her seat looking like she hadn't slept much either, and Carson rested a hand on her shoulder for a moment before he sat down. John thought he probably ought to say something, but he couldn't figure out what.

"Let me get you some coffee," Teyla said.

Keller looked up at her gratefully. "Thanks. I can get it, though…"

Teyla was already handing her a steaming cup. "I would offer you tea, but I expect you prefer coffee. It is the least I can do."

Carson smiled faintly. He had a cup of tea already, cupped in his hands as if to warm them. "My mum always makes a cup of tea whenever something terrible's happened. I suppose the idea is that if you can still make tea, things can't be that bad."

"Things aren't that bad," John said, more sharply than he meant to. "We just have a problem here we have to figure out what to do about. Where's Woolsey?"

"Not here yet," Ronon said, as if that were helpful. Probably about as helpful as the question. John took a drink of coffee and hoped the caffeine would kick in soon.

Woolsey came in last, his tablet tucked neatly under his arm.

John suspected he'd learned in some management book that
making people wait for him was better than waiting for them.
Maybe it worked. At least, everyone gave Woolsey their attention instead of making small talk about the weather. Maybe
they'd run out of things to say about it. It was still cold, and
likely to stay that way for a while.

"I'll start with the good news," Woolsey said, with a tight
smile that didn't promise too much. "I have heard both from
Radim and from… Todd."

"We can call him something else if you'd rather," John said.
Teyla gave him a sharp look, as if unsure that he was taking
this briefing sufficiently seriously.

Woolsey chose to ignore the remark instead. "Both of them
are willing to talk. Radim believes his intelligence network
may be able to determine whether Wraith worshippers visited New Athos, and possibly even find out which hive they
were working for."

Ronon was leaning back in his chair in what might have
looked like a casual pose if you didn't know him. "Do we like
the idea that Radim's got people working with Wraith worshippers?"

Teyla turned the look on him. "Would we like the idea that
he did not? We must get our information from somewhere."

"What does Todd have to say for himself?" John asked.

Woolsey looked like that hadn't been a pleasant chat. "He
is also apparently willing to talk."

That seemed too convenient. "Why?"

"I pointed out to him that having Dr. McKay in the hands
of a rival Wraith could have serious consequences for him as
well as for us."

"I'm not sure it's a good idea to play that up," John said.
"We don't want him to get the idea that it's a good idea to grab
Rodney himself."

"At least then we might be able to bargain," Teyla said.

"With a Wraith," Ronon said, looking skeptical.

"With a Wraith who has depended on our assistance in the past."

"He is at least willing to talk to us. At the moment, that's an improvement on our current intelligence. I think we may be able to persuade him that Dr. McKay could provide an unwanted advantage to whichever one of his rivals is holding him."

"Assuming it's *not* Todd," John pointed out.

"Assuming that," Woolsey granted him. "But at least with a meeting we may have some chance of finding out if that is the case."

"So what's the catch?" John said. "You said this was the good news."

"Both Radim and Todd insist on a meeting in person."

"Fine," John said. "They're welcome to come to Atlantis. Alone."

"Yes, I think we'd all prefer that," Woolsey said. "Unfortunately, we're in no position to demand ground of our choosing. Radim has requested that we send representatives to the Genii homeworld, and under the circumstances, that does seem reasonable."

It didn't seem very reasonable to John. "Because holding Dr. Beckett at gunpoint and stealing our medical supplies was just a friendly gesture."

"A misunderstanding," Woolsey said. "Which has been resolved."

"You can't blame Radim for what Sora did," Carson said. "She's a loose cannon, and always has been." He looked less troubled by the whole incident than John felt.

"Todd has proposed a site he claims to be neutral ground. PX5-422. According to the Ancient database, it's uninhabited."

"I want it checked out in advance," John said.

"Yes, of course. We'll send a team, but I want you to leave at once for the Genii homeworld. I've been trying to convey a sense of urgency about this to Radim, and it won't help to keep him waiting."

"Back up," John said. "I should go deal with Todd. Teyla and Ronon can go talk to the Genii."

"I want you to deal with Radim on this," Woolsey said. "Given what we know about the Genii, I think they'll prefer to deal with our military commander. I'd like you to take Teyla and Dr. Beckett with you. Ronon, Dr. Keller, I'd like you to handle the meeting with Todd, once our advance team reports back that the site is safe."

"All right," Keller said. She sounded a little skeptical. John was more than a little skeptical himself. "We can do that." She looked over at Ronon, who shrugged a little uncomfortably.

"You don't want Teyla to come with us?"

Woolsey looked at John. He looked tempted to say something for a moment, and then reconsidered whatever it had been. "I think it's best if Teyla accompanies Colonel Sheppard and Dr. Beckett," he said. "Our relationship with the Genii is a delicate one, and I have every confidence in your negotiating skills."

"Thank you," Teyla said, inclining her head politely.

"Our relationship with Todd could include him sucking the life out of people if he gets cranky enough," John said. "I'll go. If you want to send a military officer to go deal with Radim, send Lorne."

"Thank you for your recommendation," Woolsey said. He hesitated just for a moment, and then said, "Please be ready to dial out for the Genii homeworld in twenty minutes. Dr. Keller, Ronon, I'll let you know as soon as we hear back from the advance team."

There was an overly quiet pause.

"I'd like a word before we go, if you haven't got somewhere else to be," John said evenly.

"Not at all," Woolsey said.

"I will go and prepare for our departure," Teyla said, with a careful smile. "Carson, are there medical supplies you should bring with us?"

"I expect I could find some," Carson said, rising. Ronon and Keller were already slipping out wordlessly.

John waited until they'd all gone before he spoke. "You can't seriously want to send those two to deal with Todd. Ronon doesn't have any other setting for dealing with the Wraith other than 'shoot them,' and Keller's a little green for this kind of thing."

"She has been the chief medical officer in Atlantis for over two years," Woolsey pointed out. "And she's worked with the Wraith — and with these particular Wraith — before. Todd was generally cooperative with her attempts to find a way for the Wraith to survive without feeding, which is frankly the closest we've come to a good working relationship with him."

"I just don't think she has a suspicious enough nature."

"That would be more suspicious than Dr. Keller but less suspicious than Ronon?"

"Yes," John said, although he felt he hadn't exactly won, there.

"Colonel Sheppard," Woolsey said, looking weary. "Please believe I've thought this through. I think our chances of obtaining any useful information from Todd at this point are minimal. We don't have much to offer him, and we have no reason to believe that he has the information we need. I don't want to leave any avenue unexplored, but I think our real hopes rest on what we can find out from Radim."

"You didn't say that in the briefing," John said after a minute.

"Would you rather I had told Ronon and Dr. Keller that I think they're unlikely to find out anything? I would like them to try. If there's someone you think would be better suited to that mission — besides yourself and the team you're taking to the Genii homeworld — I'm open to suggestions."

He wished he had one. "There's not," John said.

"Then please trust that Ronon and Dr. Keller can handle this mission," Woolsey said. "I realize you haven't always had the best working relationship with the Genii in the past, but I think Radim respects you, for what that's worth."

"Probably not much," John said.

Woolsey looked at him hard. "Is it really your best assessment that we can't reach a stable truce with the Genii? I'm asking for your professional opinion."

John took a deep breath and tried for that. "I don't know," he said. "Radim keeps saying he wants one. It's just that he keeps being around when things go wrong between his people and ours. I'm not saying that he's responsible for what Sora does, or for Kolya killing our people or capturing me or generally being a pain in the ass. I'm just saying he's been involved in a lot of situations that have left me pretty reluctant to trust him."

"I'm not asking you to trust him sight unseen," Woolsey said. "Or at all. But you said yourself in the briefing for the new military personnel that the Genii are our best allies here in the Pegasus galaxy."

"We need better allies," John said.

"Maybe so, but that's not today's problem."

"Is there a quota?"

"There are priorities," Woolsey said. "Dr. McKay is the priority today. Try to get us some way of finding him."

"I'll do everything I can," John said.

"I'm sure you will."

Ronon was at the rail at the top of the steps in the control room. "So what are we doing?"

"I'm going to go talk to the Genii with Teyla and Carson," John said. "I'll get Lorne to take a team and check out the planet where Todd wants to meet. If Lorne clears it, and we're not back yet, you and Keller go see what he has to say."

"Just how fast do you think you can talk to the Genii?"

"I can talk pretty fast. How fast Radim's going to be willing to talk, I don't know." John shrugged. "I want you to stay put unless the site is clean. If it seems like Todd's trying to play us, the mission's scratched. I'm serious."

"I'm not going to let Keller walk into a trap," Ronon said. "If it doesn't look good, we'll just stay here and Woolsey can negotiate some more."

"I'll say hi to Radim for you."

Ronon snorted. "I think I'd rather deal with the Wraith. We'll get in less trouble if we have to shoot them."

"Think diplomacy," John said.

"Right."

He'd prefer to have something to shoot, too, but he was comforting himself with the thought that if this worked out, they'd have a target. That was what they really needed.

"Control, this is Jumper One," Sheppard said over the radio. "We're ready to go."

Radek looked over the console on the upper tier and pushed his glasses back up on his nose. The new gate technicians were all nervous at having to learn the ropes while everyone was under so much pressure. Of course, they would probably have been even more nervous had Rodney been here to find fault with everything they did.

"Copy, Jumper One," Airman Salawi said from her station below at the gate board. She glanced up at him for confirmation, her hand hovering over the DHD, and he came around the monitors and stood beside her chair. "Not this time," he said quietly. "We let jumper pilots dial out themselves, using the jumper's DHD. The city's systems will bring the jumper down from the bay automatically, and ensure it remains well clear of the kawoosh when the gate opens."

Salawi grinned. "Is that a technical term, Doctor? Kawoosh?"

"It more or less is." Radek smiled back. She was a good kid, come here a month ago from the SGC where she'd barely begun her training before O'Neill had sent her to Atlantis. "You people invented it. We just use it."

"Weren't you at the SGC too?"

"I was for a year or so," Radek said. He shifted from foot to foot, gauging the preparations below to a nicety. "I will tell you sometime how Dr. Jackson recruited me. But I have been here more than five years now, so this is home."

Salawi shook her head. "You must have some stories."

"I imagine that I do," Radek said. "But you had best hope that in the future I do not have stories of you."

"Only the good kind," Salawi said, grinning. "I wouldn't mind some stories about me like the ones about Colonel Sheppard."

"Possibly not," Radek said, and patted her on the shoulder to soften it. "But there is a high price for stories."

It had been a year ago that he had come back from an off-world mission, not a bad one at all, to hear what had transpired in his absence — an alien intelligence communicating with Mr. Woolsey and Rodney, Sheppard trapped on the mainland by its machinations. An alien intelligence that had at least once impersonated him to speak with Rodney.

Very weird. He had never had an alien intelligence impersonate him before. He was only sorry that he had missed it.

Or possibly not, when he saw Sheppard.

He was coming out of the mess in the morning, coffee in hand, still a little shy of six o'clock. Sheppard was sitting at one of the tables on the balcony, a mug in front of him, looking out at the sea. He was unshaved, and he slouched in his chair like a man most profoundly tired. There was no one else about.

Radek opened the door and came out, falling into the opposite chair. "Good morning."

Sheppard blinked like a man called back from dreams. "Radek."

"Yes."

"Is it really you or an alien intelligence?"

"I think that it is me," he said. "I do not feel so intelligent."

"That's what you'd say if you were an alien intelligence," Sheppard said.

"I would," Radek agreed. "But you will have to take it on faith."

The sun was rising out of the distant sea, green tropic swells rolling softly under the dawn sky frosted with pink clouds. It was unbearably lovely.

"What the hell," Sheppard said softly, not looking at him. "We get an alien intelligence, and Woolsey and Rodney both get people telling them they're great."

"You are great," Radek said seriously. Sheppard looked around at that, and Radek shrugged. "You are. If you want me to say so, I shall. Without drugs or alien intelligence or any of that. I am proud to work with you and call you my friend."

Sheppard blinked and looked away, lashes sweeping shut over bloodshot eyes, tired face heavy in profile. "It was Kolya," he said. "I know he's dead. But you know people don't always stay dead around here. It seemed...plausible."

"Of course it seemed plausible," Radek said logically. "It was coming from your mind."

Sheppard snorted mirthlessly. "Yeah, and what does that say?"

Radek settled back in his chair and took a drink of coffee. "That you are as whacked as the rest of us. We are all a little crazy. It comes with the territory. It seems to me, from what they have said, that the alien intelligence gave Woolsey and Rodney what they felt they deserved." His mouth quirked. "Which says quite a bit about the size of their egos, actually." He tried not to look at Sheppard too keenly. "It is a good thing I was not here," he said.

He felt Sheppard's glance, though he did not look away from the sea.

"I know far too well what I should have seen," he said. He considered a moment, but there was truth sometimes in morning, and to gain a truth you must give truth for truth, slice your palm to show that your blood is red. "I should have been on the satellite, not Peter."

Sheppard did not say anything. There was nothing to say to that. There was only the truth, staring back at them. The sea breeze rolled over them, cool and smelling of salt. The coffee mug was warm in his hands.

"I should have gone," he said. "But Rodney would not hear it. And so it was Peter." He took another drink of the coffee, clearing his voice again. "Sometimes I wish that it had been me. And other times I am afraid that I do not." He shrugged self-depreciatingly, dared a glance at Sheppard. "Survivor's guilt, I think they call it."

"Yeah, that's what they call it." Sheppard nodded seriously, his eyes on Radek as though for the first time this morning he were actually seeing him.

"It was a little crazy that first year," Radek said. "Intense. You know. When things are so intense, one feels things too strongly. When each day is a surprise." He looked at Sheppard sideways. "I have tried to take it as a gift."

Sheppard nodded, looked away, lifting his chin to the sea. Radek did not expect him to reply, but he thought he saw some of the tension in his face ease.

"That is all we can do," he said. "We live with it, you and I." His voice was matter of fact as he went on. "What did Kolya do? Beat you and torture you?"

Sheppard shrugged. "Basically. His usual schtick. Told me he'd killed the science team and he was going to blow up Atlantis and I had to give him the access codes. That kind of thing."

"At least you did not go there," Radek said.

"Where?"

"He did not torture your friends."

Sheppard swallowed. "I don't… This was about me."

"Yes, I see that," Radek said. "Torturing others would serve no purpose."

"No." Sheppard's profile was clean against the morning sky. "He cut off my hand."

"How very Biblical," Radek observed. "Or perhaps that is Sharia law." Sheppard looked at him sharply and Radek shrugged. "Teyla and Ronon would not know, and Rodney never reads anything that is not science."

"That's so screwed up," Sheppard said.

"Yes, well. It is your head, after all."

Sheppard smiled at that, as though the joke were on him. Which of course it was.

"There is nothing to do but live with it," Radek said. "Or die." He took a casual sip of his coffee. "And no, I do not think you are suicidal. If you were, you would only need to stop ducking."

"That's true. But I don't." Sheppard picked up his own mug and looked at it as if surprised that it were empty. "Like you said. Other times I don't wish that it had been me."

"I have tried to take it as a gift," Radek said. "I do not think Peter would wish otherwise."

"A gift." Sheppard looked out to sea, then glanced back at him, one eyebrow quirking. "And that's what you've got for me?"

"That is the thing I have that I think you will accept," Radek said gently.

Sheppard looked away again, that same smile as though he were the fool. "Right."

"I also have a bottle of Scotch, but it is six in the morning," Radek said. "It is perhaps too early to start drinking."

"Yeah, probably," Sheppard said.

Radek smiled back. "You know where to find me if you change your mind."

"Control, this is Jumper One," Sheppard said over the radio. "Dialing out."

Radek shifted out of Salawi's way. "You will see the address lighting on your board, so that you can verify they are going where they intend to. There is the first symbol, you see, the ox head…"

She watched carefully as the symbols lit, comparing them seriously to the address displayed on her computer screen, although of course there was no error. It was not like Sheppard to make careless mistakes. The gate opened in a flash of blue fire.

Salawi smiled at the sight, and Radek couldn't help smiling himself, remembering his own delight the first time he had seen the theoretical products of wormhole physics made real. It would be a shame to become too used to such sights to appreciate them.

The jumper lowered from the bay above, hovering above the gateroom floor, poised to thread the ring of blue.

"Good luck, sir," Salawi said into the radio.

"Thanks," Sheppard said. "We're probably going to need it."

CHAPTER FIVE
Radim's Proposition

THE GENII homeworld had not changed at all. In fact, for a moment, standing in the meadow full of flowers, the bees in the clover, John thought that he had stepped back in time as well, five years before to their first ill-fated trip there. Teyla stood beside him as she had then, but Rodney and Ford were gone.

Ford.

He wouldn't think about Rodney being gone the same way, never to be recovered, an MIA on his file that would never be erased.

Carson bustled up behind him just as he cloaked the jumper behind them, looking up at the pristine blue sky. "Same old same old, I see."

"Indeed," Teyla said, as three Genii scouts rose up from the long grass, rifles pointed at them. "It is exactly the same."

John spread his hands, though he kept his P90 in his right hand, holding it out on its sling. "We're here to talk to Ladon Radim," he said. "From Atlantis."

The nearest of the men, a short man with a bulldog's jaw nodded sharply. "We know who you are, Colonel Sheppard. You'll come with us."

It was a good sign that Radim's men made no attempt to disarm them, despite the fact that their weapons were far superior to the simple repeating rifles of the Genii. John cast a sideways glance at them as they crossed the meadow to the decrepit barn which held an entrance to the Genii's underground complex. Bolt action repeating rifles were a new innovation for the Genii. Five years ago they'd been single shot, more or less the equivalent of the 1853 Enfield. These were getting closer to the Brownings of the not-too-distant past. The Genii had been studying the weapons they'd captured, and pretty clearly they had the technology to understand what they'd seen. John's own automatics were half a century in the future, but the gap was closing quickly. There had been Taliban still using the Brownings when he'd been in Afghanistan, with pretty deadly results.

The barn looked just as it had five years ago too, the kind of decrepit outbuilding that John had seen along the Arkansas highways not too far from his grandparents' house thirty years ago, just a barn on a farm that nobody worked anymore, meadows left to go to seed with knee-high cedar trees. There was no reason to look inside. And if anyone did there was nothing to see except a broken down wagon minus three wheels and a pile of moldy hay.

One of the Genii soldiers scooped the hay aside with an impatient sweep, exposing the round hatch like the conning tower of a submarine. Just like Rodney had five years ago.

"After you, Colonel," the Genii said.

"Don't mind if I do." John swung the P90 onto its sling to descend the ladder, a quick glance at Teyla showing that she was right where he wanted her to be, lagging back to let Carson go between them, looking deceptively small. The Genii tended to underestimate women, a facet of a pretty male dominated society that wasn't lost on him. If it led them to underestimate Teyla, all the better. Her almost imperceptible nod told him she'd read his thoughts as clearly as if he'd spoken them. Five years of working together had rendered any original roughness smooth. Not that there had been much. They'd always been a good team.

At the bottom of the ladder a higher ranking officer was waiting for them. "Chief Radim is looking forward to speaking with you," he said politely.

"Great," John said, casting a glance back up the ladder. Carson was halfway down, Teyla silhouetted against the opening at the top. "We're looking forward to talking to him." He hoped that was sufficiently diplomatic. It had better be. God help Rodney if his life depended on John being diplomatic!

Ladon Radim's official office was underground, the same one that Cowan had used on their first visit. It was spartan, and there was nothing personal in it, not one photograph or book that spoke of personality at all. There were no messages here, unless they were in the utilitarian lines of metal desk and chair. At least there were no messages John could read.

He glanced sideways at Teyla as they were motioned into the office. She looked attentive, not tense. Canary in a coal mine, John thought. Teyla was their canary, and he'd learned to watch her reactions carefully in a situation like this.

"Colonel Sheppard," Ladon Radim stood up and came around his desk to shake hands.

"Chief Radim," John replied. He'd had the opportunity more than once to punch his lights out, and could only regret he hadn't done it. But. Rodney. He'd put up with a lot more than Ladon Radim to find out where Rodney was.

"And Dr. Beckett." Radim greeted Carson with rather more warmth. "I would like to tell you personally how much I regret the incident with Sora. She has been dismissed from our military. She was under direct orders not to interfere with your medical missions, and as I'm sure you know the breach of direct orders is a serious offense. I regret tremendously that you were inconvenienced."

"She's a bit of a loose cannon," Carson said, shaking his hand firmly. "I do not hold you responsible in the least."

Which was rich, John thought. As of course anyone under his orders was his responsibility, loose cannon or not. But. Diplomacy.

"You remember Teyla Emmagan, I believe?" he said.

"I do." Radim turned and offered his hand to her as well.

"It's good to see you again."

"And to see you, Chief Radim," Teyla said. "I am glad to see that you continue to enjoy good health."

Radim laughed. "I'm sure that you are! For the moment our interests run in tandem, something of great advantage to us both."

"And what advantage would that be?" John asked brusquely.

"We are both opposed to Queen Death," Radim said, his eyebrows rising. "Obviously she's a disaster for both of us, and for every human in this galaxy."

"Aye, pretty much," Carson agreed. "She's trouble."

"The most powerful Wraith Queen in…" he spread his hands. "Recorded history, certainly." Radim motioned to the three metal visitors chairs before the desk. "Shall I have my aide bring you some tea?"

"That would be wonderful," Teyla said, catching his eye.

"I love tea," John said, and sat down.

A quarter of an hour passed in pleasantries and tea, mostly discussion of various kinds of tea and some speculation between Carson and Radim as to how the *camellia sinesis* plant had been transplanted to the Pegasus Galaxy, while Radim's aides stood silent watch beside the door.

"Maybe the Ancients liked their cuppa," Carson said, laughing. "It's the only good reason I can think of."

"I like mine," Radim said, and his face sobered. "But you'll be wondering why I'm wasting time talking about tea."

"It had occurred to me," John said bluntly.

Teyla cast him a warning glance. He usually had more patience, and he schooled himself to a pleasant smile, seeing the corner of Teyla's mouth twitch as he did.

"We need each other," Radim said. "Atlantis and the Genii, in both the long and short term."

"Let's talk about the short term," John said.

Radim nodded. "You want information about where the Wraith have taken Dr. McKay, who has him, and where. You'd like me to bend my considerable intelligence network to that task, hundreds of agents on dozens of planets. You'd like me to retask my best men to find yours. It's a risk of considerable resources, not the least of which are the lives of my men."

"And so you want something considerable in return," John said. "What?"

Radim leaned forward, his hands clasped on the desk in front of him. "We need a pilot."

"A pilot for what?" John asked. "You guys don't have planes. Or maybe you do, in the developmental stages. Prop planes, maybe even double engine. But you don't need me for that. Surely you'd rather develop your own cadre of pilots. And those kind of aircraft aren't going to pose any threat to Wraith Darts. They'd be shot down in seconds."

"Of course they would," Radim agreed. "Building an air corps would be a tremendous waste of money and resources on something that would be no check on the Wraith. We need something considerably better."

Teyla's foot brushed against his left foot, stepping down gently. Wait, she said. Hold on and listen to him.

Radim took a deep breath, his blue eyes on John's. "We've found an Ancient warship. It's a wreck, badly damaged, but my engineers say it is salvageable. We want it. We want to repair it, and certainly we want to reverse engineer systems if possible. We're not planning to spend a century developing flight, Colonel. We don't have the leisure. We need ships that can challenge the Wraith."

John nodded seriously. He ought to have expected something like this. "You know that's not going to do it, don't you? The Ancient technology is so advanced, so far ahead of both of us, that we can't reproduce a quarter of what we see. Hell, we can't reproduce the technology of a bunch of people in the Milky

Way who were nowhere near as advanced as the Ancients! The first time we built a fighter based on reverse engineering the thing went haywire and nearly killed our test pilots. And that was based on a Goa'uld Death Glider, not an Ancient warship. This stuff isn't easy."

"We know." Radim nodded. "But we must start somewhere. Do you think my people are any less resourceful than yours at trying to jump centuries of technology in a few years? It's a leap we must all take if we're going to defeat the Wraith." He picked up his mug and took a long swallow of tea.

"What is your proposition?" Teyla asked. "We are certainly willing to consider it."

"As I said, I need a pilot. I need a pilot with the ATA gene who has flown an Ancient warship. I need you to go to the planet where the wreck is, which my engineers assure me they have already substantially repaired, get the ship in the air, and bring it back here. That's all."

"That's pretty straightforward," John admitted. "If the thing will fly. I've flown an Ancient warship before, so…" He shrugged. "But I don't think it's going to do you guys much good, especially without pilots of your own with the ATA gene."

"We have been working on that," Radim said pleasantly. "As you know, the ATA gene is uncommon in this galaxy, but not unheard of. We will find our own pilots to train once we have the ship. But that's not really your concern, Colonel. Your part of the bargain is just to bring it back here. When you bring us the warship, we'll task our men with finding Dr. McKay."

"It's on a planet full of Wraith or something, isn't it?" Carson asked.

Radim laughed. "No. It's on an uninhabited world, one that's too dry and unappealing to support human civilization anymore. Unfortunately, the crash site is a considerable distance from the Stargate, but with your ships that shouldn't be much of an obstacle. A few minutes' flight. While the Wraith doubtless know of the planet's existence, since there are no humans there and the climate is inhospitable, there is no reason for them to be there or pay the planet any special attention." He shrugged. "There are hundreds of worlds like it, essentially barren balls of rock with marginal atmosphere, of no use to anyone. Which is probably why the wreck has survived. If it had been on an inhabited world, it would have been scavenged long ago."

"But if the Wraith show up," Carson began.

"We've got a cloaked jumper," John said. "And if we get there and the Wraith are all over the wreck the deal is off. We'll come straight back."

"If the deal is off, the deal is off." Radim shrugged. "Obviously if you can't get to the ship or get it in the air, we'll have to come up with something else for you to trade for our intelligence networks."

"Ok." John nodded. "That's fair. We'll get on it. Give me the gate address."

"Of course," Radim said.

Teyla glanced at him sideways. "We will need to return to Atlantis first," she said. "We do not have a scientist with us who is experienced with Ancient technology. We will return with Dr. Zelenka and…"

"I don't think we need Zelenka," John said.

"If the ship's systems are in need of repairs," Teyla began.

That was always Rodney's job, putting things back together with duct tape and spit, complaining constantly that it would never work, it would never fly.

"We don't need Zelenka," John said.

Teyla's eyes narrowed. "But if we need to make repairs…"

"I'm sure our Chief Scientist will be happy to assist you," Radim said. "My sister, Dahlia Radim, will be accompanying you. She has been heading up our Ancient Technology Recovery program, and will be able to do whatever you need."

"Great," John said. "Then we'll get going. The sooner the better." He stood up. "Let's get a move on, people." Every moment they wasted talking Rodney was in Wraith hands.

They filed out of the office and through the halls, upstairs to the barn where the hatch led to the upper world. Radim left them at the bottom of the stairs. "Dahlia will be with you in a few moments," he said.

John looked suspiciously after him.

Carson shrugged. "If it was a double cross there would be easier ways to do it. I think it's on the up and up. So you'll be flying the Ancient warship home and I'll be flying the jumper?"

"Sounds good to me," John said. He twitched as a bird outside burst into song. Hours. This whole diplomatic thing was taking hours. And it would take hours again to get this ship and get back, but that was probably the fastest way to get Radim on the case. At least what the Genii wanted was straightforward.

"I think we should go get Radek," Teyla said quietly.

"That's going to take a really long time," John said. "Look, I'll call in and tell Woolsey what's up, but if we go back to Atlantis we'll have meetings and debriefings and it will be half a day before we get on the road again. And either this thing will fly or it won't. If it won't, the deal's off. And if it will, then we just do it. Radim isn't going to send his sister to go get this thing if he didn't think it would work."

"That's true enough," Carson said. "I had her as a patient, if you remember. Lovely girl. He was worried sick about her. I'd say if Dahlia Radim is along he expects it to go smoothly."

Teyla didn't look convinced. "As you say, Colonel."

CHAPTER SIX
Live Wires

"LOOK, HERE they go again," Lorne said in frustration as the security readout flickered. "We're having these long periods where we're not getting any data from the external sensors, and then when we do—"

"Yes, I see," Radek said, pointing out the same faint blur that Lorne had seen at the edge of the city. As long as he was hanging out in the control room waiting for Woolsey to clear him to take his team out, Lorne thought at least he might be able to pin down what was wrong with the sensors. It would be nice to be able to cross one problem off their list.

"If it's not some kind of software error—"

"It should not be," Radek said. "We have not made any modifications to the programming of the sensors since before we left Earth. It is possible that the external sensors themselves could be accumulating ice."

"Great," Lorne said. If he was remembering right, the external sensor arrays weren't anywhere that would make removing ice from them easy. "We can go out in a jumper and see if we see any ice. At least that would be a simple problem. What about these weird readings, though?"

"That is actually of more concern to me," Radek said, the green light from the display reflecting off his glasses as he leaned closer and frowned. "Our preliminary scans of the planet found no signs of habitation, or of concentrations of large animal life in the oceans surrounding our landing site."

"We didn't find out about the whales for a while, though, either."

"Well, we were not looking," Radek said.

"We scanned this planet pretty fast," Lorne pointed out. "And

I know Teyla always says that planets in Pegasus that aren't inhabited aren't inhabited for a reason."

"In this case, the reason is that there was no Stargate here," Radek said without looking up. "The only people with any way of reaching this planet would have been the Travelers, and there are few natural resources on this world that would be of interest to them."

"Or to us, it seems like."

Radek spread his hands. "We did not have a lot of choice. We had to set down somewhere." His hands were moving swiftly over the keyboard. "As much as our power had been depleted by malfunctions at that point, we were lucky to find a habitable planet and make a safe landing. And as for taking off again—"

"I'm not saying we have to," Lorne said.

"No, but you are not the only person to suggest it." Radek shook his head. "This was the best planet we could reach with the power we had at the time. And now that we have landed and would have to factor in the power required to take off again…"

"We're stuck here."

"Unless you have brought a spare ZPM in your luggage."

"Afraid not."

"All right, I have reduced the sensors' range, which should provide a stronger signal in our immediate area." He zoomed in on one of the piers. "You see here? That may be ice."

"Sea ice?" Lorne said, frowning. "It's not that cold."

"Not nearly cold enough for the sea water around us to freeze, no," Radek said. "I would like to get some samples of the ice. Assuming it is ice."

"Always assuming," Lorne said. "What are we looking for, here?"

"Saltwater ice has a different concentration of salt than fresh-water ice," Radek said, his hands sketching what might be chunks of ice in the air. "If this is freshwater ice, we are probably looking at pieces of ice that have calved off an ice shelf. Oceanography is not exactly my field, but…"

"But you're worried about icebergs." Lorne shrugged in answer to Radek's quick sideways glance. "It's not my field either, but I do know something about problems that ships can run into."

"I will ask Dr. Bryce to take a look," Radek said. He adjusted the sensors again, frowning, the display zooming in on another part of the city, high on one of the towers. "That cannot be ice."

"Probably not," Lorne said. "Switch over to life sign readings, will you?"

Radek raised his eyebrows. "I would not think… no, there is nothing. Unless…" He tapped at the keyboard again. "We keep the sensors programmed to ignore life sign readings below a certain size. That was after we found that alarms were going off every time a bird landed on the city."

"What bird's going to be out in this weather?"

"The weather is not so bad as that," Radek said, sounding a bit frustrated. "We are not talking penguins, here. And there should be few available food sources to attract birds to the city, although it could be that because of the storm…"

He trailed off as the blur suddenly sharpened and resolved itself into what looked like dozens of small, moving blobs of light.

"That's a lot of birds," Lorne pointed out.

"It could be just the local equivalent of a flock of seagulls," Radek said hopefully. "Nothing to worry about, just a perfectly natural phenomenon with no effect on the city's systems whatsoever. That is possible, yes?"

"Sure," Lorne said. They both watched the small moving forms cross and recross the display.

After a moment, Lorne sighed. "I'll get together a team to check it out."

Radek looked weary. "That is probably best."

Before he could head out to do that, alarms sounded, making Salawi's eyes widen as she looked down at her board. "Unscheduled offworld activation," Lorne prompted.

"Unscheduled offworld activation," she repeated over the communications system, her voice growing more confident as she spoke. "We're receiving Colonel Sheppard's IDC and a radio transmission."

"Put him on," Lorne said.

"This is Sheppard," Sheppard said.

"Good to hear from you, sir," Lorne said. "Mr. Woolsey just went down to lunch. Let me get him up here for you."

"That's all right," Sheppard said. "Just tell him that Radim may have some information for us, but he wants us to do a favor for him and go check out a wrecked Ancient spaceship that he thinks he can salvage. We're going to take the jumper and go take a look. We'll report in after we've checked it out."

"Yes, sir," Lorne said. He wondered what about this plan Sheppard expected Woolsey to object to. "Will you need a science team?"

"We're just going to take a look," Sheppard said. "Radim's sister has been investigating the wreck, and we think with her help we may be able to get the thing working." Zelenka's eyebrows rose, and he looked like he was about to say something, and then like it had occurred to him that doing so would mean volunteering to go wander around wreckage offworld. He frowned and bent over his console again instead. "We're waiting on her right now."

"Okay, sir," Lorne said. "I'll let Mr. Woolsey know."

Zelenka met Lorne's eyes again as the transmission cut off. "I hope they know what they are doing."

Lorne shrugged. There wasn't much he could say, and certainly not in front of Salawi, who was smart enough to pick up on any hint he might drop that he thought Colonel Sheppard might not have entirely thought this through. "I'm sure they do," he said.

Dahlia Radim didn't keep them waiting long. She was a few years younger than Teyla, in her mid thirties, blond hair pulled back in a long pony tail, wearing a serviceable jumpsuit and carrying a large pack. "I'm sorry to have kept you waiting," she said, pulling herself up the last rungs of the ladder into the barn.

"No trouble, love," Carson said, bending to help her the last little way. "We've just called in by radio and let them know where we're going." He gave her a warm smile.

Teyla approved, both of the smile, and of letting Radim know that Atlantis would know exactly what agreement they'd made and where they were going. Carson was much better at the iron hand in a velvet glove than John was. He had an iron hand and a velvet glove, but there was no meeting between the two.

"Are we ready?" John asked by way of greeting.

"I'm ready," Dahlia said, letting Carson lift her pack for her so that she could slip her arms through the straps.

"That's pretty heavy," Carson said.

"It's my equipment," Dahlia said. "I led the expedition that did the repair work on the Ancient warship. Of course without the ATA gene we couldn't initialize systems, but I think we have both sublight and hyperdrive working, though we have no shields or weapons, and only limited power outside of certain sections. There are hull breaches we haven't been able to repair, though it appears that the ship has airtight bulkheads that have sealed off those areas."

John frowned. "Are you sure this thing is spaceworthy? If there are decompressed sections and any of those bulkheads are damaged, it's going to be a serious problem."

"No," Dahlia said frankly. "I'm not sure. But I can't be sure without initializing systems. We've been all over the ship three times, and it's as tight as I can make it without being able to turn it on and get readings." She glanced from John to Carson. "That's where you gentlemen come in. We've gone as far as we can go without a pilot."

"We'll give it the old college try," Carson said.

Dahlia gave him a brilliant smile. "I'm sure you will, Doctor." She looked back at John. "If the ship proves unspaceworthy, we'll return and tell Chief Radim that it needs more work. The ship is a four day journey overland from the Stargate, so as you can imagine it's been an effort to get crews out to work on it, especially given the environment."

Teyla felt her brows rise. "Is the planet hostile, then?"

"A planetary day is forty of your hours long," she said. "And the atmosphere is thin. It's not impossible, but it's thinner than most human inhabited worlds. Given the length of day and the atmosphere, there are extremes of daytime and night time temperature, from very hot to very cold in a matter of hours, and day and night are each twenty hours long. We found it a challenging work environment."

"We're not planning on staying there long," John said. "With the jumper we can reach the ship from the Stargate in a few minutes, and then it shouldn't take too long to either get the systems running or to know we can't. Either way, it's a short trip." He opened the barn door. "Let's get going."

Teyla hung back to go last, Dahlia and Carson chatting amiably ahead of her. It was not like John to be so quick to dismiss any warning, she thought. He was worried about Rodney, imagining horrible things happening every moment that Rodney remained in captivity. She supposed he had been the same when she was in Michael's hands. She had heard as much from Sam and others. This was no different. John's team was his family. That had never been more obvious than on Earth, when he thought the team was disbanded forever. It had begun to worry her considerably, what would become of him if Atlantis did not return to the Pegasus Galaxy. He had no other home.

Teyla settled into the copilot's seat as she usually did, with Carson behind John and Dahlia in the seat behind hers that was usually Ronon's.

"Ok," John said, moving the indicators forward, "Punch the gate."

Teyla pressed the coordinates they had been given, Dahlia looking forward over her shoulder. "This ship is extraordinary," she said. "I only wish we had one like it."

"Yeah, I bet you do," John said. He didn't lift his eyes from his instruments. He knew that Teyla would take that as she did. Still, Dahlia Radim was one person, and even if her backpack held weapons or a bomb Teyla was quite sure she could take her out by herself, discounting Carson and John entirely, if Dahlia tried to take control of the jumper. The only way she could do that would be by threat, as she couldn't fly it herself.

"I didn't mean that…" Dahlia began.

"Of course not," Carson said, but Teyla heard the note of doubt in his voice.

"You can search me if you want," Dahlia said, the color rising in her face.

John glanced sideways at Teyla.

She shook her head very slightly. "I see no need for that," she said. "After all, we must learn to trust one another." Dahlia could not see her face, but John could. He could read perfectly clearly what was there. I will be watching her, never fear. And I can handle her if I must.

"Right then," John said, replying to her expression as well as her words. "Let's do it." He shoved the indicators forward, and the puddle jumper soared through the gate.

Into the middle of a flight of Wraith Darts.

"Crap!" John said, pulling up wildly and rolling like a fish in shallow water as blue fire erupted all around them. Dahlia screamed. Teyla clutched the seat arms and managed to make no sound at all.

Four Darts. No, five. They swarmed around them in a pinwheel as the jumper jinked, John looking for an opening as the ground swam beneath them, wheeling with his spins. With the inertial dampeners on full, Teyla could not have said which way was down, or how far. Not far, surely. They had just come out of the gate. There was no altitude to play with.

There was a bang and a pop, one of the displays behind Dahlia shorting out in a cascade of sparks.

"Bloody effing hell!" Carson said, grappling for the fire extinguisher behind his seat.

The jumper jinked again, and John found an opening, pulling ninety degrees straight up, a full power climb into the indigo sky. The atmosphere was so thin that even at midday the sky had a purplish tinge, a few bright stars showing through. Teyla kept her eyes on one as they climbed, growing brighter with altitude. Another shot rocked them, and then John leveled abruptly, rolled left, and began a power dive back toward the ground. He spun past a Dart so closely that Teyla could see the pilot, his silver hair held back in a dark chain, and then they were past, skimming over the red brown dirt.

"What happened?" Carson shouted, spraying foam liberally in the smoke-filled cockpit.

"We have engaged the cloak," Teyla said. On the display she could see the Darts hunting behind them, still gaining altitude along the jumper's last known course. "I think we have lost them."

"That's not all we've lost," John said grimly, his fingers white on the controls. "We've lost main propulsion and the vertical stabilizers. Carson, can you lock it down?"

Carson looked around wildly. "How do I do that?"

"Maybe I can," Dahlia said, coming out of her seat. "Where are the control panels?"

"I don't know!" Carson said.

"You'd better figure it out," John said. "Fast. Because we're losing altitude and I'm going to have to land this bird on the auxiliary steering thrusters."

"Not again," Teyla said quietly.

John spared her a sideways glance, the ghost of a smile quirking his mouth. "Been through too many jumper crashes with me?"

"The only time it is too many is the last time," Teyla said, and held on tight.

The ground came up with dizzying speed, reds and browns blurring together. The jumper pulled up, the horizon stabilizing in front of them. They skimmed over the ground heavily, like an injured bird, reds and browns and tans dissolving into canyons and peaks, plateaus and gorges carved by dry rivers.

The jumper shook and John's left hand flew over the board, a look of intense concentration on his face.

With a bone-jarring thud the jumper sunk into one of the canyons, rock scraping along one side, and came to a stop.

Dahlia and Carson were coughing, foam from the fire extinguisher around them.

John came out of his seat them moment the jumper settled, pistol in hand, pointed straight at the middle of Dahlia Radim's chest. "I want some answers," he said.

"It wasn't me!" Dahlia's blue eyes were wide, soot streaked across her face. "I swear by everything I hold holy that it wasn't me!"

"You're going to tell me that we just happened to run into a flight of Darts the moment we came through the Stargate because of pure dumb luck?" John demanded, his jaw set. "This had nothing to do with the Genii?"

"Why would I do that?" Dahlia yelled back. "Why would I set myself up to get myself killed? If the Darts had blown us to bits I would be as dead as you were! Why would Ladon do that?"

"They weren't pulling any shots," Carson said.

"Maybe Ladon didn't know about it," John said. "I don't know. But this was a set up." He didn't drop the muzzle of the .45 four feet from her heart.

"Maybe it was," Dahlia said. "Maybe my brother has a traitor on his staff! But this was not me! This was not Ladon! I had nothing to do with this!"

"John," Teyla said quietly, but he had already lowered the pistol.

Smoke swam around him in the cockpit, though the fire was out. "Nothing to do with it," he said skeptically.

"Why would I commit suicide this way?" Dahlia demanded. "There are easier ways to kill you people, you know. We get nothing out of this. Nothing!"

"Is there really an Ancient warship?"

"Yes!" Dahlia's eyes were wide. "Everything I told you is true!"

"Then why were those Darts waiting for us?" John asked.

"I don't know!"

"And why haven't they found us?" Carson asked.

"The cloak is still working," John said. "And it's about the only thing that is. We've lost the main engines and the DHD."

"Aw, crap," Carson said, his face falling. "You mean we'll have to walk back to the Stargate and dial manually?"

"With a bunch of Darts hanging around waiting for us," John said. "Oh, and we're about sixty miles from the Stargate, just to add to the fun."

Carson brushed past John and leaned over the board. "We've still got passive sensors. There's a hive ship in orbit."

"Oh yeah," John said, not taking his eyes of Dahlia. "There sure is."

"Perhaps they saw the wormhole open and came to investigate," Teyla said.

"And started shooting the minute we cleared the event horizon? That's coincidental," John said.

"I'm not saying it wasn't a trap," Dahlia said. "I'm just saying that Ladon and I weren't part of it. Look, he has a lot of enemies. They'd love to kill me and destroy his alliance with Atlantis. It's possible that someone tipped off the Wraith. But it wasn't us."

Teyla shook her head. "That is true. I do not see what Ladon Radim would gain from killing his sister and destroying his own alliance. He does not gain Atlantis merely by killing us, and he is wise enough to know that any agreement with the Wraith to leave the Genii alone will last only as long as is convenient for them."

John let out a long breath. "Ok. Teyla, search her. And then Carson, I want you to run a scan for a subcutaneous transmitter."

"Fine." A blush rose on Dahlia's face, but she lifted her chin.

Knowing how the Genii were about personal modesty, Teyla picked up Dahlia's pack and handed it to John. "Why don't you and Carson stay in the cockpit and check this while we go in the back and I search her?" John's eyes met hers and she answered his unspoken question. "Yes, it will be fine. I will call you if I need anything."

Dahlia's face was flaming as Teyla closed the bulkhead door. "I take it you expect me to disrobe completely."

"Yes," Teyla said, and her voice was cold. "It is the only way we can be certain."

"Better you than the others," Dahlia said, unzipping her jumpsuit.

"I thought you would agree," Teyla said. "I did not think you would prefer to have Colonel Sheppard search you." Her hands were quick and methodical, but still Dahlia shuddered.

"He is a hard man," Dahlia said.

"Yes." Teyla did not let awkwardness make her hurry. "He is a soldier. It makes one cruel." Dahlia would know that. The Genii were no different, Ladon Radim included.

Dahlia nodded, turning and raising her arms with only a little wince. "And you?"

"I am that which is worse," Teyla said. Let her make of that what she would.

There was a word in the language of the Genii for such as her — Bloodtainted, whose Gift of Wraith DNA had made tainted, made to glory in the mastery of others. They meant it as a mental disorder now, a name for those whose pleasure came from domination. It had been several generations since they had killed the last of those with the Gift among them. Most of those who, like her ancestors, had been the subject of those Wraith experiments had been slaughtered by the humans who came in contact with them. Only on worlds like Athos had any survived.

"You may dress," Teyla said, and opened the communicator to the cockpit. "She is clean."

"Her bag is fine too," Carson said. "When Miss Radim is dressed I'll come in and do the scan. There's nothing she needs to take off for that."

"Understood," Teyla said. She turned and gave Dahlia a reassuring smile. "It seems your pack is clean as well."

"I have told you that I was not in on this," Dahlia said indignantly, still putting her arms in the sleeves of the jumpsuit.

"Do you think we could afford to believe you?" Teyla asked.

Dahlia's eyes met hers, swimming with humiliation, but level all the same. "Of course not." Her voice was stark. "That's not the way it works."

In a moment, when Dahlia was fully dressed, Teyla opened the doors and she and Carson traded places. She heard him chatting in his best bedside manner while she slid into the copilot's seat next to John. Outside the front window there was nothing to see except the rocky side of the canyon.

"Ok?" John looked at her sideways.

"Yes." Teyla leaned forward, her elbows on the edge of the console. "What is the situation?"

"We still have the cloak," John said. "Which is why we aren't dead. There have been four or five flyovers, but they haven't spotted us. I got us down in a canyon, so there isn't a lot of surface torn up that they could see even if they couldn't see the jumper." His hands slid over the board. "But the engines are dead. We've got power, but I'm not getting anything to the main drive or the vertical stabilizers. All I've got are the steering thrusters. That might, and that's a big might, be enough to take off with but it won't get us back to the gate. It wouldn't get us a mile."

"And the gate is sixty miles away?" Teyla rested her head on her hands. "What is that thing you say when you have done something before?"

"Déjà vu," John said. "Maybe Carson can fix the engines."

Teyla looked at him sharply. "Maybe Dahlia can. You know that Carson knows absolutely nothing about fixing a puddle jumper's engines. You might as well ask me to fix them, or do it yourself."

John's mouth tightened. "Go on. Say it."

"If you had listened to me about going to get Radek we would not be in this situation."

"There. You said it." John winced. "Need to say it again? Let me help. John, you are stupid as a stupid, stupid thing."

"I only needed to say it once," Teyla said. "I am certain that you will flog yourself more thoroughly than I would flog you."

"And it will be much less fun," he said darkly.

Surprised, she couldn't help but laugh. "I hope you do not mean that! All this time I thought you were simply terrible at stick fighting!"

He had a sheepish expression on his face. "I didn't mean that! Not that way."

"You do not mean that you are throwing the fights so I will hit you?"

"Not usually." The corner of his mouth twitched and she could not be sure whether he were teasing or not.

For a moment their eyes locked, the tension in the air between them live as electricity.

The back door slid open. "She's good as gold," Carson said, Dahlia behind him. Her blush had faded, and she seemed to have regained her self-possession.

Which made one of them, Teyla thought. John looked as though he had just swallowed a frog, and she imagined she looked no better.

"Great," John said.

Teyla turned to Dahlia, her professional trader's smile plastered to her face. "I regret that we could not take your word," she said. "But as we are now all in this together, we must work together to solve our problems."

Nodding, Dahlia sat down once again in her seat, Carson almost protective at her elbow.

"Let's hear the bad news then," Carson said. "Colonel?"

CHAPTER SEVEN
Quicksilver

QUICKSILVER sat before the datascreen in his laboratory, watching numbers scroll top to bottom in a blur. Once, he thought, he should have had sense from them. But now they made no sense, going so fast, telling of things he did not remember. This the Lanteans had taken from him.

Quicksilver lifted his hands to his eyes and rubbed them with his wrists.

"You are unwell?" his brother, Dust, asked, forever attentive to his mood.

"No," he replied. "Just…" He could hardly find the words for the frustration he felt, that what should be so simple was rendered so difficult.

"It is hard, I know," Dust said sympathetically. "But perhaps your memory will return in time. You remember nothing of Atlantis?"

Quicksilver shook his head. "Nothing." Only a few tantalizing images, rooms, unfamiliar faces, as though seen through a sheen of water. "Tell me of Atlantis," he said to Dust swiftly, and when his brother began to demur he pressed. "Tell me what you know. Perhaps it will help me remember."

At that Dust nodded reluctantly and came to sit opposite him on the other bench, lifting the tails of his coat fastidiously so that they would not wrinkle. "We do not know so very much, so it is not a very good story."

"Tell me anyway," Quicksilver said.

Dust sighed and began. "They came some time ago — we do not know exactly how long — from a world of humans in another galaxy. They came to the City of the Lanteans and held it as by birthright under the control of a very great

Queen, She Who Is A Strong Place. We do not know why she came, with her clevermen and blades. Perhaps she had the losing end of a struggle in her own place, or perhaps she desired greater dominion than she could wrest from the queens there. We do not know. But we do know that she was of full years and at the height of her powers, and that her blades and clevermen were skilled. And she was worthy of her name. When a rival hive of humans captured her own Consort, the one they call Guide, she watched him tortured in front of her and betrayed nothing. That is the act of a Queen, Quicksilver! Only a great Queen would have such courage and such dignity."

Quicksilver swallowed. For some reason it left a hollow pit in his stomach, imagining the helpless man bound and gagged before the cameras. But perhaps it was only that he was a cleverman, and admiration for such dignity was the province of blades. They always said clevermen were soft.

Dust cleared his throat. "But the Asurans rose up, as they did to the detriment of many hives, and many of our lives were lost in fighting them, the enemies of all life, for they killed humans as they did us, and their ire was directed toward the Lanteans as toward us in equal measure. And they did kill She Who is A Strong Place, as they did so many of our queens, leaving the Lanteans queenless." He paused to let the horror of that sink in. "As in so many of our hives, there was no heir at hand, for the Young Queen was untried and too young yet, and was also carrying her firstborn. So the Consort, Guide, sent back to their place and made an alliance with one of the mightiest Queens of Earth, one who is called She Who Carries Many Things. And She Who Carries Many Things came to the City of the Lanteans and there she confirmed Guide as her Consort." Dust shrugged. "No doubt it was for form's sake alone, as these things often are. We have heard that she has a Consort in her own place, an older blade named Trickster, as is to be expected. She Who Carries Many Things is a warrior Queen, and in little time had pressed the Asurans to the bone and destroyed them, to the glory of us all and to the rejoicing of every hive that is — for surely all of us, Wraith and Kine alike, would be dead if not."

Quicksilver nodded, and for a moment he could almost imagine this Queen, the gleam of shiplight off pale hair over luminous eyes. "She is beautiful," he said.

Dust looked at him quickly. "You saw her?"

"I don't know," Quicksilver said quietly. "Maybe? I just know she's beautiful."

"There are many clevermen who would worship such a Queen," Dust said contemplatively.

"I don't know," Quicksilver said, but again he saw her turn toward him, her face sharp with disapproval, beautiful and forever out of reach. Yes, that must be what Dust meant.

"But She Who Carries Many Things had a greater realm and much to do in other places, so after the Asurans were defeated she went away, leaving in her stead one of her blades, called Hairy." Dust snorted. "We think it is a joke, as he is an ugly man with little hair. And so Hairy and the Consort Guide rule over the Lanteans while the Young Queen grows." He shrugged. "We do not know what assurance the Young Queen has given She Who Carries Many Things that she and her son should be let to live, but perhaps they are kin through their mothers, and She Who Carries Many Things is content to let her be her proxy. We do not know. But that is where things stand. It is this Consort, Guide, who is the power among the Lanteans, unless She Who Carries Many Things returns."

Quicksilver nodded slowly. It was disturbing. All of it. Maybe they'd tortured him. Maybe this Queen had... Something. He could not get out of his mind that he knew her, that he had desired her fruitlessly. He could almost remember, the image was so strong… "Thank you," he said to his brother. "I will try to remember. And when I do, I will tell you all I know."

CHAPTER EIGHT
Trapped

"RIGHT NOW our life signs are masked by the cloak," John said. "But the minute we step outside the Darts will know exactly where we are."

"And how long can we maintain the cloak?" Carson asked, leaning forward in his chair, his brow furrowed.

"With our present power consumption, a couple of weeks longer than we have food and water for," John said. "That's not the problem."

"And how long is that?" Carson said, looking even more worried.

"We have ten days emergency rations," Teyla said. "Carson, at worst Mr. Woolsey is not going to wait ten days before sending a rescue party. We told him the gate address where we were going."

"No, but he will wait four or five days," John said grimly. "I told him we'd be nursing an Ancient warship back to the Genii homeworld. He wouldn't be surprised if repairs took a day or two, and the trip back took two or three days in hyperspace. He won't get worried until Radim says we haven't showed up in four or five days." He looked at Teyla as if expecting her to say something about Radek Zelenka. As though she would undermine him that way before Dahlia Radim!

Teyla frowned. "Is there any chance of fixing the jumper?"

Dahlia shook her head. "I don't believe so. Not that I can do. I'm familiar enough with Ancient technology to see that the main control crystals to the engines, the DHD and the stabilizers are burned out. Two of the three of them are actually broken, one completely and one with a long lateral crack that will shatter the minute we put any current into it. We would need replacement crystals and some means of repatterning them. Dr. Beckett says that the ships' locker does not contain replacement crystals, and I have no tools to repattern them if it did. That's not something we've ever succeeded at doing." Dahlia spread her hands. "I've pulled damaged crystals from the warship, but the warship carried labeled replacements. It was a matter of switching them out correctly."

Rodney always carried replacement crystals. The thought hung in the air between them. Ever since the time they'd been stranded on Pelagia, he'd carried a couple in his pocket just in case, to good effect on Manaria. And Zelenka had been the one who had come up with the method of repatterning the jumper's control crystals more than five years ago, on the mission where John had been attacked by the Iratus bug.

"Can't we…" Carson began, then lapsed into silence.

"No. We can't," John said. "If we start messing around in the control panels doing stuff when we don't know what we're doing, we may short out the cloak. And then we're really screwed." His eyes avoided Teyla's. "We're not going to figure out how Zelenka did it. I'm not an engineer, and neither are you. If Dr. Radim says she can't do it, we'll take her word as the expert."

Dahlia blinked, as though surprised by the vote of confidence. And also perhaps by the honorary title, Teyla thought. She had not heard doctor used as an honorific among the Genii. It was solely reserved for healers.

"Where does that leave us?" Carson said. "Just sitting here until the Wraith get bored?"

"Pretty much," John said. "Sooner or later they'll have to conclude that either we're all dead and that accounts for the absence of life signs, or that we've escaped into space, which is more likely. If we can't repair the jumper, our best shot is to wait until the Wraith leave and then walk out." He looked as though he didn't like the idea much.

Carson put his head to the side. "It could be worse," he said.

"None of us are hurt, and we've plenty of supplies."

"What if the Wraith simply hide?" Dahlia asked. "That's what I would do. Take the hive ship around to the other side of the planet and wait."

John glanced at Teyla and she nodded almost imperceptibly.

"We have sensors that would pick them up," he said. "Even at that kind of range."

I would know, Teyla thought. An entire hive ship close at hand would never escape her attention, not as her Gift was now, strengthened by Todd's tutelage. But there was no need to speak of that to Dahlia, and certainly not now while they must work together in close quarters. If she took Teyla's Gift as pollution it would make things very awkward, not only for Teyla personally but possibly for their alliance with the Genii as well.

Dahlia nodded. She had no idea what the capabilities of the puddle jumper's sensors were, after all. "There is another option," she said.

"What's that?" Carson asked.

"Rather than walk back to the Stargate, we are less than twenty of your miles from the wreck now," she said. "We are more or less along the line that my repair parties trekked from the gate to the wreck. I can easily find it from here. And it would take much less time than going three times further to the Stargate."

"But if it's inoperable then we have to walk back to the gate anyhow," Carson said. "And besides, if we walk back to the gate it will take a couple of days. It will take longer than that to get the ship in the air and return to the Genii homeworld. From the gate we can just dial Atlantis directly."

"And then we will be back in Atlantis, with nothing to show for our journey," Teyla said. "Four days or more gone, and just as we were." She looked at John. "If time is of the essence, we should continue on directly to the wreck and hope to get it in the air. We are already here."

John nodded. "And complete the mission." The idea of returning to Atlantis with nothing to show for it save a lost puddle jumper clearly rankled. "That's the best plan."

"Then we wait like cornered mousies," Carson said, glancing out the front window as though he could see the patrolling Darts above. "For the cat to go away."

Seven more hours stuck in the limited confines of the jumper was making everyone jumpy. Carson prowled around looking for something to do, and Dahlia Radim was inventorying the emergency equipment, though they already knew perfectly well what they had. Teyla went from front to back again, pacing. Parceling out MREs and eating a belated dinner or an early breakfast or whatever it was did not take more than three quarters of an hour. And then she was back to pacing again.

John was the only one who seemed calm, sticking to the pilot's chair as if glued there, his eyes on the sensors as though he could will the Wraith away.

Teyla slid into the copilot's chair. "Has anything changed?"

"The hive ship has recovered Darts," he said, his eyes still on the display. "I can't tell if that's because they're powering up to leave, or because the patrol is out of fuel and they need to switch off."

"We will see," Teyla said quietly. Using the Gift in a more active way, to feel out the minds of the Wraith above looking for more specific information, would almost certainly alert the Wraith to their presence. And if they were trying to convince the Wraith that they had gone that would be a bad idea. Better to wait and see what the Wraith did.

"Yeah." John radiated tension in every line of his body, strung tight to the board. He was blaming himself for the delay, she thought. And how not? It really was his fault. If they had returned to Atlantis for Radek before coming here, the jumper would be repaired by now.

But the Wraith would still be here.

"Even if we had Dr. Zelenka," Teyla said, "We should still have to wait until the Wraith departed. We cannot challenge a hive ship."

"That's true." He took a breath and the set of his shoulders eased somewhat.

They waited what seemed an interminable time.

"You must be worried about Torren," he said.

"Not really." Teyla looked out at the same stretch of canyon wall they had been staring at for seven hours. "He is safe in Atlantis. Dr. Kusanagi is watching him, though I imagine she has traded with someone else by now."

"That doesn't worry you? That somebody or other has Torren?" He looked at her sideways.

"That is how we do it at home," she said. "Everyone must hunt or farm or trade, and once a child is weaned and is too big to carry everywhere they are watched by whoever is available and willing. Since Torren is the only child in Atlantis, there are many people who do not mind." She shrugged. "He is coming up on two years old, John. He is not a tiny infant. Children are part of the life of the city, not something kept locked away so that they will not disturb anyone. I know this is not how you do things, but I am not of you."

"No," he said. "It's not." His eyes didn't leave the sensor display. "Guys aren't supposed to want anything to do with kids. It's girly."

"How can being a father be girly?" Teyla blinked. "Is not fatherhood by definition masculine?"

"Maybe it ought to be, but it's not."

"And who does all this judging and measuring?"

"Other guys." John shrugged. "Maybe it's a generational thing. I don't know. But it's not like my dad was a great father." His hands moved over the board, never looking at her.

"It is not like my mother was a great mother," Teyla said. "She left when I was Torren's age and never returned. But I never lacked for people who cared for me. Charin was my mother." She could think with warmth of her now, and only a little sorrow.

"Charin was really super," John said, and his voice sounded like he meant it. "She seemed like such a kind person."

"She was," Teyla said. It was right to tell the stories of those who were gone. "She had a grown daughter who had a baby sixteen days old when she and the baby were taken by the Wraith in the same Culling where my father was taken. That was all her family, all there was."

John was looking at her as though cold had touched his spine, but she went on. "We are shaped by the Wraith, John. They shape who we are, the way that we live and what we value. I had no one, and neither did she. Rather than turn to bitterness, she gave her love to an orphaned child and taught me to live. But that is who we are because we have been Culled to the bone. If we were safe or even safer, perhaps we could afford to be different."

He nodded seriously. "I've seen that," he said. "It seems like there are two ways people deal with it, societies deal with it. Either they come together and differences stop mattering, or they tear each other apart. They give what they have, or they start shooting each other. That's why civilizations fall."

"It is one reason," Teyla said. "But I do not know how you can tell which a society will do beforehand, why some worlds that have been Culled help each other and others devolve into banditry, where the strong prey upon the weak until there is nothing left but chaos and starvation."

"I don't know either," he said, and she thought he was thinking of something unvoiced, some place he had been or people he had known. "The only thing you can control is what kind of person you are."

"Never leave one of your own behind. Never prey on the weak," she said. Teyla's mouth twitched. "The strong are a different matter."

"I wish I could say I was that guy," John said, toggling between sensor displays for the hundredth time.

"At least you think you ought to be," she said. "That is worth something."

"Hang on." His voice sharpened. "Look at that."

On the heads up display the marker for the hive ship accelerated, numbers flashing beneath it too fast to read. And then it vanished.

"The hive ship's gone," John said loudly enough to carry to the back where Carson and Dahlia were talking. "It opened a hyperspace window."

Teyla felt as though a weight she did not know she carried had lifted. "I think they are really gone," she whispered. "I do not sense the Wraith anymore."

Carson stuck his head around the doors to the back. "They're gone?"

"Yes," John said. He almost jumped out of his chair. "So let's pack up the survival gear and get going."

"I did that three hours ago," Teyla said. "The packs are waiting by the tailgate."

John grinned at her. "Ok then! Let's move."

CHAPTER NINE
Desert Trek

EVEN IN the shade of the rocks it was about a hundred and five degrees. John winced. "Death Valley."

"That sounds encouraging," Teyla said in a tone that he wasn't sure if it was supposed to be ironic or not.

"It's a place on Earth," John said. He looked up at the sides of the canyon, the lambent deep blue sky above. "A lot like this, unfortunately."

"We will have to get down there," Teyla said.

Twenty five or thirty feet below where the jumper had come to rest was the bottom of the canyon, a nearly dry stream bed marked by some spiny grayish plants. It would be possible to walk along the stream bed. He thought. John glanced up and winced again. Eighty feet or so to the top, broken rock all the way. Rock climbing was not his favorite thing, and he knew for sure it wasn't Carson's. Dahlia Radim aside, the idea of trying to get Carson up that cliff was daunting. He was a doctor, not special forces. "Yeah, down. Not up," he said.

"We came along the top of the cliffs before," Dahlia said, shouldering her pack. "We followed the line of this canyon but we didn't come down here. It was much easier walking along the plateau above." She looked up at the bright sky. "Though there is much more shade here."

"Well, let's get down then," John said. "Teyla, you go left and I'll go right. Let's see if we can find a place that's easier to get down. Carson, hang out here with Radim until we find a place."

The ledge thinned out about a hundred feet along, but it did slope downward gently, until it was only about fifteen feet from the bottom of the canyon. A rough fifteen feet, but if they put down guide ropes it was probably doable. "Teyla?"

"Yes?" she replied, his headset crackling.

"You got anything? I've got a fairly easy fifteen foot drop."

"I have nothing, Colonel," she said. "The canyon deepens and the drop is steeper here than beside the jumper."

"Ok, everybody down here then," he said. "Carson, you got that?"

"We're coming," Carson said.

A few moments later he and Dahlia Radim walked up, followed momentarily by Teyla. She looked at the drop. "I will get the rope from the jumper," she said.

"I'm not sure…" Carson began.

"It's easy," John said. "Teyla will climb down while I hold the rope, and then she'll belay the rest of us down. We've got a harness and everything."

"Teyla's going to hold me?" Carson looked dubious. "She's a tiny little thing."

"It's on belay, Carson," John said soothingly. "It's all pulleys. Teyla could hold Ronon that way."

Letting Teyla down was fairly easy. John didn't actually need Carson and Dahlia to help, but they wanted to so they held the end of the rope behind him while he let Teyla down hand over hand. Teyla with all her gear and weapons probably didn't top out over 150. She was, as Carson said, a tiny little thing a good ten inches shorter than he was, and fairly slightly built. It was just that Teyla always seemed to take up so much space in a room.

Once down she went about setting up the belay in a methodical fashion, and it didn't take long to let Dahlia down beside her, going cautiously as the scientist was no more of an experienced climber than the doctor was.

Carson looked doubtful as John clipped off the harness around him. "You're sure I'm not too heavy?"

"Not a bit," John said. "Just relax and lean back. You can put your feet on the canyon wall if it's more comfortable and just walk them down." Lots of people found that helpful, even if they weren't actually doing any of the climbing.

"How are you going to get down?" Carson asked as his head dipped down to the edge of the ledge.

"I'll tie the rope off through the pin up here and Teyla will let me down too."

Carson looked skeptical.

"It's ok. Just relax."

"I've a bit of a problem with heights, you know," Carson said.

"Then just look at me and keep talking," John said. Beyond Carson he could see Teyla belaying him down slowly, hand over hand. Carson's head was two feet below the ledge, so already his feet were only seven or eight feet from the ground. If Teyla dropped him that second he'd probably do no worse than break an ankle. "How are the new medical personnel working out?"

"Well, that's really Jennifer's department more than mine," Carson replied, not looking down. "She's Chief of Medicine now. I'm not sure what I am, except along for the ride."

"How's the optometrist working out?" Two more feet. Three.

"We haven't got an optometrist," Carson said. "I wish we did. We've got a PA who knows a bit, which is better than we had." Carson looked surprised when his feet touched the ground.

"There you are," Teyla said. "Let me unclip you, Carson." She smiled at him. "You see? Just as you say, easy peasy."

"Right."

His own descent was easy and fast, unclipping himself at the bottom while Teyla looked up at the dangling ropes. "We are going to have to leave them," she said.

John nodded. "Yeah. But it's just as well if we wind up having to get back up to the jumper this way for some reason. All right, people. Let's walk."

He took the point, Teyla on six with Carson and Dahlia between them without a word spoken. The late afternoon shadows had deepened. Even on a planet with forty hour days, sunset would eventually come. Maybe that's why he was so tired. The movement of the sun told him that it had only been a few hours since they landed, but… John checked his watch. Four in the morning, Atlantis time. They'd been twenty hours on this mission already, and he'd been up for twenty two. No wonder he was tired. They should have napped in the jumper while they were waiting for the Wraith to leave, but it had seemed impossible to sleep then, cornered like a mouse.

John looked up at the sun again, or rather at the sky above the canyon walls. The sun was already behind the walls, out of sight from its meridian. He hated to call a halt when they'd just gotten started. Better to put a few miles behind them first. He wasn't sure how long the daylight would last, but they might even make the Ancient ship before it got completely dark. Eighteen miles as the crow flies, or as the jumper flies. No. They wouldn't make that in one march. But they'd feel better stopping if they were a bit closer. Three six mile treks would probably do it with Carson and Dahlia, with some breaks between each one.

Out of the corner of his eye he thought he saw something move and whipped around, raising the P90 as he did. Behind him he heard Teyla flicking off her safety.

The jumbled rocks were full of deepening shadows. There was no sound. His eyes searched the rocks, glancing over tumbled stones. Nothing moved.

"Did you see it?" he asked Teyla.

"I saw nothing," she said. "I moved because you did." She took a few steps forward, coming up even with him. "What was it?"

John shook his head, squinting. "I don't know. I saw movement. That's all."

"This planet does have life forms," Dahlia said. "We encountered a few in the process of working on the wreck. Small mammals, about as long as my forearm. They eat the tuberous roots of those gray plants."

"Perhaps that is what you saw," Teyla said.

"Maybe." It could have been. He'd just seen motion. "It might have been one of those prairie dog things." John lowered his gun. "Ok. Just keep an eye out, people." It was probably nothing at all.

Shadows deepened. They followed the canyon, the stream a tiny trickle surfacing sometimes, then disappearing for a while beneath the stones. It was rough going, and John doubted they'd made three miles.

He dropped back a moment to talk to Dahlia Radim. "Do you know where this canyon goes?"

She nodded, sweat rolling down her face in the sultry heat. "It twists around to the north and then widens out into the plateau just north of the wreck."

"How much distance does that add?" John asked. It would be too much to hope for that the canyon would come out in the right place.

"I do not know in your miles, but four hours' walk perhaps? We did not come down by the canyon as I said, but cut straight across the plateau above." Dahlia looked as tired as John felt. He sincerely hoped he didn't look that tired. There was a twenty hour night coming, and he felt like he could sleep all of it. Still, a four hour walk was probably better than trying to get up eighty feet of cliffs. Going down was one thing, but he didn't think he'd care to go up himself, with nobody at the top. Rock climbing was really not his thing.

"Ok," John said. "That works."

"Are we stopping soon?"

"Yeah." John glanced at his watch. "In just a few…"

There was the movement again. He swung the gun up, pivoting right and dropping to his knee.

Carson let out a muffled sound, and he heard Teyla move behind them.

Ahead, the rocks were still and quiet. Nothing moved in the crevices of the stones. There was no noise at all, except the harshness of their own breathing.

"One of those mammals?" Teyla asked after a long moment.

"I did not see it," Dahlia said.

"Probably." John got up, dusting off his knee. "Let's go on a little further and then we'll take a breather. Maybe down there where the canyon widens out a bit and the stream looks like it comes up."

"Excellent," Carson said.

John nodded, taking the point again, conscious of Teyla's eyes on the back of his head. There was no point in saying anything. For a moment, in the shifting shadows, he had thought he saw a man.

They rested in the shade. The temperature had dropped down into the nineties, which felt good. Water was what he needed. He'd probably sweated out half a gallon. The stream was fairly clear, but he added some water purification tablets and refilled his canteen. You never knew what might be in the water on an uninhabited planet. Strange bacteria would be just the beginning.

Teyla sat down beside him, offering him one of the MREs from her pack, but he waved it away. He was too hot to eat anything that heavy. An energy bar was enough to give him a boost without turning his stomach.

Teyla apparently thought the same thing, for she was nibbling on one as well rather than the heavier rations. Above, the sky was turning purple, dotted with a million stars. Quite literally. They must be looking toward the center of the galaxy, because it was bright as a moon as night fell. She tilted her chin up, as though looking for an errant breeze that wasn't here. "It is quite beautiful," she said.

John nodded. "I've seen the Milky Way like that on Earth.

You can't see it that way in San Francisco or DC, anywhere you've been. There are too many people and too many lights. But it does get that bright."

"Where?" she asked.

John shifted, ostensibly because the stones beneath him were hard, a chill running up his spine, though his voice was casual. "In clear desert air. I've seen it that way in Afghanistan."

"Ah," she said, not turning her face to him, her eyes on the sky.

She had been with him on that planet where a Wraith mind control device had gone haywire, the only one of them immune to it because of the Gift, been with him a whole day as he slipped further and further into a hallucination. Afghanistan. He didn't know entirely what he'd said and what he'd only imagined he'd said. He was afraid to ask. But he'd probably said enough. More than enough.

There wasn't any more to say, so they sat in silence until it was time to move on, through this world's slow twilight.

Carson offered his water bottle to Dahlia Radim, but she shook her head. "I have my own," she said. "I won't need yours, Doctor."

"Carson," he said. "I think we know one another well enough for that."

"Carson," she said, her eyes skimming his face. "Then you should call me Dahlia."

"I'd be pleased to," he replied.

Her eyes went past him to where Teyla and Sheppard sat in an identical pose crosslegged on the ground, both of them looking up at the sky without saying a word. "Would he have shot me?" she mused.

"No," Carson said quickly. "Of course not. Not unless you'd been carrying a hidden bomb or the like."

"I'm not sure of that," Dahlia said. "Emmagan said that he

was cruel and she was worse."

Carson blinked. "I wouldn't say that. Not at all."

"Probably not." Dahlia shrugged. "But you're on their side."

Carson was still digesting that when Teyla got to her feet with a smooth movement and came toward them.

"Are you ready to walk a little further?" she asked.

Dahlia got to her feet. "Yes."

"We will go on a little while," Teyla said. "And then we will rest for a few hours. Carson?"

"I'm game," Carson said, getting to his feet. Beyond Dahlia, Sheppard had shouldered the heaviest pack and was taking up his weapon. He would go first, of course, and Teyla last. Carson hung back walking beside Teyla, letting Dahlia get ahead. When there was enough room not to be overheard, he leaned toward her. "Teyla, why did you tell Dahlia that Colonel Sheppard was cruel? What in the name of heaven is that about, making out he's some sadistic bastard?"

Teyla looked at him levelly. "He is the military commander of Atlantis, Carson. It is important that the Genii fear him. Do you think they would do so if I told Dahlia Radim that he is a fluffy bunny?"

Carson huffed. "Well, not a fluffy bunny! But he's not precisely Vlad the Impaler either!"

Teyla stopped, and he stopped with her. "Michael," she said.

Carson blanched.

"Yes," she said with a strange half-smile that did not touch her eyes. "And you and I bear as much taint as anyone for that. We are not harmless, even if we choose to be kind. A lion is a lion, even if you keep it as a pet or call it your friend."

He swallowed, and she touched his arm gently. "Come now. Let us not fall too far behind. It would be dangerous for us to get lost in the dark."

"Right." Carson hurried along the broken ground ahead of

her, the starlight bright enough to cast vague shadows on their path.

They had almost caught up to Dahlia Radim. Almost.

There was a blur of movement to Carson's left, a momentary brief impression of a flying body, but before he could so much as shout something hit him hard, claws scoring across his shoulder as it threw him to the ground, borne beneath hard muscle and scaly weight, its scream echoing in the night air.

CHAPTER TEN
Survival

JOHN WHIRLED around as the animal's scream rent the air, some sort of hunting call meant to strike terror into the hearts of its prey. Dahlia Radim was directly in his line of fire, running toward him as fast as she could, while all he could see behind her was a dark shape tossing around and around on the ground. Crap, he thought, his heart and legs going into overdrive, dashing toward it, trying to get a clear shot around Dahlia. Not much chance of that. Whatever-it-was was rolling around on the ground, trying to savage someone — whoever — it had got. He didn't have a shot. He didn't have anything. Opening up right now would be as likely to hit…

Fire lit the night, the bright flash of Teyla's tracers. Carson. It had Carson.

"Colonel!" Dahlia shouted, and he dodged around her.

He saw what she'd seen an instant later, a second beast on a converging path, springing toward the source of the gunfire. Teyla would never get around in time, even if she heard him shout over the sound of her own shots. John skidded to a halt, dropping to one knee for a steadier shot. Carefully.

A quick burst caught it six feet behind Teyla's back, just at the beginning of its pounce. She didn't even jerk around, still trying to get a decent shot at the one that had Carson, trusting him to guard her back. It fell backwards, twitching feebly on the ground.

He pivoted, trying to get a better angle, but all he could see was a tossing blob.

Teyla could see better. A single shot, two. The thing that had Carson scrambled up, a dark shadow against other dark shadows.

John saw the movement out of the corner of his eye. Too late. He swung back but Teyla was directly between him and the creature, coming at her from her right side while she was intent on the other.

"Teyla!"

It hit her full in the shoulder, its weight knocking her down. There was one fraction of a second, one tiny divided moment, as she fell with it on top of her that its head reared up, forelegs extended, a long reptilian head like an alligator, four clawed feet. He wouldn't have taken the shot if he'd thought about it. It was too close to Teyla. But he didn't think. He squeezed the trigger in that fraction of a second, not a burst but a single shot.

The thing went over backwards with a gurgling sound. Even as he ran up it ceased twitching, lying silent in the suddenly still night.

"Teyla?"

"I am fine," she said, already beginning to pull herself up. "Carson..." Her breath caught and she sat back down heavily. "I am fine. See to Carson."

John kept the gun in hand as he jogged over. One of the creatures was down, dead, the one he'd hit in the head. The others had vanished into the darkness. "Carson?"

The doctor rolled over, pushing himself up on his left arm. "Not fine. I need a dressing."

Kneeling down beside him, the light on his P90 flashed over Carson. His body armor was ripped and torn, the fabric gaping open to the Kevlar lining below, huge claw marks across the chest. If he hadn't been wearing the vest his chest would have been ripped open. As it was, there was a deep bleeding gash across his upper right arm, dripping down his sleeve onto the ground.

Carson leaned on his left arm. "That's lovely," he said as he saw it in the light. His voice sounded shaky.

"Here." John fumbled one handed for the field dressing he

kept in his left thigh pocket, pulled it out and tore it open. He didn't dare put the gun down, not with two of those creatures wounded and still around, maybe stalking them again just out of sight.

"That looks bad," Dahlia Radim said solemnly, coming up behind John.

"Yes, love," Carson said with a spark of his old fire. "It's not what I'd call peachy. The bicep's torn, though it didn't hit an artery. It's going to need surgery to line the muscle up and need stitches in the muscle tissue. And I can't very well perform surgery on my own right arm."

"Help him with that dressing," John said, standing up to cover them while Dahlia knelt to help Carson tie the dressing tight around his arm.

"Pressure now," Carson said. "There. I'm a wee bit lightheaded so you'll have to keep it on."

"Teyla?" John called.

"Here." Her voice sounded strained. She limped out of the darkness, her face tight in the light of his gun.

"What's the matter?"

"I have hurt my leg." She grimaced as she made the final two steps to him, not fully putting her left foot down. "That creature knocked me onto the stones. I fell hard on rocks on my left hip."

"Is it broken?"

"If my hip were broken I would not be standing," Teyla snapped, which was a measure of pain. It made Carson more determined to act normal than ever, but rendered Teyla sharper.

He put out his arm to steady her, flicking his light over the rocks around them. He didn't see any of the animals, but they were probably still here. The question was if they were too injured or had decided that the humans bit back too hard, or if they were just circling for another chance.

"Carson?"

"I'm hanging in here," Carson said. "Dahlia, pull it tighter. You've got to hurt me, love. Just go on and do it. Got to stop the bleeding."

"We need a fire," Teyla said. "Most reptiles can't abide it."

"Nothing to burn," John said. Bare rock. Some gray cactus things. No brush, no wood, no trees. "Let's hold on until the bleeding stops, then find a place in the rocks where we've got cover."

She nodded stiffly, lifting the P90 and flashing the light around them. "Perhaps this will do then."

"It'll have to." Two of them, one injured, to cover more seriously injured Carson and Dahlia Radim. Super. If Zelenka were here, he could have repaired the jumper and they could have flown to the crash site. They wouldn't be in this predicament. But he'd done it again. Shep had done it again, running off half cocked to the rescue without the stuff he needed to make it work...

"How is it, Carson?" Teyla asked, her back to the doctor.

"I expect I'll live," Carson said, but there was a tremor in his voice. "The bleeding's slowing up. I'm a bit lightheaded, but that's blood loss. Dahlia, be a love and get a pressure bandage out of my kit. Also the antiseptic and the antibiotic gel. When it's eased a bit more I'm going to take the dressing off and I'll tell you what to do."

"How's your hip?" John asked Teyla in a low voice.

Her lips were pressed in a tight line. "I can stand. Do not distract Carson with it."

He nodded. "Ok."

There was a movement among the stones to Teyla's right, and their tracers crossed as they both opened up on it at once. John had no idea if they hit anything or not, but they certainly scared whatever it was.

"How long is this night?" Teyla asked.

"About sixteen more hours," John said grimly.

"That's good, isn't it?" Dahlia Radim asked behind him. "If

those things are reptiles, won't they slow down when it gets cold? Maybe even sleep? They've got to be daytime hunters if they're cold blooded."

"Just how cold does it get here at night?" John asked. In the exertion of the fight he hadn't noticed the temperature had dropped. It was a nice, comfortable seventy five degrees or so now. But the night had just begun.

"I've never seen it go more than ten degrees below freezing," Dahlia said. "And that just before dawn."

"Super duper," Carson said in a cheerful tone that sounded a little drunk. He wasn't kidding about being lightheaded. Not good.

Teyla looked at John. "We must find somewhere to rest," she said. "We cannot go on like this."

"Yeah. Rest up for a while, get a meal into Carson and some sleep…" Twenty four hours he'd been up. Six more hours hike to the Ancient Warship. But it wouldn't take six hours. With Carson having to be helped and Teyla barely able to walk it would take twice that. That's the problem, Shep. You think it's going to take so long to walk out, but once you've got a wounded man with you the whole equation changes.

Teyla nodded. "I will cover them if you will find a place." She lifted her gun, the light flashing over the rocks around them.

"That's probably fastest." Heading out alone into the darkness with those creatures wasn't his idea of fun, but if a giant lizard landed on his back it was probably what he'd deserve. Except that if he took a hit, there's no way the wounded would get out alone. He'd done that math before, lying behind the rocks, watching three men pass close enough to nearly touch, Charlie Holland immobile behind him. He'd done that math and let them be. But had those minutes of radio silence been the critical ones? The ones that he could never recover?

"John?" Teyla was looking at him as though she'd asked something, but he couldn't remember what.

"I'm going," he said, and started off into the night.

Clear. Pleasantly cool after the heat of the day, a very light breeze picking up. Right now was an ideal time for travel. Except they couldn't. How badly was Teyla's hip injured? If push came to shove, that might slow them down more than Carson's arm.

Just leave, she'd say.

No she wouldn't. That was Holland. That was Charlie Holland. Just leave, Shep. There's nothing you can do, you stupid son of a bitch.

Behind he heard Dahlia Radim's voice, Carson answering her, though he couldn't make out the words. Cliffs. Starlight. He needed to find them a place that was sheltered, where the animals couldn't sneak up on them, a place with only one exposed side if possible so that one person could cover it. A little further along, maybe. Not too far.

At least they had supplies. He hadn't before, not many. He hadn't expected to be down. It was going to be in and out, hardly needing to get out of the helicopter, but groundfire clipped his tail rotor…There. That was better. A little scramble up five or six feet but it was a sheltered overhang, rock on three sides with a long overhang above and a vertical cliff. The only way something could approach it was like he was doing now, straight on.

John turned and looked back. He could see Teyla's light probing the darkness. It was a little way, maybe a quarter mile, but in the right direction. And deep enough that they'd all fit comfortably. Some of them could even stretch out and get some sleep.

Sleep. That was the tricky part. Sooner or later he had to sleep. And when he did…

John turned around and started back, the light dancing ahead of him on the jumbled stones.

"Did you find anything?" Teyla called as he came closer.

"Good place," he said. "Pretty much ideal. How's Carson?"

"Carson's adorable," Carson said with what sounded like a muffled giggle.

John looked at him with horror, wondering what that could be a symptom of.

"Endocet," Carson said. "It hits me this way. Thought I'd best take it before we tried to move me."

"Good plan." Carson's arm was trussed up, and he looked pale beneath a day's growth of beard. "Dahlia, can you help him up?"

Dahlia nodded, going around to get her arm beneath his shoulder on the left side. "Just lean on me, Carson."

"Here now, what are you good for?" Carson demanded. "Big, strong fellow like you?"

"I've got to have a hand free," John said. "And I've got to help Teyla."

"I can walk," Teyla said through gritted teeth, taking a few steps in the right direction, her breath hissing out in a cry cut off. She nearly fell.

"You can't. You'll take too long." He put his left arm around her back, swinging the P90 forward on the right. "I can cover us, and you can hop along. We'll all make better time."

"I didn't know you were hurt," Carson said, swaying forward with Dahlia. "I should have a look at that."

"When we reach shelter," Teyla said. "I am fine, Carson."

"You are not."

"We can't argue here in the open," John said. "Those things might still be here. Let's get under cover, and then you can argue."

Dahlia shot him a grateful glance.

It seemed like it took forever to cover the quarter mile, with Carson giggling and cursing the entire way, and Teyla's breath coming in gasps whenever her left foot took any weight, her arm over his shoulder and the P90 weighing a ton in his right hand, the light flickering over the path ahead of them. Whatever she said, she'd really screwed that hip up.

His sweat was cold on his face by the time they reached the

last little slope up, and he left Teyla to lean on a rock while he got on the other side of Carson to help him up.

"Cozy," Carson said. "Just like home."

"How much Endocet did he take?" John asked Dahlia.

She shrugged. "I do not even know what it is."

"Morphine derivative," John said. "It's a painkiller, probably the strongest one in Carson's kit."

"Perhaps Emmagan should take some as well," Dahlia said.

"I do not need it," Teyla said firmly. He was kind of with her on that one. He needed her clearheaded, not screwed up like Carson.

John let Carson down gently against the wall. "There you go."

"Now we huddle together for warmth," Carson said. "Tee hee."

Teyla shot him a look that was absolutely foul.

"You're high as a kite," John said. "I bet you're not feeling any pain."

"Son, I'm not sure I have an arm at all," Carson informed him solemnly.

"I'm only three years younger than you, Carson," John said. "You could cut out the 'son' part." He put his pack down and rummaged around. "How about an energy bar on top of all that Endocet?"

"Surely," Carson said, and reached for it with his good hand.

Teyla slithered down the wall just at the entrance, a muffled gasp escaping her lips as she touched the ground. "I am covering," she said, her light flashing out over the approach.

John nodded. "I'll get them settled." He rummaged around in his pack. "MREs. Here's one for you, Dahlia. And I've got two mylar thermal blankets in here."

"There is one in my pack as well," Teyla said.

John tossed the two he had to Dahlia. "Get one around Carson. He's lost a lot of blood."

Dahlia nodded, sitting down beside Carson with the MRE in her lap. "All right," she said, ripping open the package for the thermal blankets. "Let's keep you warm."

"You can keep me warm anytime, love," Carson said, with what might have been meant to be a Sean Connery leer.

John winced. "Dahlia…"

"I know," she said, cracking a smile. "It's the medicine. He's a perfect gentleman otherwise."

"I am the perfect model of the Scottish physician," Carson sang somewhere in the vague range of Gilbert and Sullivan. "I rely on pure science, not superstition…"

"That doesn't even scan, Carson."

"I'm a doctor, not a poet. Tee hee hee."

John boggled. "Right." He pulled out a second MRE and squinted at it. Red beans with rice. One of the better ones. There was no spoon. He edged over and squatted next to Teyla. "Share?"

She nodded, propping her gun against the rock so that the light pointed at the ceiling, diffusing a dim light over them all. He tore it open with his fingers and folded back the foil like a bowl, offering it to her. She took a pinch between thumb and forefinger as John ripped open the cracker pack, using a cracker as a scoop.

"We have been in far worse situations," Teyla said in a low voice.

"That's true." They'd been in worse. He'd been in worse. And he'd been the only one to walk out alive.

"Try to get some rest," Dahlia said to Carson behind them. "You will feel better after you've slept." Possibly not true, but still a good idea. He'd hurt when the Endocet wore off, but it would have to for them to start walking.

"You could leave us here and go get the warship," Teyla said. "Come back for us with the ship." Her voice was low enough that Dahlia couldn't hear.

John shook his head. "There's nowhere to set it down here. And if I can't get it going without Dahlia Radim, that's going to be a problem." He took a long drink of water from his canteen. "Besides, once we get to the ship we'll have climate controlled rooms that we can actually secure against those critters. I can't leave you here with those things hunting and take half the firepower."

Teyla nodded seriously, chewing another mouthful of beans and rice. "We will walk out together, then."

"Right," he said. "We'll walk out."

CHAPTER ELEVEN
Quicksilver

QUICKSILVER dreamed, and in his dreams he walked through blue green corridors lit from above, light pouring in from skylights far up on the side of white towers. Quicksilver dreamed, and in his dream he was looking for something. It was just there, surely. If only he could remember what it was he was seeking.

It might be just around this corner, or down this corridor through heavy doors ornamented with bronze, or past these windows of stained glass. It might be here. It might be just there. If he could remember what it was.

In his dreams, Quicksilver walked Atlantis.

Up a short flight of stairs, and he stood in a huge room where the Stargate waited, glittering with the cold sheen of naquadah, just as the Ancients made it. But it was not what he sought. That was further. Somewhere.

Up another flight of stairs, and consoles beckoned. He could step up to them, could do something.

She stood on the walkway beside him, a slender dark haired woman in a red shirt, and her eyes were on him. "Rodney," she said, "Wake up."

"What?"

Her eyes did not leave his, urgent and kind at once. "Wake up, Rodney. You're dreaming."

"If I just look at the consoles I can see the dialing address."

She shook her head gravely. "No. Wake up, Rodney."

Quicksilver woke.

Across the room they shared, his brother slept in his alcove, the lights dimmed for sleeping.

Quicksilver sat up, a curious sense of unreality about him. He had dreamed. He had dreamed of some strange place, and of a queen with dark eyes who spoke to him, who told him within a dream that he slumbered and forbade him the consoles. She had forbidden him. He was sure of that, for all that she had stood quietly by.

He reached for the pipette of chilled water that stood by and drank greedily. Something was wrong. Very wrong. He felt it in every bone in his body.

Dust stirred, rolled over, his eyes hooded with sleep. "Are you well, my brother?"

"I dreamed of Atlantis," Quicksilver said. His hands shook on the pipette, and he stared at them. Why should he shake? What was wrong?

"What did you dream?" Dust asked.

"I dreamed of a queen," Quicksilver said slowly. "She spoke to me."

"Dark haired or fair?" Dust asked.

"Dark," Quicksilver said. "Dark haired. Small. Slight, I mean." He pressed his hands together, searching. From somewhere he dredged up words. "Dr. Weir."

"She Who Is a Strong Place," Dust said. "You must have known her."

Quicksilver blinked. "How could I have?" he asked. "You said that she had been dead for years, but I was only captured a few weeks ago. How could I have known her?"

Dust's mouth opened and closed, an expression of dismay crossing his face. "Well, obviously not. It must have been some-one else."

"Yes, obviously," Quicksilver said sharply.

And yet. There was something about the way Dust turned from him, something in the dream that made his scalp prickle.

"Do you remember more?" Dust asked.

"No," Quicksilver said. After all, there was no need to say he had nearly seen the gate address for Atlantis. There would be time enough to tell him later.

CHAPTER TWELVE
Ghosts in the Wind

"ARCLIGHT, this is Roundhouse Zero Six. Repeat, this is Roundhouse Zero Six. Do you copy?" The sky was filled with a million stars, the Milky Way stretching from mountains to mountains, glittering like the most amazing special effect a kid ever dreamed up. "Arclight, this is Roundhouse Zero Six."

The radio crackled. There was no reply.

"It's no use, Shep." Holland's voice was labored.

"Don't start that." John thumbed the radio on again. "Arclight, this is Roundhouse."

"Tell Sabine…"

"Tell her yourself," John snapped. "We're getting out of here."

"Did you tell anybody where you were going?" Holland said. His blue eyes were shadowed in the darkness.

John let out a long breath. "There wasn't anybody to tell who wouldn't try to stop me. Not since Mitch and Dex bought the farm."

"They don't know where we are. They aren't coming," he said. "We're going to have to walk out." Holland gave a hollow laugh. "And I can't walk."

"Arclight, this is Roundhouse Zero Six."

"It's been real, dude."

"Don't start." John looked out across the broken rocks of the canyon at the lambent night sky. "Don't start with me, Charlie." There were things he could say, things maybe he should say. But it would be too much like the end. Too much like saying goodbye. At least Charlie wouldn't start with that honor to have served with you crap. "Just hang in there."

The sky pulsed with light, stars and galaxies rotating impossibly fast, spinning over the mountains like a wormhole.

He reached for Holland's hand but it was cold, cold and dry as...

He looked. A dessicated corpse leered up at him, skin aged and withered to leather over bone, the chest wound gaping where it had been fed upon, hand crumbling to dust in his...

John jerked awake, heart pounding. He was sitting up in the entrance of the little cave, his back against the wall, P90 in his lap pointed out, covering the only approach. Across the broken rocks of the canyon the night sky was lit up with the brilliance of the Pegasus Galaxy, looking toward the center, bright enough to cast strange shadows. Beside him, just where Holland had lain, Teyla slept.

He reached, touched her hand.

Cold and dry as...

His heart shuddering in his throat he grabbed it, crushing it in his, feeling the bones in her hand grind together, his breath escaping in gasp.

"John?" Her voice sounded muzzy with sleep, coming awake suddenly.

Cold ran down his back, shaking with the sudden burst of fear, everything kicking into overdrive with nowhere to go.

Her fingers moved in his. "John?"

He couldn't speak, couldn't move. Not without saying or doing something terrible. Not still seeing before him with his mind's eye...

Teyla propped up on one elbow, her brows knitting as she looked at him. Her hand closed in his, squeezing his fingers back. She said nothing. She said nothing while he breathed, while his pounding heart slowed.

Beyond her, Carson and Dahlia slept, mylar blankets reflecting dim light, side by side against each other. He had the watch, and he had dozed off. He had to sleep. Sometime he had to sleep and then…

"That is how it happened. Did it not?" she said quietly.

John nodded. He didn't trust his voice.

Teyla sat up laboriously, careful of her hip, her hand still in his, leaning against the wall beside him, her other arm sliding around his back. It was cold, so very cold. The temperature drops in the desert at night…

"I had to sleep. I fell asleep. I couldn't stay awake any longer and when…" he stopped. His own voice sounded ragged, strange.

"When you woke he was dead."

Gentle. Even. That was Teyla. He nodded.

He woke to find a corpse in his arms, already stiffening against his shoulder.

"Yes," he said.

"Ah, John," she said, and bent her head to his breast in comfort, her hand tight on his wrist.

He dropped his face against her hair, warm and real and so far from dead. Teyla.

"I grieve for you," she said, "and for all you lost."

"I can't. I don't…"

She lifted her face, a rueful expression on it. "You forget that I once spent an entire day with you believing that I was Captain Holland."

"I said…"

"You said a great many things." Her dark eyes were gentle, but her hand on his wrist was tight enough for him to feel it. "But I am Athosian, and I do not follow your stupid rules. You said nothing that made me think badly of you."

"I can't even…" His heart was pounding so loudly, one fear piled on top of another, and nothing to do, nowhere for it to go.

"Look at me." Teyla's voice was low and urgent, her hand tightening around his wrist like cuffs. He could not look away.

"You have said nothing that makes me think badly of you, then or now."

He couldn't look away. He couldn't disbelieve her. Teyla didn't lie, not like that. Not with that sound in her voice, not with her eyes snapping as they did.

"I have thought nothing ill of you, John. In all the firmament, you are my fixed star."

At that he closed his eyes. He couldn't look, couldn't see what was written on her face so plainly. There were no words. He had no words. He never did, even in the face of death. "Teyla," he said, hoping she knew it was apology, that it stood for everything that crowded round in circles, forever unsaid. He dropped his face to her hair, holding her tight, tight as though he would never let go, as though the world would end and they would still be sitting like this, his arm around her and her hand tight on his wrist, his face against the top of her head and hers against his shoulder.

"I know," she said. "I know."

She knew everything, knew him to the bone and still dared to look. He rested on her while the stars moved overhead, unfamiliar stars in strange constellations. One of them was home. One of them was Atlantis.

For as long as it could be. For as long as the powers that be allowed it. Before something happened, and he was sent back to Earth, before there was a road that led to another desert, another death where at least he wouldn't take anybody with him. Sooner or later, it always goes that way. You can't escape forever.

"They sent me home," he said. "After. They sent me home, and Nancy..." John swallowed. "One day they'll send me home."

"I will not let you go," she said, and her voice was fierce. "Do you not understand that I am stronger than that?"

"If I get hurt..." he said. "If I get hurt badly enough I'll get sent back. And sooner or later I'll be reassigned anyhow."

"If you are reassigned you can resign," she said. "And let

them hunt you through Pegasus if they wish, though I imagine Sam would have small stomach for it. And if you are hurt, do you really think that we would allow them to send you back to Earth? Do you think Ronon would allow it, having gone with you and seen your family?"

John shook his head, his face against her hair. "If the Air Force does it, you can't stop it. If it's bad enough…"

She lifted her eyes to his. "We are your family, John. When Ronon says he is your brother, he means it. We will not let anyone take you away. We will not let it happen. And do you not think that Carson would move mountains to treat you here no matter what anyone said or allowed? That Radek would open the Stargate for us even if it were locked down? That Sam would fail to find you if you did not want to be found?" Teyla smiled a long, secret smile. "And do you not think that General O'Neill knows that? Do you think he does not know what an asset you would be to the Genii or to any government of Earth as a contractor? Even if you lacked two good legs, do you think that Mr. Desai or the Ariane corporation would not hire you in a heartbeat to be their man? He is too clever for these things not to have crossed his mind. John, you need never return to Earth if you do not want to."

He let out a long breath he did not know he was holding. It was true.

"John, there is no road that leads to the places you dread. Not anymore. You have passed every turn that led there, and now it is all unknown."

He put his forehead to hers. "One of those screwed up vets who drifts from job to job, never quite getting it together, the kind of guy who dies alone in a cheap motel somewhere…"

"We are your family, and we will never let that happen." Her voice was flat. "Perhaps you will die in space, or in the cocoon of a hive ship, but you will not die on Earth, John Sheppard. That is fact."

"Ok." He took a deep breath. "I can live with that."

"Good," she said, her hand still tight on his wrist. "Now you should sleep. I will watch."

"You're tired too and you're hurt..." he began.

"I have slept for several hours." Teyla checked her watch, the luminous dial shining faintly in the dark. "Nearly six hours, actually. It is midnight here, with ten hours to run until dawn."

"And getting colder all the time." In the cave it must be in the sixties from their body heat, but outside the temperature must be in the fifties and dropping.

"Sleep a while," she said. "I can watch, and you can sleep here beside me where you will hear if I make any sound." She let go of him, lifting her head. "You must be able to fly the Ancient warship, and right now you cannot."

He nodded. Right now he wasn't sure he'd trust himself to find his way from the jumper bay to his own quarters. "Ok."

"Lie down and rest as you can," she said, pulling the third mylar blanket from around her and passing it to him. "I will call you if I see anything."

"Maybe just for a minute." He stretched out as much as he could, his knees still bent because of the narrowness of the entrance. Nice, soft rocks. Cold. He pulled the blanket up to his chin. He'd never sleep like this, not keyed up and frozen.

The last thing he saw before he drifted off was Teyla silhouetted against the stars, her chin lifted, the barrel of the P90 beside her.

John woke to darkness and soft voices.

"There. Is that better?"

"Much better, thanks."

It took a moment to place the voices. Dahlia Radim and Carson.

"I think there is another MRE in my pack," Teyla said. "Carson, perhaps you should try to eat."

John rolled over, sitting up. It was still dark. In the back of the little cave Dahlia was helping Carson to sit up. He looked drawn and pale, but far more alert than he had before. Dahlia was looking in the pack, and drew out a foil packet as he watched.

"That's the one," Teyla said from the other side of John. She was still sitting in the entrance, the gun across her lap, barrel pointing out into the night. Her breath made a cloud of steam in the cold air.

John scrubbed his hand across his unshaven face. "How long did I sleep? And how much has the temperature dropped?"

"Five hours," Teyla said. "And I think it is around freezing."

"You've been sitting there like that for five hours? You should have woken me."

"I have been warm enough." Teyla dropped her voice. "Also I am not sure I can move. My hip has stiffened up."

John swallowed, his voice low enough for Carson not to hear. "You may have a hairline fracture."

"It does not matter if I do or not," she said. "There is nothing that can be done about it, and I cannot stay off it. We are twelve miles from the Ancient warship. We must get there. When we do I will rest it."

John nodded slowly. "Ok. Carson looks better. Let's get a meal into everybody and then we'll go on. It's cold enough that those reptile things should be out of the picture. I can carry you if I have to."

"Let us hope you do not have to," she said.

Which was quite a concession, coming from Teyla. He knew better than to ask if it hurt. Obviously it hurt like hell.

"There are two more MREs in my pack," he said. "Let's split one of them. Some energy."

"Some caffeine," she said with a smile. "Even if the water is cold the granulated coffee will dissolve. And cold coffee is better than none."

"Yeah, let's not get between you and your coffee," he said.

"It is a tempting vice from Earth," she said, and her eyes danced with mischief. "Perhaps a vice we could share."

"I'm good with that." He dug out the MRE and handed it to her. "I'll get the water. Carson, how are you holding up?"

They walked on under the bright stars, through the cold night. Carson could walk, though Dahlia stuck close beside him. The bleeding had stopped, and some rest and food seemed to have stabilized his blood pressure some. It probably wasn't good for him to walk twelve miles, but he could do it.

Teyla could hobble, John's left arm around her waist to help, but it was slow going on the broken terrain. A walk that might normally take them three or four hours was likely to take twice that. And when the sun rose and the temperatures began to climb again, those lizard things would awaken.

The cold air cleared his head. Or maybe it was a few hours sleep and some coffee. But he felt more like himself.

They halted every hour for ten minutes. By the third halt John thought his left shoulder was going to freeze that way, hunched over so that he could get it under Teyla's. One disadvantage of her being so much shorter than him.

"We'll be there soon," he said.

Dahlia Radim nodded. "This is where the canyon comes out onto the plateau, just there. After that it is not far to the ship, maybe five of your miles."

"And not too long to dawn." John looked up at the sky where the stars were already paling.

"I have never seen the lizards on the plateau," Dahlia said. "Perhaps they only hunt in the canyons."

"I hope so," Carson said fervently. He was sweating in the cold air, and he looked clammy.

"Once we get to the ship you can just get comfortable," John said. "Dahlia and I will take it from there."

"If the ship will fly," Teyla said. She refrained from saying anything pointed about Radek Zelenka. Which didn't mean she wasn't thinking it. He was.

"I think it will fly," Dahlia said somewhat indignantly. "If I did not think it would, we would not have made this bargain in the first place."

"We'll see when we get there," John said.

It was a scoutship, smaller than the *Orion* had been but larger than a puddle jumper. Perhaps it had once carried a crew of fifty to a hundred, but now it lay half covered in sand. The slanting morning sunlight limned its battered hull, streaked and pitted to the color of old sand. No markings remained, blasted away by the sandstorms of thousands of years.

Carson looked gray with exertion. "That's peachy," he said, giving voice to the thought John would not. "That thing's supposed to fly?"

"We have been doing repairs for nearly a year," Dahlia said. "I have gone as far as I can without someone powering it up."

"Ok." John took a deep breath. "Let's get on with it."

Teyla set her teeth for the last little distance.

"The hatch we have been using is over here," Dahlia said.

It opened smoothly, a good sign. Or at least a sign that the Genii engineering teams knew how to lubricate a door.

Dahlia went in first, turning on a battery powered lamp that was sitting in the hall. It cast a yellow glow ahead of them. "We've been using these lamps," she said. "It doesn't appear that there's anything wrong with main power, but we can't initialize it."

"This is a job for Rodney," Carson said, leaning on the doorframe.

"Yeah," John said shortly.

Dahlia turned around. "Where do you want to go first? The bridge or main engineering?"

"Let's get our people settled first," John said with a wary

look at Carson.

"We've been using the crew lounge behind the bridge when we were here," Dahlia said. "It's this way."

Two more of the battery powered lamps illuminated what had once been a fairly small curved room with wide viewscreens along one wall and recessed lighting in the ceiling. Several metal tables and chairs had been pulled together, and some stained white cushions were piled in one corner with a bunch of grey Genii military blankets. The air was stale, but not cold.

Dahlia switched on the lamps. "We have a heater too," she said, "But it's down in engineering now since that's where we were working last. This is where we've been staying."

"It's perfect," Carson said, looking longingly toward the pile of cushions. "Just pull one of those down for me, pass me a blanket, and I'll be a happy man."

John wrestled one down, spread it with a blanket, and added a second for good measure. He patted Carson on his good shoulder. "Why don't you have a nap while I see if this baby will fly?"

Carson nodded. "Call me if you need anything."

"I will stay here with Carson," Teyla said, sinking onto a second cushion, her left leg stiffly out before her. Which said a great deal about how much this walk had taken out of her.

"Ok." John looked at Dahlia. "The bridge then."

The layout was similar to the *Orion* and the *Aurora*, but smaller as fitted a smaller ship. The panels had been carefully cleaned, but stood dark. One of them was broken, the viewscreen cracked wildly.

"We couldn't fix that," Dahlia said, her voice oddly hushed.

There were no remains. Would there not be after so long, or

had the Genii done something with them? Running his hand over the silent consoles, he had to ask.

"We didn't find any," Dahlia said. She sounded surprised. "Maybe the survivors of the crash evacuated to the Stargate and took their casualties with them."

"Maybe," John said. There was always such a sense of people in the spaces they'd inhabited, even military spaces. When he was a kid they'd gone on a World War II battleship when they were on vacation. It was restored as a museum, tied up at a busy pier next to seafood restaurants selling Calabash clams and t shirts, but below decks in the long, silent corridors he'd still had that feeling, as though all the men who had served there were waiting, and at the claxon would come running out, pulling on shirts and sidearms. They might have been pleased to know their ship was a museum. Hell, maybe they were. Maybe those old guys with beer guts and baseball caps embroidered "Navy" were the same guys. Maybe they were the survivors.

But the Ancients wouldn't be coming to reclaim this ship. He was the closest thing it was going to get.

John laid his hand on the communications panel. *Ok, baby*, he thought. *Let's see what you've got. Come on. Wake up for me.*

With a shudder the panel purred to life, screens and buttons lighting, monitors flickering as power ran down damaged conduits.

He walked left. Weapons control. Tactical. *Come on, honey. Wake up.*

Lights flickered, the panel humming, something sparking underneath.

Propulsion.

It shivered under his hand, stabilized.

Shields.

Screens lighting, buttons flashing red and yellow alarms ten thousand years old.

Hyperdrive.

Internal systems.

The overhead lights came on, the floor lights around the bridge flared to life blue and white. Somewhere there was the soft sound of air circulation systems starting, blowing cool in his face.

Wake up, baby.

Around him the *Avenger* came to life.

CHAPTER THIRTEEN
Rendezvous

JENNIFER was glad when Lorne and his team came back through the Stargate, and not only because they didn't look like they were in panicked retreat from the Wraith. They'd been waiting while Lorne sent a MALP through, checking out its transmission carefully and then taking his team through after it to make sure they weren't walking into an ambush. She wasn't going to complain about being cautious, but standing next to Ronon with her pack leaning against her feet had involved a lot of awkward silence. There wasn't much small talk that seemed appropriate to the situation.

She was finding it hard to know what to say to anyone. Half of the people who knew her were acting like Rodney was dead, which she thought was jumping the gun just a little bit. The other half kept saying things that were probably intended to be reassuring, like 'we'll find him,' without seeming to have much idea of how they intended to do that.

"So what did we find out?" Woolsey asked, coming down the stairs behind her. He looked a bit relieved, too. They were all pretty twitchy at the moment.

"Basically the Stargate is sitting in the middle of a big open field," Lorne said. "Just a big, flat grass plain, with what looks like a river and some trees way off to the north. No sign of a road. The good news is, you could see anybody coming for miles."

Ronon nodded shortly. "What's the bad news?"

"Anybody could see you coming for miles. If we were thinking about setting up an ambush, we're going to need to take a cloaked jumper through."

"That's not a bad idea," Woolsey said. "Major Lorne, I'd

like you to take a jumper and provide some backup, just as a precaution."

Jennifer glanced at Ronon, suspecting he'd argue it wasn't necessary, but he didn't. He did hesitate for a moment, as if not sure whether Lorne expected to take charge of the mission. Jennifer wasn't sure exactly how chain of command applied to the current situation; Ronon was a civilian acting on Woolsey's orders, but Sheppard and by extension Lorne were supposed to be in charge in military situations, and if this wasn't a military situation, she wasn't sure what was.

"Let's do this," Ronon said when Lorne didn't make any move to step in.

"I'm on my way," Lorne said promptly, and headed for the jumper bay.

Jennifer shouldered her pack. "Let's do this."

"I'll contact Todd once you've gone through," Woolsey said. "Don't hesitate to dial the gate if you have problems."

"Don't worry about it," Ronon said. Jennifer wasn't sure exactly which way Ronon meant that, but the gate was already boiling blue, and Lorne's jumper was descending in front of them. The event horizon rippled as it passed through ahead of them.

She and Ronon followed cautiously. She was very aware of the unfamiliar weight of the pistol in her thigh holster. She'd hesitated before putting it on, but there had seemed like too many ways this could go wrong. Just wearing the pistol didn't mean she was going to have to use it.

She still wasn't used to the tug of the wormhole, even after who knew how many trips through the Stargate in the last two years. It felt like being tumbled through cold air, like being on the carnival rides at the state fair when she was a kid with the world whipping by in streaks of color. She'd usually been too breathless to scream.

They stepped out into a warm afternoon. The grassy field stretched out in all directions, although in the distance she could see a smudge of trees on the horizon and what might be the distant gleam of water. Lorne must have already cloaked the jumper; she wished she knew where the jumper was, but it was probably better if she didn't. It meant she couldn't give its position away with an unguarded glance upwards.

Ronon turned a circle, his pistol drawn, before seeming to decide that they weren't yet surrounded by Wraith.

"What now?" she asked.

"Now we wait," he said. He backed up from the gate and lowered his pistol at it. Jennifer thought about drawing her own and decided that the situation wasn't that dire yet. She tried to look like she was totally confident about dealing with the Wraith.

They didn't have to wait long. Almost at once, the gate's chevrons lit as it activated. Jennifer braced herself, ready to move fast if she had to.

Instead of Wraith, what emerged through the gate was a small floating device of some kind, roughly spherical and gleaming metallic in the sunlight. It hung in the air, rotating all the way around its axis, and then darted toward them.

Ronon aimed his pistol in one easy motion, looking like he was about to shoot the thing out of the air. Jennifer caught his arm. "I think it's a probe," she said. "We did send a MALP."

"I know what it is," Ronon said. He didn't lower his pistol, but he didn't shoot, either. He glanced down at her hand on his arm. "Don't *do* that."

Jennifer let go. "I just think that if we shoot the probe, it's going to make them think twice about going through with this meeting."

She half-expected Ronon to say that would be fine with him, but he let out a frustrated breath instead. "They'd better know something about where McKay is."

"Well, I hope so, too," Jennifer said. "Obviously. But we're probably not going to find out if you shoot that thing."

Ronon lowered his pistol to the side and spread his free

hand with a little smile that didn't actually make him look less threatening. "I know you can hear us," he said to the probe. "We haven't got all day."

The event horizon rippled, and two Wraith walked through into the grass between them and the gate. One of them was all too familiar. She'd gotten used to looking at Todd through the blur of the stasis field. At close range without the field between them, she had to fight not to twitch as he strode toward them.

He and his companion stopped with a good ten feet still between them, well out of arm's reach if not out of reach of a flying tackle. She hoped no one was about to tackle anyone else. "Ronon Dex," he said, his rusty voice rising over the rustle of the tall grass. "Dr. Keller."

"That's us," Ronon said. He didn't like to use the names Sheppard had given the Wraith, Jennifer had already noticed. Then again, they weren't their real names, if they had real names, so she wasn't sure using them won them any points for being polite.

"Thank you for meeting with us," Jennifer said.

Todd inclined his head slightly to her. She wished she knew exactly what that meant. "As you see, I am practically defenseless. This is neutral ground, by long tradition. You may put your weapon away." His eyes flickered to Ronon as he said it, but returned to Jennifer.

"Wraith tradition," Ronon said, in a tone that made it clear exactly how much weight he gave that.

"Our traditions are older than yours, Satedan."

"We're all here to talk," Jennifer said. She suspected that if Todd started insulting Sateda, things were going to go downhill fast, and they couldn't afford that. Not when this might be the only way to help Rodney. "We have a problem, and we're hoping we can give you a reason to help us with it."

"I will be pleased to hear about your problems," Todd said. "But first, you will send the cloaked Lantean ship you have brought with you back through the gate."

Jennifer very deliberately didn't look up. She tried not to let her eyes move at all. "I don't know what you're talking about," she said.

"There's no jumper," Ronon said.

"You are wasting my time," Todd said. "I will not spare you much more of it. You do not trust me enough not to have taken precautions. You will order your ship to return to Atlantis, visibly, or we have nothing to discuss."

Jennifer glanced at Ronon, a moment before it occurred to her that it was probably as much of a tell as if she'd looked up. With reluctance written in every line of his body, Ronon thumbed on his radio headset. "They know you're here," he said. "I want you to decloak and go back through the gate. Tell Woolsey we're getting ready to talk."

"If you're sure you know what you're doing," Lorne said.

"We'll be fine," Jennifer said into her own radio. Todd laid one hand seemingly idly over the top of the probe, and the wormhole cut off behind him. The probe sank slowly to the ground.

The jumper shimmered into visibility, and the gate began to activate behind them — not the symbols for Atlantis's new location, Jennifer realized, having spent enough time since they arrived memorizing those. Of course Lorne wouldn't chance letting Todd see the gate address for their new home. If he didn't already know it.

Ronon kept his eyes on Todd, still not putting his pistol away. "What if we really hadn't brought the jumper?"

"Then you would be growing too careless to be worth negotiating with."

"No chance of that," Ronon said.

"So I see."

The jumper sank lower as the wormhole opened, and it neatly threaded the eye of the Stargate above their heads. When it disappeared, standing in the middle of the open field suddenly felt pretty lonely.

"What if we have another jumper?" Ronon asked.

Todd gave Jennifer — not Ronon — that little nod of his head again. "I will take my chances."

"Good," Jennifer said. They were certainly taking enough of a chance themselves.

"Talk," Ronon said. He kept his pistol out, ready to level it on Todd if he made a single wrong move. The other Wraith was watching them both, his long braided hair shifting with every slight movement. Ronon wondered if they made him nervous. He hoped so.

Todd met his eyes. If he was nervous at all himself, he wasn't showing it. "You are the ones who wanted to ask for a favor."

"We want to trade," Jennifer said. "We might be able to do you a favor if you'll share some information."

"There was a raid on New Athos four days ago," Ronon said. He was getting tired of pretending this was a friendly conversation. "Three darts came through the ring. One of them took McKay."

"That is unfortunate," Todd said. "What do you expect me to do about it?"

"Share some information," Jennifer repeated.

Todd exchanged glances with the other Wraith. He thought they were communicating, in whatever way they did. The other Wraith bent over the probe and activated it again, his fingers moving across its surface like he was petting it. Ronon leveled his pistol on it, although it looked like the standard ones that only had cameras and transmitters, no weapons.

"It is essential that we move away from the Stargate," Todd said. "You may follow us." He turned his back on Ronon and began walking toward the treeline. The other Wraith followed him, but kept glancing behind.

It was awfully tempting to just shoot them both. If he killed the other one, he could probably take Todd down but leave him alive. There was just a little too much chance of Jennifer getting caught in the crossfire.

"We're not going anywhere," he said.

Todd turned. Ronon hated the way they always moved, like snakes trying to fascinate their prey into freezing. "We are not the only ones who use this meeting place," he said. "I cannot afford to be seen treating humans as people to be negotiated with."

"You mean treating humans as people," Jennifer said. Todd didn't bother to respond. "You could tell them we were your prisoners."

"Will you allow me to restrain you, then?"

"No," Ronon said flatly.

"Then that will be difficult to believe. If we are to negotiate, we will not do it standing next to the Stargate."

"Fine," Ronon said. He nodded to Jennifer. "Dial the gate. We're leaving."

"No, we're not," she said. "We're not done here."

"Yes, we are," he said. He stepped backwards until he touched the DHD with his left hand, not taking his eyes off Todd. He found the first symbol by feel, the plate warm under his hand.

"No, we're not," she said, her voice low and hard the way he'd only heard from her a few times before. He hadn't liked any of those times. She turned to Todd. "You don't want to stay by the gate, fine," she said. "We'll come with you."

"He said himself more Wraith could come through the gate," Ronon said. He wasn't sure why she wasn't understanding how bad that would be. "We'd be cut off."

"Then we'll find a way to deal with them."

"No," he said. "End of discussion. We're dialing out." He pressed the first symbol in the address for New Athos.

"Fine," Jennifer said. "Dial out if you want. But I'm not leaving until we know for sure they can't help us find Rodney."

"Follow or not," Todd said, turning his back on them again. "But I would not remain at the gate if I were you."

"I thought you said this was neutral ground," Jennifer said.

"I am willing to treat you as if those rules applied to you," Todd said. "Others will not be."

Jennifer looked at Ronon. He could see her wavering. "It's got to be a trap," he said. "We aren't doing this."

She set her jaw. "I am," she said.

There was a moment where he could have caught her arm to stop her. He probably would have if she'd been Teyla, but he hadn't been raised to push women who weren't soldiers around that way. That was probably going to get them both killed. Jennifer set off through the long grass, and Ronon swore under his breath and went after her.

They should be leaving enough of a trail for someone to follow. At least, he could have followed their trail. Lorne would at least be able to track them by their subcutaneous transmitters. That was something.

Todd and the other Wraith seemed unconcerned with whether they were following or not, keeping to a slow enough pace that they could follow without running, but not making any effort to drop back to join them. Ronon kept his eyes on them, but he could feel every step they were putting between themselves and the Stargate.

"We probably should have told someone that we were moving away from the gate," Jennifer said under her breath. He wondered if that was supposed to be some kind of peace offering. It didn't work, if it was.

"Can't," he said shortly. "Unless we shoot the probe first. It'll record the gate address."

"Right," she said.

"You should listen to me," he said. "This is a bad idea."

"We can't do this now," she said, her voice a hiss barely above a whisper. They could probably hear her anyway. "We need to be together on this."

You mean we need to do what you want, he thought, but he was all too aware that the Wraith were listening. "Fine," he said.

"Where are we going?" she called to Todd.

"Be patient," he said without turning.

"We're not," Ronon said.

"I know," Todd said. "Just beyond the trees."

They walked for a while in silence. The flat plain was beginning to slope down toward the line of trees, and the grass was shorter, brushing against his ankles. That made him frown, but he didn't want to take his eyes off the Wraith to look closer.

"What?" Jennifer asked.

"This field's been grazed," he said. "Maybe just some kind of herd animal that roams wild here. But maybe not."

She glanced down underfoot. "I think you're right," she said. "You don't think there are people here, do you?"

"No cooking smoke," he said. "But not everybody keeps fires lit all day when it's this warm."

"We are here," Todd said, and actually stopped and waited for them to catch up. "You will be better received if you stay close to us. Most humans are not welcome here."

"I thought this planet was uninhabited," Jennifer said.

"Then you have been badly informed," Todd said. As he spoke, a man stepped out from behind the trees. He was wearing robes and high cloth boots that looked weirdly familiar. After a moment, Ronon realized they were imitations of Wraith clothing, or maybe even the real thing.

"Wraith worshipper," he spat.

The man spread his hands. "You travel in the company of the gods yourself." His left hand was painted in what Ronon realized to his disgust was an imitation of a Wraith's feeding slit. His hair fell down his back, clearly once dark but beginning to gray.

"They aren't gods," Ronon said.

"*Ronon*," Jennifer said. "It doesn't matter what he thinks they are."

"Yes, it does."

"You may find this entertaining," Todd said. "But my time here is limited. If your blade cannot keep a civil tongue, you would be wise to silence him."

It took Ronon a moment to realize the Wraith was talking to Jennifer. His free hand clenched into a fist.

"I'm sure we can all be civil, here," Jennifer said.

"Of course," Todd said. He looked about as skeptical as Ronon felt.

CHAPTER FOURTEEN
Blood Secrets

"AH, THAT'S better," Carson said as the overhead lighting came on. He burrowed under a pile of Genii blankets. "Getting the ship up and running, I see."

Teyla thought his face looked strained. "Are you in pain, Carson?" she asked.

He let out a deep breath. "More than a bit. But I didn't dare take another Endocet this morning. I wouldn't have been able to walk."

"You do not need to walk now," Teyla pointed out. "All you need do is lie there while Colonel Sheppard flies the ship. So you may as well take another and rest a bit."

"And make a cake of myself again?" Carson looked embarrassed.

"We have all been injured," Teyla said. "And we have all said things we wish we had not. But there is no reason for you to lie there in pain. If I were the patient that is what you would say."

"There you've got me, love," Carson said. "I've more in my kit."

"I will get it," Teyla said. Carson's pack was across the room, clearly distinguishable from the others by the red cross on it. She crawled the few paces to it and snagged it with one arm.

Carson's eyes were sharp. "How is your leg?"

"It is fine." She held the pack out to him for him to find the medicine.

"It isn't." Carson frowned. "You hurt that much worse than you let on, or you would never have let Colonel Sheppard help you this morning. It could be a hairline fracture or a splinter that's not impacting the hip socket."

"And can you tell anything about it without an X ray, or do

anything for it?" Teyla shook her head. "When we are back in Atlantis you may do with it as you like. But until then there is nothing to do about it."

Carson frowned deeper. "You ought to stay off it."

"I am staying off it."

Carson opened a little plastic bottle and poured two white pills out on his hand. "You could have one of these yourself, you know."

"Perhaps I will later," she said, and took one from him while he swallowed the other. "When we are in the air."

Carson nodded. "All right." He followed his with a gulp of water from his water bottle, then carefully lay down on his good shoulder. "I'll just stay out of the way."

"Sleep," Teyla said. "I will call you if anything happens."

Carson pulled the blanket up to shade his eyes, turned away from her. Teyla let out a long breath, the white pill sticky in her palm. It would be good to take it, to relax, but she could not fully do that until they were back in Atlantis. Too many things could still go wrong. Just because the lights went on did not mean the ship was spaceworthy. They might still have to walk back to the Stargate.

I will just lean back against this bulkhead, Teyla thought, positioning the cushions around her more comfortably. I will lean back and rest a few minutes while I may. There were too many things that crowded her mind—Carson first, a few feet away. Rodney, who was in the hands of the Wraith, who might this moment be withering in a Queen's hands. Torren, who might… Who knew what Torren might do? He could walk well, run faster than anyone expected on his cute little baby legs, wanted to get into everything. And many of the people who might be watching him had not the slightest idea how to take care of a child his age.

Torren was probably the least of her worries. He was in Atlantis, with no more danger than any child might face from inexperienced caregivers. They all meant him well, and they would all care for him as best they could. She was gone longer than expected, but no one would neglect him. They would pass him around, vying for the privilege of feeding him and playing with him. Torren was in more danger of being spoiled than neglected.

I will just rest a moment, Teyla thought. I will put these things from my mind and conserve my strength. I will rest a moment.

Teyla woke to the sound of careful footsteps. John had come in quietly and was getting his canteen from the packs. There was the sound of ventilation systems, but no deep purr of engines. Teyla pushed herself up on one elbow. "John?" she whispered.

With a glance at Carson he came over and dropped down beside her cross-legged. Three days growth of beard made him look different, like a man of her people. He took a long drink of water and nodded in Carson's direction. "Has he been out long?"

"He has been sleeping the entire time," she said. "He took another pain pill. I am afraid I went to sleep as well. How long has it been?"

"Three hours." John closed the canteen carefully. "I've initialized everything. There are some power problems here and there, but Dahlia thinks she can fix them. So she's trading out crystals and moving stuff around. Until she's finished there's not much for me to do." He took a deep breath, not looking at her. "You were right and I was wrong. If we'd gone back for Radek we'd be sure of getting the ship in the air."

"You may have to go back for him yet," Teyla said. "If the ship will not fly, then Dahlia and Carson and I should wait here, where there is shelter, and you should go back to the Stargate and return with Radek and another jumper." Sixty miles by himself across this rough terrain in daylight, in the searing heat, with hunting reptiles. But Teyla knew she could not do it. Not now.

John nodded, running his hand over his chin absently, as though already seeing the trail. "If it comes to that. Dahlia may be able to fix the power problems. It doesn't seem like there's anything actually wrong with the propulsion systems. It's the hull breaches that forced them down, and it looks like the Genii have patched some of that, or that the bulkhead doors are sealed. Lousy structural integrity, and when we're ready to take off we should all get in sealable compartments and vacuum suits. I'm not going to lay any bets on staying pressurized."

Teyla's eyebrows rose. "And how long are we to spend in Ancient vacuum suits? Do not they have a limited supply of air?"

John nodded. "Yep. But we'll only be in hyperspace for a little less than six hours."

"Surely the Genii homeworld is much further," Teyla said, trying to picture it on the moving map in Atlantis. She was used to knowing worlds by their gate addresses — finding them by their physical location always seemed strange to her.

"Atlantis isn't."

"We are going straight back to Atlantis?"

"We need to get Carson to a doctor. And the *Avenger* needs a lot more than we can do here before she's spaceworthy." John put the canteen down on the other side.

Teyla shook her head, seeing a course through the politics as he did through space. "Ladon Radim will be very upset."

"Ladon Radim would like to get his sister back breathing." John glanced at her sideways. "It's too far. And the ship is in crap shape. I don't think a bunch of these bulkheads will hold when exposed to vacuum. We're going to have decompressions. This stuff is just too old and too beat up. Dahlia's done a good job, but she doesn't have the right materials. And propulsion's all she's got. No shields, no weapons control, no long range communications. It's stuff we can't replace on the fly. We've got no transmitter dish for communications. Dahlia can't pull one out of her back pocket."

"Why do we simply not fly the ship to the Stargate?" Teyla asked. "Then Carson and I could go through and send a science team back."

John shook his head. "The terrain around the Stargate is pretty broken up. Canyons and plateaus, nowhere near flat enough to land a ship this size. If I could even be sure I can land it in one piece. In Atlantis if the landing goes sour I can ditch it in the ocean and there will be a rescue jumper there in minutes. If I try to put it down on a bunch of rocks with no backup? It won't be pretty."

"That is true," Teyla agreed. "But if we do not arrive with the warship in good time, Ladon Radim will take it as a breach of your bargain."

"We'll give him the *Avenger*. But we've got to make Atlantis first. Dahlia will see that."

"I hope so," Teyla said. She leaned back against the bulkhead again, and he sat beside her, stretching his legs out tiredly. For a long moment they sat there in companionable silence.

He apologized for not listening to her, not for bringing her here in the first place. He was not sorry she was here. It was her place. This was who she was, Teyla Who Walks Through Gates, Teyla Who Would Never Return to New Athos, who could never again be satisfied with a smaller world. Not when two galaxies in their courses stretched before her, filled with people moved by familiar motivations. How could she be satisfied trading furs for silks when there were trades to be made that dwarfed anything she could once have imagined? There were trades that changed the lives of millions, saved them or squandered them. Elizabeth had called it diplomacy and Woolsey called it The Great Game. Ladon Radim called it politics, the world as it is. The art of the possible. How could she go home and raise tava beans, and hope that the deluge would not come?

"Kanaan has asked me to release him," she said.

John looked at her sideways. "I'm sorry."

"Are you?"

"No?" His expression was somewhere between sheepish and startled. He took a deep breath, as though hunting carefully for the right words. "I mean, I'm sorry it didn't work out the way you wanted it to. It's rough, getting divorced."

Teyla smiled ruefully, leaning her head back against the wall. He would think what he would think. "We never made those promises to one another."

"But you…" He sounded confused, but she would not look to see. "You planned to have a child together."

"We planned no such thing. Torren was…an unexpected blessing." She would not look at him. She did not want to see a change in his face, the loss of respect in his eyes.

John's voice was low. "You could have told me that to start with."

"And was it any of your business?"

"No." That had come out harsher than she intended. He sounded hurt.

Teyla shook her head. "I knew what you would say. What your people would say. Do you think I do not hear the things that people say, the jokes they make? About breeders and people who are wasting their lives with children? About women who might have amounted to something? Do you think I did not hear what Rodney said about Jeannie? Do you think I do not know the words ho and baby-mama?" She looked at him and he was wincing, but this anger had been building in her a long time, and it would not be stopped now. "Do you think I wish to be a figure of fun? Do you think I do not know that everything I do reflects upon my people? That is a responsibility I accept. I will be their representative. I will be their ambassador. But I know what that means."

John looked down at his lap, at his big hands resting on his thigh. "Teyla, you've got to understand that these people aren't typical. The original expedition — they're all a little crazy. People with any kind of functional relationship don't sign up for a one-way trip. The people who came were the people who were too screwed up to have anybody to leave." He looked at her, frowning. "Maybe kids like Ford weren't. They were real young and thought it would be an adventure. But all the scientists, everybody older… Most people on Earth aren't like that. Most people on Earth aren't basically dysfunctional to start with. Most people would have somebody who would miss them."

John shrugged. "The new people aren't like that. All these Air Force guys O'Neill pulled in — it's another deployment for them. They've got girlfriends, husbands and kids at home, parents, friends. But the original ones who took a one way ticket like me and Rodney and Radek and Carson — that was kind of different." He looked up at the ceiling. "It's like Rodney, you know? He goes on about Jeannie and how she could be doing something else, but he's the guy in a hurry to get married, the one wondering if he missed the boat."

She knew what was unspoken in those lines of tension in his face, all the worry for Rodney he would not voice, the fears he would not give shape to, lest naming them make them real. "We will find him," she said, and squeezed his hand.

"Yeah." He nodded, his eyes on their hands. "Yeah."

"And you?"

"I sunk that boat." John swallowed. He did not look up. "But I want you to know that I don't think anything bad about you. There's nothing you said that would make me lose respect for you or something."

His hand in hers, her fingers against his wristband. "Truly?"

"Yeah." He gave her a lopsided smile. "You know. Stuff happens. Life happens."

She could not help but smile back, finding his words. "I think it is possible…that I am kind of dysfunctional too."

"Yeah, probably."

"We are ready to go." Dahlia Radim stood in the doorway, her jumpsuit streaked with oil. "Or at least as ready as I can make us." She looked from one to the other of them, and to Carson, rolled insensible in a mound of blankets. "Is Dr. Beckett all right?"

"He took another pain pill and he is sleeping," Teyla said, releasing John's hand as though it were nothing. "But I will have to wake him up to get him in a vacuum suit."

"A vacuum suit?" Dahlia looked at John.

"There are some in the forward locker that check out," John said. "And I think we'd better all get into them. I'm not confident about how much pressure the *Avenger* can take."

Dahlia nodded. "That's prudent. Though we should not seal them unless a failure seems imminent. It is much too far."

John got to his feet. "Not to Atlantis," he said.

Dahlia went pale. "What?"

"Not to Atlantis," John said. "It's seventeen hours in hyperspace to your homeworld and just under six to Atlantis. We're going to Atlantis."

Dahlia took a step back. "You planned this all along. This is a double cross. You want the warship. All of this talk of your missing man was nothing but a ruse." Her eyes snapped with anger. "You knew we had an Ancient warship and you made this up so that you could take it!"

"No," John said. "It's not…"

"The warship is yours," Teyla broke in smoothly. "Colonel Sheppard will take you and the *Avenger* both to your homeworld. But you can see very plainly that Dr. Beckett needs medical attention as soon as possible, and you know that the *Avenger* is barely spaceworthy. We will go to Atlantis, and there you may call your brother and speak with him. Then you and our engineers will make certain that the *Avenger* is spaceworthy, and Colonel Sheppard will take you home."

"And you will copy the specs of the *Avenger* while you are at it," Dahlia snapped.

"We already have the plans for an Ancient warship," Teyla said. "We have had one in our possession before, as you know. But we are no more capable of building one complete than you are."

"You've got to trust us," John said.

"As you trusted me?" Dahlia demanded. "If I body search you, will I find your intentions?"

"You will have to see from what we do," Teyla said. "It is dangerous enough to take this ship into space at all. To take it three times further than we must is folly. I give you my word that when we are in Atlantis you may use the Stargate to contact your brother and tell him where you are and all that has transpired."

"So that you may show him I am your hostage," Dahlia said.

"I give you my word that you are not," Teyla said gravely.

Dahlia's eyes met Teyla's firmly. "And should I take your word for it, Bloodtainted as you are? What is your word worth?"

It was as happens when sparring, when there is an unexpectedly solid hit that takes your breath away, leaving you gasping for the next thing. Teyla drew in a breath sharply.

"We have heard a great deal of Atlantis, and of you, Teyla Emmagan. We have heard how you set upon a soldier called Bates who feared you Bloodtainted, and how you nearly beat him to death." Her eyes flicked to John. "And how it was covered up by your lover."

"She had nothing to do with Bates." John looked as though he were scurrying to keep up. "That was a Wraith commando loose in the city."

"That is not what the soldiers said who gossiped in front of Sora Tyrus. In the three months she was in your charge she learned many things. Not the least of which is that you bear a Bloodtaint that should have been stamped out many years ago, madness and cruelty that the galaxy is better off without." Her eyes slid to John, and there was no anger there, only wonder. "Do you not know what perversions it leads one to? The last Bloodtainted among the Genii killed seventeen women over a period of three years. The one before that killed his mother and his father, and then two officers of the peace who came when people heard the screams. They are criminals, Colonel Sheppard! They are mad criminals who love to cause pain, and who do it for their pleasure, or because they hear voices that urge them to kill. There is no rehabilitation that can be accomplished with the Bloodtainted. They are not safe. If you take such a one to you, one day you will wake with a knife in your chest while she drinks your blood."

John gulped, and she thought she saw uncertainty in his eyes, though his voice was level. "I know Teyla."

Though cold ran down her back, she must focus on the matter at hand. "It does not matter at this moment what you think of me. We must do what will best accomplish our mission without anyone dying. And that is to take this crippled ship into Atlantis, where there can be more extensive repairs and Dr. Beckett can get medical attention. Then Colonel Sheppard will take you home and deliver the warship to Chief Radim, as we promised. You may choose not to believe us, but that is what will happen." Her eyes met John's for a moment. "When the colonel says he is ready, we will go."

"And if I do not consent, you will kill me?" Dahlia asked, her chin high.

"I'll have to lock you in one of the empty crew quarters until we get there," John said. "You can't override the locks, not if I tell the ship not to let you. I'd rather not do that. But I will if I need to."

"Then we will make ready to go," Dahlia said sharply. "And you may know that Chief Radim will have a great deal to say." She turned on her heel and headed for the bridge.

John started to say something, but she forestalled him. "John…"

He turned and looked at her.

"There is no need," she said quietly. "The things she said are true. That is why those with the Gift were so often hunted. So Charin told me, and so I believe." She raised her eyes to his, braced for the reaction there. "I am part Wraith. You know this."

"It wasn't a problem five years ago, and it's not a problem now." His mouth quirked. "If you start turning into some kind of crazy serial killer, I'll be the first to know."

"Do you not think that is what I fear?" she asked, and to her horror her voice shook. This was not the time and place for this conversation. Not with Dahlia Radim, not with everyone so exhausted and strung up.

"I know you, Teyla." He rested his hand a moment on her shoulder. "It's ok." He squeezed it once, then let go. "I'll show you where the suits are. You should probably get Carson into his suit before takeoff. The first problem moment is going to be when we leave the atmosphere. That's when anything that's not going to stand up to vacuum will go."

"Very well," Teyla said. "Let us do this and go home."

CHAPTER FIFTEEN
The Houses of the Dead

"WE ARE honored by your presence," the Wraith worshipper said, and then went to his knees in front of Todd. Jennifer could feel Ronon move beside her, and she put out a hand to arrest whatever move he was about to make.

"We have come to negotiate," Todd said, as if he found the idea a little amusing. "Do not expect to be rewarded for nothing."

"Of course not," the man said, but Jennifer thought she could see his jaw twitch. She didn't dare look at Ronon.

"I'm Dr. Jennifer Keller," she said. "This is Ronon Dex. Do you have a name?"

The man got to his feet before he looked at her. "I am called Carlin," he said. "You have come to the Houses of the Dead."

Jennifer couldn't help feeling that sounded less than good. "We're here to talk," she said.

The man nodded. "Many come to talk. Here in the land of the dead, there is no war among the gods."

"Or among humans," Jennifer said. "I hope."

"The living do not walk among us," Carlin said.

"Unless your gods wish it," Todd said.

Carlin nodded, although he looked a little skeptical. "As you say."

Todd smiled. It wasn't a friendly expression. "Will you not make us welcome?"

"You are welcome," Carlin said. "Come with me." He led them down the easy slope toward the water.

Jennifer followed, trying not to look as thrown as she felt. So, Todd had lied to them. Well, that wasn't exactly a big surprise. Or maybe not actually lied—he'd promised neutral ground, and it sounded like this was some kind of traditional neutral ground for warring factions of Wraith. That didn't make their position any better if they were surrounded by Wraith worshippers, though. She was pretty sure they'd take Todd's side if it came down to a fight. So it had better not come down to a fight.

What had looked like rolling hillside proved to be a small cluster of dugout buildings, their tops grown over with grass, or maybe they'd been hollowed out of the hillside without disturbing the sod. Jennifer saw a few people moving from house to house, all with the same long hair and somber clothes Carlin wore. More than one of them moved haltingly, as if even crossing the short distance from house to house was painful.

"We can offer medical assistance if that's something your people need," Jennifer couldn't help saying.

"These are the Houses of the Dead," Carlin said. "They await rebirth. The dead do not seek healing from the living."

"Well, okay," Jennifer said. She still didn't see any smoke, but there were animal tracks in the soft ground that ran down to the river, and enough footprints that she thought there must be plenty of living people around.

"What kind of rebirth?" Ronon said from behind her. Jennifer had already pretty much decided that it was best not to ask that question. It figured that Ronon couldn't let it alone.

"The gift of the dead gods," Carlin said.

"Okay," Jennifer said quickly. The Wraith could heal as well as kill, feeding humans the same energy they drained when they fed on them. She knew Ronon had experienced that firsthand, over and over as torture until he finally broke under it and then had to painfully withdraw from his body's addiction to the process, craving it like a drug. She knew he had every reason to hate the Wraith, but they were here for a reason, and she wished he'd act like he remembered it. "We'd like to hear more about your people another time, right, Ronon?"

"Sure," he said. He sounded angry. She hoped it was at the

Wraith and not at her.

"It's just that we're a little busy right now," she went on firmly.

"Carlin's people have served us at this meeting place for many generations," Todd said. "It is useful to us to have a place to meet where misunderstandings are less likely to take place."

"You mean where you're less likely to stab each other in the back," Ronon said.

"I believe that is what I said." Todd stopped in front of what looked like a small hill until Jennifer saw the weathered wooden door set into the curve of the hillside. "This will serve our needs."

Carlin hurried to open the door for them. Jennifer stepped back, letting Ronon check it out first. He didn't look like he particularly wanted to step across the threshold, but after a moment he did, looking around with his pistol drawn.

Todd and the other Wraith hung back, making no move to go in until she and Ronon had assured themselves that it was safe. She wished she were more sure whether that was courtesy or just a hunter waiting for the mouse to walk into the trap.

"It's clear," Ronon said finally.

"After you," Jennifer said.

Todd's lips twitched in an unreadable expression. "As you wish," he said. He glanced at the other Wraith, who preceded him in, and then ducked inside himself. Jennifer followed, trying not to think about mousetraps springing shut.

Inside there was a trestle table laid with a pitcher and stacked cups. The floor was swept earth, and the ceiling was high and arched, supported by what she hoped were interlaced tree branches. It was possible that on closer inspection they would prove to be bones, but she wasn't planning on inspecting that closely. The room was dim, lit only by the light filtering in from a pair of small skylights covered in what might have been glass or plastic.

In one corner, there was a teardrop-shaped device with coils winding across its face that looked suspiciously like a battery-powered heater of some kind. It suggested that the reason there weren't any fires lit was probably that the locals had better ways of cooking their breakfast. She wasn't an expert, but she would have bet on its being Wraith technology.

Todd seated himself at one end of the table, his hands on his knees. She waited for Ronon to sit, but he leaned against the wall, his pistol out to cover the table. The other Wraith took up a position behind Todd, his hands spread as if ready to reach for a weapon himself.

Apparently it was going to be that kind of negotiation. Jennifer sat down at the other end of the table, hoping that would look like she was insisting on equal status rather just that she preferred having the length of the table between them. It was a relief to shrug off her heavy pack. She rested it against her knee where she could reach it in a hurry.

"Now talk," Ronon said.

Todd spread his hands. "What would you like me to say?"

"We want to know who took Rodney," Jennifer said. "We're willing to make a deal for any information that will help us find him."

"I have no idea who took him," Todd said. "It was not any of my doing."

Jennifer thought he sounded just a little too innocent. "You're telling me that you don't have any idea who attacked New Athos, or where they might be now?"

Todd seemed to grow suddenly interested in inspecting the water pitcher. Jennifer waited, as patiently as she could. She didn't think he'd be going to all this trouble if he thought there was no chance of making a deal.

"There have been new developments," Todd said finally. "Many of our territorial arrangements have broken down. We had placed New Athos off limits for the time being. If that is no longer being respected, it is beyond my control."

Ronon smiiled like he didn't believe that at all. "Why would you do that?"

"Maybe they don't want to have to deal with us," Jennifer said.

Todd spread his hands. Ronon's hand twitched at the motion, and Jennifer silently willed him to be still. He wasn't making this any easier by acting like he was ready to start shooting at any moment. "New Athos is Lantean territory," Todd said. "We felt it unwise to challenge you for it at present."

"It's not our *territory*," Ronon said. Jennifer could have kicked him. "But they're our allies. You're right that we'd come after you if you attacked them. We will, if you just did."

"We have no interest in New Athos," Todd said. "The Athosians have been too recently culled. It would be poor husbandry for us to drive them to extinction through greed, though admittedly leaving the genes for certain — peculiar talents — in existence has its risks."

"You sound like an environmentalist talking about bears," Jennifer said. Ronon shifted his weight again, and she shot Ronon a look that she hoped communicated *this is not the time to ask me what an environmentalist is.*

"It is in our best interests to preserve our... environment," Todd said. He looked amused. "Unless we intend to seek a new and unspoiled feeding ground."

"I think it would get spoiled pretty fast," Jennifer said.

"For you, at least," Todd said.

"Somebody sent those darts," Ronon broke in. "It wasn't a culling. They wanted one of our people."

"It looked to us like they were after Rodney in particular," Jennifer said. "He's got a lot of information that could be damaging to both of us."

"If that is the case, the queen who took him will be extracting the knowledge from him as we speak," Todd said. "There is little chance that he can be retrieved before he reveals what he knows."

"You'd be surprised," Jennifer said, fighting to keep her voice level. "Rodney's tougher than he looks."

"It doesn't matter if he's already talked or not," Ronon said, somewhat to her surprise. "He's ours. We want him back."

"That is wasteful of you," Todd said. He sounded less critical than thoughtful, his eyes on her speculatively.

Jennifer raised her chin. "I think that's our call."

He shrugged. "Perhaps," he said. "But if he has already revealed what he knows, I do not see that I have much incentive to become involved."

"Maybe we can give you one," Jennifer said. "We've worked together in the past."

Todd snorted. "And we have seen what great advantage I have gained from that arrangement."

"You're still alive," she said. "We have information, technology—"

"None that is of interest to us."

"You used to find Dr. Beckett's retrovirus pretty interesting."

"It doesn't *work*," Todd said sharply. "We learned that at our cost."

"It doesn't work *yet*."

There was an abrupt mechanical noise, and she and Todd both glanced up at the other Wraith, who was looking at some kind of readout on a device he wore on his arm. The Wraith looked sharply at Todd, and for a moment she thought Todd's eyes showed a flicker of alarm.

Someone knocked on the door outside, and then opened it. "More gods have come through the ring," Carlin said. Jennifer thought he was the only one in the room who looked pleased.

Ronon gave him a sharp look. "How would you know

that?"

"There are transmitting devices in the gate field, well dis-
guised," Todd said when it was clear the man was planning to
offer no explanation. "We may need to postpone any further
discussion until they leave this place."

"No," Ronon said. "You said we'd be safe here. Now you're
just jerking us around."

"Ronon," Jennifer said.

"I've been patient," he said.

"No, you haven't," she said. "If we need to wait—"

"Because they say so?"

"Remain where you are," Todd said, and strode out of the
room. The other Wraith bared his teeth in a smile that didn't
look entirely confident. Jennifer didn't feel up to meeting it
with one of her own.

"We should get out of here," Ronon said.

Jennifer turned up her hands. "It sounds like the other
Wraith are between us and the gate."

"Like I *told* you."

"If Todd wanted us dead, we'd be dead by now," Jennifer said.
It seemed obvious enough to her. "He'd have had these people
ambush us, or have set some kind of trap—"

"If that's what you thought, then why did we come?"

"Because I don't think he wants us dead. There's something
he still wants badly enough to—"

"He's a Wraith. He wants us dead."

"If you're not even going to listen to me, why am I on this
mission?"

Ronon was smiling a little, but it wasn't a friendly expression. "That was Woolsey's idea, not mine."

That hung there for a moment, and then as Jennifer started
to speak, the door slammed open.

"Do not waste time in foolish questions," Todd said. "Move
quickly if you want to live. The Wraith who have come through

the Stargate are followers of Queen Death. She must not know I have met with you."

"Why?" Jennifer asked.

Todd glared at her. "That would be a foolish question."

"Fine," Jennifer said. "What are you suggesting?"

"There is a hiding place."

"If these people know about it, it's not exactly going to do us much good."

"I have made arrangements," Todd said. "You may trust me."

"Right," Ronon said.

"I don't see that we have a lot of choice," Jennifer said.

"You're right. We don't," Ronon said. He didn't say and whose fault is that, but she was pretty sure he was thinking it.

"Then let's go," Jennifer said, and shouldered her pack again. It seemed like it was getting heavier every time.

CHAPTER SIXTEEN
Tomb

TODD LED them along the river, under the shelter of the trees, leaving the other Wraith behind, presumably to explain his absence if he didn't get back before the other Wraith arrived. Ronon kept his pistol in hand, more than ready to shoot at any sign that they were being led into a trap. At this point, shooting Todd wouldn't solve their problems, but it would at least make him feel better.

"How much farther?" he demanded.

"Far enough that you will not be heard even if you persist in talking," Todd said.

"I think we're that far already."

Todd ignored him.

"Ronon," Jennifer said. He pretended he hadn't heard.

Finally Todd stopped, peering closely at the ground that led up from the river, and then began making his way carefully up the bank.

"Where are we going?" Ronon asked.

"The tombs along this side of the river are rarely visited," Todd said. "They are too old for the humans here to believe that the dead in them will rise."

"Oh," Jennifer said a little faintly. "Well, that's good to know."

"They bring their dead here hoping that you'll revive them," Ronon said. "Only you don't."

"Those who reside here consider themselves dead," Todd said. "Those who serve us well may be rewarded."

"I'm guessing whoever's in this tomb is not going to be doing that," Jennifer said.

"You are probably correct," Todd said. He stopped in front

of what looked to a casual glance like an undisturbed curve of hillside, but Ronon could see the depression in the grass around the edges of something with sides too straight to be a rock. He bent and dug his fingers in, finding an edge and tugging. A trap door lifted free with some effort, earth showering down into darkness.

"There won't be enough air in there," Jennifer said.

"There is an exhaust fan, and light as well," Todd said. "I told you, I have made arrangements."

"For us?" Ronon said. "That's considerate."

"In case of emergency," Todd said.

"I thought you said this was neutral ground," Jennifer said. "According to ancient Wraith tradition."

"Times change," Todd said. Now that he looked, Ronon could see wires running across the bottom of the wooden trap door. Todd pressed a button tangled in the wires, and a faint green glow lit what seemed to be a pit dug into the hillside, wide but not more than three or four meters deep. There were shapes in the dim light, but he couldn't make them out clearly. They could have been anything.

There was also a low whisper of noise that set Ronon's teeth on edge. It might be a fan. It was probably mechanical. Not at all like the sound of something breathing in the darkness where nothing ought to be breathing. Not at all like the sound of something moving down there, whispering papery-dry against the walls—

"This is not my idea of a great hiding place," Jennifer said, but she was already clipping a line to her pack and fastening her flashlight to it. She lowered it down, peering down after it. "I don't suppose there's a ladder?"

"There are hooks for one on the door," Ronon said, pointing them out. "You can fasten the rope."

"My day really needed a little rope-climbing," Jennifer said. She secured the rope with a better knot than he'd expected her to tie; it looked Athosian in style, so maybe Teyla had been trying to make up for some of the things Jennifer had apparently never learned in school.

"I will return when the others have departed," Todd said.

Jennifer sat on the edge of the trap door and wrapped her hands inexpertly around the rope. He started to tell her to let him go down first, and then hesitated, because that would mean leaving her up here with a Wraith.

Before he could tell her to do one or the other, she was already descending the short distance to the floor of the pit. She picked up the flashlight and shone it around her, adding its bright beam to the green glow. "It looks clear," she said.

"If this is a trick, I'll kill you myself," Ronon said.

"If this were a trick, you would not get the chance," Todd said. "Descend now, so that I can close this entrance behind you."

"I don't take orders from Wraith," Ronon said. It was intensely tempting to just pull the trigger. This wasn't the first time someone had wanted to trust Todd, and it probably wouldn't be the last time. He could put an end to all that right now. Jennifer couldn't see him from down in the pit. He could kill the Wraith, see him fall twitching at his feet and watch him finally go still, and then he'd say—

That was where it broke down. Jennifer might believe him if he said that Todd had drawn a weapon on him, but Sheppard would be skeptical enough to ask him outright if it was true. He'd have to lie, which would be wrong, or else have to admit he'd disobeyed orders and live with Sheppard's disappointment. His hand was clenched on the pistol, his finger shaking with the effort not to squeeze the trigger.

"One of these days I'm going to kill you," Ronon said.

"Not today," Todd said. Ronon holstered his pistol in one fast move before he could think better of it and swung himself over the edge of the pit, dropping down to the floor without bothering to use the rope. It was cooler down there, and it smelled dank, although he could feel the air moving in a way that suggested they would be able to breathe.

The trapdoor closed without warning, dirt raining down onto Ronon's hair. He managed not to flinch, closing his eyes for a moment and breathing out sharply to avoid breathing the stuff.

Jennifer shone the flashlight around, tracing the curve of the walls. Above them, the roof was reinforced by the same bleached tangle that had strengthened the longhouse roof. He thought some of it looked like the antlers of some herd animal, but some of it was clearly old bone, weathered in the open for some years.

The green light was coming from a lantern set into one wall, its wires running up the wall to the trap door in the ceiling. At one end of the long pit, there was a raised platform of earth with a shape lying on it, wrapped in cloth. It didn't move, no matter how long Jennifer shone her flashlight on it. That was a good thing.

"All right," Jennifer said, shining the light on a pile of rough wooden boxes at the other end of the pit. "What's this stuff?"

"Probably stuff he wanted buried with him," Ronon said. "It sounds like he was planning on getting to use it later."

"Right," Jennifer said. "This is creepy." She climbed up on one of the boxes anyway, crossing her legs and leaning back against the earth wall. "You're not going to pace like that the whole time we're down here, are you?"

"I don't know. Are you going to talk the whole time?"

"I don't think anybody can hear us down here."

"I can hear you," Ronon said.

Jennifer actually looked like that stung. He'd wondered what it would take to get it through to her that he wasn't happy with her.

"Okay, we don't have to talk," Jennifer said. She wrapped her hands around her knees and switched off the flashlight. To conserve the battery, he told himself. Not just to get on his nerves.

The green light threw weird shadows across her face, hollowing her cheeks and the backs of her hands. He didn't really want to look at that, but there wasn't much else to look at. Probably the stuff in the tomb said something meaningful about their culture. Teyla would have said they should take pictures for the scientists back in Atlantis, but Teyla was probably sitting in Radim's office right now being really polite while drinking endless cups of tea.

That was actually starting to sound pretty good.

The silence grew unbearable pretty fast. Staying quiet was made even harder by the fact that for the first time since they'd arrived on the planet, Jennifer felt like it was actually safe for them to talk. For the moment it looked like there wasn't anyone watching them, at least assuming they weren't being monitored by some hidden piece of Wraith technology. There wasn't any way to tell, so she figured there was no point in worrying about that.

This wasn't how she'd wanted this mission to go. She'd hoped they could make some kind of deal quickly, and get back to Atlantis with a way to find Rodney. She'd also hoped that Ronon would back her up while she tried to make that happen. Instead he seemed determined to argue with her every step of the way.

She couldn't put off having it out about that any longer, not when they were going to have to work together when Todd returned. She wished she felt like she could. She would have much rather had this talk in her infirmary, surrounded by all the proofs of her own competence, not sitting here in somebody's tomb.

"I'm sorry," she said finally. "I think we do have to talk."

"Fine," Ronon said, after enough of a pause that she was pretty sure that wasn't a conventional phrase on Sateda for I'm about to say something you won't like. He spread his hands. "Talk."

"You can't just decide things like 'we're going back to the Stargate' for both of us," she said. "You can't tell me we're giving up on the mission and expect me to accept that without even talking about it first."

She could just barely see Ronon shrugging in the dim light, his face in shadow. "Sheppard's not here," Ronon said. "It's my call."

"We're supposed to be working together," Jennifer said. "And maybe you don't like the fact that I'm here, but I am here. It's my mission, too, and if you aren't willing to work with me, then you're the one who shouldn't be here."

"You think I want to be here? We're not getting anything useful, and we never were going to —"

"Then go!" Jennifer snapped. "If you want to try to get back to the Stargate, or whatever it is you think would be better than what we're doing right now, then go. I'll stay here and —"

"And wind up as dead as that guy?" Ronon jerked his head toward the wrapped corpse at the other end of the pit without looking at it. His whole body was tight with anger, his fingers twitching where they rested against the grip of his holstered pistol.

That didn't seem right. She could see that he was mad at her, but she didn't think he wanted to shoot her. She flicked her flashlight back on so that she could see him more clearly. He was breathing too fast, and suddenly she wondered if they had adequate ventilation after all. Hypoxia would bring on shallow, rapid breathing, loss of coordination, diminished judgment.

Her own breath was coming easily, though, and she felt fine. He didn't look fine. If it hadn't been Ronon, and if he hadn't seemed fine up until now, she would have said he was terrified.

She wouldn't have gotten away with 'seemed fine' in her clinical training, some critical part of herself pointed out. He hadn't complained. It was possible that he wouldn't, no matter how he felt about having to be at close quarters with the Wraith. And after everything they'd done to him, she probably ought to figure that he wasn't entirely fine about that.

"We're okay right now," she said, shifting to the tone she used with her patients. "It's probably pretty safe down here. There's only one way in or out, and we'll certainly notice somebody opening that door."

"If there's air circulating, there's another way out," Ronon said.

"So, let's take a look." She shone the flashlight carefully over the walls. It caught the glimmer of metal in two places, both toward the other end of the pit. "It looks like the fans are set into the wall. There must be ventilation shafts, but..."

"They're small," Ronon said. "So, only one way out."

"Which is a good thing, right? Because that means there's only one way in."

Ronon nodded, although he still looked like he was waiting for someone to leap out at him. It occurred to her that it might actually be normal to have a problem sitting around with some-body's dead body a few meters away. She hadn't been particu-larly spooked by cadavers since med school, but a lot of people did find tombs pretty creepy, in more than a 'haunted house at the amusement park' kind of way.

"So, sit down and let's talk about this. We're both in this together. I just want us to make decisions as a team, not have you tell me what to do."

Ronon looked reluctant, but he did come to sit down on one of the other boxes, his back to the wall so that he had a clear view of the trap door above. "It's my call," he said. "We're in the field, and you're a civilian."

"I'm a civilian, sure, but I think I may be better at handling the Wraith than you are."

"I can handle the Wraith."

"Kill them, sure," Jennifer said. "I'll be the first to say you're awfully good at that. But I think right now what we need to do is talk to Todd, and try to get him on our side about this—"

Ronon shook his head sharply. "He'll never be on our side. They're Wraith. We're food to them."

"Maybe most of them think that way, but I don't think Todd thinks of all of us as food," Jennifer said. "Teyla's not just food to him, because he still sort of thinks of her as a Wraith queen. And Sheppard… actually, I have no idea what goes on there, but maybe Todd thinks Sheppard is, I don't know, our version of him."

"Sheppard's nothing like a Wraith," Ronon said.

"We have to find the ways that we are like them," Jennifer said. "The ways they are like us. Because we need their help right now, and to get them to help us, we have to talk to them. Like we're all people."

Ronon let out a breath in the darkness. "They're not people."

"Then let me do the talking," Jennifer said. "I can do this. Just… let's work together, here. Let's talk about what to do, and we can decide together. Don't just tell me what you've decided we're going to do."

"Like you do?"

Jennifer frowned. "What?"

Ronon shook his head. "We've talked enough." He looked a little calmer, but he still didn't look very happy with her.

"I don't think so," Jennifer said. "What are you talking about?"

"That's what you do," Ronon said. "You're the doctor, so you tell people what's going to happen. When McKay had that brain parasite—"

Jennifer remembered those days all too well, how it had felt to watch Rodney slowly deteriorate before her eyes and not be able to stop it, to make anything better for him, no matter how hard she tried. Ronon had wanted to take him to the Shrine of Talus, a folk remedy to give him one more day with his mind intact. She hadn't believed there was anything more to it than wishful thinking until it was nearly too late. To give up her search for a cure to take him to a magic shrine—

"I was trying to save his life," Jennifer said.

"We told you what would work, and you wouldn't listen to us. To me."

Jennifer felt her cheeks heat, and was suddenly grateful that he couldn't see her face. She searched for the right words. There were right words, words she'd learned for dealing with difficult patients, difficult people. She'd been told often enough not to let them push her around because she was young and pretty and looked harmless. I'm the doctor, she told herself.

"You didn't think yourself that there was any chance of saving Rodney's life," she said.

"You're the doctor. It took you, what, fifteen minutes to figure out how the place worked once we got there?"

"I am the doctor," Jennifer said. "I made the call based on my experience and my judgment." She was tempted for a moment to add it's hard enough for me to trust either one.

"If I were a doctor, would it have mattered?"

"Of course it—"

"If it had been Melena telling you, or any of the doctors from Sateda, would you have believed it then? She didn't know exactly how it worked either. But she knew it did work. Everybody knew that."

"Sometimes the things everybody knows are wrong," Jennifer said. "Folk remedies can be dangerous. At best, they're usually harmless, and that's when they don't involve taking a critically ill patient to a planet full of Wraith. It's magical thinking, a way for people to feel better when they can't really do anything to make a situation better. Like sleeping with the lights on when you're scared." That was probably not a very useful way to put it, she realized. "Not that I expect you—"

"When you saw it, you didn't think it was magic," Ronon said. "You thought there had to be some reason for it, some scientific thing you didn't understand."

"That's right," Jennifer agreed, but cautiously. Ronon's tone suggested there was a catch somewhere in that question, like the questions in med school that sounded simple and ended with congratulations, you've just killed your patient.

"But you didn't believe it when I said I'd seen it."

That would be the catch, then. Jennifer hunted for words. "It's not that I don't trust you," she said finally.

"You don't trust me," Ronon said. "You're like McKay that way, at least the way McKay used to be. You won't do what people tell you because you think they don't know what they're talking about. You won't ask people what they want to do because you think if you do what anyone else wants you to, you'll get hurt."

"I am not like Rodney," Jennifer said.

"You think?"

There was a long silence after that. It was too quiet in the underground space. That was probably good, though. It was probably too soon for the other Wraith to have left, so footsteps above them wouldn't mean anything good. She wasn't sure whether they'd even be able to hear footsteps through the thick earth ceiling above them. Ronon would probably know.

"If that's what you think, then why..." Jennifer began. It took her a minute to figure out how she wanted to finish that sentence, but Ronon waited while she did. She got the feeling he would have waited much longer if he'd needed to. "Why are we still friends? If we, you know, are."

"I can live with that stuff," Ronon said. "In a friend."

"Right," Jennifer said. She smoothed back her hair, feeling it trying to work its way out of its ponytail. Teyla always managed to come through these kinds of situations looking neatly put together. Jennifer always suspected she looked like anything but a professional.

"The thing is, I'm not Carson," she said finally. "He has enough experience that if he says he has no idea what to do, people are just going to think it must be a tough problem. If I say that, they're going to think I'm not ready for this job. If I ask other people what to do — if I act like I'm not in control of a situation that's gotten scary — then I don't think anybody's going to take me seriously."

She stopped, struck by how well the words applied to more than just herself. She glanced over at Ronon, wishing she could see his face better in the dark. "You get that, right?" she said tentatively. "How maybe it might seem like a good idea to just tell people what to do, so they won't doubt that you know what you're doing? And maybe so you won't look scared."

"Maybe so," Ronon said after a while.

"But, you know, maybe I could do a better job of listening to people who might actually have useful ideas about how we could get out of the bad situation," she said. "You think?"

"Yeah, maybe."

"Is that a deal?" Jennifer asked. She held out her hand hesitantly, not sure if it was even the right gesture to make, but after a moment Ronon clasped her arm, squeezing hard before he let go.

"So," he said. "We're stuck down here. There's a bunch of Wraith up there. We don't know if it's a trap. What do you think we should do?"

Jennifer took a deep breath. "I think we should wait a while and see if Todd comes back," she said. "If a bunch of Wraith burst in here trying to eat us, then we can probably move on to plan B."

"Plan B being 'shoot the Wraith and fight our way back to the Stargate.'"

"That's the one," Jennifer said. "You guys seem to get a lot of use out of that plan, to read your reports."

"It's simple," Ronon said. "I like simple plans."

"So do I," Jennifer said. "They just never seem to work out that way for me."

CHAPTER SEVENTEEN
Quicksilver

AFTER FIVE sleeps, Quicksilver went with Dust to the gaming room. He felt stronger, though the sense of unreality continued to plague him, things being difficult that should have been easy.

"Perhaps the company of other men will make you feel more settled," Dust said, and though he was uncertain, Quicksilver accompanied him. "We need not stay long."

Thus they sat at one of the tables that dotted the room, a gameboard between them, while Dust explained the rules as though to a child. Looking around the room, at blades and clevermen relaxing over dice or over other games like theirs, the sheen of shiplight on white hair, the soft colors relaxing and pleasant, Quicksilver thought he ought to be at peace. The ship *Bright Venture* cruised through hyperspace, its passage smooth and effortless. They had taken no damage, and there were no wounded men missing from their number. All should be well.

And yet he bent over the board and could not remember a single move.

It was a simple game, Dust said. It should be simple, a logic puzzle of strategy and counterstrategy, but he could not remember. What moves did the purple pieces make? Was it that they were the ones who only went backwards from their initial placement? He could not remember.

"It will come to you in time," Dust said soothingly in a low voice. "Just play as best you may. It will strengthen your concentration."

"Of course." Quicksilver nodded, bending his head over the board again, caressing the purple piece with his feeding hand.

Its edges felt sharp as glass against the sensitive tissue.

Sitting on the floor a few paces away, a group of blades clustered about a low table, a dice game in progress. Their voices were loud, almost loud enough to be impolite in the quiet gaming room.

"He might have been sharp once, but I doubt his blade's half so sharp anymore!" one of them laughed, a suggestive waggle of the hips leaving little to doubt. "Not for a pretty young queen like that!" He was slight and pale faced, a slight greenish tone to his skin that spoke of the lineage of Night.

One of his companions snorted. "If Queen Steelflower isn't dead. She probably is, you know, and Guide is just keeping up the pretense. He gave no account of her absence when he was here. Stranger things have happened than a Consort carry on pretending to act in a Queen's name."

Quicksilver's ears pricked, and he looked at Dust across the board. "Isn't Guide the Consort in Atlantis?"

Dust scanned the board casually, thinking of his next move. "They are speaking of a different Guide. The one they mean is an old blade who is Consort to Queen Steelflower, one of the lesser queens who has only recently joined our alliance. Guide was here not long ago to pledge himself to Queen Death, but his Queen did not come." Dust shrugged. "Perhaps it is politics, so that if she wishes later she may disavow Guide and the alliance. But she will learn that such a course would be suicide."

"I'm just saying she could do with a better!" the original wit suggested. "Come, what can that dried up corpse give her?"

"Better service than you," one of the others said, laughing, his teeth bared. "Let us know when you get your full growth!"

The wit hissed, his fingers flexing, but his companion held his ground.

"Don't be silly, Ardent. You're not ready to be Consort yet. Not even to a minor queen such as Steelflower."

"They said she was beautiful," the third blade said. "Tiny

little feet and a spill of hair like midnight. And she took out one of Locust's hives without quarter when they trespassed on her feeding grounds."

"That story's probably exaggerated," the one called Ardent said, the slender blade who had spoken first. "Anyhow, it was probably Guide's battle, not hers."

"He's a dried up corpse and he commands his queen at once?" the second blade said, rolling a dice between his long fingers. "Which is it, Ardent?"

"I'm saying that she'd do better with another," Ardent said smugly, lifting his chin so that his hair fell in soft waves of silver. "And who better to seal a magnificent alliance than myself, our Queen's own brother?"

"Our queen's own fruit-fed brother," the second snorted. "When you are a man you may speak of such things."

"I am man enough now," Ardent said, getting to his feet, his long leather coat flicking against the cushions. "As you will see if you try me."

The second looked him up and down, and then closed his feeding hand deliberately. "I'll try you now if you like. Just take it like a good boy."

Ardent sprang, but there were hands to pull them apart, the third blade grabbing Ardent while Dust leaped to his feet.

"The Queen will not like this quarreling," he said quietly, "Nor knives pulled in the zenana."

"Be quiet, Cleverman," Ardent snapped. "You are above yourself." His eyes flicked over Quicksilver. "And you bring that among us, to sit among men!"

"Watch your tongue," Dust said, his tone still even. "Quicksilver has the Queen's favor."

Ardent twisted about, shaking off the blade's hands, and his eyes raked Quicksilver from toes to crown. "Queen's favor!" he spat, his handsome face contorting. "Ha!"

Quicksilver got to his feet, his heart pounding. "I do not

know what bad blood there is between us," he said carefully. "I have been ill and cannot remember. But I do not wish to name myself your enemy."

Ardent shook his head, his feeding hand contracting. "You do not wish to name yourself my enemy! That is rich! As though you would for a moment be worthy of being the enemy of a blade of the lineage of Night, misbegotten..."

"Ardent." The third blade put his hand to Ardent's shoulder. "That is enough. Your sister will not like it."

"My sister is foolish to listen to such as Dust," he said, and spun about on his heel. "I will not stay in the gaming room when you bring in such creatures!" He left in a flurry of leather and silk, the heels of his boots hard on the floor.

"Come," Dust said quietly, and took Quicksilver by the arm.

He did not protest. He felt their eyes on him, their guarded glances.

In the corridor outside their sleeping room he stopped, his hand to Dust's sleeve. "My brother," he said softly, "What have I done?"

Dust shook his head. "Quicksilver, it is nothing. Ardent is the younger brother of the Queen, and he is hot blooded. He speaks without thinking and he has little respect for clevermen and the battles that can be won with the mind rather than the knife."

"Oh," Quicksilver said. "I have heard of such. But it seemed that rather he held some personal grudge against me."

"There is nothing," Dust said, but his eyes did not meet Quicksilver's. "Put it from your mind."

And so they spoke of it no more.

CHAPTER EIGHTEEN
Avenger

"OK, LET'S do this thing," John said. The vacuum suit was ungainly as he sat in the helmsman's chair. He'd prefer to be in the captain's seat, but they didn't exactly have a helmsman.

Teyla had come to take the other forward terminal, which could be done sitting down, though most of the systems that terminal controlled were inoperable. They had no shields or weapons. For that matter, they had no long range communications. So there wasn't really a lot Teyla could do.

Dahlia Radim stalked around the back of the bridge, checking the various power control consoles. "We're as ready as we're going to be," she reported.

John wondered if it wouldn't be better to lock her in one of the crew quarters, given everything. But the fact remained that she was the only engineer he had.

Carson was in one of the seats to the side, the one usually reserved for the communications officer. He looked pale inside the helmet of his vacuum suit.

"Ok," John said. "Sealing the bridge." The heavy bulkhead doors slid shut, and the faint draft from the overhead ventilation ceased as ducts and automatic shut offs closed.

Dahlia looked up. "You will have to restore active life support to the bridge before long."

John nodded. "Yes. But there's plenty of air in here for a couple of hours. Let's get out of the atmosphere and see what holds before we open up any connections again. I'd rather not have to go on suits if we don't have to."

Teyla ran her hands over the console, clumsy in the suit's big gloves. "I will watch damage control."

"I will watch damage control," Dahlia said from the back.

"You do not know what to do."

John glanced at Teyla. "Dahlia will take it," he said. "She knows how to reroute the power if we need it." He hated to trust the Genii scientist that way when she had made her opposition to the plan so clear, but he didn't see that he had any choice. Yes, Teyla had trained on the *Daedalus'* equipment, but the Ancient interfaces were entirely different and the systems were put together according to different protocols. Damage control, especially with a dangerously crippled ship, required someone who understood Ancient systems more than it required someone he could trust.

And if he had Radek Zelenka here...

John put that thought out of his mind. If they got back to Atlantis in one piece he could get Radek for the longer run to the Genii homeworld. Nobody knew the Ancient systems better than Radek, with the exception of Rodney. And ok, Rodney was better with code, no doubt about it, but Radek was the go-to guy on the hardware.

"Starting main engines." John watched the power indicators climb, the *Avenger* shuddering as it began to lift, sand flying from superstructure half buried for centuries. The main thrusters hovered on the threshold of critical strain for a moment, then cleared as the *Avenger* shook clear of the sand, roaring into the sky. The ship trembled, inertial dampeners overcompensating, then steadied.

John gritted his teeth. They were going to have to watch the inertial dampeners. That wasn't something he could afford to lose at speed.

Propulsion hovered in the clear, well above the caution marks.

"Ok, let's try for some altitude," John said, as much to himself as to anyone else. "Button up, people." He heard the hiss of Teyla's suit sealing a moment before his.

The *Avenger* gained altitude, the sky outside the main forward window darkening purple, stars appearing one by one.

There was a pop and a shudder, and John leveled it off, hands sweating in the heavy gloves. "What's going on over there?"

"We had a decompression in deck two on the starboard side, just aft of main engineering," Dahlia reported. "Two compartments have vented to space, but the seals to adjoining compartments seem to be holding."

"Aft of engineering?" He couldn't spare a look at the ship's schematics, but he didn't think that was good.

"I don't see any damage to the propulsion systems," Dahlia said. "It's near the hyperdrive, but those systems are designed to work in vacuum if necessary. And right now the decompression is limited to just those two compartments."

"Ok. Taking her up." Come on, baby, John thought. You can do it. Not so far. We'll get you home to Atlantis.

Had Atlantis originally been her home port? Or had it been one of the other worlds settled by the Ancients in the Pegasus Galaxy, one of the worlds where they had seeded humanity? It hadn't been the most important thing, knowing how the Ancients had settled this Galaxy. It hadn't been the field of study that seemed the most rewarding, not these last years with the Wraith breathing down their necks. He supposed there was information in the database in Atlantis — lots of it. But since Elizabeth had been lost, no one had made it a priority. There was always so much else going on, so much to do with the here and now. Nobody had time to figure out how many ships had called Atlantis home. Nobody had time to figure out where else they might have been built, or who might have crewed them.

Who had *Avenger* belonged to originally? Who had sat in this chair last, made the last log entries? They would find some information in dry facts held in her data banks, but they were likely to find as much truth in Teyla's old stories, stories of colonies left to fend for themselves as inexorably the Wraith advanced. Maybe some stood a few years, solitary Camelots above the flood, but they all fell long ago. Did this ship come from those waning days, as the *Aurora* had? Or had it been lost early in the war, when these fringes of the galaxy were the battleground? Maybe someday he'd find out.

The stars were bright outside. The last vestiges of atmosphere streamed away.

Another shudder, another alarm.

"We've lost one of the storage tanks on the port side," Dahlia reported, moving around from one console to another almost behind Teyla. "Potable water and water reclamation."

"We can do without that for five hours," John said. "We've got supplies inboard. Let's give her a few minutes to get used to vacuum and see what else goes. Besides, it's going to take a little while to run the course given the corrections to the database to make up for stellar drift." He ran his hands over the console. These big fat gloves drove him crazy, but it would only be for a few hours. "Ok. Navigations to run the course for Atlantis."

"That's incorrect," Dahlia said evenly.

It took a moment for him to look around.

"That is not the course you will be setting," she said, a pistol to the back of Teyla's head as Teyla sat before her in the navigator's chair. "You will set a course for the Genii homeworld."

John did the math. Normally holding a gun to Teyla's head was a really bad idea. She was the wickedest hand to hand fighter he'd ever seen, and he'd give her even odds with Ronon. With a woman her own size who was more scientist than soldier he wouldn't even stress. But Teyla was sitting down, fouled by the confines of the chair built into the console. And her hip was loused up badly enough that she was having trouble limping around. Kicking anything was not going to happen. And she was wearing a vacuum suit, which definitely impeded movement. No, for once he couldn't count on Teyla to get herself out of this.

He could pretty much figure Carson out of the equation. He wasn't a fighter at the best of times, and with his right arm messed up there was just nothing there. Not to mention that he wasn't exactly at his most alert. It was Carson's pistol that Dahlia had.

So it was all him.

"You will set course for the Genii homeworld," Dahlia said calmly. The gun's barrel just touched the back of the head of Teyla's vacuum suit.

He had to get out of the chair. It was modular with the console, not a loose separate piece that could fly around the bridge if the inertial dampeners failed, a smart move on the Ancients' part, but awfully hard to start something from. John lifted his hands. "Just put the gun down."

Dahlia didn't even flinch. "You will stay where you are, Colonel Sheppard. And you will compute the course for our homeworld. You will not be able to betray my people this time."

"Look," John began, "We're not trying to double cross you. We're going to keep our deal. But we've got to go to Atlantis first."

"And you would have me believe that you will then just give us the warship?" Dahlia's eyebrows rose. "Why would you do that?"

"Because we have an agreement," John said doggedly.

"And that's worth what to you?" Not so much as a waver in her voice. He wasn't getting anywhere. Teyla was frozen, perfectly still, waiting for him to do something...

"If you shoot her, then what?"

John looked around in surprise. Carson was standing by his own chair, a rueful expression on his face. "Oh sure, you can blow Teyla away," he said. "There's none of us can stop the shot. But then what have you got?" He paused a moment, his eyes on hers. "If you think that once you've shot her, Colonel Sheppard will fly the warship for you, you've got another thing coming. You'll have to kill him too, shoot him in cold blood as you stand there. But you could do it. There's a full clip in the gun. You could probably take him down before he'd get to you."

Carson stopped, letting that picture sink in. "And then here we are, lass. Just the two of us with a pair of corpses and an Ancient warship falling apart about our ears that neither of us knows how to fly. We'd certainly not make the Genii homeworld. I doubt I could land it in one piece. We'd die here too, trying to get back down, and no one would have the warship." Carson shook his head sadly. "My old mum used to say it was better to live to fight another day. You've got nothing. Fold your cards and live to come back to the table. You know we daren't kill you, seeing as you're Ladon Radim's sister." He saw her hand move, and gave her a grave smile. "You could kill Teyla, sure. But it gets you nothing. And you're not Kolya, to do it in sheer cursedness."

John saw her waver, hardly dared to breathe.

"Put it away," Carson said. "And let's get out of here."

Slowly, with a look of abject defeat, Dahlia lowered the pistol.

Carson crossed the room slowly and took it from her hand. "There now," he said with his best bedside reassuring smile. "Let's get on with it then. Set course for Atlantis."

Teyla twisted around in her chair, her eyes furious, but Carson forestalled whatever she might say.

"Miss Radim and I are going back to the crew lounge. It's an internal compartment and the pressure seems stable. We'll pass the voyage there and see you in Atlantis, Colonel Sheppard." He gestured for her to precede him to the back and the main bridge doors, a gesture that would have seemed pure courtesy if not for the pistol in his left hand. The doors opened before him, and they passed through, sliding shut behind with the soft sound of seals connecting.

John blinked, adrenaline still surging through his veins with nowhere to go. "What the hell was that?"

"It is called talking," Teyla said ruefully. "And I thank the

Ancestors we have someone who can do it!"

John looked toward the doors. "You think Carson will hold her at gunpoint for the next five hours?"

"Knowing Carson, he probably will not need to." Teyla took a deep breath, as though she too were trying to still a racing heart. "She had not thought the plan through. She got Carson's gun while he was sleeping, but she had nothing to bargain with."

"Except destroying the ship," John pointed out.

"With her on it?" Teyla shook her head. "She is not Kolya, and she is neither mad nor suicidal. Is death preferable to being held prisoner for five hours and then returned to her brother?"

"But we're not actually trying to steal the ship!" John protested. "I keep telling her that! We're not planning to double cross the Genii! We made a deal to trade piloting the ship for them for their information about Rodney. We've never planned to not keep the deal!"

"She does not know that," Teyla said. "An Ancient warship for one man?" Her eyebrow lifted. "It does not seem rational."

"This is Rodney," John said flatly.

"I know," Teyla said. "But she was not there when you diverted the *Daedalus* to Sateda for Ronon, nor when you dared Michael's laboratory to come after me." She shook her head as though the joke were on her. "She does not know you. And I out-clevered myself, telling her of your cruelty. I rendered the truth unbelievable."

"Why the hell did you do that?" John asked. She didn't think he was cruel. Probably?

"I thought…" Teyla put her hands to her face, or would have, except that the faceplate of the vacuum suit helmet was in the way. "It does not matter what I thought. You and I have both made mistakes. Let us try to get back to Atlantis before we make any more!"

"Right." John looked down at the board, the course corrections nearly completed. "You're going to have to handle damage control.

And hope we don't come apart when we enter hyperspace."

"Because hoping is about all I can do," Teyla said with a flash of black humor. "I will hope very hard for you, John."

"Thanks." The board cleared, the corrections completed. "Ready as we'll be." *Hang in there, baby,* he thought to the ship, and slid the indicators forward.

The hyperspace window opened before them, and *Avenger* slipped through.

CHAPTER NINETEEN
Snowbound

AFTER four years in Atlantis, Lorne had learned better than to assume that any deviation from the city's normal routine was harmless. The problem was defining normal. They'd gotten a lot of strange sensor readings over the years, which had turned out to be — on various occasions — nothing, dangerous natural phenomena, various hostile invaders, Ancient devices someone turned on by accident, freak weather, and alien lifeforms trying to communicate with them.

This time, Lorne would have bet on 'nothing', followed by 'weather', but Colonel Sheppard didn't keep him around to gamble. He gestured to the security team to spread out, taking up positions along the length of the corridor. The life signs detector in his hand was still showing multiple small objects on the other side of the storage room in front of them. It looked like whatever they were, they were out on the balcony.

He opened the door, P90 at the ready, and gestured for Jacobs and Hernandez to follow him in. They were both new, and he hoped he and Sheppard had impressed on them firmly enough that pretty much anything could happen at any moment. He'd been trying to walk a fine line between making it clear what the new people were in for and completely freaking them out.

The room was dim enough that he could just make out the shapes of stacked pallets. Across the room, only a little gray light filtered in through the glass in the balcony doors. It looked like it was still snowing out there.

General O'Neill had provisioned them generously but a little weirdly, having clearly transferred over whatever supplies he could get his hands on given the short notice, and they'd opened up new storage rooms for everything from spare bed linens to more breakfast cereal than he hoped they'd be going through anytime soon. He brought the lights up, and heard rustling, and then silence.

He glanced back at Jacobs, who nodded his head sharply; he'd heard something too. He motioned Hernandez up on his other side and moved slowly across the room. There was another rustling noise, fainter now. He tracked it around the side of a pallet, and leveled his P90 to reveal nothing but the crushed corner of a box.

More rustling. This time he thought it sounded like it was coming from the other side of the wall. He glanced down at the life signs detector. There were enough moving forms on the other side of the wall to account for quite a lot of noise.

Where the box was broken, something was strewn across the floor. He nudged it with the toe of his boot and decided it was cereal.

"We might have rats," he said quietly. They hadn't had a pest problem in the last few years, but then they'd been bringing in supplies either by Stargate or aboard the Daedalus. With all the trips back and forth on tenders while they were in San Francisco Bay, he wouldn't be surprised if they'd picked up some unwanted guests.

Or it could be an infestation of alien bugs that would try to suck out their lives the moment they opened the door. The beauty of life in the Pegasus galaxy was that you never could tell. "Let's just stay ready for whatever's out there," he said, and opened the balcony doors, letting in a rush of cold air.

There was a wild rustling and an eruption of movement. Winged things were beating against his legs and blundering against his chest and face, and he swung his P90 to track them by instinct, just barely managing not to fire. To his right, machine gun fire sounded like thunder, way too close on the narrow, icy balcony.

"Hold your fire!" he yelled. Feathers swirled around them in the wind. Hernandez lowered his weapon, already starting to look sheepish.

"Way to blow away those pigeons," Jacobs said. "Could have been a real threat to the city there."

Lorne waved him quiet. "It could have been," he said patiently. He caught a feather as they started to swirl downwards from the balcony and considered it. Off in the distance, he thought he could see small dark forms arrowing their way through the snow. "It just looks like this time it wasn't."

"It was a flock of unknown alien organisms, sir," Hernandez said. "Apparently avian." Lorne felt that he got points for trying to dig himself out, and also for using the word *avian* correctly in a sentence, but also that there was a time to accept that you'd done something stupid and live with it.

"I think they were pigeons," Lorne said. "Regular Earth pigeons." He was pretty sure the biologists were going to consider this a problem, in the 'let's not contaminate other planets' ecosystems' kind of way, but he was also pretty sure it wasn't going to be a problem from his point of view. That made one down, and a very long list to go.

The wind was shrieking against the tops of the towers, the lights of the city shining through the snow. Lorne lowered his P90 and turned back toward the doors. "Come on, and I'll show you how we fill out a report," he said.

He felt the tower shudder at the same time that he heard the noise, a distant thud and then a low groaning sound that made him think about ships grinding over rocks. They weren't moving, and there weren't any rocks. He turned to lean out over the balcony, trying to see any signs that something was amiss, but it was impossible to see the ends of the piers clearly through the snow.

The balcony was steady under his feet now. He could almost believe that he'd imagined it. It was just that he knew where that line of thinking usually led, and it wasn't anywhere good.

"Never mind," he said. "We've got another problem. Come on."

"Where are we going?" Jacobs asked.

"Jumper bay," Lorne said. "We're going to do a little reconnaissance."

Hernandez caught up to him on the other side, still cradling his P90 as if he expected more hostile pigeons. "What are we looking for?"

"I'm not sure," Lorne said. "You'll get used to that." He caught the muzzle of Hernandez's weapon and lowered it firmly. "Try to be a little less twitchy."

"Yes, sir," Hernandez said. Lorne suspected it might take him some time.

Eva Robinson swirled the last of her coffee around in her cup, looking out her office's tall windows at the snow. It was certainly a very comfortable office, although she suspected Dr. Heightmeyer had originally chosen it for the view, which — when you could see anything but falling snow — was certainly breathtaking.

It was just that at the moment it was also empty. She'd spent the morning unpacking her books and arranging her desk the way she wanted it, but there was only so long that stayed interesting. She checked her appointment schedule on the computer again, just to make sure something hadn't miraculously added itself. It remained blank for the rest of the day.

She'd met a few members of the expedition already, a handful of bewildered Marines who wanted reassurance that they weren't crazy for believing that the city was flying through space and a few scientists who were having trouble settling back into their daily routine after so many unsettled months. She'd also spent a long hour with Dr. McKay, who mainly seemed to want to interrogate her about her suitability to deal with what he referred to as 'the complicated and delicate workings of his psyche.'

She'd wound up liking him more than she'd expected to by

the end of the session, and actually hadn't minded the prospect of seeing him on an ongoing basis. He mainly seemed to want help managing stress, and possibly to want to talk about his relationship with his girlfriend, both of which seemed like nice simple problems compared to some of the things that apparently happened in the Pegasus galaxy. Like being captured by the Wraith.

It was part and parcel of working with people in combat positions, she knew. One day they were telling you about their feelings about joint pet ownership as a step toward commitment, and the next day they were listed as missing, which was usually just a way of saying 'dead, but without any reasonable sense of closure for anyone involved.' It would have been easier if she'd had other regulars to see, to remind her that life went on.

She put the cup down with determination. At least she could go meet some of the people she'd be working with. It would be more productive than sitting in an empty office trying to figure out how much trouble she'd be in if she installed Plants vs. Zombies on her laptop.

She decided it wasn't too early for an early lunch, and the mess hall seemed likely to be full of other people. She filled her tray with food that, for being served in another galaxy, seemed distinctly familiar from every military cafeteria line she'd ever seen, and poured herself another cup of coffee.

Few of the people whose names she felt confident she knew were in the mess hall. She did recognize one of the scientists eating at a table by the window as Dr. Zelenka, who'd been helping Dr. McKay give the orientation lecture to the science staff. He'd spent a lot of time in the meeting trying to soften McKay's predictions that they'd probably all be dead inside of six months.

Only if you do not pay attention, Zelenka had said, his eyes on the younger and more nervous-looking of the new staff. *Which we are sure you will.* She wasn't convinced he actually was sure, but he was at least comforting.

She put her tray down on the opposite side of the table. "Mind if I join you?"

"Not at all," Zelenka said. "But I will not be here long for company. I have a very long list of places I should currently be." He gestured to his mashed potatoes as if apologizing for the necessity of eating them.

"I'm sure you do," she said. "It's been an interesting first few weeks in the Pegasus galaxy."

"You should see it when it really gets interesting," Zelenka said. "We have only had minor catastrophes so far. If we cannot get Rodney back, or the city is overrun by strange alien lifeforms, or we are attacked by many Wraith, then we will have real problems."

"I can see that you'd have to develop a sense of perspective."

"That, or entirely lose your mind," Zelenka said. "But I have not yet, so you do not have to worry that I will add to your workload."

"I'm happy to talk to anybody who'd like to talk," Eva said. "It's actually pretty quiet right now from where I'm sitting. I'm hoping I can get to know people better and just get a sense of how everyone's doing."

"The same as usual," Zelenka said. "We are stressed and overworked and underpaid. Everyone has had traumatic experiences that should have us all hiding under our beds, but there is too much work to do. Half the people in the city are having regrettable romances, and the other half would not know how to begin one without an instruction manual."

Eva found herself asking "And which category would you be in?" even though she knew she probably shouldn't.

"I prefer to be regrettable," Zelenka said, meeting her smile with one of his own that suggested a wicked sense of humor she hadn't suspected him of having. "In the last few weeks there has not been time."

"I expect it's hard for the science staff with Dr. McKay missing."

Zelenka spread his hands. "Sheppard's team goes missing a lot. And of course we are always very worried, but we try not to —" He broke off, putting a hand to the radio headset he wore. "Zelenka." He listened for a moment, then stood abruptly. "I must go," he said. "There is a problem. Big surprise."

"It was nice to meet you," Eva said to his back as he hurried away, talking into his radio in low worried tones. She was getting the feeling a lot of her conversations in Atlantis were going to end like that.

Dick Woolsey sighed and looked at his open laptop. The databurst from Earth had just come in, and his inbox now showed 282 new messages. Most of them were not things he wanted to see — official messages from the IOA asking for clarification of one thing or another, screams of annoyance from various people he'd rather not talk to. He had seven days to answer them all before the next scheduled dial out, once weekly to conserve power, unless events warranted otherwise.

Three emails from General O'Neill. He opened the earliest first. It was a simple confirmation that the *George Hammond* had left Earth on time, Pegasus bound. Good news, but hardly unexpected. Another, three days later, confirming that the *Hammond* had checked in at a Milky Way gate and was still on schedule. By now it would be between galaxies, out of communications from both ends. *Daedalus*, on its return trip, would be reaching the edge of the Milky Way today, checking in with Stargate Command at the first gate. It always made Dick a little nervous to have all the warships out of reach.

He was going to have to write to Dr. McKay's sister sooner or later. He'd put it off, missed this week's databurst, telling himself that it hadn't been long enough yet. They'd find Dr. McKay soon, and there was no reason to alarm his family unnecessarily. But another week and he would have to. There would be no excuse. He would have to start one of those letters that began with 'regret to inform you…'

But not today. They'd find him before the next databurst. Surely.

Dick wished he truly believed that. He wished he had that kind of faith in the way the universe worked.

CHAPTER TWENTY
Tip of the Iceberg

"DR. ZELENKA, this is Lorne," Lorne said as he steered the jumper out of the bay and up through the hatch out into the snow. The wind was gusting unpredictably, and it took concentration to keep the jumper level. "We just had what felt to me like some kind of impact, like maybe something hit the city. I'm taking Jumper Two out to have a look."

"Yes, seismic instruments are recording an impact on the south-east pier," Dr. Zelenka said. "The currently south-east pier —"

"I got you," Lorne said, swinging the jumper around. Sheppard had landed the city oriented with a different facing than they'd had on New Lantea, and everyone who had gotten used to calling things 'the east pier' and 'the north side of the city' for the last couple of years was having to learn to adjust. He'd asked Sheppard if he couldn't have parked straighter than that, and Sheppard had snorted and told him that next time he could drive.

Lorne thought that he'd get the chance to do that approximately the same time that pigs flew. Or when everybody with a better chair interface rating was out of commission and they had to move the city, which wasn't a set of circumstances he could really hope for. Beside him, Hernandez was looking more cheerful. Flying spaceships seemed to be more what he'd been hoping for out of this posting.

"I think the most likely thing is ice," Zelenka said. "The sensors on that part of the city are out again, though."

"So it could be anything," Hernandez said.

"You're getting the picture," Lorne said.

"Did you get a chance to check out those life sign readings?" Zelenka asked.

"We have pigeons," Lorne said.

"Come again?" Zelenka said. "Communications may also be—"

"Pigeons," Lorne said again patiently. "Papa, India, Golf, Echo, Oscar, November, Sierra. As in small birds."

"Yes, I know what a pigeon is," Zelenka said. He sounded testy, which Lorne figured was reasonable at this point in the day.

"We were parked on Earth all that time," Lorne said. "And since we had the shield up when we launched, it's not like we gave them a chance to leave. So, no crisis on that front. Just a few casualties among the pigeons."

"What did you do to the pigeons?"

"It was kind of an accident," Lorne said. "Involving weapons fire."

"You shot at defenseless birds," Zelenka said, in a tone that made Lorne wince. "It is that they were threatening you in some way? You feared for your life if they pecked you with their little pigeon beaks?"

"I said it was an accident," Lorne began, and then broke off as he brought the jumper down just past the end of the pier, hovering over the waves. "Okay, I think I see what we hit," he said. "We've got a lot of ice in the water here, and there's one big piece that's jammed up against the pier. It looks like it's maybe five meters across and about as high at its highest point." The jagged chunk of ice rose unevenly out of the water, its top looking like it had been sculpted by the wind that was still buffeting the jumper as Lorne tried to hold it steady.

"How bad is it?"

"I can't see much damage right now—maybe it'll leave a dent, but it's not like there's a big gaping hole. The actual city wall's pretty thick. The only thing is, these things are bigger underneath, right?"

"Yes," Zelenka said. "The majority of the ice will be below the waterline."

"I'm just afraid that if the current, or the wind, or whatever ran it up against the pier in the first place drags it down under the city—"

"There are delicate mechanisms that could be damaged, yes," Radek said. "The hyperdrive propulsion systems, a variety of underwater sensors—which mostly are not working right now, which could mean there is already damage."

"Hang on," Lorne said. "I'll take the jumper down and have a look."

"These things go underwater?" Hernandez said.

"Read the freaking manual," Jacobs said.

Lorne ignored them both and brought the jumper down gently to touch down on the water, watching the display to make sure its systems were switching over smoothly to its submersible mode as it sank beneath the surface. What had looked like a chunk of ice from the surface was a wall of ice below it, its clouded surface reflecting back the jumper's lights.

"We may have a little problem," Lorne said. "It's definitely bigger underneath." He dove until he could clear the bottom of the ice, turning the jumper's lights on the underside of the city. "It looks like it's jammed up against the end of the pier pretty good; I think part of it may have broken away when it hit us. It's not doing anything but scraping up the bottom of the hull, but if the rest of it breaks away, there's a lot of stuff for it to hit down here."

"Even if we raise the shield, it will not protect against an object that is already within its extent," Radek said. "We could maybe modify that, but that is probably the most costly way of dealing with the problem in terms of power."

"We don't have to do that," Lorne said. "If I come back and fit a grapple onto the jumper, I can grab hold of this thing and tow it out of the way. But if this is going to keep happening, that's going to be a problem."

"Tell me about it," Radek said. "That is a question for the

oceanographers, but at this point I am not expecting to hear good news from them."

"The thing I don't get is, if the city used to be in Antarctica, shouldn't there be some way of keeping it from getting damaged by ice? They have a lot of ice in Antarctica."

"I know that, too," Radek said. "We think the city was resting on an ice sheet on land, not on the surface of the Antarctic ocean, so maybe this was not a problem for them. Or there may have been some defense mechanism that is not operating properly."

"Oil rigs use spikes to fend off big chunks of ice, but we'd have noticed something like that before now," Lorne said. "Unless they're supposed to extend when the city senses that there's ice."

"Which it may not, if the underwater sensors are inoperable because of the water temperature," Radek said. "Very ironic."

Lorne brought the jumper under the city slowly, sweeping its underside with the lights. They hadn't spent a lot of time down there, except for a cursory look after they'd landed on Earth to make sure that the hyperdrive engines weren't showing any external signs of damage.

"It's kind of a mess down here," he said. "There's no visible damage to the hyperdrive array, but I'm seeing some hull damage on the southwest side of the city that I don't think was caused by ice — it's pretty dented up in some places. Did we ever take a really good look down here after we moved the city the first time?"

"I wish I could be sure," Radek said. "I was busy with critical systems, and by the time we had stabilized those .. yes, well, now we must make sure. You may as well bring your team in and let me see what I can find out from here."

"I'll come get a grapple fitted on the jumper," Lorne said. "I think you're going to have to come down here and take a look, though."

"I expect so," Zelenka said, adding something in Czech that

Lorne would have bet good money didn't translate as *that sounds like what I'd love to do with the rest of my day.*

"Postříleli holuby! Zbrklí idioti!"

"Beg pardon?" Airman Salawi blinked at him, looking up from her board with a concerned expression.

"Nothing," Radek said. "Nothing of any great importance. Now…"

At the far end of the control room, one of the monitors let out a shriek. Banks looked up from her board, her voice urgent. "Dr. Zelenka, a hyperspace window has just opened!"

Radek lunged for the keys at the same moment he spoke. "Major Lorne, you had best get inside now. We are raising the shield!" He spared a quick glance to make certain the puddle jumper was not at that moment passing through the area the shield would occupy and punched it with one hand, the other flying over the scanner keys. "It cannot be the *Hammond*. They are not due for a day and a half yet."

Amelia Banks hit the all-systems alarm. "Mr. Woolsey to the control room!"

Woolsey came tearing out of the conference room like a scalded cat, followed by Dr. Robinson, Dr. Bauer, and the new physician's assistant. "What happened?"

"We have a hyperspace window opening. Unidentified ship," Radek said. He leaned over the instruments. "It is an unfamiliar type. I have the shield up."

"Not the cloak?" Woolsey covered the last few steps to the control area.

"If they know where we are, they may start shooting immediately," Radek said. "I thought it was prudent."

Woolsey didn't disagree. "Hail them then."

"We have a signal coming in," Salawi said.

"Put it through," Woolsey replied.

"Atlantis, this is Colonel Sheppard." Radek thought everyone in the room sagged visibly at the sound of the familiar voice. "We need to land this thing. Can you clear the north pier and have a medical team standing by? And also a rescue jumper if I put it in the drink."

"What's happening?" Woolsey asked as Dr. Bauer took off at a run for the transport chamber, cupping his headset as he did, presumably calling for the rest of the medical team to meet him there.

"We've got the Genii's Ancient warship," Sheppard said. "But it's in bad shape and the landing's going to be dicey. I'd rather overshoot and hit the water than hit the city if I have to abort."

Woolsey looked like he was holding himself in physically. "I thought you were assisting the Genii in taking the ship to their homeworld."

"We are. But we've got technical problems with the warship and a medical emergency."

Banks looked at Radek and he looked at her.

"Understood, Colonel. Bring it in," Woolsey said. "If Dr. Beckett says it's an emergency, we've got a crew standing by."

"Dr. Beckett is the patient," Sheppard replied.

Woolsey looked as though he wanted to ask for more details, but thought better of it. He gestured to Radek. "Drop the shield."

Radek nodded to Salawi, who paused with her fingers over the buttons. "How do we know it's not a trap and that he's not a hostage or something?"

Radek smiled. "He didn't report formally. When something is very, very wrong Colonel Sheppard will do it by the book. Which is what anyone holding him might expect. So it is clever, you see. He would not need to say something wrong. He would only need to say something right. So drop the shield, that is it." He switched channels on the headset. "Major Lorne, you may as well not get out of the jumper. Colonel Sheppard needs a jumper in the air for open water rescue if he aborts the landing and drops an Ancient warship in the ocean."

There was a long pause on the radio, clearly Lorne digesting the new twist and turn of events. "Copy that," he said laconically.

"You see, that is how it is," Radek said to Salawi. "One moment you are checking for icebergs and the next you are preparing for an open water rescue in freezing temperatures. There is never a dull moment around here."

"I'm seeing that," Salawi said.

Robinson and the new physician's assistant were hanging around the back of the control room, but there was no reason to get rid of rubberneckers. They were not in the way. Dr. Robinson looked as though she wanted to ask questions. Radek gave her an inviting little head wiggle, indicating she could come closer if she wanted. It was certainly no more dangerous. If Sheppard miscalculated and crashed an Ancient warship into the city, a few meters would not make any difference.

"We are go for open water rescue," Lorne said on the radio, the jumper once again clear of the tower. "And we have a visual on Colonel Sheppard."

Now the city's remote cameras had a picture as well, a glowing light streaking like a meteor toward them from the southern horizon.

"Are they on fire?" Robinson asked quietly behind him.

"It is just reentry," Radek replied. "It flares off the skin of the ship like that, the interaction of superheated gasses and the ablative material of the ship." He shook his head. It was awfully bright. He supposed those Ancient ships were made to withstand reentry without energy shielding in the event of damage, but it was not pretty. Not pretty at all.

But it was slowing. "Airspeed four hundred miles per hour and slowing," Banks said from her monitor.

Now it looked less like a meteor and more like an aircraft, though it was still glowing reddish gold in the gray sky, cutting through the last wisps of low hanging cloud.

"Too fast," Salawi said under her breath. "Damn."

It would be too fast for an airplane, where normal g forces acted upon the occupants, but the inertial dampeners allowed for braking thrusters at speeds that would be lethal otherwise. Too fast for a passenger plane, surely, but only about twice as fast now as a fighter jet would be coming in for a carrier landing, ready to hit the wire.

Only of course there was no wire. There was only the concrete platform of the pier. And the city.

Radek found himself tightening his fists. "Come on, Sheppard," he breathed. He watched for the twitch, for the warship beginning to pull up, an abort to skim the pier and ditch in the water on the other side. At that speed they would sink like a stone, and the water was very deep here. Nevertheless, airtight compartments would hold underwater as well as in space, and Major Lorne could be there with the jumper to mate with the wreck in minutes.

There was no twitch. Reverse thrusters fired, bright white against the gold, seven or eight g's absorbed by the inertial dampeners. The warship slowed, her pitted form streaked black from something burning off in atmosphere, belly down at a slight tilt, landing gear deploying, like a goose coming in for a landing on the smooth surface of a pond.

Reverse thrusters fired again, tilting like a harrier jet to the vertical, and the Ancient warship settled onto Atlantis' pier gracefully with fifty feet to spare.

The control room broke into applause, and Salawi grinned as though she were swallowing a lump in her throat.

"Major Lorne, the rescue will not be needed," Radek said into his headset.

"Copy that."

Below on the pier the medical team was rushing out, gurney at the ready.

"Atlantis, we're down," Sheppard said. He sounded as relieved as he ought to be.

"Good to hear that," Radek said, and hoped the warmth in his voice carried.

CHAPTER TWENTY-ONE
Time

IT SEEMED like the Wraith had been gone all day, but when Ronon glanced at his wristwatch, it had apparently only been a few hours. Assuming it was working properly. He'd looked at some with mechanisms that made sense to him when he was on Earth, but they were a lot more expensive than the plastic ones that ran on tiny computers or however they were supposed to work.

He'd rather have one with hands that ticked around its dial to show that it was working rather than just glowing numbers. He might be able to trade for one with the Genii; they made good clocks. The question was whether the Genii would still be speaking to them after Sheppard got done being diplomatic with them.

"What?" Jennifer said.

"Just wondering how the other team's doing."

"I'm sure they're doing fine," Jennifer said. "They've dealt with the Genii a bunch of times before now."

"The first couple of times didn't go so well," Ronon said. "The next couple of times didn't go so well either."

"They can handle it," Jennifer said. "Right?"

"Sure," Ronon said. It couldn't be easy for her just waiting around not knowing what was happening to Rodney. "We'll find McKay."

She nodded without looking at him, playing unhappily with her unlit flashlight. "It's my fault," she said abruptly.

"You weren't even there when they took him."

"It's my fault we even came back," Jennifer said. "We talked about staying. After everything the IOA put us through... well, it just seemed like there were more useful things we could do on Earth without getting jerked around as much. If I hadn't changed my mind—"

"There's not anything more useful you could be doing on Earth," Ronon said. "You knew this was going to be dangerous."

"I did," Jennifer said. "Believe me."

"So, you have to decide whether it's worth it."

He wouldn't have thought badly of her if he'd thought she was going to cry, but she was dry-eyed, her face turned up at the shadows around the roof's tangle of bone. "You think it's worth losing Rodney like this?"

"We haven't lost him yet," Ronon said. "We're not going to."

"But if we do," Jennifer said, her voice going flat again. He thought maybe that was her way of not letting it break.

"Then he'll have died fighting the Wraith," Ronon said. "Protecting Torren and Teyla's people on New Athos. You going to say that's not worth doing?"

Jennifer rested her forehead on her fingers. "No," she said. "I just wish…"

"I know," Ronon said when she didn't finish the sentence.

She took a shaky breath and let it out. "I know there's a lot we can do here that makes a difference."

"Yeah," Ronon said. "A lot of places don't have doctors."

"I know humanitarian relief isn't a priority for the IOA, but you'd think they'd at least be interested in building some good will out here," Jennifer said. She glanced at him like she wasn't sure he'd follow that.

"You mean that if we help people, they'll like us."

"It's a theory," Jennifer said. "And there's always the chance of finding some local pharmaceuticals that can help us back on Earth."

"I thought you didn't believe in that stuff," Ronon said.

Jennifer winced. "That's really not what I meant."

"Okay."

"I'm getting the feeling I lost some serious credit with you and Teyla there."

"Teyla's over it," Ronon said. "She thinks you're just weird like the rest of the people from Earth are weird."

"We didn't get off to a really great start, so I think that's an improvement," Jennifer said.

That was probably true enough. "She wasn't even mostly upset about you not believing her about the shrine, because she'd never seen it herself. But she thinks you didn't treat her like family."

"Well, she's... I mean, I hate to say it, but she's not," Jennifer said. "Neither is Colonel Sheppard, although from all the time he spends in the infirmary when he's not the one I'm treating—"

"You don't know the Athosians," Ronon said. "They've been culled every generation lately, sometimes more than once. Most people don't have the family they're born with. They have whoever they have, whoever takes care of them."

"I'm not asking for anybody's birth certificate," Jennifer said. "But I can't know who people want to be considered family members unless they tell me. I give people forms, and then they don't fill them out."

"I'm telling you," Ronon said.

"Have you filled out the forms I sent around?"

"You sent around forms?"

Jennifer looked like she wanted to throw her flashlight at him, until he let the hint of a smile show. She returned it tentatively, her face seeming to waver in the dim green glow of the Wraith lantern.

"It doesn't seem like the Athosians are so different from you people," Ronon said. "A lot of people in Atlantis don't have any family back home. Or might as well not."

"A lot of people in Atlantis don't have family, period," Jennifer said. "I'm lucky that my dad's still around."

"That's not McKay," Ronon said. "It's not going to be, even if he didn't have a sister."

"Okay," Jennifer said. "I get that. That's a good thing." Now she kind of did look like she was going to cry. He didn't think she'd like that, so he hunted for a distraction.

"So, you and McKay going to get married?"

"Well, we…" Jennifer said, looking flustered. "We hadn't really… I think it's a little too soon to…" She looked up at him. "Why do you ask?"

He shrugged. "No reason. I just—"

There was a noise from above them, muffled enough by the soil that Ronon didn't think Jennifer heard, but he froze, drawing his pistol in one smooth movement and covering the trap door above. He motioned for Jennifer to stay back, and she nodded, and then drew her own pistol, holding it inexpertly but steadily.

The trap door opened, pouring more dirt down in front of Ronon. He waited as someone crouched by the entrance. It wasn't one of the Wraith, but one of the locals, a pale-haired woman with a tracery of lines painted across one cheek like the ridges that would have been etched into a Wraith face.

"You may come out," the woman said. "The dead god who brought you here wishes to speak with you. He bids you follow me back to the place where he awaits you."

Ronon looked at Jennifer. She shrugged. "Why didn't he come himself?" Ronon called.

"I did not question him," she said. "The dead gods do not reward us for idle questions."

"No, they reward you for being—"

Jennifer made a frantic throat-cutting motion and shook her head. Ronon took a deep breath and let it out. If there was anything to find out here, she was right that they shouldn't screw that up just for the pleasure of telling these people what was wrong with them.

"Fine," Ronon said. "I'm coming up first." He glanced at Jennifer's pack. "Can you climb wearing that?"

Jennifer looked at the rope dubiously. "I don't know."

Ronon nodded and looped the straps of her pack around one arm, pulling himself quickly up the rope. He hoped it wasn't obvious how grateful he felt when he got his first breath of fresh air. He heaved himself up over the side of the opening and rolled up to a crouch, holding his hand down for Jennifer. "Come on," he said.

Jennifer was struggling with the rope, but she managed, reaching up gratefully for his hand. He supported her until she could scramble to her feet. As he stood up, he felt something hard press between his shoulder blades.

"Don't move, or I will shoot," the woman said.

Ronon's hand was already reaching for his pistol. He made himself hold still, his eyes on Jennifer's. Her eyes had gone very wide, but she was watching closely, as if taking in every detail. "What's she got?"

"I don't know," Jennifer said. "It doesn't look like a stunner."

"You don't want to do this," Ronon said.

"Greatest of all the gods is Death," the woman said. "Her enemies will be destroyed, and those who serve her will taste eternal life." The weapon dug in harder at his back. If it was some kind of stunner, he could slap it out of her hand as she shot him, and give Jennifer a clear shot when he went down. If it fired bullets, he'd probably end up dead.

Jennifer's eyes were steady on his. *Trust me*, they said. He spread his hands the tiniest bit. *If you have an idea, go for it.*

He hoped she did.

"You can't cover both of us with that thing," Jennifer said.

The woman looked at her around Ronon's shoulder. She slid her hand around to spread it flat on Ronon's chest. Jennifer could see him flinch, even though he knew this was a human holding him. "If you try to run, I will kill him."

"Then the dead gods will restore him," Jennifer said. "Won't they?"

"You wear the uniform of Atlantis," the woman said. "The people of Atlantis do not trust in the mercy of the gods."

"Not all of us," Jennifer said. She didn't dare come any closer, didn't dare go for her pistol. She wasn't sure what she'd do with it anyway; she'd done a fair amount of damage to some paper targets, but she didn't think she could shoot the woman without risking hitting Ronon. "We serve the one we call Todd." Ronon's jaw tightened, but he didn't argue.

"That is not his name."

"He hasn't yet honored us with his true name," Jennifer said. She tried to channel every henchman ever in all the bad horror movies she'd seen. "When Atlantis falls to the Wraith, he has promised us that we will be rewarded."

"I cannot wait so long," the woman said. Jennifer looked her over with a physician's eye. Her color was bad, and there were dark circles under her eyes. She moved like she was in pain.

"I'm a doctor," she couldn't help trying. "I might be able to help you."

The woman stiffened, and jammed the pistol hard enough against Ronon's back to make him wince. "Death will reward me when I deliver you to her," the woman said.

"I think she'd like you to deliver us both in one piece," Jennifer said. "It would save her the trouble of having to bring us back to life. And you know we might not…" Jennifer reconsidered. It was entirely possible that these people believed the Wraith could restore any dead body to life, if it had taken them a while to give up on someone they'd already buried. "She is more likely to give you the gift of life if she hasn't already had to revive us."

"You serve a god who keeps secrets from her," the woman said. "I can't trust you to come with me quietly. We have little time before her servants depart through the Stargate." She sounded more rattled, the formal cadence of her speech slipping a little.

"You could tie us up," Jennifer said. "There's a rope tied to the door there."

"Get it," the woman said. Jennifer knelt and struggled to unfasten it, her hands shaking. That probably wasn't a bad thing. It didn't make it look like she had a plan, here.

"I can't get it untied," she said. "There's more in my pack."

"Throw your weapon down first," the woman said. Jennifer drew her pistol carefully, knowing Ronon would probably manage to shoot the woman in the same movement. She tossed it away.

"I'm getting the rope now," she said in the same voice that she used to explain what she was doing to terrified patients. "See?" She drew it out, turning over her right hand to show it empty except for the rope. It took her too long to find what she was looking for by touch and jam it up her left sleeve, but she hoped she covered it by fumbling with the rope.

"All right," she said, holding out the rope. Ronon would have noticed the way her sleeve hung wrong now, and the awkward way she was keeping her hands high, but she didn't think this woman was really a fighter. "Tie us up."

The woman shook her head. "You tie him," she said.

She'd bet on that. There wasn't any way the woman could tie either of them up and still cover Ronon. "Okay," she said. "I'm going to tie his hands."

She came up in front of Ronon, looping the rope around Ronon's wrists, praying that she remembered the knots Teyla had showed her. If she was doing it right, it ought to look sound, and still slip free at a single tug. She saw Ronon's eyes flicker to the knot, and thought he saw that it wouldn't hold.

Jennifer edged closer, wrapping the rope around his waist. It was tempting to go for his pistol, but she was afraid she wouldn't even get it clear of the holster before the woman fired. Instead she tied one last ineffective knot and slid the weight from her left sleeve into her right hand. She hoped Ronon could see what she was doing and that the woman couldn't, but she didn't dare look up to be sure. "All right," she said. "You're going to have to tie mine."

"No tricks," the woman said, stepping around to cover her, and it was the hardest thing Jennifer could remember doing to wait until she saw the muzzle of the pistol clear of Ronon's side before she pulled the pin on the flash grenade. She squeezed her eyes shut and dropped it, knowing it was too close to both of them, but afraid to try to toss it further away.

The world went red, the crash of the grenade stabbing through her ears. She flung herself to the ground and clung to it as the world reeled. That was the noise, the effect on her inner ears. She made herself open her eyes, and was pleased that despite black spots swimming in front of her, she could actually see.

When she managed to sit up, she saw Ronon down on one knee next to the woman, who was sprawled unmoving on the ground. The rope was still looped loosely around one of his wrists, but he'd clearly made short work of the knots.

"Good thing you saw the grenade," Jennifer said.

"I didn't," Ronon said. His voice seemed to be coming from a long distance away. "Can't see anything."

"Your vision should improve pretty fast," Jennifer said, moving to his side as fast as she could without falling over.

"It had better," he said, but he didn't actually sound angry.

"Is she dead?" She ought to be able to answer that question, being the doctor, but she was feeling a little slow at the moment. She was going to have one serious headache.

"Not sure," Ronon said, spreading his hand on the woman's back as if trying to feel her breathing. "I think her pistol went off, but it was hard to hear anything."

Jennifer leaned over the woman, feeling for a pulse, but when she rolled the woman over, it was clear there wasn't much she could do. Her stomach roiled, which she tried to tell herself was because her balance was still off. "She's dead," she said. "I'm afraid we just attracted some attention."

"Depends on how close people were," Ronon said. He sat back on his heels, closing his eyes. If he was as disoriented as she was, he was trying hard not to show it. "Tell me if you see anyone coming."

"Or we could try to get back to the Stargate."

"If we're lucky, that's where the other Wraith just went," Ronon said. "If we're not, they're between us and the Stargate, and I can't see to shoot."

Jennifer retrieved her own pistol from where it lay on the grass, and collected the Wraith worshipper's weapon as well, shoving it into her pack.

Ronon was undoing the knot around his wrist. "Pack up the rope, too," he said. "And what's left of the stun grenade. No point in leaving evidence we were here."

"It's still hot," Jennifer said.

"We've got a minute. I hope. If we don't, it doesn't matter."

"I'm sorry," Jennifer said. "I couldn't think of any other way to—"

To her surprise, Ronon grinned. "You did good," he said, standing up and drawing his pistol. "Do you see a whole bunch of Wraith running toward us, or are we all right for the moment?" He actually sounded like he was happier than he'd been the entire rest of the mission.

"All right for the moment," Jennifer said, and then she did catch sight of movement in the trees ahead of her, from the same direction they'd come. "Somebody's there," she said.

"Great."

"Can you see anything yet?"

"Not a whole lot," Ronon said. He was still smiling. "So this could get interesting."

"We could run for it," she said, and then, "Wait—that's Todd."

"Are you sure?"

"I'm sure," she said, but she didn't lower her pistol.

"I told you to hide," Todd said sharply when he came in sight. He looked down at the woman's body and then at them as if at children who'd broken something fragile that he'd unwisely left in their reach. Not something precious and irreplaceable, but something that had made a loud noise and left a mess. *Can't I leave you alone for a minute?* she remembered her mother saying.

"That was when we weren't being attacked by crazy Wraith worshippers," Ronon said.

"Do the other Wraith know we're here?" Jennifer asked, since that seemed to be the more pressing question.

"They had already left to make their way back to the Stargate," Todd said. "If we are lucky, they did not hear you."

"She said Death would reward her if she handed us over," Jennifer said. "Whatever arrangements you made with these people, I don't think they worked so well."

"This one is the sister of Carlin," Todd said. "He swore she was trustworthy, for a human. He seems to have been mistaken."

"You think?" Ronon said. Jennifer couldn't really blame him.

"He will regret it. He had hoped I would reward him."

Jennifer really hoped they weren't around to watch Todd tell Carlin he wasn't going to 'reward him'. She expected that wouldn't be pretty, and she really didn't want to make Ronon watch the man beg for the Wraith's healing touch. She couldn't help glancing down at the dead woman, thinking, now that their lives weren't in danger, of how desperate she must have been. "Can you heal her?" she asked.

Todd gave her a sharp look. "Why would I do that? She has already betrayed me. If you wished her alive, you should not have killed her."

"If we hadn't killed her, would you have left her alive?" Ronon said.

"No," Todd said. "I will take you back to the Stargate as soon as the others have passed through. You have been a great deal of trouble to me."

"Why were Queen Death's people here?" Jennifer said. "What did she want to talk to you about?"

"She has taken a prize," Todd said after a moment's hesitation. "A prize belonging to the Lanteans, which she believes will be of great use to her and her loyal followers." He didn't sound like he much liked the idea of being one of them.

Jennifer tried to keep her voice steady. "What kind of prize?"

"I have my suspicions," Todd said. "As do you."

Ronon was staying quiet this time, letting her play her cards. Either that or he was just feeling worse than he let on, although she thought his vision was improving. His eyes were starting to track Todd as he moved. "If she has Rodney, and you can help us get him back—"

"Why would I do that?"

"What if she does learn everything Rodney knows?" Jennifer said. "Not just a handful of codes. She could have that by now if she wanted, but it sounds like she's planning to keep him until she gets everything from him." She suppressed her fierce surge of joy at that. As long as Rodney's captors still had a use for him, there was still hope. "The retrovirus that destroyed your entire hive. How to program nanites to take over people's brains. Everything he knows about jamming your shield technology and infiltrating your computer systems—"

"You have made your point," Todd said. "It is still an unacceptable risk. She already does not trust me, and if there are humans here who serve her personally, they may tell her things that will inspire more distrust."

"That's too bad," Ronon said, with an unfriendly smile.

"If I betray her position, I will be under suspicion at once."

"So tell her you know who actually betrayed her," Jennifer said.

"The Genii have spies all over the galaxy. Tell her they've infiltrated her supposedly loyal Wraith worshippers. Blame them for telling us where her hive ship was going to be."

"It will still be a risk," Todd said after a moment.

"All we need is information about where her ship is going," Jennifer said. "That's got to be worth it to you."

"It would be better for me if McKay were killed," Todd said.

"But we aren't going to do that. And if you try it yourself, then you're really taking a risk."

"And then we'd have to kill you," Ronon said.

"It will take me some time to gather the information you require," Todd said.

"The longer it takes, the more she's finding out from Rodney," Jennifer said.

Todd's hands clenched. "I am aware of that." It occurred to her for the first time that he might find this whole situation frustrating too.

"We'll keep checking in with you," Jennifer said. "As soon as you find out where they are, we'll be ready to move."

"I do not suggest you remain here in the mean time," Todd said.

"We'd rather not," Ronon said.

Todd looked him up and down in what looked like amusement. "You seem somewhat damaged," he said. "That could be remedied."

"Touch me and I'll kill you."

Jennifer wished it seemed like a good idea to stop and take something for her worsening headache. "Let's just all take a nice walk back to the Stargate now."

CHAPTER TWENTY-TWO
Duty

EVA ROBINSON was still in the control room when Colonel Sheppard came in escorting a blond woman in her thirties who looked none too happy to be escorted. Though he didn't touch her, her body language was stiff and her angry stride and clenched jaw spoke volumes. Sheppard, for his part, sported a heavy growth of beard, and sand had caked and dried in his graying hair. There were dark circles under his eyes, and he moved with wary tension, like a man who needs to be given a wide berth.

Dr. Zelenka did not hesitate to approach him. "How is Carson?" he asked.

"He tore up his arm pretty bad, but he and Teyla are both on their way to the infirmary," Sheppard said in a low voice.

Zelenka frowned. "What happened to Teyla?"

"She hurt her hip. Might have broken something."

Sheppard was interrupted by Mr. Woolsey coming out of his office, his right hand extended. "Miss Radim! It's a pleasure to welcome you back to Atlantis."

"It would be more of a pleasure if your intentions were not so perfidious," the woman replied. "This blatant disregard for our alliance will not be tolerated by the Genii. This warship…"

"Perhaps you will join me in my office," Woolsey said smoothly, with a glance at Colonel Sheppard. "And we can get to the bottom of this. I assure you that we value our alliance with the Genii greatly." His eyes fell on Airman Salawi at the near board. "Airman, will you arrange for a courtesy tray? Right this way, Miss Radim."

The woman preceded him into the office, followed by Sheppard. The door hissed shut behind them.

"What's a courtesy tray?" Airman Salawi appealed to Zelenka.

At the other end of the terminals Banks stood up. "It's a tea and coffee service with some light snacks. You call it down to Sergeant Pollard or whoever's in the kitchen and then run down and get it. It's a thing they do when they have important visitors. I'll show you."

"Thanks," Salawi said, going down to join her.

Zelenka looked worriedly toward the office door, where behind the glass Sheppard and the woman were taking seats in Woolsey's visitors chairs.

"Who is she?" Eva asked him.

"She is Chief Scientist Dahlia Radim," Zelenka said. "She's a Genii engineer, and also happens to be the sister of their head of state. And she does not look happy."

"Perhaps this mission didn't go well," Eva said.

Zelenka gave her a rather penetrating gaze over the top of his glasses. "You think not? Two people injured out of the team of three we sent, and Colonel Sheppard looking like something the cat dragged in? An unexpected Ancient warship almost crashed on our doorstep, and never a word about the information they went to get? And the Genii furious?"

"I thought the Genii were our allies," Eva said, dredging the memory out of the reams of briefings she'd read in the past few weeks.

"That is the present theory, yes." Zelenka pushed his glasses back up on his nose.

"Two people injured," Eva said slowly, seeing again the way Sheppard had stopped and dropped his voice to talk to Zelenka. "That's not good."

"No, it is not." Zelenka went around her to examine something on the board behind her, looked up at her swiftly. "They are friends, both of them. Close friends. Teyla and Carson both. We have been here more than five years together. We are like family. I watch Teyla's son for her. For Carson I was a pallbearer. I would be off down to the infirmary now to see how they are, but…" He spread his hands, gesturing to the control room and the Stargate beyond. "I am on duty. I have the watch, and you have seen how fast things can happen around here."

Eva grabbed at the thing she thought she must have misunderstood. "A pallbearer?"

A flash of a smile illuminated his face. "It is a long story. I do not have time for that one just now, but I will tell you another time."

"Ok," Eva said. "I'd like to hear it."

Everyone in the control room was trying not to stare at the windows of Woolsey's office, stealing occasional glances, passing the word to others or speaking quietly into headsets. By now half the city would know who was injured and who was here. Nothing ran as quickly as gossip in a small world where everyone mattered to one another. A unique community, she thought, like the seed of something entirely new.

At the SGC she had never forgotten that she was in a real place. Yes, it was a little strange going to work in Cheyenne Mountain, knowing that there was a gate to other worlds a few floors away, talking to people who went back and forth through space like it was nothing. But at the end of the day you got in your car and you drove home. You were in Colorado, in an ordinary American city, a not very famous or interesting city where people went to the dentist and had baby showers and visited their Aunt Erma in the assisted living place out on the interstate.

Atlantis was something entirely different.

Eva looked through the window, frowning. Sheppard moved stiffly in his chair, as though everything hurt. The scientist, Dahlia Radim, was talking, anger evident in every gesture. Woolsey was placating. His bland attentive expression was exactly what one is supposed to learn to convey neutral interest. He had been to school, that one. He knew all the tricks. But this had to count as the management school of hard knocks.

Airman Salawi came up the steps with a tray, coffee and hot water and tea bags and a plate of little cookies looking like they'd just been taken out of a box. "Should I just go in?" she asked Zelenka.

"Knock at the door and Mr. Woolsey will motion you in if it is appropriate," he said. "He can see you. Don't be nervous."

Salawi gave him a big smile. "Thanks, doc. You're swell." She walked over to the office door, balancing the tray carefully.

Zelenka shook his head. "Kids today. Do they say swell again? It sounds to me like something out of an Andy Hardy movie."

"I guess they do," Eva said. She glanced at Salawi, who had been beckoned inside and was trying to put the tray down on the desk without dropping it in Sheppard's lap. "You like the training? Like the kids?"

"Let us say I am gentler about it than Rodney would be."

"Than Rodney would be," she repeated.

Zelenka shrugged self-deprecatingly. "It is a mania with me. I will not stop speaking of the lost. I will not say their names in hushed voices, as though I were afraid to invoke them. I will not paint them saints or less than they were."

"You don't think they're going to find Dr. McKay?" she asked quietly. That was the question that everyone had, but no one would ask.

Zelenka's blue eyes were frank, though his voice was low. "I think it is very unlikely that Rodney is still alive. It is unlikely he survived his first interrogation. I have seen the Wraith drink from someone, from a prisoner bound to a chair. I have seen how it goes. And I am not certain that I can wish Rodney still alive for days and days of that."

Eva swallowed hard, but she had to ask. "And the prisoner. Did he die?"

Zelenka's mouth twisted wryly. "It was Colonel Sheppard. So, no."

Dick Woolsey opened the door to his office courteously. "Banks, will you show Miss Radim to guest quarters where she can rest? Also, please see if you can find her some clean clothing while her own is washed." He gave Dahlia Radim his best smile. "We will make arrangements immediately to contact Chief Radim and apprise him of the situation. You are welcome to speak with him of course, and there will be no constraints whatsoever on your conversation."

"Thank you," Dahlia Radim said. Her voice was still frosty, but she was no longer shaking with anger.

"Banks?"

"I'd be delighted, ma'am," Amelia Banks said. "Right this way."

"Colonel Sheppard, if you would stay." Woolsey kept his voice neutral until the door closed again. Sheppard looked ragged. By his own admission he'd only slept five hours in more than three days. That knowledge tempered him somewhat. But.

"Sure," Sheppard said, dropping back into the visitor chair as Dick went around his desk to resume his own seat. "I know what you're going to say, and…"

"Colonel Sheppard," Dick broke in. "What were you thinking? Do you have any idea what the ramifications of bringing that Ancient warship here are?"

"We can't keep it," Sheppard said, scrubbing his hand over his chin. "We've got to give it back to Ladon Radim."

"Of course we have to give it to Ladon Radim!" Dick was finally starting to lose his temper, and he reined himself in. "We can't possibly do anything else under the circumstances. Keeping it would be a declaration of war for all practical purposes!"

"Then I don't see what the problem is," Sheppard began. "I told her we'd give it to them."

"Do you understand the political consequences of having an Ancient warship and then just giving it away? Do you have any idea what the IOA or General O'Neill are going to say about how we found an Ancient warship that could be critical to us, an operational Ancient warship, and then we gave it to the Genii? We gave spacefaring capability to our shakiest and most powerful ally?"

Sheppard blinked. "You didn't say that when I called in and told you what the deal was."

"That is because what you told me was an entirely different circumstance. It's one thing for us to render technical assistance with a salvage operation in order to build good will with an ally. It's another thing to give them a goddamed warship!" Dick never lost his temper, but it was gone now. "As long as we never had it, as long as it was a Genii salvage project we were assisting with, we could go along. But the minute you brought a functional Ancient warship here and landed it in Atlantis, you changed the entire game!"

"I had to," Sheppard said. "The ship wasn't in good enough shape to make the Genii homeworld, and Carson and Teyla both needed medical attention. Dahlia couldn't fix the ship, and it was barely spaceworthy enough to get here."

"And do you know why you couldn't fix the ship?" Dick asked sharply. "Have you thought through that one? Why you were wandering around in the desert in the first place being attacked by wild animals?"

Sheppard nodded, his face closing. "Because I didn't return to Atlantis to get a technical crew to accompany us."

"Yes." Dick took a deep breath and let it out slowly. Not so hard. No point in belaboring the point. "I know that you don't want to replace Dr. McKay on your team, but the lack of technical skills nearly got all of you killed. It is essential that you maintain a team that is able to deal with the common challenges you face, and at present without Dr. McKay that is not the case." He folded his hands on the desk before him. "Therefore, as of now, Dr. Zelenka is on the gate team."

Sheppard lifted his eyes. "Radek Zelenka isn't…"

"Qualified to be on the gate team? Then name someone else. Dr. Kusanagi? Dr. Sauneron?" Dick was adamant. "You have to have someone with the requisite technical skills on the gate team. That's not negotiable."

He expected Sheppard to argue, but instead he nodded slowly. "Ok. It's Zelenka then. Until Rodney gets back."

"Until Dr. McKay returns and is able to resume his duties," Dick agreed.

"Dobrý Bože! You are shitting me," Radek said. He stared at John, wishing that he were more certain it were a joke.

"No." John looked terrible, and as he hadn't been to his quarters yet to clean up, he smelled like four days in the field.

"I have a bad leg," Radek said. "And I have not fired a pistol in four years. I have never fired a P90 in my life! I cannot see across the gate room! I cannot see you standing there without my glasses! Čím jsem si tohle zasloužil, John! I am forty-three years old, not some strapping young Marine!"

"You'll do fine," he said. "You always do fine when you go offworld."

"Which I try not to do unless I absolutely have to!" Radek snapped. "And when I do I have to be carried about like a parcel! I am not Rodney McKay, action hero!"

"You're exaggerating," John said patiently. "You don't have to be carried around like a parcel."

"All of this running and jumping and shooting things…"

"That's not what we need you to do," John said. "We need you to fix the jumper. You can do that, right?"

"Well, of course I can do that. Who do you think fixes the jumpers when you bring them in torn to hell and back because you have done something bizarre and courageous? But you are talking about going to combat situations. I am useless in that. I am nothing but a dead weight." Radek kept talking faster and faster, as though the sheer number of his words could wear John down. "I do not do the hand to hand combat, the stick fighting! I am five foot four! Do you think I will be karate chopping people?"

"Teyla's five-foot four."

"Teyla is a very cute and adorable tank dressed up as a beautiful woman," Radek said. "She could break my neck with her little finger."

"Well, right now she's stuck in the infirmary having an x ray to see if her hip is broken because we couldn't fix the jumper," John snapped. "Look, you don't have a choice. I don't have a choice. This is the way it's going to be. So haul yourself up and get with the program." He turned around and walked off, leaving Radek gaping after him.

Radek stood for a long moment, until he could stop breathing quite so hard. The entire gate room was trying very hard not to stare at him.

"Well," he said casually, and wandered back toward his station on the upper tier. Dr. Robinson was still standing there, looking like she was trying as hard as anyone not to appear to be listening to things that were not her business. And yet of course she'd heard every word. "Well, I seem to be on the gate team."

There. He said it, this thing that scared him to death. "I suppose there is nothing for it." Was that what Rodney would say, casual and cool as a pickle? Was that how a hero would sound when asked to do something far beyond his physical capabilities? Sure, yes, I will do it, no problem.

"I guess so," Dr. Robinson said quietly.

"It is very inconvenient," Radek said with a shrug.

CHAPTER TWENTY-THREE
Home

JOHN HEADED for the infirmary, every step seeming to take forever. His feet felt like wood. He'd been a little hard on Zelenka. Yes, ok, he hadn't wanted Zelenka on the gate team for all of the rational reasons Zelenka had said. He knew perfectly well Radek wasn't a soldier. And he knew perfectly well that somebody was going to have to look after him when they ran into a firefight. No two ways about that.

But he was brave. When the chips were down he always came through. John had seen that more than two years ago on a space-walk that had nearly turned deadly. They'd been engaged in a repair that everyone's lives depended on when micrometeorite had gone through Radek's leg like a bullet, a serious enough wound in the field even if it hadn't left him bleeding in vacuum. Radek had kept going and finished the repair. John figured he had what it took when it really mattered.

Yeah, Radek would rather not go offworld. They all had things they'd rather not do. He'd rather not deal with the Genii. But he had to. It was just that everyone was going to have to stretch a little bit, get outside their comfort zone.

The infirmary was pretty quiet. John glanced around. There were lights on and voices from one of the operating theaters in the back, so he ducked around the screen.

Teyla lay in the far bed, her dirty hair spread on the pillow. Sound asleep.

"Colonel Sheppard." Marie Wu, the Australian nurse who had been with them from the beginning, came around the corner.

"Just wanted to check on my folks, Marie," John said. "How are Carson and Teyla?'

"Dr. Beckett's back in surgery right now," she replied. "His arm is fairly torn up. He's going to need the wound completely cleaned and then the muscle lined up and sutured with self-absorbing sutures, then the subdermal layers realigned and sutured the same way, then the wound closed with staples." Marie's eyes smiled. "Dr. Bauer knocked him out so he'd stop telling him how to do it. Dr. Beckett is the worst patient on the base!"

"I guess he is," John said. "How's Teyla?"

Marie glanced back toward her bed. "Her hip's not broken. It's a pretty serious bone bruise, but there's no fracture. I'm sure it's very painful. She'll need to take it easy for a few weeks, but there's not anything we can do for it except let it heal and give her ibuprofen to reduce pain. She doesn't actually need to stay overnight, but we gave her a shot of Demerol to take the edge off while we did the MRI, and she was out like a light."

"Yeah, she hasn't had much rest in a few days." He looked around Marie at Teyla, who looked very small in the white bed, her face relaxed in sleep.

"She can go when she wakes up," Marie said, "But she's going to need to be careful and ease back into activities. I'm not sure if Dr. Bauer will clear her for offworld missions yet."

John nodded. "Well, the next thing is taking this Ancient warship to the Genii homeworld, so she could sit this one out. That's probably the best thing. She could get some rest and have some down time."

"Da!"

John spun around. Dr. Kusanagi was in the doorway holding on to Torren, who was appropriately wearing a t-shirt with a wrecking ball on it. Dr. Kusanagi certainly looked wrecked.

"Colonel Sheppard," she said, her hair coming out of its long black ponytail in disorderly clumps, "Can you please take Torren? I have had him for several hours, but Dr. Zelenka is shouting at me that I must get out there with a team and start repairing the Ancient warship, and Torren wants his mother and he has destroyed the lab and..."

John reached down and scooped up Torren, who grabbed his ear as an easy handle and threw his other arm around his neck. "Sure. How're you doing, buddy?"

"Momma!"

John held him so that he could see around the screen. "Your mom's asleep right now. She got very, very tired on the mission, so let's let her sleep."

"He's been changed, not that it did much good as he had an accident in the lab and…" Dr. Kusanagi was still running on harriedly.

Torren turned big brown eyes to him. "Momma hurt?" he asked. He'd probably already heard that she was.

"Your mom fell and hurt her leg. You know how we always tell you to be careful and not fall because you might get hurt?" John asked. "She's going to be ok, but her leg hurts where she fell on it and she needs to rest."

"She ok?"

"Yes, she'll be just fine," John said. "She was very brave, and she walked a long way after she got hurt, until she couldn't walk anymore."

Torren regarded him solemnly. "Then what?"

The simple answer was the truthful one. "I carried her."

Torren nodded. "Ok."

"He hasn't had his dinner, and Dr. Zelenka is yelling at me on the radio every three minutes…" Dr. Kusanagi was still going. Obviously Radek was passing on his bad day too.

"It's ok," John said. "I'll take Torren. Thank you for watching him. I know Teyla appreciates it a bunch."

"You are very welcome." She essayed a smile, unclipping her hair clip and trying to smooth her hair back into some semblance of order. "I do not mind watching Torren some. It is just that today…"

"I know. It got busy. Thank you." Torren grabbed his hair for balance. "Have fun with the warship. She's a sweet ship!"

"I will enjoy it a lot," Kusanagi said, retying her hair. "I like the Ancient systems better than many things. And they like me."

"Yeah, that gene thing comes in handy," John said. "The *Avenger's* pretty friendly, if you know what I mean. I think she's kind of glad to be salvaged. She's a mess, but you know, glad to be back."

"I do indeed know what you mean," Kusanagi said with a smile. "They have personality, the Ancient things. They know what they like."

He wouldn't normally talk this way, not like things were people, but Miko got it. He thought the city talked to her too. Not really talking, of course. But almost.

She leaned forward and planted a kiss on Torren's brow, looking considerably more cheerful. "Have a good dinner and good night, sweet boy. I'll see you soon."

"Bye bye," Torren said cooperatively, looking as though he'd been a little angel all along.

There was nothing in the world John wanted as much as his own bed, except maybe a shower, but Torren hadn't had his dinner. "Ok, buddy. Let's go to the mess and find some food." He looked at Marie. "When Teyla wakes up, would you tell her I've got Torren, and I'm going to get him some dinner and put him to bed?'

"Of course," Marie said. He wondered why she and Kusanagi were smirking at each other like that, except maybe that Torren was very cute.

Dinner.

One hot dog, plain, hot dog and bun clearly separated on the tray so that they didn't touch each other. One fruit cup. One carton of 2 per cent milk. One plate of spaghetti with…tava bean sauce? John regarded the sauce curiously. Yep. Those were tava beans. Kind of like a puttanesca sauce, only with tava beans instead of olives. Ok. Why not? Sometimes Sergeant Pollard got creative with local ingredients with disastrous results, but this actually worked pretty well.

John ate one handed, the other one trying to keep a slithering toddler from sliding off his lap and running through the mess hall with hot dog in hand. The world was all getting a little blurry, but food would help. Food, shower, sleep.

"You know," John said contemplatively, "You could try sitting in a chair and being still. Some people do that while they eat?"

"Why?"

At the moment John couldn't think of a single good reason. "I dunno."

"Ok then," Torren said in exactly Teyla's tone of voice.

Torren's elaborate Athosian cradle was long since outgrown and returned to New Athos for some other baby to sleep in. Now he slept in what John couldn't help but think of as a playpen, a framework full of blankets and stuffed toys on the floor in the front room of Teyla's quarters. Teyla said the framework was to keep Athosian children from straying, which pretty much made it a playpen.

Diaper. Footy pyjamas. Giant stuffed frog. John turned the lights down. "Now get some sleep, buddy. Ok?"

Torren sat watching him like he had every intention of wreaking havoc the moment John was out of sight.

"I'm going to take a shower. I'll be in here." Where presumably he'd hear bloodcurdling screams.

Teyla had a nice bathroom. He'd always thought so, even when he wasn't quite so loopy. The lights were starting to get coronas around them. At this rate they were going to start getting the wedge of lime too.

But the city made the water just the right temperature, and he stood under it for a long time, letting the sand and the mission wash off. Ok, it was a little weird to smell like Teyla's jasmine shampoo, but that's what there was. And she'd probably kill him for messing up her razor, but he had to shave if he was ever going on duty again. Which he was. Sooner than he'd like. Though mercifully Woolsey hadn't called him to the gateroom for Dahlia to dial out to the Genii homeworld and talk to her brother. Or maybe Dahlia actually wanted some sleep too.

When he got out of the shower Torren was asleep, curled up with his big stuffed frog. John tucked the blanket around him and put on a clean t shirt and sweat pants. Bed. Teyla wouldn't mind. He'd be up and out of here long before she was awake, with a shot of Demerol. And she wouldn't care if he slept in her quarters when he was keeping an eye on Torren.

He left the door open to the outer room and fell onto her bed, still present enough to tug the coverlet up before his eyes closed on sheets that smelled like her.

Once back in Atlantis, the debriefing felt to Jennifer like it took nearly as long as the mission itself had taken, but when Jennifer finished telling him what they'd said and done, she thought Woolsey was at least cautiously pleased with their results.

"I sincerely hope Todd actually can provide us with information about the location of Queen Death's ship," Woolsey said.

"He said he'd contact us when he knew something. But even if he doesn't actually come through with anything, at least now we know which hive ship we're looking for," Jennifer said. "If this Queen Death is the leader of a big alliance, there have to be people out there who know where she is."

"Unless he's lying about who's got McKay," Ronon put in. "I don't think he'd be very sorry if we could take Queen Death out of the picture for him."

"That may be, but if he were trying to encourage us to launch a full-scale attack against her hive ship, this isn't the best way," Woolsey said. "We can't just go in guns blazing and have any chance of pulling off a rescue. I'm going to ask Colonel Sheppard for his recommendations for getting a small strike team aboard a hive, once we're actually in a position to find it."

"Is Sheppard back?" Ronon asked.

"He is," Woolsey said. He didn't look particularly pleased. "I suppose you haven't had a chance to see the Ancient warship parked out on the pier."

"Is everyone all right?" Jennifer asked.

"Actually, no," Woolsey said. "Dr. Beckett sustained a fairly serious injury to his arm, and Teyla is also in the infirmary, although I'm told she mainly needs rest. We've also been given twenty-four hours to return the warship to Ladon Radim, and not incidentally return Radim's sister along with it, or face unspecified unpleasant consequences."

"Well, okay," Jennifer said. "It sounds like everybody's been busy."

Woolsey smiled tightly. "Very."

"I should go down and check on Carson and Teyla," she said.

"And then you ought to get some rest," Woolsey said, with a more genuine smile. "This is the best lead we have so far, and we're definitely going to pursue it."

Jennifer couldn't help wishing their return had been just a little more triumphant than that. On the other hand, they had returned in one piece, which had seemed like a close question for a while. Ronon followed her out of Woolsey's office, and there was a moment as they walked toward the transport chambers when neither of them seemed sure what to say.

"Are we good?" Ronon said finally once they'd stopped to wait for the transport chamber to be free.

"We're good," Jennifer said, with as much of a smile as she could manage at that point.

Ronon nodded. "I'm going to go get some sleep," he said, and stepped into the transport chamber. "You headed the same way?"

"I'm actually going down to the infirmary, so..." she said, trailing off a little awkwardly and letting him go on without her. It was actually tempting to head straight for her quarters; it was early morning now Atlantis time, and she'd have to be up again later in the day. But patients came first. She waited until the transport chamber was empty again and took it down to the infirmary.

Carson was more than happy to tell her the whole gory story of his injuries, giant carnivorous reptiles and all; he made a restless patient, and it probably didn't help that he knew full well he was going to be staying put for a while. She rummaged around while he talked until she found an energy bar and an abandoned fruit cup that she could consider dinner. Or maybe one was lunch and the other was dinner.

"You should be off to your own bed," Carson said finally. She didn't say that she would have been happily in it by now if he hadn't been so eager to tell her his war stories. She'd learned by now that listening to everyone's war stories was part of her job.

"Try and get some more sleep yourself," she said.

Carson leaned back discontentedly. "Well, I haven't got much else to do, have I? I should have let my mum teach me how to knit. She always says it helps her pass the time."

"I can sort of knit," Jennifer said. "Maybe we could get some craft supplies in here to improve patient morale."

"I can just see Colonel Sheppard doing a nice bit of crochet," Carson said. "Perhaps a sort of a gun cozy."

"I don't think they make knitting patterns for holsters," Jennifer said. "I could ask around."

CHAPTER TWENTY-FOUR
Carter Inbound

AT LEAST Ronon and Dr. Keller had returned with useful intelligence, Dick Woolsey thought as he watched them walk away. Unlike Sheppard, who had brought him a colossal headache and nothing to show for it. He walked back toward his office, thinking longingly of breakfast. He'd been up since before five, when Ronon had dialed in, and it was now after eight. Perhaps the universe could spare him long enough to get breakfast...

"Unauthorized offworld activation!" Banks said loudly, and the alarms sounded all over the place. Major Lorne and his Marine team dashed out of hiding like so many birds out of a cuckoo clock, automatic weapons covering the gate. Ronon Dex was down there too, of course.

"Shield up," the young Airman said very seriously.

"We're getting a video signal," Banks said, looking over at him. "It's Chief Radim."

Of course it is, Dick thought to himself. Who else? They hadn't spoken in nearly twelve hours. "I'll take it," he said.

The image of Ladon Radim stabilized as he made his way to the screen. "Mr. Woolsey."

"Good morning, Chief Radim."

"I hope that you can give me the timeframe in which I may expect my sister and our warship to return to us," Radim said. His voice was pleasant, but the way he asked the question left no doubt that it was an ultimatum.

"My scientists tell me it will be a day or two before the warship is spaceworthy," Woolsey said, cringing inwardly as he said it. It sounded false to his own ears even though it wasn't. Dr. Zelenka swore that it would take them forty eight hours to make the ship safe to fly — absolute truth of the unpalatable kind.

"As soon as the repairs are completed adequately, our crew and Chief Scientist Radim will embark."

"I am sure your men can accomplish much in little time," Radim said with a friendly smile. "I will look forward to hearing that they have left in twenty four hours."

"We will do our best," Woolsey said, but the transmission was already cut at the other end. Smooth. Very smooth. The Genii thought they were lying, all the more galling since they weren't.

Woolsey opened a radio channel. "Dr. Kusanagi? How are the repairs to the warship coming?"

"They are in progress, Mr. Woolsey," Dr. Kusanagi replied, the sounds of heavy equipment in the background. "We are currently repairing hull breaches just aft of the engineering section. They are fairly serious breaches, and it is requiring a good deal of welding and heavy labor. And even so I would not say that it is a good job."

"Just do your best," Woolsey said. "It doesn't have to be perfect. It just has to get to the Genii homeworld."

She sounded exasperated, as much as Dr. Kusanagi ever did. "There are no shortcuts in hull repair, Mr. Woolsey. Either it holds in vacuum or it does not."

"Understood," Woolsey said. And they certainly couldn't afford to lose the ship. They'd never explain that to the Genii.

Woolsey stopped himself. Of course, he would never risk his people on a ship that wasn't safe. Or that was at least so unsafe as to amount to negligence. Unsafe was something his people did every day. If he never let them do something unsafe… And where was the line between cavalier disregard of human lives and safety? That was the question that Sheppard had wrestled with on the mission. When is prudence the better part of valor, and when does it make it impossible to function?

These equations looked very different from Earth. These decisions seemed cut and dried to those who had never made them. No matter where his career carried him from here on out, he would not forget that. He would not forget the agony that went into the decision, and the guilt when it went wrong.

He should probably have Sheppard back in here at some decent time and talk over the personnel changes on the team. Sheppard had done the math wrong, and probably no one felt it more keenly than he did. But that was part of being in charge, of moving from a field command into greater responsibility. It was a big change, and some people couldn't make the transition. No disrespect to them. There were many fine field people who were not cut out for supervisory and policy positions, and many people who'd never done their time in the field who wanted to make policy. Dick Woolsey knew that. He'd been one of them. He'd learned the hard way, and he'd made some enemies in the process. He only hoped that now they were more generous to him than he had been to them.

Case in point, Colonel Samantha Carter. He'd botched her relief in Atlantis, but that wasn't the first time he'd gone to the wire with her. That had been over the SG-1 mission that had cost the life of Dr. Janet Fraiser. He hoped some of the bad feeling had been made up in goodwill over Atlantis' departure from Earth. He hoped. Because now he was going to have to work with her as commander of the *Hammond*, a position that answered neither to him nor to the IOA, but only to the Air Force. She couldn't tell him to go to hell in so many words, but there would always be excellent reasons not to cooperate if she didn't want to. He had enough of that already with Caldwell. And with Caldwell none of it was personal.

Also, Sheppard didn't get along with Caldwell, while Sheppard and Carter were close. Dick had no illusions that if he told Sheppard to do one thing and Carter told him another that he'd keep control of Sheppard for ten minutes, especially since Sheppard could hide behind the excuse that Colonel Carter ranked him.

He hoped that it wouldn't come to that. But when Weir and Caldwell had clashed, the only thing that had shored up the civilian authority in Atlantis was Sheppard's backing, tacit and implicit. He could rely on none of that.

And any moment now he would have Carter here, returning to the Pegasus Galaxy for the first time since her precipitous and no doubt embarrassing departure. A welcome would be in order, something to allow everyone to vent their feelings, their chance to say nah-nah-ni-boo-boo. He could be gracious and allow everyone to make their thinly veiled comments about how nice it was to have Carter back in Atlantis and how much they'd missed her with the distinct implication that everything had gone to hell in her absence and that they would rather have her in the driver's seat than Dick Woolsey. He should let Carter rub it in his face however much she wanted. It might diffuse the tension in the long run.

The presence of Dahlia Radim provided the perfect excuse for a welcoming dinner. Atlantis was short on formal social life, and pulling out the stops would serve both the diplomatic situation with the Genii and soothe Colonel Carter at once. Yes, that would be ideal. The sort of formal dinner for senior staff that less chaotic postings held more regularly. Ostensibly in Dahlia Radim's honor, such a dinner could be replete with tributes to Colonel Carter, which would doubtless also impress upon Radim the importance and power of Earth's new battlecruiser.

Yes, Dick thought, folding his hands. That was a plan. Now to see if the redoubtable Amelia Banks could put it together on twelve hours notice…

Jennifer's quarters were mercifully quiet for all of thirty seconds, and then Newton peered out from the bedroom and began mewing piteously. She'd left out extra food for him, and Marie had promised to come by and feed him today if she'd still been away, but he twined around her legs wailing as if he'd been abandoned for days.

She picked him up, stroking him with a flicker of guilt. He'd been more Rodney's pet than hers, acquired in a spirit of 'if I can't have Atlantis, at least that means I can have a cat,' and now Rodney wasn't here to feed the kitten too many snacks and let him sleep on a warm laptop case at night.

"I'm sorry," she murmured, scratching him under his chin. Newton switched from complaints to a rattling purr, writhing against her hand in kitten ecstasy. At least there was someone around whose problems were easily solved.

She slipped off her radio headset, and then winced as it almost immediately chirped at her. She settled it hurriedly back in her ear. "This is Dr. Keller," she said.

"Banks here, Dr. Keller. Mr. Woolsey has asked me to inform you that you're requested to attend a dinner he's giving for our Genii guest Dahlia Radim at 1800 hours tonight. He said formal dress," Amelia added.

"Oh," Jennifer said. She was aware that a better response was required. "Tell him… tell Mr. Woolsey that of course I'll be happy to attend. Formally dressed."

"I'll do that," Amelia said, cutting out.

Jennifer put the kitten down on the bed, in hopes that would keep him from immediately wrapping around her ankles again, and briefly contemplated the contents of her closet. The only thing that could remotely be considered formal was the black dress she'd worn to the conference she'd attended on Earth with Rodney. They'd both nearly frozen to death, and she'd ended the evening with Rodney's tuxedo jacket around her shoulders and his arm around her waist, holding on very tight—

"It's a perfectly good dress," she said grimly to Newton, "and I think all the water stains came out, and it's the dress I have, so I'm going to wear it. So that settles that."

She glanced over to see that Newton was curled into a tight

ball in the middle of the bed, his tiny eyes shut. Rodney was trying to be strict about not letting the kitten sleep in the bed, but
Jennifer wasn't planning to leave her laptop on as an alternate
source of warmth, and anyway she didn't mind the company.

"Rodney will say I've been spoiling you," she said, and tried not
to wonder whether he was ever really going to get the chance.

"Sheppard, you're in my parking place!"

John grinned at the viewscreen in the control room, now
showing Sam Carter with an impish smile on her face. "Sorry
about that, Colonel. I happened to pick up this Ancient warship
somewhere, and it takes up the whole driveway. We're doing a
little classic car restoration around here."

"Where do you want me to put the *Hammond* then?" she
asked, and John didn't miss the caressing note in her voice on
her ship's name. If the shiny sleek *Hammond* were his, he'd be
in love with it too.

"Think you've got room to bring it down over on the south
pier?" he asked.

"The pier that's to the south, or the pier that we used to call
the south pier?" she replied, glancing forward at the control
panels of the helmsman ahead of her. Or possibly out the main
forward window at Atlantis on approach over a cloudless cold
sea, weak afternoon sun casting the shadows of the towers long
over the water.

"The pier we used to call the south pier which is now the west
south west pier," John clarified. "I think there's room, though
it's tighter."

"We can put the buggy in a pretty small space," Sam said,
grinning back. "Improved reverse thrusters."

"Send me to school, Colonel," John said. Her smile was infec-
tious.

"Believe I will, Sheppard." She cut the transmission cheer-
fully.

John switched to the external cameras to watch the *Hammond* land. Built on the same lines as the *Daedalus*, she incorporated the most recent generation of features, including more heavily armored superstructure around the bridge and larger and wider landing bays for 302s. With her paint shiny and every antenna trim, she was indeed a beautiful ship. It was a pleasure just to watch. He could only imagine how much fun she'd be to fly.

John glanced back toward the office door. Woolsey had his head buried in his laptop. John shrugged and looked at the controller on the gate array at the near board. "Sergeant, will you tell Mr. Woolsey the *Hammond* is in? I'm going down to the pier to greet them." Woolsey wouldn't want to go down anymore than Elizabeth had. She'd always made a point of making Caldwell come to her. But he could damn well go down if he wanted to.

"Yes, sir," Sergeant Taggart replied. "I'll let him know."

The wind was gusting as John came out of the tower and onto the pier, low clouds scudding in from the west, where the sun was dipping into purple shadows. More snow on the way, he'd bet. He'd seen those kinds of clouds over the Rockies as a boy, and it always meant another blow. It was well below freezing, so every flake would stick.

Sam Carter and several of her crew came down the ramp from the hatch. She shivered as she stepped out of the shelter of the ship wearing only her flight suit. "Nice climate you've got here, Sheppard." Her hair was more bronze than golden now, caught back in a long tail instead of severely braided as it had been when she first came to Atlantis.

"Welcome to Atlantis, Colonel," he said formally. It was what he'd said the first time, more than two years ago, now. He'd been glad to see her then, worn out from those sleepless and hopeless days after they'd lost Elizabeth. Having Carter step through that Stargate was like getting a real grownup, and he hadn't realized how relieved he was until, those first briefings completed, he'd fallen into bed and slept the clock around.

"It's nice to be back." Sam looked up at the bright towers, a smile on her face as though she'd missed them. "Really nice."

"Please let your crew know to make themselves comfortable," John said. "We've got the locker rooms open with unlimited fresh water showers and there's still the lunch line in the mess for another hour. Airman Dees there has maps of the city and transporter codes for your people, so they don't get lost. But of course you know where everything is."

Sam turned to her first officer. "I'm sure we'll be glad of the showers after twelve days in space." She gave John another smile. "Colonel Sheppard, this is Major Tyrone Franklin, the *Hammond's* first officer."

"Major."

"Colonel." They shook hands. "I've heard a lot about you," Franklin said. He was a young black man in his thirties, rather short and squarely built, with a solid handshake and a direct gaze.

"Some of it good, I hope," John replied.

"All of it, sir," Franklin replied.

"Franklin comes to us from flying a Lancer in Iraq," Sam said. "And he did a tour at Kandahar a few years ago."

"Oh," Sheppard said. Suddenly he realized why the guy looked familiar. Lieutenant Franklin had just arrived at the base when Mitch and Dex went down. He remembered him now, looking grave and spooked in the background while Colonel Chapman explained that what they had to send home was less like remains and more like forensic evidence. He felt the cold suddenly, and it didn't come with the rising snow-laden wind.

Sam had seen the change in his face, and she'd been around the block enough times to read it. "Franklin, it's quite a city," she said.

"My first alien city," he said with a look like he still didn't quite believe it. Last year he'd been in Iraq. Now he was flying a spaceship to an alien city in a different galaxy.

"The city's pretty safe," Sam said. "But bear in mind we're still in a forward base. Something can come up any minute. We need to keep a full watch on board at all times. The other two watches can enjoy some liberty. You'll arrange the rotation."

"Yes, ma'am," he said. "I'll go do that now."

"Sounds good."

Franklin turned and hurried back up the ramp, and Sam turned to him. "Franklin's a good guy, John."

"Yeah," John said, moistening his lips against the wind. "I didn't really know him in Kandahar. He came in right before I left. Just three or four weeks, something like that." He made himself focus on her face. "How'd the *Hammond* shake out?"

Sam's eyes lit. "Oh, she's a beauty! You have to come aboard and let me give you the tour! She makes the good old *Prometheus* look like a Wright glider!" She glanced back toward her ship fondly. "The only thing is that we don't have our 302s aboard yet. Homeworld Command didn't want to delay our launch, given the problems you guys had getting here, to wait on our 302s when we had a glitch with them."

"A glitch?" John raised an eyebrow.

"A glitch involving the Tok'ra and a very long story."

"That kind of glitch." John nodded. They had moved to the door of the tower, out of the wind. "I'm glad to see you, Sam."

"It's good to be back." She put her hands on her hips, nodding fondly at the doors and the scoured concrete of the pier beyond. "I'm really sorry about Rodney."

"We haven't given up," John said tightly.

"I know," Sam said, and her eyes were grave. "And I'm here to help."

John swallowed. "Thanks." Franklin and four of her crewmembers were coming down the ramp again, walking toward them. "And you're not going to believe what's up."

"What?"

John shook his head. "We're giving you a formal dinner."

Sam hesitated a moment, as though wheels were turning in her head, and then burst out laughing. "And here I left my Class A's in Colorado Springs!"

"It's officially for Dahlia Radim," John said.

"Then I'd better hit the showers, hadn't I?" Sam said.

CHAPTER TWENTY-FIVE
Shapes in the Snow

"ALL RIGHT, ma'am?" Major Franklin's brow was furrowed as he met Sam at the *Hammond's* main hatch, though his flight suit was spotless. "I'm sorry I don't have service dress with me."

"Neither do I," Sam said, gesturing down at her own flightsuit. Given that her closet on the *Hammond* was ten inches wide, her class As were at home, neatly shrouded in plastic in the closet, just like her bike was in Jack's garage. Somehow she hadn't thought she'd need them in the Pegasus Galaxy. "You look fine."

"I've never gone to a formal dinner in an alien city," Franklin said. "With aliens."

"The aliens won't seem very alien to you," Sam said encouragingly as they hurried across the pier to the door. The wind had picked up as night fell, and it was going to start snowing any minute. "The humans in the Pegasus Galaxy look just like us, give or take ten thousand years of separation. They're not really any different. You've got the same kind of politics, the same motivations. People are people anywhere. It's just their customs that are different."

He followed her along the corridor. Left here, she thought, to the transport chamber. If she remembered correctly.

"The Genii are a fairly conservative society. Very structured, very rigid in their collective labor. Their science and technology belong to the state, as does their agriculture, and the free market is limited to crafted items and consumables. Big families, fairly strict gender roles, low tolerance for homosexuality. Chief Scientist Dahlia Radim is the first female Chief Scientist the Genii have had. They say it's because she's the head of state's sister." Sam shrugged. "They're probably right. The Genii don't often let women rise to those kinds of positions of authority unless they've got powerful patronage. But I would not underestimate her, Franklin. Just because she's the only woman in the boys' club and she got there because she knows nuclear physics…"

"I follow that, ma'am," Franklin said fervently. He could see the direction that was going.

The transport chamber was exactly where she remembered it was. A good thing, as these corridors were freezing. Probably because her people had been flapping the doors all afternoon.

"Any other aliens I should know about?" he asked.

"I'd go with citizens of the Pegasus Galaxy if I were you," Sam said, stepping in. "And the only other likely to be at the dinner is Teyla Emmagan. She's been a contractor with us for more than five years, and her people, the Athosians, are the best friends we've got out here."

"And she's Colonel Sheppard's wife?" Franklin asked.

Sam blinked. "Where'd you hear that?"

"One of the IOA members at the launch," Franklin said.

"Nechayev." Sam rolled her eyes. "He was hitting on her when she was on Earth, so Sheppard told Nechayev she was married to him. You can disregard that."

"Yes, ma'am." Franklin grinned. "But you hear some pretty wild things about gate teams."

"None of which bear repeating," Sam said sternly, and Franklin's grin vanished.

"Yes, ma'am."

The transport chamber doors opened on a different part of the city entirely.

It was, Sam thought, fairly surreal. A long table and chairs had been set up in the top room of one of the towers, a round dome that Sam had always loved for its 360 view of sky and sea, nothing but glass all around, an absolutely stunning view with Atlantis lit up like a Christmas tree, every tower blazing white and blue and green.

Woolsey was in a dark suit, while Sheppard looked uncommonly scrubbed in his class A's. Sam didn't think she'd seen him wear them except for funerals, a blast from the past right there.

Teyla came forward to greet her like an old friend, forehead to forehead, as though she had not seen her on Earth only six weeks ago. "Colonel Carter, it is good to have you back."

"Teyla," Sam said, her forehead inclining to Teyla's, as she was considerably taller. "And it's wonderful to be back. May I introduce you to Major Tyrone Franklin, the *Hammond's* first officer?"

"It's a pleasure, ma'am," Franklin said, bobbing somewhere between a head butt and a handshake.

"Major Franklin." Teyla offered her hand, thereby resolving the dilemma. "Welcome to the Pegasus Galaxy."

"I'm happy to be here, ma'am."

"You may call me Teyla," Teyla said with a smile, "as I hold no military rank."

"I should speak to Jennifer," Sam said to Teyla quietly, having just seen Dr. Keller across the room, standing by herself looking out at the city, forlorn looking in a black cocktail dress.

"Of course," Teyla said, and her eyes were grave. "You know…"

"I do." Sam nodded. "It's rough. Rodney…"

"We will get him back," Teyla said firmly.

"Yes," Sam said, and refrained from adding, if he's still alive. There was never any good reason to add that.

She excused herself to Teyla, leaving Franklin in her care, and made her way over to stand beside Jennifer. "Dr. Keller?"

"Colonel Carter." Jennifer looked pale, but her face was set.

"I just wanted to say that I'm terribly sorry about Rodney."

"We'll get him back," Jennifer said.

"Of course. And if there is anything I can do personally as well as professionally…" Sam ran out of an end for that sentence. She was never any good at these kinds of conversations.

Thankfully, Jennifer didn't seem to be either. They stood there looking dumb at each other for a long moment.

"How's Atlantis?" Sam dredged up.

"Good. Good." Jennifer jumped on it nervously. "Ronon and I just got back from talking to Todd…"

"Miss Radim, I'd like to introduce you to Colonel Carter," Woolsey said behind her. "Colonel Carter is in command of our newest battlecruiser, the *George Hammond.*"

Back on safe ground. She never knew how to have these conversations with anyone who hadn't drunk the Kool Aid, how to make the formulaic responses to premature condolences that might not be premature at all, and Jennifer hadn't. Conversations with her usually seemed to land on weird ground, teetering back and forth between too distant and too personal. It always worked that way with women not in the service. Except for Teyla, but she didn't really count. She might not have drunk it, but she was pretty darn familiar with the Kool Aid by now. Sam supposed this was why most of her friends were men.

Major Franklin had fetched Teyla a drink very properly, and now he was rubbernecking while trying to look as though he weren't, a thing almost all the men from Earth did when they first came to Atlantis. It did look spectacular, Atlantis amid the falling snow, white towers shining like beacons through the blowing gusts. Outside it would be very unpleasant, the winds blowing nearly gale force over whitecapped sea, whipping around the towers with a cold that would cut like a razor blade. Inside, they ate pickled ciano berries and drank vermouth martinis like so many children left in the house of their parents while their parents are away.

"The City of the Ancestors is beautiful, is it not?" Teyla said softly.

"It's gorgeous," Franklin breathed, his eyes on the skyline bright against the dark sea.

"I admit that sometimes it still takes me by surprise," Teyla said.

"You aren't from here?"

Teyla shook her head. "My people — the Athosians — are a pastoral people. We have not built cities like this since the great war. We cannot defend them, you see, and a settled people are an easy target." She gestured with her glass to Dahlia Radim, who was staying pointedly across the room from her. "The Genii, on the other hand, hide their cities underground in the hopes that they will escape the attention of the Wraith thus. There are many civilizations in this galaxy, Major, and as many ways of living as human beings can invent. The only constant is that we are hunted. Here, human beings are prey."

Franklin nodded. "And so you want our help."

"Some of us do, and some of us do not. Since Sateda fell, the Genii have been the strongest human civilization in the galaxy, so you must not think they will be glad to see you. Why should they be? If it were not for you, they might be the next short lived empire."

"I don't understand."

"Do you not have empires on your homeworld, Major Franklin? It is human nature for civilizations to expand, and there are some that absorb others. On your world they fight, or so I have read, until one or another fails. Here, it is more often that the strongest is leveled by the Wraith. Whenever it seems that we will come together, either by force or by treaty, the Wraith destroy it. If they do not, then sooner or later they know that we will successfully resist them. But as long as they keep knocking down the strongest, that will not happen." She raised her glass and took a quick sip. "Sateda was the most recent one. They had radios and electric lights, trolley cars and energy beam weapons, steel mills and antibiotics. And so they were killed, even those the Wraith did not feed upon, so that there would be no one who knew how to make those things. If you are here long, you will meet my friend Ronon Dex, who was of the Satedan Immortals, stood in their last battle against the Wraith, and endured much in the years after."

"I would like very much to meet him, ma'am," Franklin said.

"He often works out with the Marines in the morning," Teyla said. "Perhaps if you are in the gym you will see him." She took a step toward the window, unexpectedly feeling her hip give way. She stumbled and nearly fell, catching herself against the glass.

Franklin grabbed for her elbow ineffectually. "I'm sorry. Ma'am, are you ill?"

"I am fine," Teyla said. "I injured my hip on the last mission, and it is tender. Dr. Bauer has said I should stay off it, but I think that I can stand up and drink a martini." She smiled, making light of the pain. It would stop in a moment, when she had not put her weight on it wrong.

"What did you do to your hip?"

"I was knocked down by a charging carnivorous lizard while shooting at the rest of its pack with a P90."

"Ok." He swallowed nervously. Franklin looked a little overwhelmed glancing around the room. So many new people, Teyla thought. And Atlantis was rather overwhelming.

"You will come to know us quickly," Teyla said reassuringly. "I know it is confusing to meet so many and know no one."

"I've met Colonel Sheppard before," Franklin said. "In Afghanistan."

Teyla did her best not to flinch. "Oh? Did you serve with him there?"

"Not for very long." Franklin's eyes searched her face. "I'd only been there three weeks when he was sent home. You know, the thing… The court martial board stopped short of a dishonorable discharge, because it wasn't a direct order he disobeyed. And they cleared him of Captain Holland's death. There wasn't enough for the other charges to stick. I mean, nobody actually had anything but hearsay, so…" He pulled himself up short and swallowed hard. "I mean, I'm glad it worked out okay for him, because he seemed like a nice guy, and sometimes stuff happens."

"Sometimes it does, Major," Teyla said gently. "As I am sure you know by now."

"I figured he'd get the short end of the stick somewhere," Franklin said quietly. "I never thought I'd run into him here. He was a great pilot."

"He is a great pilot," Teyla said. "As you will probably see firsthand sooner than you wish. I do not imagine it will be long before you are under fire. Colonel Carter is…what is the term? A fire-eater?"

Franklin laughed. "She sure is! We're looking forward to it."

"It was an honor to serve with her," Teyla said.

Franklin's face stilled. "You have been around us quite a while, haven't you?"

"More than long enough to know your words for that," Teyla said softly.

The dinner lasted about as long as all formal dinners held on base lasted in John's experience, which was to say about an hour longer than anybody wanted to be there. Woolsey and Sam spent the whole time being so polite to each other that it was probably clear to everyone in the room that they couldn't stand each other. Teyla looked like she'd rather be taking a nice hot bath, although she did keep determinedly launching new lines of conversation every time they ran one entirely into the ground.

She spent some considerable time pretending to be interested in the *Hammond's* long-range scanner system, while Jennifer and Woolsey pretended to be interested in the Genii's recent developments in nuclear power. John couldn't think of anything to talk about that it seemed fair to make people pretend to be interested in, so he put on his best social smile, the one that made Teyla look at him a little strangely, and waited the evening out.

Eventually the party broke up, with Teyla heading off to collect Torren from wherever he'd spent a nicer evening, and Jennifer offering to show Dahlia Radim to guest quarters in what was probably an attempt to persuade her that not everyone in Atlantis was an axe murderer. Franklin said goodnight with the expression of someone grateful to have survived his first social occasion under the eye of his new CO.

That left him and Sam lingering in the corridor once Woolsey exchanged one more round of probably insincere pleasantries with Sam and finally called it a night.

"Whew," Sam said when he was well and truly out of earshot. "I think I'm out of practice at this kind of thing."

"You think you're out of practice. Around here, we usually only dress up for funerals," John said. "It gives formal occasions that extra added touch of depressing."

Sam looked him over frankly. "Bad week, huh?"

"We've had better," John admitted after a moment. "You want to go have a real drink?"

"That sounds good," Sam said. "Can I tell you about our new railguns?"

He grinned. "Can I stop you?"

"Oh, admit it, Sheppard. If she were your ship—"

"Then I'd probably sound like I had a new crush, too."

He handed her a beer when they got back to his quarters, and pulled out one for himself. It was way too cold to go sit outside, even on the balcony. Sam settled into a chair and put her feet up on another.

"Woolsey's trying," John said, folding himself into a chair himself. "I think this was supposed to be an olive branch."

"Complete with olives," Sam said. "I had followed things that far, yes." She shrugged. "He's made it pretty clear that getting sent out here wasn't his idea, and for what it's worth I believe him. I was never going to make the IOA happy, because I wasn't going to let them call all the shots. So they replaced me with someone who would."

"I think the honeymoon's worn off there," John said.

"I think you're right," Sam said. "It wasn't until after you left that it dawned on the IOA members — at least, it did on the brighter ones — that Woolsey and General O'Neill had been playing them all along. Nechayev is probably Woolsey's only remaining fan, along with the president. Neither of them wanted us to get stuck with Atlantis on Earth."

"How mad are they?"

Sam shrugged. "I'm not the best judge of that, obviously, or I'd have seen what happened to me coming. I think it'll blow over if he can do some things out here that they actually like. I hear some of the cooler heads have been pointing out that if General O'Neill and the president hadn't made a grab for Atlantis, someone else would have at some point. It was an open invitation for somebody to start a war."

"With whoever jumped first having a big advantage," John said. "Fun times."

"Oh, yeah." Sam hesitated for a moment. "Listen, John, I'm sorry I didn't tell you what we were planning."

"I'm sure you had good reason," John said, although it was a little scary how close he'd come to walking away from Atlantis for good.

"Well, to start with, we weren't sure it was going to work. I didn't want to make promises I couldn't keep. Beyond that, we both know about gate teams. If I'd told you, you can't tell me you wouldn't have told Ronon and Teyla and McKay."

"You could have ordered me not to."

"Come on."

"All right, I might have been tempted to slip them the word."

"And then they would have each wanted to tell somebody else, and in twelve hours the whole city would have known," Sam said.

"I know what the rumor mill is like in a place like this."

"Tell me about it," John said. He drained the last of his beer and opened the fridge again. "You want another beer?"

"Sure, hit me again," Sam said. "Let me tell you about our hull modifications. You don't let your eyes visibly glaze over like some people I know."

"She's a really sweet ship," John said.

Sam looked immensely proud, whether of herself or of the ship John wasn't sure. He figured she deserved both. "I know."

The hull modifications carried them through that beer and halfway through the next.

"You ready to tell me about it?" Sam said finally. "Because if I drink any more of these, I'm going to fall over before I get back to my ship, and that's not really the reputation I want."

"Sam Carter, intergalactic drunk," John said.

"Yeah, no." She was watching him, her eyes kind.

John leaned back in his chair so that he could look at the ceiling instead of her. "I screwed up," he said, forcing the words out and taking a bitter pleasure in how much each one stung. "We should have come back to Atlantis and gotten Zelenka instead of going out there without a scientist. Only I didn't want—it would have been like—"

"Like admitting that Rodney's really gone," Sam said.

"He's not dead," John said.

"I know, and that's good. But it's still hard to replace somebody when you know that, in a lot of ways, you can never replace them."

"It almost blew the mission," John said. "And then Teyla and Carson got hurt, and it was starting to look like we wouldn't make it out—"

"But you did."

"I got lucky," John said. "It would have been my fault if they'd died."

"You screwed up," Sam said. "I'm not going to beat you up

about it. I think you're doing enough of that yourself."

"I can't afford to screw up," John said. It was possible that a martini, two different wines with dinner, and the better part of three beers were making him excessively honest. "It's my job to get it right."

"Everybody screws up," Sam said. "You can't win them all, and if you think we ever won them all, you haven't read our old reports closely enough. We came up with some pretty astonishingly bad ideas sometimes."

"Yeah, but you're…" John gestured inarticulately with the bottle. "You don't let this stuff get to you."

"The only people it never gets to are the people who don't give a damn, and we try not to keep them around," Sam said, with enough heat in her voice that he thought she meant it. "Rodney used to be one of those himself, although he did get better."

"He was pretty frantic when Teyla was missing," John said.

Sam gave John a look that felt like she was seeing through him way too much. "You mean compared to the way you were when Teyla was missing?"

"When Teyla was… I let it get to me," John said. "I was off my game." And that wasn't the way you were supposed to do it. You were supposed to be able to let it go, to say *it was an honor serving with you* and get up and walk away—

"You did what you needed to do," Sam said. She smiled as though the joke were on her. "It's not actually an Air Force regulation that you're not allowed to have any feelings."

"I was pretty sure about that one," John said.

"A lot of people seem to think that," Sam said. "We ought to send out some kind of memo." She smiled crookedly. "Did I ever tell you about the time General O'Neill smashed in General Hammond's car windows with a hockey stick?"

"General O'Neill did that."

"It was Colonel O'Neill then, but, yeah," Sam said. "That was when we thought Daniel was dead. Well, one of the times."

"What happened?" John said. He was having a little trouble visualizing that.

"General Hammond told him he had to pay to get his windows fixed," Sam said. She smiled at him as if amused by his expression. "I'll tell you now, if you break my windows, it's not going to be cheap to get them fixed."

"I think I'd need more than a hockey stick to break your windows," John said.

"Try a tactical nuke," Sam said. "Which is to say, don't. I don't want to mess up the paint job. You could try giving yourself a break, here," she added more gently. "It's not actually supposed to be easy."

John tried a smile. "I thought it said that in the regulations, too."

"Not even close," she said.

CHAPTER TWENTY-SIX
Origins

TEYLA WAS awake quite early in the morning. Not an unusual thing with Torren, but it was unusual to see him to the Stargate. She had promised Kanaan these next few days with Torren, and Kanaan had offered kindly to come and get him, sparing her the walk to the settlement from the Stargate on her injured hip. And so there was an awkward scene in the gateroom, before the sun had even risen, in which they were gravely courteous with the care of people who are afraid that any gesture may be misinterpreted, who are trying so very hard.

Once they had been easy together. Once their friendship had been unstrained. Perhaps it would be again, when they were not learning how to be people who shared a child but not a life.

After he and Torren had departed, Teyla made her way to the mess hall. In days past she could always count on Rodney to be there at this time of day, drinking his endless cups of coffee and catching up on his email before he went to the lab or wherever else they needed to go.

He was not there, of course.

Nor was John or Ronon or Radek. John had been up late the night before talking to Sam Carter, Ronon was probably beating up Marines, and Radek was doubtless out in the snow repairing hull breaches on the Ancient warship. It was a thankless task, and he would be utterly foul when he was finished. Climbing around on the ice covered hull with a blowtorch was not his idea of fun.

Carson was in the mess hall though, his right arm in a sling, looking distinctly sporty despite having not shaved since their mission began. Presumably he hadn't essayed it with his left hand. "Good morning, Teyla!"

She got her coffee and sat down with him. "You're looking well, Carson. The beard is different."

"A bit of the Sean Connery look, I thought," he said. "Do I look like a dashing adventurer?"

"Exactly like one," Teyla assured him, and they laughed. The coffee was hot, and there was real milk for it. Jinto had come with Kanaan, to bring the milk in trade.

"You're up early," Carson observed.

"I have seen Torren off to New Athos with his father for a few days," Teyla said.

"You don't sound pleased about that."

Teyla cupped her hands around her mug. "It is not that I do not want Torren to be with Kanaan," she said slowly. "It is only that I cannot relax when he is on New Athos. There have been so many raids, and New Athos is so vulnerable." She raised her eyes to Carson's. "Nor can I deny Kanaan his son on the grounds that it is too dangerous when Torren runs no greater risk than any other Athosian child, no greater risk than that which Kanaan and I faced growing up." She shook her head. "When Torren is in Atlantis, I feel that he is safe. Perhaps it is not true. The city has its own dangers, and more than once enemies have penetrated. But I feel he is safe and I can go about my work. When he is on New Athos, I am poised for trouble, and I do not know how to stop worrying so."

Carson nodded gravely. "Part of developing judgment is knowing what to worry about and what not to. The last time Torren was on New Athos, the Wraith raided New Athos and took Rodney. Of course you're worried! Last time he was there you lost a friend. It could as easily have been your son, and you're not able to deny that to yourself. You're worried because there's something reasonable to worry about."

"I suppose when you put it that way," Teyla said. The first rays of morning sun were coming in through one of the slanted windows high up on the walls, picking out shades of bronze and green in the ceiling. "It does not seem...neurotic."

Carson snorted. "Now I know you've been around us too long when you start using words like neurotic! You're about the least neurotic person I know."

"Do you think?" Her words came out unexpectedly solemn.

He looked at her keenly. "Something bothering you, love?"

"No. Yes. I suppose so." Teyla took another long drink of her coffee. "You are a geneticist, so perhaps you can tell me..." Carson waited, and she drew a breath, not looking at him. "The Genii believe that the people with Wraith DNA, the descendants of the humans who were part of that Wraith experiment, are what they call Bloodtainted. That they are mentally...wrong. We know, we Athosians, that some of the Lost who then returned went mad. They heard voices, they made no sense, and some of them even killed. Among the Genii, they believe it is because of the Wraith DNA. That humans with Wraith DNA are inevitably wrong. They are twisted in ways that cannot be fixed. They cannot help but kill. And what is most obscene, they take pleasure in it."

Teyla laced her fingers around her mug tightly. "To my people that is the greatest evil. One may kill in self-defense or the defense of another. One may kill in passion or anger—this is bad, but it is understandable. People kill in fights or injure one another, and that is bad, it is a crime, but it is not evil. Evil is being like the Wraith. Evil is killing or tormenting another for pleasure." She looked at him, at his worn, patient face. "I do not want to be thus. This Gift..."

"Teyla. Love." Carson unwound one of her hands and squeezed her fingers. "Why would you ever do such a thing? I've known you five long years now, and you're completely rational. I've never seen you do any such thing." He sighed as though he marshaled his thoughts. "The Genii don't yet have the technology to examine genetic code, and while I've no doubt that the original Bloodtainted that you describe were survivors of Wraith experiments, there is no way they could possibly have diagnosed any more recent cases as resulting from genetic abnormality. They simply don't have the technology to get that kind of information. So what they're going on is presenting symptoms. Every human society produces sociopaths and psychopaths. Regardless of their technology level, it's part of being human. There are always some few people who aren't quite right, regardless of their genetic heritage. Every society on Earth has dealt with killers. How we frame that, as possession by evil spirits or genetic abnormality or witchcraft or poor upbringings, is different from society to society, but it's a problem all humans have when they live in large enough groups. I'm sure it's a problem the Genii face too. But that has nothing to do with Wraith DNA. It has nothing to do with you or with your Gift."

Her eyes searched his face. "You are certain of this?"

"Absolutely," Carson said. "There is no cause whatsoever to think that your Wraith DNA makes you any less moral or rational than any other human being."

Teyla swallowed. "And yet I fear sometimes what I will do," she said quietly.

Carson squeezed her hand in his. "What are you afraid of?"

She could not look at him and still speak. "When we are in a fight, there is nothing for me but that. Even when it is only sparring. There is a satisfaction in hitting Ronon hard, in landing a solid blow and seeing him wince. I like it."

Carson smiled. "I think Ronon is perfectly capable of taking the hard knocks he asks for. If you whale on Ronon a bit, I don't see the harm in that. He can always stop playing."

"That is true," she said, and it was. "There is no reason he must spar with me if he does not want to. But." She took another deep breath. "What does it say about me that I like to do it? That I find it pleasant to hurt someone?"

"There's many a person I'd like to smack from time to time," Carson said. He smiled encouragingly. "It's a way of blowing off steam, I'd say. Mind you, I'm not the psychologist. That would be good Dr. Robinson. But as long as you're playing a game with another consenting adult, with someone who can certainly adequately defend themselves or who can stop whenever they want, I don't see how it's wrong. Giving Ronon or John a few bruises isn't the end of the world. Mind you, I'd object if you were putting Colonel Sheppard in the infirmary with a broken arm! But he's had stitches often enough from sparring with Ronon and none from you, so I'd say there's nothing to be concerned about."

Teyla felt a furious blush rising in her face for reasons that made no sense whatsoever. "They play too rough with one another," she said. "I do not like to need stitches."

"Nor do I," Carson said. He shrugged. "I suppose it's manly or something. But I truly think you have nothing to worry about. Your Wraith DNA is a useful quirk, and nothing but that."

Teyla met his eyes firmly. "Then you do not believe the Wraith are evil."

Carson swallowed hard, and she knew he was thinking of Michael, of the misbegotten crew of the hive ship he had first tried the retrovirus on with such disastrous results. They had seemed men. And yet, in the end, they had slaughtered them because they were too dangerous. Because they were Wraith.

"No," Carson said quietly. "I don't think any sentient creature is inherently evil. Maybe that doesn't make me a good Scots Presbyterian, not seeing the separation between the elect and the damned, but I do not believe that any person is inherently evil."

"And they are people?" Her eyebrows rose and her stomach churned. "The Wraith are people?"

"How can you doubt that?" Carson asked. "Ninety-four percent of our genetic code is the same. They're much more closely kin to us than Rodney's cat or a bird or one of those lizard things that attacked us. Their physiology is clearly based on human physiology, their brains on our brains. Compared to something like the Asgard, there's no doubt we have common origins."

"How is that possible?" Teyla clutched at her coffee cup, and it was bitter in her mouth.

Carson dropped his voice. "I told you years ago that my first theory was that the Wraith were an accident. That human colonists on a planet with the Iratus bug accidentally gave rise to a hybrid. It was a good theory, but it's wrong."

He waited a long moment for that to sink in, and Teyla gasped. "Then where did they come from? You were certain that the Iratus bug…"

"I am certain that the Iratus bug plays a role," Carson said. "But there's simply not enough time after the Ancients return to the Pegasus Galaxy for that to happen. This kind of evolution requires millions of years, not a few tens of thousands. I believe there had to be a human element involved."

"You mean that the Wraith were genetically engineered," Teyla said.

"My guess, my working theory at present, is that human colonists were placed on a world where the Iratus bug was native. But as you know, it's very deadly, and because it never releases its prey until the prey is dead, it's very unlikely for anyone to survive an attack. My thought is that there was an attempt to create an immunity to the Iratus bug, a blood marker that would prove unattractive to the creatures so that when they attached themselves to an inoculated human they would find the human unappealing and drop off, something that would prevent them from killing. We know that the bugs will not bite one another, and when Colonel Sheppard was contaminated with the Iratus DNA that time we saw that they would not bite him. Perhaps the Ancients intended to create a vaccination against them."

"That is entirely sensible," Teyla said. "Because it is not that the bite itself is so bad, but that the feeding process continues."

"Exactly. If they bit, found the human unappetizing, and dropped off, they would become a nuisance, not a deadly danger." Carson's blue eyes met hers ironically. "And you know those wacky Ancients. They were completely cavalier in their relations with humans, as we've seen from their social engineering experiments, entire peoples left to spend their lives in a game for watchers in Atlantis. Ascension devices, nanites designed to kill, not to mention the entire Replicator situation! Do we believe that they would not have mixed human DNA with that of the Iratus bug in the laboratory and inoculated a population with their experimental vaccine?"

Teyla let out a long breath. "No," she said. "We cannot believe that. What you suggest is entirely in keeping with what we know of the Ancients, and with the other things that they have done."

"And then the experiment went wrong," Carson said.

"As it so often seems to have."

He nodded. "And you know what happened then?"

"The same as with the Replicators," Teyla said grimly. "The same as we did with Michael and his crew. They tried to kill them." A chill ran down her back. Her imagination was not so clear as John's, but she could not help but look backward to those experiments now discarded, human beings twisted into Wraith and then hunted as dispassionately as the Ancients did everything in their clean, bright ships. "But they did not succeed," she said.

Carson's eyes were grave. "They didn't. And their experiment came back to bite them in the arse."

"Carson," she said, "You know you cannot say these things. You are standing on C4."

"I know. That's why I've not spoken of this, and will not until I've got some better proof."

"If you say we are kin to the Wraith..." Teyla shook her head. "I can not even begin. That challenges everything we believe about ourselves, everything we know about our place in the universe, about good and evil and our reason for existing! You are uttering what is, to many of the people in this galaxy, the greatest possible obscenity. What you are saying…"

"Makes Charles Darwin look uncontroversial," Carson nodded. "I get it. But there it is." He leaned forward. "We already know the Ancients engineered life forms in the Milky Way, and that they messed with the genetic code of our ancestors. We know that they messed with yours too, and that they brought some not inconsiderable number of humans to the Pegasus Galaxy from Earth around 10,000 years ago, in the last days of the war, and that those humans mixed with those already here. That's written in our blood, yours and mine. My ATA gene, derived from some Ancient on Earth, your mitochondrial DNA arising on the steppes of Central Asia. Do we really think it's unlikely that the Wraith are a third iteration?"

She let out a long breath. "It is not unlikely. As little as I wish to believe you, as little as I want to believe that the Ancestors would have done this…" Teyla blinked eyes suddenly full. "I saw how they treated the Replicators, their creation. I saw how they treated my people when they returned to Atlantis, shuffling us off Lantea without even speaking with us, as though we were no more than cattle who had strayed into the yard! They sent us from our homes, from our crops in the field, when we had waited for them and praised them. We would gladly have served them. We would gladly have died for their city. But we were so little to them that even our deaths would be worth nothing to them." Her voice choked. "And now we are a people bereft. We do not know what to believe. We are ripped from our anchors and are adrift on the sea."

Carson took a drink of his own long cold tea. "It was like that, when I was Michael's prisoner all those long months. You look things in the eye. You lose your faith. It trickles away down some dark hole. And what it leaves is what you really are, the things you really believe in."

She reached for his bad hand. "And what do you believe in, Carson?"

"I'm a doctor," he said. "I try to alleviate human suffering. I can't know the meaning of it, nor the rhyme or reason, but I do know that's what I must do." He closed his fingers around hers. "There's a poem by Leigh Hunt, about a man who asked an angel if his name was on the list of those who loved God. The angel told him no, it wasn't. Well then, said the man, put me down as one who loves his fellow men."

"And was that the right answer?"

"I expect it was," Carson said.

Teyla put her head to the side. "You are very much like John," she said. "If he can only save everyone, then he will be worthy."

"You can never save everyone," Carson said gravely. "There are always some who are beyond your help."

"I know that," she said, "but he does not believe it. It is always a failure in him, a fatal imperfection. If he saves ninety nine people out of a hundred, his thoughts are always on the one who was lost."

"The good shepherd," Carson said ironically. "A play on words, my dear."

"I suppose I have translated it differently," Teyla said. "In our language Sheppard doesn't translate as farmhand, but as guide." She stopped, ice against her spine. "That is Todd's name, in his own language. I learned it when I masqueraded as his queen, Steelflower."

"I always thought they had a bit in common," Carson said. "And speaking of the devil…"

John and Sam Carter were making their way across the mess hall toward them, trays in hand. "Good morning!" Sam said brightly.

"Good morning," Carson replied. "What's on your plate today, John?"

"I'm taking the Ancient warship to the Genii as soon as Radek and Kusanagi sign off on it," he said, sliding in beside Teyla with his eggs and bacon. "You can sit this one out, Teyla. Keller said to stay off that hip, and there's not really anything for you to do. Kusanagi is coming with us along with a full Marine team, and the *Hammond* is escorting us just in case, but basically I'm spending two days driving the bus."

"Some bus," Sam said with a sideways smile, sitting down beside Carson. "Pity we can't keep it."

"And start a war with the Genii," Teyla said.

"I didn't say keeping it was a good idea," Sam replied. "Just that it looks pretty sweet." She grinned at John. "Race you there?"

"You're on, Carter."

CHAPTER TWENTY-SEVEN
Below Decks

EVA ROBINSON glanced up at the burst of laughter from the nearby table, the coffee stirrer in her hand. Colonel Carter, the commander of the *George Hammond*, seemed to be good friends with a number of the senior staff in Atlantis. The relaxed humor at the table occupied by Carter, Colonel Sheppard, Teyla Emmagan and Carson Beckett spoke of long friendship. She hadn't known Carter well at the SGC, despite the fact she'd heard it was Carter who recommended her for this job, but of course she knew of her. Who didn't? At that point, Carter had been in her tenth year with SG-1, the flagship gate team, the pride of the SGC. She was extraordinarily hard to miss, and incredibly difficult to know.

Eva had learned a lot from having worked as a consultant at the SGC about the breadth of bizarre things that could happen that nobody had ever learned about in school. Gender swapping. Mysterious alien agencies in one's mind. Time dilation. Mind probes. Ancient devices that dropped databases full of knowledge in one's head. She'd learned that you had to stay on your toes, keep an open mind, and above all listen to the people. Some of the things that really did happen were unimaginable.

And she'd learned that everyone had a different face from their official persona. How well people coped with both the bizarre happenings and the not so bizarre griefs and stresses had a lot to do with how supported that private face was, with how well equipped they were to process things. And so her job description evolved. One of the most important things was helping people find that private face, helping them to develop the things in their lives that allowed them to cope, and to endure the worst the universe could throw at them. It was a lot more

proactive than the job description had been, a lot less to do with
mulling over the latest reason why Dr. Jackson was curled up in
a fetal position mumbling in a dead language and more to do
with encouraging people to actually have lives.

Friendships were a good thing. Emotionally isolated people
were more vulnerable, more likely to make deadly mistakes. It
was easy for people in positions of great responsibility to become
isolated. They had few peers, and friendships within a supervisory position or up and down the chain of command were always
fraught. Colonel Sheppard was hardly going to pal around with
a second lieutenant twenty years his junior, or Dr. Beckett with a
new medical assistant. Carter couldn't be chummy with anyone
who served on the *Hammond*. Not only were those friendships
rendered complex if not actually inappropriate by the supervisory relationships, but they were unlikely because of age and
life experience. Teyla stood outside the chains of command, but
surely being the only Athosian besides her son currently living in
the city was isolating enough. Seeing the four of them laughing
and talking over the breakfast table was a good thing.

The milk jug was empty. Eva tilted it all the way up, but only
a couple of drops fell out. And coffee without milk was like a
morning without…she would say sunshine, but the high windows of the mess hall showed nothing but an expanse of purplish gray sky heavy with snow.

Milk. The serving line was open, but the two young soldiers
were busy helping people. She might as well go refill the pitcher.
Her coffee cup in one hand and the thermos pitcher in the other,
Eva ducked through the kitchen door.

It was immediately obvious why the original Atlantis expedition had chosen to use this room as the kitchen, though it
wasn't like any kitchen she'd ever seen. It was high and airy, a
ceiling fully two stories high, with broad windows in a curved
wall looking out onto a panorama of other towers, a Fortune 500
CEO's office view in New York or London. Down one wall ran

what appeared to be a long bronze trough, but on closer inspection was one long, slightly tilted sink, a dozen faucets and buttons providing water of various temperatures. The opposite wall had several heavy doors in it, freezers or supply lockers or something else. And in the middle was set up a modern stainless steel field kitchen, stoves and prep surfaces and deep fryers and a steam table.

It was an interesting juxtaposition. Boxes stacked neatly for easy access identified themselves as Chicken and Gravy Meal, use before 10/22/2012, property of Strategic Air Command, Nellis AFB. Next to it was Hot Dog, Lunch, Sausages and Condiments, ship to NORAD Lot number 7475. An open case beside it proclaimed itself MREs (Kosher and Halal) Florentine Lasagna with a hand-lettered sign on it that said, "Please do not take more than two at a time unless you have permission. Our quantities are limited." A sign below it read, "For permission talk to Sgt. Pollard." Another sign below that one read, "And he really really means it."

Eva couldn't help but smile. She looked around, wondering where milk would be.

"Need something, doc?" A man her own age, his graying hair cut in a buzz so severe he looked almost bald, came around the corner of the steam table, drying his hands on his apron. Beneath it he wore the red shirt of Atlantis support services.

"Sergeant Pollard?" Eva asked. She waved the pitcher around. "I was just looking for some milk."

"That's me." He snagged the pitcher from her. "Over here."

"How did you know I was a doctor?" she asked.

He grinned at her, his face seamed with premature lines. "You're not military, so you're a doctor. Doctor something."

"Dr. Eva Robinson, the new psychologist."

"Oh." He filled the pitcher from a nearby tin jug. "Got your work cut out for you, don't you?

"People keep saying that," she said.

He shook his head. "I came out here with the second deployment. Third, if you count Colonel Everett's. He lasted four days, God help him! I came out on the *Daedalus* with the second bunch, right after the siege. Been in the United States Marine Corps nearly thirty years, and it was one of the damndest things I ever saw! And I've been some interesting places, let me tell you. It runs you pretty crazy around here. So if you're looking for crazy, we've got our own special brand of Pegasus crazy, right here." Sergeant Pollard handed her the milk back. "That's what I tell these new Air Force kids. At least we've got a proper support unit now. We didn't, back in the old days."

"It seemed like there were a lot of new people," Eva said. "And I had no idea there were kosher and halal MREs."

"Oh yeah. They're pretty good. They're always available as alternatives to the main meal, whatever that is, though most folks keeping kosher or halal usually go down the line and just try to avoid certain foods." He looked with some pride at his kitchen set up. "We're only serving 200 breakfasts, though there's 417 in Atlantis, well, plus the baby and Teyla and Ronon, and right now the crew of the *Hammond*. So it varies. But a lot of people don't eat breakfast, or they just want coffee or something. So we only make 200 portions." Pollard grinned. "Today it's pork sausage links, creamed beef, hashbrowns, coffee cake, grits, scrambled eggs with salsa, orange juice, and instant Irish cream cappuccino. Not that the eggs are really eggs, but the salsa helps disguise that some. Also sliced Sila fruit and teosinte cakes with sour cream."

"Excuse me?" Eva blinked.

"We're supposed to supplement the A rations with local fresh food. Which sometimes is easier said than done." Pollard reached for what looked like a knobby yellow potato. "This is a sila. They grow on a lot of planets around here. Tropical fruit, high in vitamin c, taste something like a tangerine. We got these guys from Pelagia last week." He gave her an encouraging nod as she smelled it. "You can keep it. The teosinte cakes…" Pollard put his bullet head to the side, thinking. "I guess you'd call it kind of an heirloom corn. Dr. Parrish says that when the Ancients brought stuff from Earth before the war they brought a lot of domesticated and semi-domesticated plants that they liked. Teosinte is maybe kind of like corn was ten thousand years ago. Little bitty ears as long as your finger, reddish brown kernels, like the ornamental corn people use for flower arrangements and stuff on Earth. Anyhow, people here grow it for food and as animal feed, just like they do at home. Most of it's ground up for grain. Grain's always one of our problems here. We get a certain amount of flour from Earth, but it doesn't even begin to touch what we use. So we trade for a lot of it here, stoneground and all. Makes kind of crunchy corncakes. You ought to try them."

"I'll be sure to," Eva said, fascinated.

"The biggest problem is always milk," he said. "We always need milk, and it's hard to get." He gestured to the pitcher in her hand. "That's Athosian goats milk, from those pygmy goats they keep. Jinto brought eight gallons the other day, so we're set for the rest of the week."

"I had no idea," Eva said. "What did he trade them for?"

Pollard leaned back on his counter. "Well, the Athosians are our oldest trading partner, so it's a long running agreement that Teyla and Halling keep track of, who owes who what at any given moment. They trade fresh food for a variety of things — plastics, metals, stuff they can turn around and trade through the gate to other folks. Plastic is worth a lot, since it doesn't seem like anybody can make it here anymore. Ronon's people used to, but they're gone now."

"You must know a lot of people from Pegasus," Eva observed.

"Oh yeah!" Pollard grinned again. "They say the gate team is the tip of the spear and all that, but I'm the one spends tons of time talking to people, trying to figure out how to cook this stuff, dealing with everybody who supplies stuff on a weekly or monthly basis. I handle the established trades and the regular merchants, check out the markets of allies who have them, make sure we've got what we need."

"That's…incredible," Eva said. So many networks, so many contacts. And such unique experiences for a tech sergeant, a cook who didn't on the surface have a very interesting job. "You'll have some stories to tell when you get home."

Pollard's face fell, and his voice dropped. "I hope not," he said. "I'm trying to figure on that."

"You don't want to go home?"

"Not if I can help it," he said quietly. "I've got a friend, you see… Her name's Osalia, one of Halling's cousins that got rescued from Michael. She's the one who makes the goat cheese. I've been thinking that if I had my druthers I'd retire to New Athos. She says she could use me about, with those two teenage boys of hers and twenty two goats. But I'm not thinking the Marine Corps would like that."

"Maybe not," Eva said. But wasn't that always the case? There were always people who didn't want to come home, people who made a home where they hung their hats, who made new lives. What was the policy about people staying in Pegasus? Had anyone tried it yet? Or tried taking home a bride from another galaxy? A whole kettle of fish, a whole new series of questions…

"Anyhow." Pollard straightened up with the air of a man who's said too much to a suspect psychologist. "Got lots to do. Stop in anytime, doc."

"Thanks," Eva said, and made a retreat with her milk in hand, wondering who the proper person on Earth to put these questions to was, or if questions would in themselves create problems. Often something wasn't officially prohibited until it was brought to the attention of authorities. She would have to tread very carefully indeed.

"So, what's the sensor situation looking like?" Lorne asked, coming up behind Zelenka to look at the code scrolling across his screen. It was meaningless to him, but at least it suggested that progress of some kind was being made.

"We are still having problems," Zelenka said. "Now that we have cleared some of the ice off the external sensor arrays — thank you for that, by the way — "

"No problem," Lorne said. He'd spent the day before towing the baby iceberg out of range of the city where the Marines could practice their demolitions skills by blowing it up, followed by painstakingly supervising ice removal by teams in climbing gear. "Next time we move the city, though, how about somewhere tropical?"

"If only to stop everyone complaining, yes," Radek said. "We are getting better short-range data, but the sensors directly below the city are still showing blind spots."

"Kind of inconvenient if we're going to keep getting chunks of ice jammed down there."

"And there is the part that is really a problem." Radek's fingers moved swiftly across the keyboard. "This is what we are picking up from the short-range sensors, and by that I mean the ones that tell us about the surrounding ocean, not about things happening in space. This is themal imaging, showing the temperature of objects in the surrounding water — "

Lorne whistled. "That is a lot of ice," he said.

Radek nodded. "It is. Dr. Bryce has set up a subroutine for the sensors that will alert us when objects of alarming size approach the city. For example, here — " He pointed to one of the larger spots of icy blue on the display. "This we suspect is on course to hit the city. It will have to be diverted."

"Well, we can do that," Lorne said. "It's going to be a pain having to spend our time going out and towing icebergs around, but as long as we have plenty of warning, we should be fine, right?"

"In the sense that we are unlikely to be struck by an iceberg the size of a tall building without warning, yes," Radek said.

"The problem is that there are so many smaller pieces of ice in the water. We think this is a result of the high seismic activity in the area. There are many small earthquakes," he added when Lorne looked quizzical. "Ice breaks free from the ice sheets on land, and so we get many small chunks of ice striking the city. And by small here I mean maybe the size of a car."

"Which would be okay, except that there's stuff under the city that's apparently getting banged up."

Radek nodded. "You were right, by the way. According to the Ancient database, the city was once equipped to reshape itself if it was in cold water to prevent ice from being swept under the city. It is a fairly low-tech solution, a network of spikes and grid-work that is supposed to extend below the piers."

"I guess even if the Ancients could have run the shield all the time, they didn't want to waste all the power it would use if it had ice hitting it all day long."

"We do not think they planned to run the shield all the time, even when they had easy access to ZPMs," Radek said. "It uses a tremendous amount of power. Whatever their process was for making ZPMs, it was not likely easy or cheap."

"Okay," Lorne said. "Can we turn this thing back on?"

"In a way, it is on," Radek said. "The subroutines that are intended to trigger the extension of defenses against ice are running. The trick is, they think that there is no need for the defenses."

"Because the underwater sensors aren't working right," Lorne said.

"Yes. If we were on land, trying to extend the defensive mechanisms would probably damage them. Not to mention that anything that happened to be under a five-meter spike when it extended would get skewered. The built-in safety protocols are trying to save us from ourselves by insisting that we cannot modify the city's shape in areas of the city where sensors are not operational."

"Don't we keep having that problem?"

"I think the actual builders of the city did not much trust those who ran it to make good judgment calls about its technology," Radek said. "This is not an attitude unique to the Ancients, believe me. There is a tendency to assume when building any mechanism or program that your users will be idiots."

"Which in our case might be a good thing."

"Most of the time I think it is," Radek said. "The safety protocols kept us from doing serious damage to the city or to ourselves many times when we did not know what we were doing. But this one is not helping." He ran a hand through his disheveled hair in frustration. "If we had Rodney, he could maybe interface with the part of the city responsible for modifying its structure and make this work. It will not work for me."

"Which leaves what?"

"We will have to repair the sensor inputs below the city," Radek said. "It is impossible to tell if they were damaged by ice or by the battle with the hive ship that attacked Earth or years ago when we first moved the city, but they have been damaged by something. I have a team building replacements that should work. The entertaining part will be installing them."

Lorne didn't have many illusions about who was going to wind up taking a team to do that. "I don't suppose we can fit a jumper with remote manipulators so that we don't actually have to get out in the water?"

"It is a good idea, but, no," Radek said. "The connections required are delicate, and I doubt you can keep the jumper stable enough in the water in these currents."

"The currents and the water temperature are what I'm thinking of when I'm thinking about doing this as a dive," Lorne said. "Not to mention all the ice."

Radek shrugged apologetically. "Yes, I know. I wish there was another good option, but I think this is it. Once the sensors are back online, the city's own defense mechanisms should keep ice from being swept under the city, and we will only need to worry about very large pieces of ice."

Lorne rubbed the back of his neck. "Okay. If we set up a video feed, can you walk a team through what needs to be done?"

"Yes. I hope this is the only time you will have to go diving."

"Knock on wood," Lorne said. "Just out of curiosity, how big do very large pieces of ice get?"

"A couple of hundred meters in length we would say was very large," Radek said. "Hopefully we will not run into anything bigger than that."

"Great," Lorne said. "How big are the ones we're hoping we won't run into?"

"Closer to the size of a city," Radek said reluctantly. "But that is very rare, so I would not worry about it too much yet."

"I try not to," Lorne said. There were usually plenty of current problems to worry about instead.

CHAPTER TWENTY-EIGHT
Proving Ground

THEY DIDN'T actually race to the Genii homeworld. That would be irresponsible, and John and Sam were both very responsible people. Maybe they were a little competitive, but not quite that competitive, at least John wasn't when he was flying a ship that might fall apart any minute, and that anyhow Sam could dust with one hand tied behind her back.

For once, nothing terrible happened. Despite being on tenterhooks for the whole thirteen hours in hyperspace, there was nothing more dire to report than a few power fluctuations that had Dr. Kusanagi crooning and muttering over the crystals as if she could talk them into behaving. Maybe she did, because everything held together, and they came out of hyperspace exactly where they were supposed to, twenty two minutes after the *Hammond*. It was a good thing it wasn't a race, because that would have been pretty embarrassing.

Carter had spent a good twenty minutes trying to explain to Ladon Radim that she was there full of good will and happy thoughts, and that the Ancient warship and Dahlia were just behind. He'd pretty much stopped believing her and the rhetoric was escalating when John dropped out of hyperspace and Dahlia called down to report that both she and the *Avenger* were in great shape.

After that things warmed up a bit, and there were a few hours of changeover as they landed on a camouflaged field and the Genii crew came aboard. Then there was a hastily prepared meal with Ladon Radim in a farmhouse that looked like it was straight out of Amish country, built over an underground bunker that generated nuclear power. John really didn't have enough words to express how glad he was that he wasn't the ranking officer in the party, so all the making nice and polite conversation that would be scrutinized for secret clues to Earth's intentions was on Sam.

The Genii clearly had a problem with that. The way that some of the senior officers looked straight through her or posed their questions to John instead was pretty obvious. If he'd been feeling a little more charitable, maybe he would have done something different, instead of giving everyone what Teyla called The Smile of Wrongness and deferring to Sam on every answer, like he couldn't tie his shoes without her permission. He wasn't sure what the Genii made of that little performance, but it seemed to amuse Sam to no end.

Dahlia Radim made polite conversation for a few minutes, clearly more at ease now that Teyla wasn't around. She kept giving him pitying looks, like a guy you expect to get killed in some awful way any day now, but that you can't say you didn't warn. Or maybe like the looks you give a guy who's blowing up his career by getting serious about the wrong person, but hasn't realized it yet. He'd seen that kind of thing back on Earth, and he didn't like it any better here.

It was hours before Sam managed to shut the festivities down on the grounds that they had to get back to Atlantis. There was nice flat bunk waiting in the *Hammond's* guest quarters, and he sacked out and took a long nap while they left the Genii behind, homeward bound. It was the best sleep he'd had in quite a while.

Radek looked at Ronon over the rim of his glasses as they entered the armory. "You know I think this entire thing is a bad idea."

"I know that," Ronon said. He refrained from pointing out that Radek had said so more than once in the last fifteen minutes. "But we need a scientist. If we get the jumper shot up, or we wind up on a planet where there's something wrong with the DHD, or there's some weird radiation that's going to make us all mutate if we stay too long—"

"It would more likely just kill you," Radek said. "I understand that you must have someone on the team with an understanding of Ancient and Wraith technology. I just wish Sheppard would choose someone else."

"But given that he hasn't..."

Radek sighed and squared his shoulders. "Given that he hasn't, I sense that my future will involve much more shooting at things than I would prefer. So here we are."

Ronon smiled a little. "Lorne said you did a pretty good job beating up his Marines that time everybody had amnesia."

"I had the element of surprise," Radek said. "And my goal was not to overpower an entire Marine team, but to buy time in which to run away."

"A lot of the time that's us, too," Ronon said. "If we get into it with the Wraith, the main thing is for you to be able to defend yourself as we retreat. Teyla will be covering you while me and Sheppard hold them off. You and Teyla are supposed to get back to the gate and dial out for us."

"Believe me, I will not hesitate in that," Radek said. Ronon handed him the pistol and watched while he loaded it. He did at least know how to do that competently, which put him ahead of where some of the scientists had started.

It had taken a while for Ronon to make it clear to Sheppard when he first came to the city that he knew how to train people with no combat experience at all, and that he wasn't going to break them by accident. He always felt wrong teaching people to shoot before how to fight with their hands—you were supposed to teach the foundation skills before you worked with any weapons—but he could see that sometimes it was a necessary evil.

"Okay," he said. He demonstrated the beginner's firing stance Sheppard's people taught, shoulders square and feet apart. He'd learned a sideways stance, body angled away from enemy fire, but this way was better for bracing against the pistol's recoil. "Keep a firm grip onto the pistol. Don't jerk the trigger. It's going to be loud."

"I am not afraid of the gun," Radek said. "I am just a bad shot." He sighted along it and fired. It was a hit on the target, but just barely. Not close enough to the center.

"You want to at least hit within the rings," Ronon said. "Hit between here and here," he said, sweeping his hand down his own body from the hollow of his throat to his groin. "It can take two or three chest shots with one of these pistols to drop a human attacker. More than that for a Wraith."

"Wonderful," Radek said. He shot twice more, sighting carefully each time. The first shot went way too low, and though Ronon could see him trying to correct with the second one, he over-corrected, missing the target entirely. "I told you I was a terrible shot."

"You need practice," Ronon said.

Radek made a noncommittal noise and emptied the rest of the clip, without much improvement.

"Did you teach Rodney to shoot?" Radek said as he was reloading.

"Sheppard did," Ronon said. "Sheppard's pretty patient as a teacher."

"Rodney is not," Radek said wryly. "If he were, perhaps the rest of you would have learned something of jumper repair these last few years."

"None of us are scientists," Ronon said. "And Sheppard's the only one who knows anything about your technology."

"It is not our technology. The Ancients built many things we are lucky if we can even use. And, yes, we have needed our own scientific knowledge to determine how things work and how they can be repaired. But it should not require an education in nuclear physics to make repairs we have made a hundred times already.

Not everything is a fascinating new unique problem."

"Maybe we can learn something," Ronon said. "Right now you're stalling."

"Yes," Radek said with resignation. "Here we go again."

Radek was trying, Ronon thought, but it wasn't getting him very far. With the target up very close, he was a fair shot for a beginner. At any distance, he'd be more of a danger to them than to the Wraith. He wasn't shooting any better at a normal distance by the end of the practice session than he had at the beginning, and Ronon had expected at least some small improvement.

The standard-issue pistols kicked but not too badly, not compared to something like Sheppard's .45, and Ronon had seen tiny women handle bigger weapons and still shoot accurately. He'd watched the precision with which Radek worked with fragile things, his hands moving surely; he didn't think he was one of those people who could never make hand and eye work together.

He considered that, and then took the pistol from Radek and drilled a hole neatly into the outer ring at what Sheppard's people called nine o'clock. "Where did I hit?"

Radek glanced at the target, but didn't answer. After a moment he smiled without humor, as if he'd been caught out at something.

"You can't actually see the where the bullet hole is at that distance, can you?" Ronon said. "I thought that was the point of wearing glasses."

"It is," Radek said. "Without them it is much worse. It has been a number of years since I had these prescribed. I should most likely see Dr. Keller for an eye examination to see if new glasses would improve my eyesight."

"But?" Ronon prompted, when the fact that he didn't go on to actually offer to do it made it clear that there was apparently some complication.

"If it is bad enough that they cannot correct to 20/20, to normal vision, then the rules will say that I am not qualified to be part of this expedition," he said. "By the book, I should be sent back to Earth and replaced by someone who has not had five years to learn the city and all her quirks. I think right now that would be a fairly big problem."

"It would."

"Dr. Weir would have pretended she knew nothing," Radek said. "I think she bent the rules a number of times when she hired the first expedition members. Of course we would like everyone here to be healthy, but there are not so many experts in wormhole physics that she could really pick and choose. Mr. Woolsey I think has a different philosophy."

"He let McKay keep the cat," Ronon said.

Radek shrugged. "There is that." He still looked reluctant to risk it, and Ronon could see why. It had surprised him when he'd first come to the city how healthy everyone was, and how unscarred the soldiers were. He'd expected to see missing fingers or eyepatches to cover a blinded eye, and to see worse on the soldiers assigned to things like cooking dinners and organizing supplies. Those were things a man could do when he'd lost a leg or worn out his body with too many small hurts over the years, ways to stay in the fight.

At first he'd taken the fact that everyone in the city was young and strong as a sign of how much of an advantage their technology gave them. Then he'd seen one Marine after another come back through the gate with terrible wounds and be sent through it again back to Earth. Most of them didn't come back to the city. From what Sheppard said, the worst injured weren't even kept on in the service back on Earth. You get a nice pension, though, he'd said with a smile that didn't touch his eyes, in the tone of a man who'd rather die.

It wouldn't mean losing as much for Radek, but losing the city would be no small thing, and losing him would be no small thing for the city. And now they needed him on the team, and for that he needed to be able to see what he was shooting at, and it was all tangled up in the paperwork and regulations that everything on Earth seemed to require. There were times when he felt like dealing with it took half of the energy he had for dealing with anything.

"All right," he said when he realized Radek had been waiting for a while for him to say something. "Let me talk to Sheppard. Maybe he can fix it somehow."

"If you think it will do any good," Radek said wearily.

Ronon shrugged. "It's worth a try."

CHAPTER TWENTY-NINE
Quicksilver

QUICKSILVER dreamed, and in his dreams he was far underground. The chamber beneath the earth was vast, vast enough to hold a glittering Stargate. It turned, red chevrons flaring, symbols rotating like a ring of fire.

She was standing next to him, the Queen he remembered, her dark hair pulled back severely, her arms crossed over her chest, watching the gate turn.

"Why am I dreaming you?" Quicksilver asked. Banks of lights danced behind her, strange machines humming and jumping. "Why am I dreaming you?"

She turned to him with a secret smile. "Because you want to, Rodney," she said.

The gate opened, blue fire erupting like water.

"Where does that gate go?" Quicksilver asked.

"Where do you think?" The Queen who was called Dr. Weir looked at him, her eyes on his. "Do you remember the nanites? Do you remember the first time I was infected? Where do you think it goes?"

"I don't know," he said. There was something profoundly disturbing there, something just out of reach. Something he didn't want to know, didn't want to remember. "Can you go with me?"

She shook her head sadly. "No. You have to go through that gate alone."

"Oh," he said, the surface reflecting before him like ripples of light on water. "Why?"

"Because you're not dead, Rodney," she said. "You're only sleeping."

"Are you dead?" He didn't want to ask, but some part of him had to.

There was that smile again, secret and rueful. "Why don't you ask Dr. Jackson about that?"

"Who's he?" He felt he ought to know, but the memories ran away from him like droplets of water through his hands.

"Walk through the gate and see." Her voice was gentle, but also steel.

Quicksilver looked toward the gate, cold blue light flooding over him, and yet he could not take a single step. It faded as he woke.

He worked in the laboratory later that day, bending his head over the datapad, trying to make sense of things that should have been easy, and anger welled up in him. How could they have taken this from him, these Lanteans? Was it not enough to hurt him, to break his body in a thousand ways? How could they have taken from him his mind as well? What if he could never relearn it? What if it never again became easy?

Dust had named him the cleverest of clevermen, and he knew that was true. He was the smartest. Without that he was nothing. Without the quicksilver grace of his intellect, how should he be worth anything to anyone? He would be worth nothing to himself.

There was a stir at the door, and one of the blades he had sometimes seen in the gaming room came in, his midnight blue leathers ornamented with jet, and spoke to Dust in low tones. "We have had word from one of our worshippers with the Genii," he said. "And as you can imagine it is a matter of great concern, worth a very carefully placed operative."

Dust straightened. "You have come from the Queen?"

"Just," the blade said, "And she is disturbed."

"What is the nature of it?" Dust asked, casting a quick glance around the room. Quicksilver bent his head, blinking as if he made little sense of their words.

"She Who Carries Many Things has returned," the blade said.

"With a new warship, one that is said to be deadlier than any before. She and her Consort were with the Genii, meeting in secret, and all is well between them. He took nothing on himself, and seemed to have many marks of her favor, so any hope of a falling out there is nothing but hope."

"She and her Consort both?" Dust shook his head, and worry was evident in every line of his face. "That is ill news indeed. What can the Lanteans be up to?"

The other blade might have spoken, but Quicksilver broke in. "Is there no way to probe my mind for the information you seek? I am sure I know the gate address to Atlantis! If it is that the Queen is concerned about hurting me, I beg you to think no more of that! I would gladly suffer whatever is necessary to help!"

Dust came round the table to him, and put his hand to Quicksilver's cheek in affection. "My brother, I know that you are brave and that you would like to help, but there is nothing that can be done. Your mind is so damaged that even the Queen can reap nothing from it. We have only to hope that as you heal you may remember. Give yourself time, and tell me of each thing that comes to you, for even the smallest thing may hold a clue, no matter how unimportant it may seem."

Quicksilver nodded. "I will do that," he said eagerly. "And perhaps if I try very hard to remember, I shall find more." Perhaps, if he disregarded the words of that queen he dreamed, he could find the information that hung just out of reach...

CHAPTER THIRTY
Interference

THE DOOR signal to his quarters jolted John awake. He had a moment of disorientation, the gray light from the windows making it hard to remember what time it was. By the time he'd decided it was early evening, he was already up and at the door, trying not to resent being woken up at a time when he shouldn't actually have been asleep. Torren was the only one in Atlantis anyone would expect to be in bed at seven.

"Here's the thing," Ronon said without preliminaries, leaning in the door as it opened. "Zelenka's a bad shot because he can't see well enough. He won't go see Jennifer about it because he thinks if he fails the eye test, Woolsey will send him home," Ronon said.

"That's a problem," John said, shaking his head to try to clear it. He always hated getting the scientists shot at, and it helped if they were at least armed and able to shoot back.

"I thought maybe if you talked to her…"

"Yeah, maybe," John said. "You know Keller, though, she plays things by the book. If we still had Carson—"

"We do still have Carson."

It was tempting to take this to Carson, but John was pretty sure that Carson couldn't sneak this by under Keller's nose in her own infirmary, especially when it would mean borrowing whatever equipment he needed for an eye exam. "I'll work something out."

Ronon looked a little skeptical. "So you're going to talk to her."

"I'm going to work something out," John said. "Trust me."

He headed out to the pier where the *George Hammond* was docked instead of down to the infirmary. It wasn't a pleasant stroll in the evening with snow whipping across the pier, although apparently someone had been out long enough that afternoon to build a snowman that was now guarding the *Hammond* at icy attention.

He found Sam in the *Hammond's* galley, nursing a cup of coffee. She waved him to a seat and pushed the paperwork she'd been reading aside. "What can I do for you, Sheppard?"

"I was wondering if I could get someone on your medical staff to do an eye exam for Zelenka," he said. "It's probably no big deal, but just in case there's something that might be a problem according to the letter of the rules…"

"Well, okay," Sam said. "I'd think Dr. Keller could do that, though."

"Well, then it's official, and if she doesn't put it in her paperwork, she could get in trouble. If it's just one of your people taking a look when they're off duty, though—"

"Yes, all right," Sam said. "I can arrange that. You owe me, though."

"Absolutely," John said, with his most charming smile. He figured that ought to take care of it. There might not be any problem after all, but better safe than sorry.

The morning briefing for the new military personnel on Ancient weapons technology was easy to do pretty much on autopilot, because it really boiled down to 'we have some drones and some weird devices that we don't know what to do with, and that are equally likely to be actual weapons and to be things that we're just using in all the ways it says not to on the warning label.' The fun part would be getting to actually play with the drones, which would be a later and much smaller training session.

John was thinking hopefully of coffee when his radio headset sounded.

"Colonel Sheppard," Jennifer said. "Would you stop by when you have a moment? There's something we need to talk about."

He considered getting the coffee first, "I'll be right there," he said instead. It was never a good thing when a doctor said there was something you needed to talk about. It probably wasn't about him, unless he'd managed to contract a deadly disease in the last couple of weeks, but if one of his people had managed to wind up in the infirmary with something embarrassing and contagious, or, worse, something that suggested serious mental health issues, it was going to be his problem.

He was not really in the mood to deal with either 'contracted a social disease while the rest of us were trying to get some work done' or 'probably crazy.' Of course, Jennifer wouldn't put it that way. She'd talk about PTSD and the pressure everyone was under, and he'd nod and agree that of course whoever it was needed to go home. Or maybe send them over to Dr. Robinson, and let her find fancier words for 'couldn't put up enough of a good front.'

John was beginning to think he should have fortified himself with coffee first, but it was too late now that he was almost at the infirmary doors. He squared his shoulders and walked in, looking around to see who was here and what they'd done to themselves.

The infirmary was quiet except for a young Marine who was getting stitches on his cheek from one of the nurses. He relaxed a little; Jennifer had called him down here before to point out that the Marines inflicted an unnecessary number of injuries on one another in physical training, which John agreed was probably true but disagreed that he was in a position to do anything about. It wasn't like telling them to play nice was likely to have much effect.

"Colonel Sheppard," Jennifer said, standing in the door of her office. He was alarmed by how grim she looked. "Come into my office, please."

"What's wrong?" he asked, coming in.

She shut the door without answering, but made no move to

sit down behind her desk, where her laptop still sat open. She had coffee, some part of his mind noticed enviously, although it looked like it had gotten cold.

"I received a transfer of medical records from the *Hammond* this morning," she said. "The records of Dr. Zelenka's eye exam. Does this ring any bells?"

John considered *I don't know what you're talking about* and *they weren't supposed to send you the records* as possible answers, and struck out for some middle ground. "How'd that go?"

"He's cleared for active duty. Is that your question?"

"He's been having trouble with firearms practice," John said. "It was my advice that he should get his eyes checked."

"It looks like that was good advice," Jennifer said. "Now I want to ask you a really direct question, and I'd appreciate an honest answer. Was it Zelenka's idea to do an end run around me on this, or was it yours?"

"It was mine," John said after a moment.

She shook her head. "Somehow I figured that."

"We need him," John said intently. "With Rodney missing, if we lose Zelenka, we're totally screwed. You can see that, right?"

"Yes," Jennifer said. "I can. His corrected vision is really borderline according to the regulations, and I'm going to keep on ignoring that, because we do need him."

"Great," John said. "If that's all, I have a busy day." He could see her expression tighten at the sarcasm in his tone, and knew it wasn't helping matters, but he couldn't seem to stop.

"Is that really how you want this?" She was keeping her voice low, but he suspected it was with an effort. "Do you think I haven't noticed that there's a little tension right now between Woolsey and Colonel Carter? How do you think Woolsey would like to hear that you're going behind his back to get her to do you favors that he's not supposed to know about?"

"I really hope that's not supposed to be a threat," John said.

All of a sudden he thought she looked more tired than angry. "It's actually not," she said. "I actually thought maybe we could talk about this like reasonable adults who are supposed to be on the same team. Was I wrong?"

He eyed her coffee cup to avoid seeing her face. "You weren't wrong."

"Why didn't you come to me about this? It could have been handled discreetly."

He glanced back at her. "I didn't think you'd be willing to play it that way."

"I'm not willing to keep people on active duty if in my professional opinion they're a danger to themselves or others. That's not every situation that breaks the rules." She spread her hands. "Nobody is going to die because somebody has 20/30 vision rather than 20/20. I know on paper we have to draw a line somewhere, but I'm willing to use my judgment in what falls on which side of that line."

"I wasn't sure," John said.

"You didn't ask. There's not a lot I can do to help people if they don't trust me."

"Now you sound like Dr. Robinson."

"And that's a big coincidence right there."

"My people are going to be kind of reluctant to bring things to either of you that they don't want to go down on their permanent records," John said. "It's not that they don't trust you. It's that they don't trust 'the doctor.'"

"That's me," Jennifer said. "I'm really not out to get anybody."

"It's not just you," John said. "It's whoever reads your files. It's guys back home who have no idea what we're going through out here and who are just looking for some reason — " He stopped, hands clenching, abruptly out of words.

"I can run interference for you," Jennifer said. "If somebody back on Earth wants to try to make trouble for me, I'm okay with that. The number of people who actually want this job is smaller than you'd think. But if I'm going to do that, you have to trust me to make the calls. And that means your people need to give me enough information to make them."

He took a deep breath and let it out. "That's fair."

"I think so," Jennifer said. "Let's try this again. I've looked at the results of Zelenka's eye exam. With an updated prescription for corrective lenses, I think he's fine to be on active duty. I may have accidentally neglected to make a note of precisely what his corrected vision score was, but I'm considering it acceptable."

"The IOA won't like that much if they ever notice," John said.

"Since when does the IOA like anything?" She shook her head. "You let me worry about that."

"Okay," John said. It was a relief to think that maybe he could. Jennifer seemed to be watching him, her expression rueful. "What?"

"Atlantis has been my first experience treating military patients," she said. "I'd appreciate it if you'd let me know when there are special concerns."

"I don't want people on active duty when they're so burned out they're going to get somebody hurt," he said. "I also don't want to end somebody's career because they've had a rough week. Sometimes people just need a little time."

"Or a little help," Jennifer said. "Even big tough military guys, right?"

John smiled without humor. "We see all the most exciting parts."

She nodded with what looked like real sympathy. "I bet. You know, if people are having problems, I really want to see them. Or I want Dr. Robinson to see them. Let us figure out what we can do, and then we'll figure out what the best thing is to put in people's files."

He shrugged. "Fair enough."

"Not exactly the most rousing vote of confidence I've ever heard," she said dryly, "but right now I'll take it."

"I trust you to keep us all from getting killed," John said. "I'd probably be dead about five or six times otherwise."

"At least," Jennifer said. "I don't actually enjoy sewing you up, you know. It's not my idea of a fun day at work."

"I thought it kept you from getting bored."

"If I get that bored, I'll read a magazine," she said. "Go on, go shoot things, or whatever you have on your busy schedule." Her tone was dry rather than angry, though, and he smiled crookedly in return.

"Training exercises. I'll try not to send you any new patients."

"You do that," she said. "I'm going to start charging extra for any injuries your guys inflict on each other."

"Just put it on my tab," John said, and went to find that coffee.

CHAPTER THIRTY-ONE
Beneath the Surface

THE WATER was relentlessly cold, a full-body punch that made Lorne's hands cramp almost as soon as he left the jumper. Dry suits made the dive bearable, but he had to wear light enough gloves to be able to do the actual repairs. He turned slowly in the water, making sure that Campbell and Green were ready to follow him, and then kicked off from the jumper's side. They were both avid divers, while Lorne felt this wasn't really his idea of a great way to spend the day.

Below them, Lieutenant Miller was holding the jumper steady, its lights turned upward to illuminate the underside of the pier. It had been tempting to use the jumper's shield to create a bubble of air for them to work in; it would have meant they could stay down longer without worrying about the cold. It would also have meant trying to keep the jumper steady right under the part of the city they were trying to repair. The idea was to avoid doing any more damage.

Green was carrying a video camera, and she flipped it on as they approached the damaged section of the hull. They'd been down here with a camera mounted on the jumper to take video of the damage, and Zelenka had identified three sensor arrays that needed to be switched out. They'd brought all three replacements down with them, hoping not to have to do this again.

"I am receiving your transmission," Zelenka said. "Major Lorne, are you ready to proceed?"

Lorne leaned into the camera's field of view and gave a thumbs-up. He and Campbell approached the first damaged sensor array, steadying themselves on either side. The camera's light was at a bad angle, throwing more shadows than anything; he took hold of Green's arm and pushed her gently back, getting the light where he needed it.

Campbell unfastened the first replacement from the back of Lorne's suit. It wasn't that big, a metal box with a sensor vane on one side, and on the other side, a row of control crystals that should slide into place easily once they got the damaged one out of the way. Or so Dr. Zelenka said.

"You can see the mechanical damage to the sensor array," Zelenka said. He certainly could. The sensor vane was crumpled, and one corner of the box was twisted up out of alignment with the city's hull. "I've deactivated the power to the array, so try to gently pry it free. Gently, please."

Lorne found a screwdriver in one of his suit's pockets and pried at the other corners. He wasn't sure he was exactly being gentle, but he was making some progress. He wrapped his fingers around it and tugged, hoping it didn't come free quickly enough to send him tumbling. It was possible he should clip on to something to brace himself, but he didn't see anything to clip onto other than the sensor vane itself, which wasn't very helpful.

Green swiveled suddenly in the water, the video camera turning with her and throwing the box in front of him into shadow.

"What are you doing?" Zelenka said into his radio. Lorne spread his hands, but since Zelenka couldn't see him, it hardly mattered. Green turned the camera back toward him, and he shrugged one shoulder in a question.

She spread her hands as if there were something she wanted to say but couldn't, and pointed below them. He looked down. He didn't see anything but the jumper, and if he put his back to the jumper, there was only dark ocean beyond the reach of the jumper's lights.

She shook her head and signaled 'okay.' Lorne hesitated. They could always scratch the mission, but he hated to have it all to do over again.

"Lieutenant Miller says he is reading nothing on sensors but some life form readings, barely large enough for him to detect," Zelenka said. "We have not had much chance to catalogue the ocean life on this world, though, so if you see anything that looks dangerous, it may be wise to return to the jumper."

Thanks for the advice, Lorne wanted to say. He nodded and tugged doggedly at the sensor array. It finally came free, and he managed to keep hold of it, waiting for Campbell to stow it on the back of his suit before he started edging the new one into place.

"It should click into place," Radek said. "We think."

He wasn't sure it clicked, but it did at least fit, which was the first big step.

"I'm going to initialize the sensor array," Radek said. "It should first clear the water from around the crystals." Lorne nodded. He could see bubbles in the water around the edges of the sensor array, which soon stopped. "Now we are turning the power on."

All along the sensor vane, small lights began to twinkle red. Lorne signed an enthusiastic thumbs-up for the camera.

"Perfect," Zelenka said. "Two more to go."

On the way from the second to the third, a flicker of colored light caught Lorne's eye. He thought for a moment he'd gotten disoriented, somehow turned a circle in the water. The cold was starting to make his head ache, and his hands were nearly numb to the wrist. He looked up, reassuring himself that he was following the line of the pier, directly below it.

He clapped Green on the shoulder and gave her a questioning look when she turned. She nodded and pointed down, flicking the camera's light on and off pointedly. They were almost at the last sensor array; Lorne glided up to it and caught at the bent vane to stop his movement in the water, looking down.

He couldn't see anything past the jumper's lights. When Green turned the camera on Lorne again, he pointed down toward the jumper and turned his own flashlight on, then pointedly off.

"Lieutenant Miller says he is getting some indication that there may be a fairly large life sign approaching," Zelenka said. "He is maybe a little concerned."

Wonderful. Lorne tugged experimentally at the damaged sensor array. It showed no signs of coming free easily. He was sure he saw another flicker of light somewhere in the murky darkness. He pantomimed turning off the jumper's lights again.

"You would like the jumper's lights off?" Zelenka asked skeptically.

Lorne nodded firmly. After a moment the jumper's lights switched off. He turned off his own flashlight, and after a long moment's hesitation, Green switched off the camera light.

It took a while for his eyes to adjust. He could see the dim light filtering down from the cloudy sky outside the shadow of the city. Beneath him, there were definite flickers of colored light moving in the darkness, and then brightening lights, like something rising toward him.

"Miller feels that you should perhaps return to the jumper," Zelenka said, and then exclaimed, startled into his native Czech, "Co to, do pekla, je? Gigantická chobotnice?"

Lorne backpedaled instinctively as something rose in front of him, traced with patterns of light that shifted and merged. It looked like a gigantic squid, he realized after a moment, its upper body spread out like a hood in front of him, nearly twice his height. Its tentacles trailed far below it, a few tipped with light.

It was glowing, soft white light chased with patterns of red, whole patches blinking out into darkness and then relighting themselves again. He couldn't help a sense of fascination, even as he wondered what it ate and if he might look like food to it.

"Okay, it is some sort of cephalopod," Zelenka said. "The biologists will love this. You should probably not make any sudden moves."

Lorne wasn't planning to. He turned the flashlight on experimentally, on the theory that might discourage the creature from sticking around, although he couldn't help watching it in fascination.

The tip of a tentacle rose toward him. He kicked backwards, wondering if he could actually get out of reach. Then it lit, the light playing over him like its own flashlight beam.

To his left, Lorne could see Campbell prying the damaged sensor array loose. Lorne made a mental note to thank him for that. He motioned for Green to help him, and she unfastened the last replacement array from Campbell's back with one hand, still filming with the other. Green let go of the damaged array and let it sink beneath them, which Lorne thought was forgivable under the circumstances.

He thought he could see the thing's eyes, or what passed for its eyes, dark patches that turned to follow his movements. He turned the flashlight experimentally off and then back on. The tentacle went dark, and then lit again.

More tentacles rose toward him, one reaching out toward the flashlight. Lorne considered his options, and let go of the flashlight. The creature curled its tentacle around it, tilting the flashlight back and forth in the water.

"The last array is in place," Zelenka said. "I am turning it on." There was another rush of bubbles, and then the sensor vane lit with twinkling red light.

The glow of the creature's body shifted, dimmer red lights spreading against skin that had gone suddenly dark. It looked a lot like the sensor vane.

One for the biologists, Lorne told himself, and pushed off from the hull, trying to kick toward the jumper without making sudden movements. Green and Campbell followed. Green started to switch on the light on her camera, but Lorne motioned for her to leave it. They didn't want to draw the creature's attention as they tried to make their retreat.

It stayed where it was, and Lorne thought he could see the glow of the flashlight's beam moving erratically through the water along with the light shed by the creature itself. Then it moved, faster than he would have thought possible, rushing past them into the darkness, the flashlight tumbling abandoned through the water behind it.

Lorne heard the noise a moment later, a grinding that he hoped wasn't an iceberg about to send giant chunks of ice tumbling toward his team. Green caught his arm and pointed toward the edge of the city, and he looked up toward where the water was lit by the gray sunlight.

A ring of spikes were sliding down through the water, meters long and angled out to deflect any impact. Between them, cables stretched to make an underwater fence that would catch anything small enough to slip between the spikes. Here and there Lorne thought he saw gaps, but they could take a look later, and mend anything that looked the worse for wear.

"That is perfectly lovely," Zelenka said. "Now come inside and get warm."

Lorne wasn't about to argue with that.

… and returned the ship to the Genii, thereby ensuring the continuation of smooth diplomatic relations, Dick typed. He hesitated, and then deleted the last part of the sentence. Not strong enough, and anyway he felt that describing their relations with the Genii in the past as smooth was probably more of a creative interpretation of the truth than the IOA was likely to swallow. *Thereby avoiding a diplomatic incident that might well have…*

The trick was making the consequences sound significant enough to justify handing over an Ancient battle cruiser, but not so dire as to make the IOA question the wisdom of trying to make a deal with the Genii in the first place. He very much suspected that couldn't be done. He wasn't looking forward to the IOA reading this report. *A diplomatic incident that…*

…that would have been very embarrassing, Dick typed, and

then deleted the words with a sigh.

He looked up at a diffident knock on the doorframe, feeling grateful for the distraction. "Dr. Zelenka, please come in. What can I do for you?"

"Well, I have good news and bad news," Zelenka said.

"At least there is some good news," Dick said.

"A bit, yes," Zelenka said. "We have managed to reactivate the Ancient systems intended to protect the city from damage by floating ice. We may still have problems if we encounter extremely large icebergs, but Major Lorne says there is no problem with towing those out of the way, or even just blowing them up."

"Is blowing up icebergs entirely safe?"

Zelenka shrugged. "I think not particularly, but he says that the demolitions experts could use the practice, and I suppose it is not more dangerous than blowing up anything else."

"I suppose that makes sense," Dick said. He had been dealing with the military for decades, now, and he still sometimes found their perspective a little hard to grasp. "Any more good news?"

"Not really," Zelenka said. "The biologists are concerned about the pigeon issue."

"I'm sorry?"

"They sent you memos? We have pigeons?"

"Of course," Dick said. "The pigeons." He'd seen an email about pigeons, he was fairly sure, but it hadn't seemed to be a priority compared to the offworld teams that still hadn't reported back at the time. "And they're concerned because…"

"It could be damaging to this planet's ecosystem," Zelenka said. "Pigeons can be an invasive species. However, as far as we can tell there are no native birds, and I am skeptical that the pigeons can survive outside the city in this weather. Here they have warmth, and they seem to be finding sources of food."

Dick frowned. "Would that be our supplies?"

"We have taken measures to make our storerooms pigeon-proof, so we will see how that goes. They are resourceful birds."

"Is there something else we should be doing?"

Zelenka shrugged again. "I think poison would be more likely to harm the ecosystem than the pigeons, especially if the pigeons were eaten by any of the native sea life. We have a sort of giant squid, apparently. There are various strategies for driving pigeons away, but as there is essentially nowhere for them to go, that is unlikely to be effective."

"Back up a moment," Dick said. "Giant squid?"

"They seem to be doing no harm, although they were alarming for our divers to encounter unexpectedly. They are probably interesting to the marine biologists, but in terms of their effect on city systems…" Zelenka made a dismissive gesture, possibly indicating that as long as they didn't pose a technical problem, he didn't consider them a priority.

"And essentially you're recommending that we do nothing about the pigeons."

"Yes. I think the pigeon situation is not really a crisis."

"Let's do that, then," Dick said. He was very much in the mood for problems that could be solved by doing nothing. "Was that the bad news?"

"That would be nice," Zelenka said. "No, the bad news is much worse. I have been working on trying to ensure that the Wraith cannot access Atlantis's computer systems using information they have gained from Rodney." Dick nodded. "It is a bigger problem than I thought. I am finding multiple back doors into the system, and this is suggesting that there are many I am not finding. Right now in my opinion the computer system is not secure."

Dick let out a breath. "All right. What do we do?"

"I will need help on this one," Zelenka said.

Dick had a sinking feeling about where this one seemed to be going. "I suppose we could ask Colonel Carter if she could spare any time to our computer security," he said. Asking the person who'd had his job before him for help wasn't exactly a position he wanted to be in, but neither was having the Wraith with free access to Atlantis's computers. "I know she plans to keep the *Hammond* on station here for at least a few more days in case we do hear from Todd."

"That would be helpful. I am just thinking that if we do not, we will need help for more than a few days. The *Daedalus* should be leaving Earth shortly on its way here—"

"Yes," Dick acknowledged. "Unfortunately, I think we're in no position to request additional staff. The IOA has made it very clear that they will not authorize any further expenses this fiscal year, and that was before they read the report I'm about to send them."

Zelenka's eyebrows raised. "Is it that bad?"

Dick spread his hands. "I have to tell them that we let Todd escape, that Dr. McKay is in the hands of the Wraith and may be handing over the access codes to our computer system as we speak, and that we just gave a functional Ancient battle cruiser to the Genii. Let's just say they won't be happy."

"It was worse the first year," Zelenka said, with the ghost of a smile.

"Most of the first year, Dr. Weir was entirely out of contact with Earth," Dick said. "I'm beginning to envy her."

"I am not suggesting we hire someone new," Zelenka said. "Frankly what I need as much as someone with Rodney's computer skills is someone who understands how Rodney thinks. Myself, I try not to think like Rodney most of the time. It is better for my peace of mind."

"What are you suggesting?" Dick asked as patiently as possible.

"Jeannie Miller," Zelenka said.

"Dr. McKay's sister?"

"She has worked with him in the past, and she understands

him as much I suspect as anyone does. If anyone can figure out what back doors Rodney has left for himself and how to close them, I suspect it is her."

"I should really write to her in any event, to inform her... I was planning to wait a little longer, but I'll go ahead and ask if she's willing to come out and give us some assistance."

"That would be very helpful," Zelenka said. "It will be at least couple of weeks before the *Daedalus* can get here, but if we wait and it leaves without her, it will be a month or more."

"I'll see what I can do. And then figure out how to explain it to the IOA in a way that doesn't overly emphasize Dr. McKay's unauthorized modifications to the computer system."

"I will leave you that in your hands," Zelenka said quickly, and left.

"I'm sure you will," Dick said to no one in particular, and began typing again.

CHAPTER THIRTY-TWO
Dangerous Passages

TEYLA STRETCHED, trying to find balance. Her left hip was still tender, though the range of motion was back. The problem was weight. When she tried to stand on her left foot and extend her right foot straight out in front until her toes were level with her shoulders, her left hip gave. It was very frustrating.

Dr. Keller had said that the bone bruise would heal well eventually, but a matter of weeks seemed like such a long time. "It has only been six days," Dr. Keller had said. "You have to give it time." And yet time was the thing it felt there was so little of. Every day, every moment that flew by, was another moment that Rodney remained in captivity, was another day that he might be giving the Wraith everything they wished to know, was another day he might be in torment while they had no idea where he was or what they might do.

It weighed upon them, knowing there was nothing to do. How do you search the galaxy for one man?

Teyla stretched, extending her arms in counterpoint to her legs, each extension graceful and controlled, her long thin slitted skirt opening in flowing lines.

Mr. Woolsey said that they must give their sources time to work. John had only returned from returning the *Avenger* to the Genii day before yesterday. It would take time for their intelligence networks to be cast wide to bring in useful information, even if Ladon Radim acted immediately to keep their bargain. Teyla did not doubt that he would at least bend some effort to keeping it, but how much and how quickly was questionable. And so they must prepare and wait, make certain that everything was in readiness when the call came.

It seemed like so little. It felt like doing nothing, and how could they do nothing even for a few hours? It was worse with Torren on New Athos. When he was here, Teyla never lacked for something to do. Every moment was filled and more so. While he was with Kanaan, she might sleep with no regard for his schedule, eat with her friends, go to the gym. And yet this day seemed to be taking forever.

Though it was only ten in the morning.

Stretch. Concentrate. Surely even if her mind were too disordered to meditate, she could find release for this tension in movement. Eyes closed, stretching toward the bright snowlight that came in through the stained glass window, the city's heating systems purring softly...

The sound of the studio door opening.

"Oh, sorry," John said.

She opened her eyes to see him standing just inside, clad in sweat pants and a black t shirt, his gym bag in his hand.

"I didn't realize you were here," he said.

Which was an out and out lie, Teyla thought. If he had not known she was here he would not be carrying his bantos sticks. Also, he would have knocked on the studio door before entering if he truly did not know who was using this room.

John at least had the good grace to look sheepish. "I can come back," he said.

For a moment she was almost tempted to say, yes, you can, so foul was her mood. But it would be unfair to take it out on John, when he was as worried as she was and probably equally keyed up. "I do not mind sharing the room," she said, her shoulder cracking as she completed the stretch and sank into her last posture. Thankfully, her hip held, though it twinged rather painfully.

John shrugged, his sticks protruding from his gym bag. "Want to spar? I promise I'll take it easy with your hip."

"Will you?" Teyla's eyebrows rose. "Will you take it easy on me?" Absolute nerve, as though she didn't clean the floor with him nine times out of ten.

"Yeah, I mean, you're just getting back into it and all…" He gave her a sideways smile. "Maybe I'll win for a change."

"I would not place any bets on that," Teyla said, going over to the bench for her sticks.

"Think you can take me with your hip messed up?"

Teyla turned around, lifting her sticks into guard, her eyes meeting his in challenge. "I can take you anytime, any way I want."

"Ok then." He lifted his, a smile transforming his face, reminding her suddenly of that so much younger man who had come to Athos nearly six years ago, who had said that he liked tea and Ferris wheels and things that went very fast. "Come and get me."

"I will," she said, beginning a long, wide circle around him, sticks at the ready.

There were ways to compensate for an injury. In real fights this happened all the time. More than once she'd had to take on an opponent when she was already wounded. Of course John had both the height and reach on her, not to mention the strength, but it had never done him that much good before.

Circling, circling. She saw the movement in his eyes an instant before he lunged, and she sidestepped it easily, spinning around him on her right foot, bringing the stick down in a stinging blow across the back of his thighs.

"Yow!" He twisted around, dropping out of guard as he did, his left arm rising.

Perfect. A straightforward forearm blow, right across the inside of his left arm.

John dropped the left hand stick, and Teyla backed off, circling, a little smile on her face. "Are you going easy on me? Or perhaps I should go easy on you?"

He bent and picked it up, his eyes not leaving hers. "That wasn't fair."

"Wasn't it?" she asked airily. "You can surrender anytime you like."

"I don't think so." He was grinning as he picked up the stick, though she could see the long red welt standing out on his forearm. "We're not done."

"No, we're not," she said. Circling. Circling. This time he was going to wait and let her come to him. Which was smarter, actually, give the difference in their heights. Playing defensively was a better strategy for him, but one he almost never used.

A feint, and she dropped below his response, letting the momentum of his movement carry him sideways to her as she once again stepped behind him. Both sticks, in swift one-two motion, right across the seat of the pants. No doubt it was less painful than the forearm blow but more embarrassing.

He backed off, scrubbing his sweat soaked hair back off his forehead. "What's gotten into you today?"

"Merely blowing off some steam," Teyla said. It felt so good to move like this, to feel each connection solid and real. "If it is too much for you, you can retire."

"It's not nearly too much," he said, circling again. "I can take a lot of punishment."

"I'm sure you can." Reversing direction, stalking sunward around him. "But you do not have to."

"Think I'm going to back down?"

"You could." Circling, circling. The tips of their sticks touched, just grazing each other in passing, her eyes on his.

"Gonna have to do better than that," he said, and exploded into motion, a furious feint and lunge toward her bad side. She caught his stick on hers, though the weight behind it nearly pushed her to her knees, arms straining, a foot apart.

"Your fly is unzipped," Teyla said.

He looked and in that moment she disengaged, slipping under his stick like a whisper, laughing as she went.

John straightened up, a sheepish expression on his face. "I

can't believe I fell for that! I'm wearing sweat pants."

"You are too easy to distract," she said.

"Yeah," he said, his eyes smiling into hers.

"You had better be careful," she said. "An unscrupulous opponent could take advantage of you."

"They might," he said. "Lucky for me, I don't like playing it safe."

"Don't you?" Another feint, and this time she slipped to the left, dodging his riposte neatly. The left stick caught him in the back of the knees and he dropped before her, the right stick going around his throat as she leaned forward, her right knee in his back and his shoulders pulled back against her, the back of his head against her belly.

"Erk," he said as his knees hit the floor, and he looked up at her, the stick at his throat, taut as a bow in her hands.

"Will you yield to me at last?" Teyla asked quietly, feeling his pulse thrumming in his neck, hammering in time with hers.

His eyes met hers. "Oh yeah," he said as she bent over him.

"Colonel Sheppard to the gateroom! Colonel Sheppard to the gateroom! We have an incoming transmission from Todd." Amelia Banks switched the radio back out of transmit and looked up at Woolsey leaning over her shoulder.

"Put Todd on," Dick Woolsey said grimly. "Let's see what he has to say."

The viewscreen stabilized, a grainy picture that showed nothing but a headshot of Todd. "I only have a moment, and I will only say this once," he said. "Dr. McKay is being held aboard Queen Death's hiveship. Most of the time he is in the forward laboratory section. You are fortunate, as that section is less heavily guarded than most of the ship." He gave what might pass for a Wraith smirk.

"Good information," Dick said, "But useless without the location of the ship." He made himself keep his voice light, though he felt a surge of excitement run through his veins.

"Of course," Todd said. "And what is it worth to you to know the location of the ship?"

"It's to your advantage to tell us and have us do your dirty work for you," Woolsey said calmly. "Or not. But you don't seem to have time for a long discussion about it."

Todd snarled.

Sheppard came bounding up the stairs from the transport chamber wearing gym clothes and looking distinctly flustered. He crowded in beside Dick at the monitor. "I'm here."

Todd's expression changed to something like amusement. "And how is the Young Queen?"

"Huh?"

"The ship's location," Dick said patiently.

"In seventeen of your hours Queen Death's ship will be at the following coordinates. The planet is unimportant and uninhabited except for a small garrison we keep there extracting some precious minerals from the world's soil. With our biotechnology it is necessary to provide the ship with the proper building blocks for it to use to expand and repair, and indeed to continue in good health."

"You have to feed your ship?" Sheppard asked keenly.

"From time to time," Todd said. "Even the largest ships must consume new materials and enter a brief period of digestive dormancy while they assimilate them. During that time a ship is exceedingly vulnerable. It is asleep, for all practical purposes. Its defenses are down, it is not prepared for hull regeneration, and engines and weapons are offline. Queen Death has been using her ship hard. She must bring new material aboard and give it time to consume it."

"And how long does this take?" Dick asked.

"No more than a few hours, typically," Todd said. "So it is our practice to go to some remote spot and complete the entire process in less than one of your days. Her ship will be at this location in seventeen hours, and it will stay with certainty no more than four or five, though it may stay as long as eight depending on the amount of new material to digest." Todd looked down at his hands as though they were moving over a console. "I am sending the coordinates. Now." There was a brief databurst, and the transmission dissolved into static. An instant behind that the Stargate cut out.

Dick drew himself up. "Whew."

"I've got a set of coordinates," Banks said. "It's a planet a little less than an eighth of the way around the galactic rim. There's a Stargate, but we've never used it but once to send a MALP through. There's nothing there."

Radek Zelenka looked down from the board above, pushing his glasses up on his nose. "It could be a trap," he said.

"Todd doesn't know we have the *Hammond*," Sheppard said. "He's assuming we'll have to send a jumper through the Stargate."

"Banks, ask Colonel Carter to meet us in the briefing room at her earliest convenience," Dick directed. "We need to talk about this. And then call Dr. Keller. Sheppard, get your team together." He looked at his wristwatch. "Let's say ten minutes."

"It's the only real lead we've got," Sheppard said, settling down into one of the conference room chairs, a cup of coffee in his hand. He hadn't taken this ten minutes to go get changed, and he still looked disheveled.

"What is?" Dr. Keller asked as she came in, followed by Dr. Zelenka.

"Todd's tip," Zelenka said, sitting down opposite her on the near side of Sheppard. "He says Rodney is on Queen Death's ship and he says it will be parked and dormant at a certain place." Zelenka put his travel mug down before him and looked around expectantly. "I feel I must play devil's advocate here and say that it may very well be a trap."

"It may be," Dick said. "And that's one thing we need to discuss. But let's wait for everyone to get here."

"What about the Genii?" Keller asked, frowning.

"We haven't heard from them yet," Dick said.

Sheppard shifted in his seat, but said nothing. Ladon Radim, for all his promises, had as yet delivered nothing, while unexpectedly the meeting with Todd had borne fruit. Still, Dick thought, the Genii might come up with something of importance down the road. One could not say that their diplomatic overtures were entirely wasted, even if nothing had come of them so far.

Colonel Carter and Major Franklin came in a few moments later, Ronon in animated conversation with Franklin about some sort of target shooting competition, and Teyla slipped in behind them, her hair soaking wet as though she had just come from the shower. She sat down unobtrusively beside Ronon, while Carter took the chair beside Sheppard.

There was a lengthy recapping of the facts, complete with playback of Todd's message. When it faded everyone sat in silence for a long moment. Carter was looking down the table with the expectant air of someone who thought the facilitator ought to get on with it, but who doesn't feel like they ought to be the one to go first.

"Colonel Carter," Dick said. "You look as though you have an idea." He might as well get it out in the open and get started. Everyone was looking at her anyway.

"Just a thought," Carter said. "Unless Todd has better intelligence than we think, he doesn't know about the *Hammond*."

Sheppard nodded, leaning forward with his elbows on the table. "If they're expecting a cloaked jumper, or if this info is on the up and up and they're not expecting us at all, the *Hammond* could do some serious damage."

"If it's on the up and up and they really are powered down, we could destroy Queen Death's hive ship," Carter said. "And possibly take her out too, if she's onboard."

"That would be the best case scenario," Dick said. "And while that's certainly desirable, let's look at the worst case."

"The worst case is that they're waiting for us," Carter said. "And that they do know about the *Hammond*. But even if they are, even if we drop out of hyperspace and the hive ship is powered up, or if there are half a dozen hive ships, our shields can certainly take it for the few seconds it will take us to open a new hyperspace window and get out of there."

"But isn't the plan to get Rodney off the ship?" Keller asked. "Not just destroy it?"

Sheppard looked at her across the table. "We jump in, we see if the defenses are down, if everything is on the up and up. If it is, Carter beams a team aboard the hive ship, we grab Rodney, she beams us out, and then shoots up the place."

"Sounds good to me," Ronon said gruffly.

"And if the hive ship brings its defensive systems back online while you're aboard?" Dick asked, his eyes on Sheppard.

"Then Carter's got to get them down again. Or we do. Or get to the Dart bay. There are a lot of options."

It didn't sound like a lot of good options to Dick. But this was the best lead they'd had, perhaps the best they were going to have. And Carter was unlikely to risk her ship on its maiden run if it looked like the entire situation was a set up. She'd jump out if it seemed like the hive ship wasn't actually powered down.

They were all looking at him, waiting for him to be the kind of decisive leader they expected and deserved. He glanced at Sheppard. "What if you can't find Dr. McKay? Surely the Wraith have removed his subcutaneous transmitter."

"If he's not in the labs where Todd said he was, he's probably in one of the holding cells," Sheppard replied. "We check them as a backup plan. And if he's not aboard or we can't get to him..." He let his voice trail off.

"I beam the team off and we jump out," Carter said. "I can keep a lock on their transmitters. As long as the hive ship's jamming device stays down, I can pull them out anytime I need to."

"And if the hive ship activates its jamming device after transport?" That was the catch. That was the really big catch. "Todd did not give us any idea how long it would take for a ship to come out of dormancy."

Teyla cleared her throat. "If we can find a command terminal, I may be able to speak with the ship. While I probably cannot override Queen Death's orders, I will certainly be able to find out what its status is and whether or not it is powering up."

Franklin looked down the table boggling at her, but Carter didn't even blink. Of course she was familiar with Teyla's Gift.

"That's good enough for me," Sheppard said.

Of course he thought so. Sheppard was ready to jump on any half-baked plan that offered to rescue Dr. McKay, but it was Dick's job to knock holes in things that didn't stand up on their own. It was his job not to throw tens of lives away on one. Carter was eager to get her ship into action against the Wraith and see how it performed. She wasn't going to be the voice of sanity.

Still, this was hopeful. This was the best lead they'd had, and the opportunity to do Queen Death some actual damage. It was in Todd's best interest to play straight with them. If his information was genuine, they might get rid of his enemy with no effort to himself. And if the information were false, the loss of Sheppard's team would not actually cripple Atlantis, though the double dealing would destroy any relationship between them, any tentative truce. If Todd did not wish to betray Queen Death, he could simply have said nothing, rather than risk making an enemy of one or the other. No, Todd had every reason to be telling the truth. Dick could parse that out.

"You have a go, Colonel Sheppard," he said. The timeframe to get into position was short enough as it was.

John stopped Woolsey on the way out of the conference room. "I've got one more concern," he said, letting everyone else go ahead. Teyla very carefully did not look back at him, her back straight, deep in conversation with Radek. He waited until they were out of earshot. "It's about Zelenka."

Woolsey nodded like he'd been expecting it. "You don't want him on this mission."

"This is a combat mission," John said. "A straight up combat mission. And we don't know what kind of shape Rodney's going to be in. If he's hurt or drugged or something Ronon's going to have to carry him while Teyla and I cover. We can't take care of Zelenka too. I'm good with him being on the team, and I know he's been working with Ronon on the shooting range, but this is a military assault. He doesn't belong in it. Teyla and Ronon and I will handle it."

"Would you be surprised that I agree with you?" Woolsey smiled mirthlessly. "Dr. Zelenka stays in Atlantis this time. I never meant that he should turn into Rambo."

"Good," John said. "And once we get Rodney back, he'll be off the hook."

"As soon as Dr. McKay can return to duty," Woolsey reminded him.

CHAPTER THIRTY-THREE
Bright Venture

THE *George Hammond* eased out of orbit of Atlantis' new planet, gliding through space with a grace Sam wished she could record and keep forever.

"The course is plotted, ma'am," her helmsman said.

Sam nodded, her hands on the arms of the captain's chair. "Punch it."

Ahead the hyperspace window opened in a green flash, and the *Hammond* lunged forward like an eager hunting dog let off the leash, charging ahead. All systems were go, everything optimal. Probably the last time that would be the case, Sam thought. They were going to go scratch the factory paint.

It was nearly sixteen hours to their rendezvous with the hive ship, timing that if Todd were correct should drop them out of hyperspace an hour after Queen Death's ship powered down for its feeding process. Sam certainly wasn't going to stay on the bridge the entire time. They'd rotate through the entire duty roster before they arrived, passing through a full afternoon and night for the *Hammond's* crew.

And for Sheppard's team as well. It was good to have friends out here. Sam was a team player. She'd spent most of her career embedded in a collegial structure, working with people whose skills and talents complimented hers. Solitary responsibility wasn't her ideal command style. The crew of the *Hammond* were all new. They weren't a team yet. So far they were strangers who were just beginning to work together. And tomorrow they'd be tested for the first time. She'd find out how they came together, what the gaping holes were, what their strengths and weaknesses were.

It was an intimidating thought, but Sam knew better than to

let any of it show on her face. She waited until everything was
running smoothly, their hyperspace passage as uncomplicated
as the one that had brought them from Earth, and then returned
to her quarters and her waiting laptop to do paperwork.

Her thoughts strayed. They'd uploaded to Atlantis' databurst
while they were in the city, electronic reports and private emails
coming and going in fractions of a second through the wormhole opened once a week at tremendous cost in power. She'd
had fifty eight incoming emails.

Her brother, Mark, had sent pictures from her niece's soccer
game and asked if she'd buy some Girl Scout cookies.

Cassie, her foster daughter, had sent three emails back to back,
one asking her if she'd seen Band of Brothers, one asking if she
knew anything about airborne training in Toccoa, Georgia in
1943, and one talking about how she hated her very boring job.
She had been there three months, and of course it was boring.
Sam didn't think Cassie would be satisfied with nonprofit work
in the long run, no matter how worthy the cause.

Teal'c had not sent one, a sure sign that he was off in trouble
of his own. Otherwise he would have replied to her last one, sent
from the last Milky Way gate outbound, a remote planet where
once they had hunted for the Lost City of the Ancients, hoping
it held weapons or secrets that would help them against Anubis
and the Goa'uld. It held nothing, now or then, but it was the
last Stargate, the last outpost of the Ancients in the Milky Way,
before the long, cold void between galaxies.

Jack had sent seven emails, one each day since the last transmission, one for her to read each day until the next one. *Hey,
Carter...*

And Daniel... There was a long ramble about Phoenician
gods, a request for samples of alphabets now current in the
Pegasus Galaxy, and the half humorous question of whether or
not she'd been shot yet.

She'd reply to Daniel.

Sorry, Daniel. Not shot yet. Maybe tomorrow. We'll see. We're flying straight into Queen Death's hive ship and it might be a trap or maybe not, so same old same old here. Listen, you've got the letters if you need them, right? I sent them to you instead of Mitchell. You know what to do with them if it comes to that. Which it won't. I won't bore you again telling you what a sweet ship Hammond is, but I'm still in love and familiarity isn't breeding contempt but then it never does with me. Lots of beautiful Ancient buildings send their regards. I wish you were here. I truly do.

"We're getting ready to exit hyperspace," Sam said, standing up from her chair and coming around to where John and his team were waiting. "It's about to be showtime."

"We're ready," John said. They'd slept for a while, or at least he and Ronon had slept, in bunks in the cabin Sam had given them, and he expected Teyla had too, from the fact that she wasn't yawning. Then they'd spent the rest of the trip trying not to pace and get in the way of Sam's people. Now Ronon and Teyla looked as eager as he felt to get moving.

"As soon as we jump in, I expect they're going to start trying to power up the ship," Sam said.

"And our clock starts ticking, I know."

"I'll radio you if it looks like it's starting to go bad. If they get their defensive systems back up, it's possible that we can disable them. If it looks like that's not going to happen, and we start taking a pounding, we're going to have to jump out."

"I know," John said. "We're ready."

"Preparing to exit hyperspace," the *Hammond's* helmsman said.

"Okay," Sam said. "Good luck." She glanced over at a waiting technician. "Beam them down."

The shimmer of the Asgard beaming technology was always disorienting for a moment. It took a couple of heartbeats before the hive ship corridor resolved itself clearly around John. Ronon

had already put his back to John's, covering the length of the
corridor behind them. Teyla stepped to John's left, her P90 at
the ready, taking in their position.

The corridor was empty for the moment, the red light that the
Wraith seemed to prefer tracing the weirdly organic shapes of the
walls. John glanced down at his life-signs detector. There were
moving forms nearby, but there was no way to tell if they were
separated by walls or if they'd run into them in moments.

Sam had beamed them into what they'd guessed was the laboratory section of the ship, but it was hard to tell from feature-
less corridor if they'd gotten it right. The holding cells should
be up and forward. If Todd's tip was good, though, that would
be a needlessly dangerous detour.

He chose the direction that promised fewer Wraith ahead, and
signaled Ronon to take point. If they ran into one or two isolated
Wraith, Ronon's pistol would make less noise than P90 fire. If
they ran into more than that, they'd take that as it came.

Teyla followed Ronon, her eyes searching the walls for signs of
a door or side passageway. She was moving easily enough, showing no signs that her hip was bothering her. He just hoped this
wasn't going to end with them having to retreat at a sprint.

Ronon lifted a hand to stop them, and gestured to an opening
in the wall. John glanced down at the life signs detector. There
was no one in there. It looked like a laboratory when he looked
inside, with benches and consoles and what might have been a
large display screen against the wall, although it was dark.

"If the ship has powered down completely, it may not be possible for the scientists to go about their normal work," Teyla said
under her breath. She stepped forward, running her hands over
one of the consoles. "I do not believe the main databanks are
currently operable."

John glanced up at the dark display screen. "You think they
gave everybody the afternoon off?"

Ronon was still covering the corridor outside from the doorway. "Then what'd they do with McKay?"

"Put him back in a holding cell, maybe. Or maybe they aren't going to stop asking him questions just because their computers are down."

"Perhaps their scientists are needed to put the ship into its state of hibernation, and to restore it to its normal function." Teyla spread one hand across the console, her fingers moving purposefully. "I am trying to activate this console, but the ship is not responding. It is as if it is sleeping."

"We'd like it to stay asleep," John said.

"We would also like to know how long it will take to power up the ship."

"We can't waste time trying to find that out," John said. "The important thing is finding Rodney. If the defenses go back up, we'll figure out something."

"Would we not like to know where he is?" Teyla asked, not yet stepping away from the console.

"Can you get that thing to work or not?"

Teyla frowned, her hand moving on the console almost as if she were trying to push it along. John was reminded, in the sudden vivid way that irrelevant things rose into memory, of a herdsman trying to clear cows from a road.

"No," she said finally in frustration. "I cannot."

"Then let's go."

He waved them back out into the corridor. The next two openings were also empty rooms, one a storage room of some kind full of containers of liquid that didn't seem to bear investigating, the other another laboratory, also deserted. He spared a glance for the life signs detector, and swore under his breath.

He tapped Ronon's arm and gestured for him to hold up. They were going to have company. Ronon nodded, smiling sharply, and held his pistol at the ready, his whole body expectant. He looked almost happy at the prospect of getting to shoot something.

John tensed, waiting, painfully aware of the seconds passing. They must already be starting to power up the hive ship. They had to find Rodney before that happened, or else they had to figure on making their own way off the ship, and with the ship on alert that wasn't going to be easy. Still, maybe they could get to the dart bay, take a dart out in the confusion and signal the *Hammond*—

The life signs detector showed their glowing dots almost on top of each other, and then he saw the movement, pale hair catching the light as the Wraith stepped around the corner. Ronon fired twice, the first shot making the Wraith stagger backwards, the second dropping him.

John caught Teyla's eye. "Teyla?"

She took a deep breath and frowned for a moment as if looking at something he couldn't see. "I do not know if he was able to communicate our presence to anyone," she said. "There is too much alarm and confusion."

"Let's hope he wasn't," John said. He scowled down at the life signs detector. There were too many moving forms, and no way to tell if any of them was Rodney. "Let's go."

The corridor branched off into two others, one slanting upwards, the other down. John picked the upward one, moving quickly and checking every opening. There were too many deserted rooms, too many branching corridors. They could wander around a fleshy maze for an hour, all their time slipping away—

Teyla caught his arm, and he looked down at her. "This will take too long," she said. "We must find out where he is being kept."

"You have an idea?"

She squared her shoulders as if bracing herself for something. "They will know we are here soon enough already," she said. "Let me try to get the knowledge from one of them. I think I can do it."

He gritted his teeth. He hated asking her to risk touching one of their minds that way, but it was true that they weren't getting anywhere. "What do you need?"

"I will need to be close," she said. "We will need a prisoner."

They took the next turning, following a single bright spot making its way down the corridor past several more serpentine bends. John gestured for Ronon to cover their rear, stepping out in front. They needed a prisoner in good enough shape for Teyla to do her thing, not stunned into unconsciousness or with large smoking holes in him.

He came around the corner behind the Wraith, its head bent over some kind of device in its hands, and put one shot through its shoulder. It screamed, the noise inhumanly loud in the cramped corridor, but Ronon was already moving, throwing the Wraith hard against the wall and then wrestling its arms behind it. That wouldn't hold it for long, and if it broke free, it would be easy for it to spin, to jam its feeding hand against Ronon's chest—

Teyla stepped out from behind John, her face as calm as if she were sitting cross-legged in meditation back in Atlantis, beautiful in shadow. The Wraith's eyes locked onto hers, and both of them tensed. Ronon jammed his pistol hard against the Wraith's side, and John trained his P90 right between its eyes, but he held still, heart hammering in his chest, waiting.

Fear. Confusion and fear. She felt it like ice within her, cold as the barrel of Ronon's energy pistol against his side.

Once, under Todd's tutelage, masquerading as his Queen Steelflower, she had learned to speak this way, to modulate the tones of her mind to what passed for conversation, to speak as a Wraith would speak rather than shout. This was different. This was as different as speech was from interrogation.

And yet she felt his fear lessen by some small amount. The touch of her mind did not send him burning in agony to his knees. It was imperative and order, the vise-like strength of the mind of a Queen.

You will tell me where the scientist McKay is kept she demanded, and he felt almost a moment of relief, as an unsure soldier would be steadied by John's voice snapping an order, decision taken away, uncertainty resolved in the reliance on someone who ought to give the orders, who by right could command.

He did not resist, but the images were jumbled, corridors and doors, Wraith and more Wraith. People that he knew, others aboard the hive ship, with no clear picture of Rodney. Not useful, not coherent.

Tell me what room. He could not deny her. She was a Queen, and her mind was on his. No mere cleverman could conceal his thoughts from such, even if he might wish to. *I am a Queen* Teyla said, mind to mind, as though her hands ringed his wrists like iron. *Show me the chamber where the prisoner McKay is.*

Power and the thrill of power, the bright yielding of his mind to hers, as though he bent like a supplicant, head down before her beauty and her strength. The corridor, the room, not so far from here. Two turnings, and then the door.

You will kill me. He stated it as fact. Of course they would. When he had rendered her what she wanted, he would die, surely as a sacrifice beneath a sovereign's hand.

Yes she said.

She pulled the energy pistol from Ronon's hand, thumbing the settings, her fingers small around the large grip, the barrel against the cleverman's ribs, and squeezed the trigger. The Wraith sprawled first to his knees, then collapsed to the floor in an ungainly heap, a pool of shadow in the darkened hall. She held the pistol out to Ronon.

He took it, glanced down at the stun setting, and frowned. "What did you do that for?"

"Because I wanted to." In Teyla's voice she heard the echo of a Queen's tones, and Ronon's frown deepened.

"Later," John said, forestalling any further discussion. "Did you find out where Rodney is?"

"Yes. It is this way. Todd was right that it is a laboratory." Teyla gestured to the left. "It is not far. Come."

John let her lead, following after with the life signs detector, while Ronon took six. It took only a moment, which was probably a good thing. She knew that time always seemed to run unevenly in a mission, minutes seeming hours, elongating with strain and adrenaline, but even so they must have been aboard the hive ship for some minutes. Sooner or later it would awaken. Sooner or later they would activate their defensive systems, and then the *Hammond* might be seriously outclassed.

"It is here," she whispered, gesturing to a closed door.

John squinted at the life signs detector in the dim light. "Two," he said. "Rodney and somebody else. And there are a bunch one corridor over who are going to be here any second. Ok, let's do this thing. Ronon, cover us."

Quicksilver was in his laboratory when the alarms sounded. Doors slid shut all over the ship, panels of bone and cartilage connecting with the quiet hiss of ventilation systems sealing. The laboratory lights flickered and then came back to life as it went to internal emergency power.

"What has happened?" Quicksilver said.

Dust shook his head, but he looked disturbed. He cocked his head for a moment, listening to the great network, to the other minds aboard. "An unidentified ship has just come out of hyperspace," he said. "And we are powered down while the ship restores himself. We have no external power. The *Bright Venture* sleeps."

"That's not good, is it?" Quicksilver asked, cold running through his veins. Fear. That's what it was.

"It might be rival hive," Dust said. "Or it might be..."

Quicksilver turned to the viewscreens, trying to get sensor readings. There they were, green and red on the screen, the dipping, weaving shape of a ship the size of a cruiser, approaching with evasive jinks and bobbles though the *Bright Venture* did not return fire.

The alarm tone changed. Pilots to the Dart bay. Though how they should get the bay doors opened with the ship dormant…

In the hall there was a burst of sound, the bright pure buzzes of stunners, and the heavy rattle of something else, something that seemed oddly familiar to Quicksilver. Terrifying. And yet he felt his heart lift inexplicably.

"We must get down," Dust said, and pulled him to the floor behind one of the long tables. "Their weapons will pierce the door!" He drew a small stunner from a compartment in the wall behind them.

"I did not know you had that," Quicksilver said. Weapons were the province of blades. Clevermen did not generally use them.

"It is for emergencies only," Dust said with a joyless smile. "And this is an emergency, my brother. This is the worst kind of emergency."

They were trapped in the laboratory, no way out except through the door, and no one with them, no blades or drones to defend them. He felt this had happened before, and though the fear clawed at him, it could not hold him.

"We will have to resist them as long as we may," Quicksilver said.

Dust looked at him with surprise. "You are brave."

"Not really," Quicksilver said. "Unless I have to be. This is also for emergencies only." He squared his shoulders as the door blew in.

Two humans burst into the room, their black clothing dark against the wreathing white smoke. Their weapons were held high, and their lights cast a fitful and piercing brightness, almost searing to look at. A third remained in the hall, his hulking back slightly visible behind them as he covered the corridor outside.

Quicksilver froze, his pulse hammering in his head.

The taller of the two humans swept his weapon around. "Rodney?"

"Hurry!" the one outside shouted. "I'm not going to be able to hold them long, Sheppard!"

"Rodney?" the smaller of the two called. "Rodney, are you here?"

Dust gave him a sideways look, a swift half-smile that Quicksilver knew he would keep in his memory forever. And then he darted out from the end of the table, firing his stunner at the intruders, narrowly missing the smallest one.

The other swung around, the beam of light from his weapon catching Dust just as he opened fire. Blood blossomed, and he jerked in the rain of hard things, six, eight catching him full in the body, tearing through velvet and cloth and flesh and muscle and bone, shaking him like a rag caught in a tornado, flinging him useless and broken to the floor, one final spark of pain flaring in his eyes before they fixed.

"No!" Quicksilver was hardly aware of himself, unconscious of any fear at all, rising up from behind the table and leaping for the stunner thrown from Dust's opened hand. "No!" He dropped to the floor, across his brother's blood, and his fingers closed around it. Once, twice, three bright bursts erupting at the dark figure who had slain Dust.

Quicksilver rolled, getting out of the way of return fire, and squeezed off another shot and another, pumping blast after blast into the human where he lay, just as he had torn Dust, grim determination in his face and bile in his throat. The smaller human dove behind a piece of equipment, and he threw shot after shot at her, pinning her and the one in the doorway both. His shots could not penetrate the metal of the equipment nor the frame of the door, but he could keep them thus, keep them until blades came.

The smaller one was screaming something, calling out to him or to her fallen packmate, he did not know. That one lay insensible, blood seeping from his ears, stunned again and again, his head lolling back. Quicksilver blasted him again for good measure. This is for Dust, he thought. This. Above, the ship's alarms began to shriek in a high voice, overhead lights slowly warming.

Bright Venture was waking up.

CHAPTER THIRTY-FOUR
Endgame

THE *George Hammond* swept wide, rail guns blazing as she burned a streak down the hive ship's lateral surface, rotating on her own axis as she spun off the end, flipping around to come about for a dorsal pass. A cloud of Darts parted before her, reforming behind her and peppering her aft shields with flowers of fire.

Sam knew better than to direct her helmsman. The reason Lt. Chandler was a helmsman was because he was a hot pilot, hotter than she'd ever been. And so, other than the imperceptible tightening of her hands on the arms of the chair, she did not react as they rolled through a flashing waterfall of fire, diving behind the hive ship's bulk.

Depressurization alarms must be hooting all over the hive ship, inner compartments sealing. Their sensors read massive damage. If they could just refrain from depressurizing sections where they had people aboard…

"Sheppard?" she said into her radio. "Status report, please." There was no answer.

"Ma'am, aft shield at 40 per cent," Major Franklin said from the station behind her. "We are rerouting power, but it appears that the starboard ventral emitter has taken physical damage."

Trouble, but by far not a mortal wound.

"Sheppard? Status report."

The *Hammond* dove, rotating 280 degrees as she evaded another flight of Darts.

"The hive ship is powering up!" Franklin said, his voice cracking as he bent over his display. "All systems are coming online!"

That was their cue. Once the hive ship's defenses were active, their team would be trapped.

The *Hammond* shook, shuddering from bow to stern.

Sam snapped about as a shower of sparks flew behind her. "What was that?"

"The damaged starboard ventral emitter blew, ma'am," Franklin called. "We've lost the entire rear shield!"

For a moment Sam wished she were the type who swore under pressure. Power reroutes they could do. External physical damage was beyond their repair capability in the middle of a battle, and depending on the damage possibly more than they could do without significant down time at a base.

"Cut the power to the damaged sections," Sam directed. "So we don't have anymore surprises back there." She cupped her headset. "Sheppard? We're out of time."

Ronon's voice came through loud and clear, blasts and the sound of gunfire behind him. "Sheppard's down."

Ronon fired and fired again, and Wraith after Wraith fell, but they kept coming, their stunner fire spitting down the corridor toward him. He flattened himself against the wall as best he could. No way to get past so many of them, and they would be pouring down the corridor from the other direction now, cutting off their escape.

"I can't give you any more time," Carter said over the radio. "We're about to open a hyperspace window. I can beam you out *now*, or you're going to have to find your own way home."

No more holding them off. He crouched and dived in the door of the room, rolling as he came up, taking in a series of images — Sheppard down, unmoving, Teyla swiveling her P90 toward him, startled by the sudden movement — and then he saw Rodney, firing off blast after blast from the Wraith stunner in his hand.

It was Rodney, and at the same time he had the ridged markings of a Wraith's face beneath bone-white hair, and the hand clenched around the stunner had claws. It was Rodney, firing again and again at Teyla as if he was afraid to stop. The table she was sheltering behind crawled with stunner fire.

For a moment Ronon froze. It was like something out of a nightmare, and for a moment he thought *this can't be real.* Then he knew it was, and even as he rolled to one knee, raising his pistol, he remembered watching a Wraith writhe in restraints in the isolation room, watching its face become human as their engineered virus worked its destruction through its body.

"Our hyperspace window is open," Carter said in his ear, her voice level like the seasoned soldier she was. "You've got about ten seconds before we jump to hyperspace."

"Rodney!" Teyla cried. "It is us, we are here to help you—"

Rodney threw himself behind a piece of equipment, and Ronon's shot stung harmlessly against the metal. He was crouching to dive over the tables, preparing to roll wildly out of the way of the stunner blasts when he got close enough.

"Ronon!" Teyla called, and he heard the thunder of her P90, spraying the doorway behind him with bullets. He fired once, twice, and readied himself to spring.

"We're leaving now," Carter said. "Ronon, make the call."

With Sheppard down, they didn't have a pilot, but it didn't matter. They'd never make it out of this room. He wanted to stay, to keep fighting to get to Rodney, even if all he could do was die with his teammate. It was the right thing for a soldier to do.

It wasn't the right thing for the team leader to do. Teyla was still firing, pausing only to jam another clip home. Sheppard lay unmoving, one hand outflung as if in sleep. He couldn't throw away the lives of his team. He had to keep them safe.

"Pull us out," he said, his voice rough in his own ears. "Carter, do it now!"

He felt the pull of the transport beam, his stomach twisting as the world changed around him. They were on the bridge of the *Hammond*, Sheppard sprawling across the deck, Teyla dropping to her knees next to him. His face was pale and streaked with blood.

"Get a medical team up here," Carter said. "Franklin, punch it!"

There was a slight jolt, and the view outside the forward window changed, stars elongating into the azure of the hyperspace field as the *Hammond* passed through the window, leaving the battle behind.

"He was hit by a stunner many times," Teyla said urgently, her hands on Sheppard's neck, checking the pulse at his throat. "I think he is not breathing as he should."

"They're on their way," Carter said. "What happened?"

Ronon didn't think either of them wanted to say it. It was Teyla who finally answered.

"He is Wraith," she said flatly. "Rodney is a Wraith."

The blue shifted stars of hyperspace slid past the *George Hammond*, while within the thin envelope of the hyperspace field a spacesuited repair crew swarmed over her surface, conducting a visual inspection of the damaged shield array.

Master Sergeant Luciano, the *Hammond's* chief structural engineer, frowned at his captain through the video link to the station beside her command chair. "It's not good, ma'am. The shield emitter is basically blown away. There's nothing left but the twisted backing plate attached to the brackets. We've got replacement internal electronic components for repair purposes aboard, but we're going to need a full machine shop to rebuild the titanium alloy casing."

"And until then we've got no rear shields," Sam said, her fingers drumming on the chair arms. "I read you loud and clear, Sergeant. Bring your crew in. We'll see what we can rig up in Atlantis. They've probably got what we'll need for the casing."

"Yes, ma'am."

It wouldn't be that simple, of course. Rebuilding a

major external system was not going to take a few hours. It might — might — take a few days at best. More likely a week or more. Still, it was something well within their capabilities to do. The *Hammond* carried titanium alloy hull plates for repairing breaches. The problem would be machining the spare hull plates into the proper structure for all the fiddly little parts that made up Asgard shielding. It was a week's work for skilled people with Atlantis' facilities to use.

"Major Franklin, you have the bridge." Sam stood up, making her way to the infirmary.

Her people were in pretty good shape. A medical corpsman was treating three or four people for mild electrical burns from the shield control panels shorting, and Sam stopped to say an encouraging word to each of them. If the worst to show for her ship's first battle was a damaged shield array and some second degree burns that wouldn't keep people off their feet a full day, you had to call that a win.

Only it wasn't, of course. They didn't have McKay back, and they hadn't destroyed Queen Death's hive ship, though Sam thought they'd fairly well crippled it. She thought they'd taken out the hyperdrive and all of the forward weapons systems and done some major structural damage. That wouldn't be easy to fix either. It would be months before that ship was flyable again. But Death was queen of a big alliance. She'd probably shift her flag to another ship.

And then there was Sheppard. Sam looked around the screen in the infirmary, where Sheppard was hooked up to monitors and drips. Teyla sat on the metal stool at the beside, her feet up on the rung and her arms crossed over her stomach. Ronon leaned against the wall behind her, his head back against the bulkhead and his eyes closed.

The doctor came over as Sam approached. "How's he doing?" Sam asked quietly.

The doctor glanced back at him. "Not too bad for someone

stunned that many times. He's still out cold. I've got him on a drip to replace electrolytes, and a heart monitor because we detected arrhythmia as a result of the amount of electrical current his body absorbed. It's pretty much the equivalent of being struck by lightning."

"Lovely," Sam said. She looked over at Ronon and Teyla. She'd spent a lot of hours waiting like that.

"He'll be ok," the doctor said. "I think it's unlikely he'll suffer any permanent effects. But even a stun beam can be dangerous if you do it over and over. The Wraith don't usually fire more than necessary to incapacitate a human being."

"It was Rodney," Teyla said harshly, and Sam came over to stand on the other side of the bed. "Rodney did not know us. He resisted. John…" She shook her head, her eyes falling to Sheppard's face. "I do not think he ever realized what had happened. That Rodney was…not himself."

"It's some kind of medical thing," Ronon said. "Like Michael. I don't know. I don't know what it was. But he was a Wraith."

"A retrovirus?"

"I don't know," Ronon said again, shaking his head, anger plain in his voice. Not anger at her, Sam thought. Anger at himself, that he had not somehow parsed the impossible.

"We couldn't have known," Sam said. "Todd may not have known."

"Or he was playing some game of his own," Teyla said, and there was a bitter edge in her voice. "I do not think he serves Queen Death. I do not think he truly serves anyone's interests besides his own."

Sam nodded. "We'll be back in Atlantis in nine hours and a bit. Sheppard may be up and awake by then, and we can all sit down and debrief. But until then you might want to get a meal and some rest."

"I think we would prefer to stay here," Teyla said. Unsurprisingly. Sam had sat that watch herself way too many times.

"I'll have somebody bring you up something," she said, and turned to go.

Night had come, and the towers of Atlantis glittered through the falling snow. The debriefing was over, and Teyla left the conference room, Woolsey and Carson still talking behind her. Yet everything that could be said had been said and said a thousand times while she and Ronon and Sam and Mr. Woolsey and Radek and Carson and Jennifer had deconstructed everything over and over. There was nothing more to be said. There was no more information to share. There were only empty, gaping questions.

Through the glass doors of the control room balcony Teyla thought she saw a familiar figure outside despite the cold and darkness. She hugged her jacket about her as the doors opened before her, but the wind hit her like a punch in the chest as she stepped out of the shelter.

"John? I thought you were in the infirmary."

He didn't turn around, just stood at the rail, his shoulders hunched against the cold. "Keller let me out. I'm not sure she wanted to see me any more than I wanted to see her."

Teyla drew a deep breath and came and stood beside him. "How are you feeling?"

He shrugged. "I still can't feel my toes. How many times did I get stunned, anyway?"

"Six," Teyla said matter of factly. She shook her head. "At least we know so much of Rodney remains. He has always been overkill!"

John snorted mirthlessly. "That's true. I suppose I should just be glad he had a Wraith stunner, not a P90. You wouldn't be bringing much home if he'd shot me six times with that." He shook his head, looking out into the night. "I don't know what happened, Teyla."

"It all happened very fast," she said. "I did not have any way to incapacitate Rodney except to shoot him, and if I had tried that I probably would have killed him." Teyla shook her head. "I could not risk it."

"You did the right thing," John said, and she knew he was thinking of Ford, of the time he had not taken the shot when he might have.

Teyla took a step closer, her shoulder against his arm, side by side at the rail. "We will get him back."

"You know that's not very likely, don't you?" John looked at her sideways.

"In that other reality, Rodney spent twenty five years trying to find a way to change the past and save me. Do you think I will give up on him?" He was silent, so she continued, lacing her hands together in the cold. "You looked for a long time before you found me when I was Michael's prisoner, and you nearly succeeded once before you at last did. We did not know what we were up against this time. We did not know that Rodney would not come with us willingly. We had no reason to expect what happened. Next time we will know."

"And how are we going to take him down without killing him?"

"Ronon's stun pistol." She shook her head. "We will get a zat gun from the SGC. Something else. We will figure it out. But we are not going to give up. We will get Rodney home." She nudged him with her shoulder. "You may be sure of that."

John looked away. Whirling snowflakes landed on his dark hair, sticking whole and complete. "Teyla, is there something we need to talk about?"

He sounded so strained, so uncertain. "No," she said quietly. "There is nothing you need to say. There is nothing you could say to me that your actions have not said a thousand times."

His eyes closed, and she thought the faintest hint of a smile played around the corner of his mouth. Or perhaps he was laughing at himself, inarticulate always in the face of so much to say. "Ok," he said. He lifted his arm and she slid under it, warm against his side as the cold wind swirled around them, his chin resting on the top of her head.

Beyond, the snow fell soundlessly into the sea.

ACKNOWLEDGEMENTS

A BOOK is never written alone, and this one was very much a team effort. We'd like to thank Melissa Scott who has put so much of herself into this book even though her name doesn't appear on the cover of this volume. We'd also like to thank Mary Day, who helped immensely with Dr. Robinson, and Katerina Niklova, who translated Radek's lines into Czech for us. Also, we are indebted to Anna Kiwiel, whose comments and continuity assistance have been invaluable.

We'd also like to thank our early readers who lived and breathed The Lost for an impossibly short period of time, Rachel Barenblat, Gretchen Brinckerhoff, Imogen Hardy, Anna Lindstrom, Jennifer Robertson, Lena Sheng, Lena Strid and Camy. We live for your screams of "Oh no! What have you done to Rodney!"

Lastly we'd like to thank our wonderful editor, Sally Malcolm, for giving us this wonderful opportunity to continue the story of *Stargate Atlantis*.

SNEAK PREVIEW

STARGATE ATLANTIS: Allegiance

Book three of the LEGACY SERIES

by Amy Griswold & Melissa Scott

"LET'S TAKE stock," Dick Woolsey said, looking across the conference table at the weary team. No one looked very happy, but then they didn't have much reason to. He wasn't expecting much good news.

Everyone at the table had believed that the raid to recapture Dr. McKay from the Wraith would succeed. Instead, not only had the mission failed, with the *Hammond* sustaining serious damage in the process, but Colonel Sheppard's team had come face to face with McKay, and made the grim discovery that he had somehow been transformed beyond recognition.

"What's our present situation?" he prompted when no one seemed eager to speak up.

Dr. Zelenka, Colonel Sheppard, and Colonel Carter exchanged glances. He didn't think any of them were dying for the chance to report first.

"Not great," Sheppard said finally. He looked like he'd recovered fully from the series of stun blasts that had left him confined to the infirmary the day before, although he hadn't apparently managed to shave. "Rodney's still in the hands of the enemy. We're not sure what they did to him, but he looks like a Wraith, and he wasn't acting like he remembered he was on our side."

"We have some theories," Dr. Keller said, glancing at Dr. Beckett beside her. If so, they'd been up early developing them. Dick had called the meeting as early in the morning as he'd thought was reasonable, given that people did need to eat and sleep.

He wasn't sure Dr. Beckett had taken the opportunity to do either. "Aye," he said without enthusiasm. "Go on and tell them all about it."

"We've been working for some time on a retrovirus we originally hoped could physically transform Wraith into humans," Dr. Keller said. "That didn't exactly work out as well as we hoped. We've since moved on to trying to find a way to give the Wraith a more human-like metabolism that would allow adult Wraith to survive on normal food rather than feeding on humans."

"We know that," Teyla said, with a smile that was encouraging but not particularly patient.

"Sorry," Dr. Keller said. "Just trying to get everyone up to speed, here."

"Which those of us who haven't been here for a while appreciate," Carter said.

Jennifer nodded and went on quickly. "It seems pretty likely that the Wraith have found a way to reverse engineer one of the versions of the retrovirus that we tested on live subjects. They've created a way to transform humans into Wraith."

"As Michael did with his hybrids," Teyla said.

"Something like that," Jennifer said. "But he was trying to create an intermediate form between humans and Wraith. Here..." She looked across the table at Sheppard and his team. "From everything everyone's said, Rodney didn't look much like any of the hybrids."

"He was Wraith," Teyla said. "If I had not known his face, I would not have believed he was anything else."

"He had a Wraith feeding hand," Ronon said.

"That would be necessary for a complete transformation," Dr. Keller said. "Of course, it could be cosmetic. We've faked that ourselves. It would be nice if it is."

Dick frowned. "And if it's not?"

"Then he probably has the ability to feed on humans. And he may not remember why that would be bad."

Sheppard broke the silence that settled around the table. "But that's not going to happen, because we're going to get him back. Right?"

"That's the idea," Dick said. He was on his third cup of coffee, but it wasn't making up for not having had much sleep. "The problem is, he doesn't remember that we're trying to rescue him."

"That could be a side effect of whatever process they used on him," Dr. Keller said. "Our first version of the retrovirus produced complete amnesia as long as the dose was kept at a high enough level. Which, when you think about it, may actually be a good thing for us."

Ronon gave her a look. "How is that good?"

Dr. Keller shrugged. "If he was afraid of you when you tried to rescue him because he didn't remember who you were, then he might not remember his access codes for the computer."

"Or where this planet is located," Sheppard said. "Or the location of Earth. Or how ships using Ancient technology can penetrate our shields. Or—"

"I get the picture," Dick said.

"We are already working on securing the computer system," Zelenka said. "There are many ways Rodney could access the system officially, and we have already found numerous back doors. We will keep working."

"I'd be happy to help if you could use another pair of eyes," Carter said. "We dealt with a lot of security problems when I was at the SGC."

"Yes, please," Zelenka said before Dick could say that they were grateful for the offer and would take it under consideration. It probably didn't matter at this point. Any tension between himself and Carter over her help being needed in Atlantis would be beside the point if McKay effectively handed Atlantis over to the Wraith.

"Sure," Carter said. "After the meeting, why don't you show me what you've been doing?"

Zelenka nodded. "It would help if you could also read Rodney's mind."

"I don't know about that," Carter said. "But I'll see what I can do."

"As we are speaking of reading Rodney's mind," Teyla said, a little reluctantly. "Things happened very quickly, but I believe I was able to sense Rodney's presence as if he were a Wraith. I might be able to make contact with him if I were close enough."

"Something to keep in mind when we're at a point where another rescue attempt is practical," Dick said. "At the moment, though, we have no idea where Death's hive ship went after the *Hammond* entered hyperspace."

"We have no clue," Carter said. "I don't expect they're still sitting around at the repair facility waiting for us to come back, though."

"I think that's a little much to hope for," Sheppard said. "We can check back with the Genii, see if they've come up with anything."

"I'll get in contact with Radim," Dick said. "In the mean time, I want our first priority to be securing the computer system. If the Wraith can lower our shields, or lower the iris, there's nothing to keep them from dropping a nuclear bomb on us at any time."

Carter and Sheppard exchanged glances.

"They probably won't do that," Carter said.

"We've got a ZPM," Sheppard said, in answer to Dick's questioning look. "And lots of tasty people for them to snack on. Blowing us up is probably plan B."

"I don't think I like plan A any better," he said. "Assuming it's invading Atlantis and taking us all prisoner to feed on later."

Radek shifted restlessly in his seat. "You know, the longer we are sitting here talking, the longer we are not working on computer security."

"Go," Dick said. "Colonel Carter, any assistance you can provide would be appreciated."

"It's my pleasure," she said. "I've got time right now while we're repairing the damage to the *Hammond's* shield emitters. By the time that's done and I can take the *Hammond* back out, Jeannie Miller will be here to assist Dr. Zelenka."

"She is coming out aboard *Daedalus*," Zelenka said. "I wish she could have come through the Stargate, but apparently that was not possible to arrange."

As Dick was the one who hadn't been able to arrange it, he felt it was worth pointing out why. "Since the Wraith destroyed the ZPM installed in the weapons chair at Area 51, Earth's only ZPM is aboard Odyssey," Dick said. "The Odyssey is on a deep-space mission, and even if it had been possible to recall it, it would take nearly as long to reach Earth as *Daedalus* will to reach Atlantis."

"You can't ever get a cab when you need one," Sheppard said.

"Well, let us hope that the delay is not critical to preventing Atlantis from being invaded," Zelenka said. "That would be nice to think."

Dick let the door close behind Zelenka and Carter before he raised his eyebrows. "He doesn't seem optimistic."

"We are all worried about Rodney," Teyla said.

"Of course," Dick said. He suspected that his decision to assign Zelenka to Sheppard's gate team might also have something to do with Zelenka's mood, but he still didn't see any alternative. They couldn't go on as though McKay might walk through the gate at any minute. "I'd like you to think about the best tactics for another rescue attempt, should we be in that position."

"I'll do that," Sheppard said. "And also get some extra security teams to keep an eye on critical areas of the city, just in case."

Dick turned to Dr. Keller. "Assuming for a moment that we do get Dr. McKay back, what happens then?"

"We don't know," Dr. Beckett said before Dr. Keller could answer.

"If the process they used is based on our original retrovirus, it should simply wear off once the virus is no longer being administered," she said.

"Yes, but we don't know that it is," Dr. Beckett said. "It could just as easily be based on the process I developed for Michael, or they could have designed it from scratch after we gave them the idea."

"Whatever they based it on, I think we should go back to your original work as a starting place," Dr. Keller said. "It's the best chance of figuring out what they did and making sure it's fully reversible."

"Please keep me posted," Dick said.

"I will," she said. "If that's all…"

"One more thing," he said. "I hate to have to be the one to say so, but we can't put all our energies into this. I am not saying that we should stop trying to recover Dr. McKay. That has to be a priority. But we came out here to do any number of important things, and we can't stop doing them just because one person is missing."

"I think we all understand that," Teyla said after a moment's pause. He hoped it was just that she was the quickest to speak, and not that she was the only one at the table who agreed with him.

"All right," Dick said. He stood as people began to push back their chairs. "Colonel Sheppard, if you've got time this morning, I'd like to discuss your team's schedule for the rest of the week."

"I'm not exactly booked up," Sheppard said as the others made their way out. "I'd like to have a word with Lorne about security first."

"Of course," Dick said. "There's also plenty of time for you to go shave."

"I expect there is," Sheppard said after a moment.

"We can't act as though we're in a state of crisis all the time,"

Dick said. "I just think we need to send the message that things are getting back to normal."

He could see Sheppard bite back whatever sharp reply had first come to mind. He might not like it, but he knew it was true. "Yeah, but what if we *are* in a state of crisis all the time?" he said instead.

"We still act like we have things under control," Dick said. "At least, I always understood that to be part of my job description."

"Which is why I'm glad you have the job and not me," Sheppard said.

Dick was tempted to point out that it was a good question whether that would still be true once he heard from the IOA about his most recent set of reports. That problem could wait, though. He thought they had enough to keep everyone busy for the day.

STARGATE ATLANTIS: BRIMSTONE

by David Niall Wilson & Patricia Macomber
Price: £6.99 UK | $7.95 US
ISBN-10: 1-905586-20-5
ISBN-13: 978-1-905586-20-2
Publication date: September 2010

Doctor Rodney McKay can't believe his eyes when he discovers a moon leaving planetary orbit for a collision course with its own sun. Keen to investigate, he finds something astonishing on the moon's surface — an Ancient city, the mirror of Atlantis…

But the city is not as abandoned as he thinks and Colonel Sheppard's team soon encounter a strange sect of Ancients living beneath the surface, a sect devoted to decadence and debauchery, for whom novelty is the only entertainment. And in the team from Atlantis they find the ultimate novelty to enliven their bloody gladiatorial games…

Trapped on a world heading for destruction, the team must fight their way back to the Stargate or share the fate of the doomed city of Admah…

STARGATE ATLANTIS: DEATH GAME

by Jo Graham
Price: £6.99 UK | $7.95 US
ISBN-10: 1-905586-47-7
ISBN-13: 978-1-905586-47-9
Publication date: September 2010

Colonel John Sheppard knows it's going to be a bad day when he wakes up in a downed Jumper with a head wound and no memory of how he got there.

Things don't get any better.

Concussed, far from the Stargate, and with his only remaining team mate, Teyla, injured, Sheppard soon finds himself a prisoner of the local population. And as he gradually pieces the situation together he realises that his team is scattered across a tropical archipelago, unable to communicate with each other or return to the Stargate. And to make matters worse, there's a Wraith cruiser in the skies above…

Meanwhile, Ronon and Doctor Zelenka find themselves in an unlikely partnership as they seek a way off their island and back to the Stargate. And Doctor McKay? He just wants to get the Stargate working…

Sometimes the nightmare starts when you wake up

STARGATE ATLANTIS

DEATH GAME

Jo Graham

Based on the hit television series created by Brad Wright and Robert C. Cooper

Series number: SGA-14

STARGATE
SG·1.

STARGATE
ATLANTIS™

STARGATE UNIVERSE™

Original novels based on the hit TV
shows **STARGATE SG-1,
STARGATE ATLANTIS** and
STARGATE UNIVERSE

AVAILABLE NOW

For more information, visit
www.stargatenovels.com